The death of Terri Shiavo should be known as the battle of Terri Shiavo. Her tragedy became her husband's nightmare because she did not sign her name and make her wishes known with a Living Will. The war between her family and her husband struck a sentimental cord around the world. Everyone formed an opinion, but in the end, a single man – Michael Shiavo, defeated the United States Congress, the President, and numerous appeals. The family knew her longer, but he knew her intimately, and she had given him and him alone her love.

A simple one-page document could have prevented the years of battle. The document is called a Living Will, but in fact, it appoints a sole person with the trust of carrying out your desires on how you wish to live or die when you can no longer make that decision on your own.

The Will was begun years before the Shiavo case became headlines around the world. Nonetheless, it is a battle gay partners have faced daily for many years. In times of tragedy, loving partners are banned from hospital rooms and medical consultations, shunned from expressing their partner's desires to live or die, and when concluded, blocked from planning their lover's funeral, and in some cases, banished from the final ceremony.

Chase and Brett's story begins with plans for an exotic tropical vacation, but their difficult journey takes a tragic turn within ten miles of their house. Their story is fiction, but unfortunately, the events of their story continue with gay lovers all around the world.

Books by TJ Johnson

The War Apart - Part I

The War Ahead - Part II

The Will

Stranded

The Raceboys

Coming soon:

A Writer's Fantasy
(About His Favorite College Basketball Star)

The Blackfeet Boys

Gay Grifters

The War Beyond - Part III

Forever Alone…Again

Web Site and Release Information:
WWW.ItsFiction.com

THE WILL

By
TJ Johnson

Brett and Chase were complete opposites when they met and fell in love. Brett, tall and handsome, worked hard every day, never bounced a check, and continually looked towards a better future. Chase went from job to job, could not balance his checkbook, and did not think about the future. Brett loved watching Chase ramble on like a kid on maturity hold forever. He would not have changed a thing about Chase, and like many others, watching him dance with such pure frivolity and happiness, always brought a smile to his face, and joy to his heart. Their love exceeded their differences, and the ensuing painful tragedy created a stronger love and deeper commitment.

Dedication

To all couples gay or straight, may your moments of joy and happiness far exceed any seconds of sadness life may afford you. My personal goal was simply to seek someone who could and would love me, as much as I loved him. My simple test was to see if he took as much joy in leaving the last piece of chicken, cake, or scoop of ice cream for his lover, as I did for him.

Sadly, my original writing companions passed away, but my new partners bring immense fun to my life. I am writing of course about my beloved beagles Huckie and Mickey. Every day when I first open my eyes, they are there smiling back at me. They give me doggie kisses, beg me to rub their ears, and despite my cooking imperfections, they'll eat just about anything I attempt! Boy, they are clever!

ONE

He awoke slightly but heard nothing. Their house, rarely still and quiet, produced only the mild hum from the ceiling fan over the bed. Installed throughout the house were fourteen pairs of stereo speakers, capable of producing the sensational sounds of satellite digital radio, the latest compact disk, downloads or the mp3 player, or the surround sound of a new DVD. The latter often had the floors vibrating from the deep bass woofer, and magically created the feeling a plane, helicopter, or space warriors just crashed into the great room. Sometimes, but not often, he awoke to the sounds of the dogs barking at a squirrel in the backyard. The ceiling fan ran three hundred sixty-five days a year, successfully drowning out the sounds of crickets or birds, and sometimes the dogs. However, today at this early hour, there were no sounds at all, and the puppies were snoozing. He twisted his head slightly on the pillow to be sure he could not hear a sound, but everything inside and outside the house had shut down for the night. There were no cars moving, no truck delivering the newspaper, no music, and no television. He could actually hear the slight intake and release of air through his nostrils.

Chase gently turned to his right, while still beneath the warm cozy bedcovers, and managed to open one eye. After a long minute, he focused with difficulty on the red numbers on the clock radio. "4:50," he muttered in a whisper. He sighed; he knew he had only ten more minutes of sleep before the alarm went off, and the entire house erupted in comedic chaos like a bad firehouse drill. Most days he would have dreaded the piercing sound of his alarm clock, for it would have meant time to get ready for work, but not today. Then he grinned slightly, because today he did not have to go to work—nor tomorrow. He did not have to do weekend chores around the house, nor cut the grass or wash the car, because today began the beginning of a big adventure—a long planned dream vacation to the tropics.

"Nine minutes," he whispered after another glance at the clock. Slowly and gently he turned and snuggled up close to the warm, smooth, soft, magnificent body lying next to him. The arousing nude bed partner remained asleep while lying on their side and turned away from him. Gently, he allowed his warm hand to caress the silky, well tanned back while sliding farther down to roll his hand over his friend's gorgeous, melon-shaped buttocks or buns as he affectionately called them. His hand glided down to the glistening legs shaved so sensuously keeping the flesh startlingly soft and tender. To him, the pair of delicious legs put Marilyn Monroe to shame. His confident opinion came from close observation as he had gently kissed almost every square inch of those exotic legs in their previous rendezvous of lovemaking. The mere

11

moment of rekindling his thoughts of those wonderful limbs made his member stiffen.

Tenderly he moved in closer, allowing his erection to slide on its own between the cracks of those stunning melons until he was planted perfectly between those beautiful legs just as they entered the torso. He wrapped his right arm around the upper chest while planting a butterfly kiss to the bare shoulder, and once again pulled himself even closer. Satisfied with just spooning, he stopped moving and stalking, but finally allowed his eyes to close and savor how lucky he was to be next to the person he loved most in the world. He felt ecstatic to be lying together all warm and toasty and in the nude on their wonderful waterbed. He pushed downward with his right foot and released to create gentle movement in the water.

The moment lasted all of ten seconds—way too short for Chase. The sleeping body suddenly snorted, uncharacteristically grunted, and began turning towards him. Chase moved his arm, as the body kept moving like a house rolling down a hill in a Los Angeles rainstorm. A knee slightly bumped his balls but not harmfully. The body stopped moving after facing him. A head full of beautiful brown hair fell loosely onto Chase's face, tinkling his nose, but he did not dare sneeze. He watched his friend, his lover, carefully. One eye opened and then the other, to reveal even in the early morning predawn hue, the most beautiful blue eyes he had ever seen.

Suddenly, the body glanced up at the clock and said, "God, it is 4:55 in the morning!" The sound of the voice could have awoken the dead. "We have to get up in five minutes!"

Chase quickly planted a kiss to the dry lips of his lover's stunning face. Then a second one to the cheeks followed by whisper kisses to the now once again closed eyelids before returning to the sensuous mouth. This time the mouth parted slowly and a wet, exciting, delicious tongue slid through the teeth barriers into Chase's mouth. The previously started erection instantly reached certified, flagpole, governmental regulation standards. Their hearts picked up a beat or two.

Breaking the kiss off, the partner said, "Chase, you horny dog. In three minutes, we have to get up, shower, feed the dogs, and jump into the SUV and head to the airport. Today we begin our exciting vacation to the jungles of Costa Rica and …" Chase felt a warm hand around his member, gently squeezing him, "and you're ready for action at 4:57 in the morning?"

"Sorry, can't help myself when I'm with you." Chase planted additional warm and welcomed kisses again to those wonderful luscious lips.

"I don't think we can do it in just three minutes."

"I think we should try to break our record. Three minutes is plenty of time."

The remarkable face broke into a wicked grin. "Okay, I am ready." He paused just slightly, "One, two, three, GO!"

12

Chase laughed, broke the embrace, and threw back the covers, rolled to his left and grabbed a condom from the basket on the nightstand. He tore it expertly open with his teeth, flipped back towards the naked body, and pushed the unrolled condom into his lover's expecting mouth. The lover then leaped over to Chase's erection and in a flash pushed down securing the condom. An Olympic official would have given the lovers a score of ten for executing such an important skill so...so...skillfully!

The lover fell back to the mattress. Chase scrambled between the beautiful legs. He noted the little chill bumps, scooted up close, leaned forward, and though his target remained in the dark, he deftly slid his penis into the target with same perfection a sailor might use to load a torpedo into a launch tube on a submarine.

The lover moaned with delight and began contractions on Chase's member causing it to expand even larger. The rhythmic primal pumping began. He leaned forward and began rolling his tongue around his lover's bare tummy, swirling the tongue into the crevices of the belly button, feeling the hole tighten even more on his penis. He slid his wet tongue upward, exploring, deviating to a rib, and yet returning upward until he could gently bite a hardened nipple. He heard yet another moan of delight as he thrust even deeper. He planted a deep wet kiss and received a pulsating flickering tongue in return. The volume of the moans increased along with the speed of the pumping.

Their hands continued caressing, pulling, and pinching, while the rubbing and thrusting accelerated. The moment of orgasm approached. Chase leaned up to allow his body to push deeper. A hand reached up and began pinching his left nipple. He moaned in delight and pumped even faster like his turbo button had been flipped on.

Chase knew he was about to run out of time, but refused to allow his eyes to open. He had reached a sexual plane far higher than ever before. He reached down and dragged his fingertips down the chest of his lover's soft tender belly. The fingers played with the pubic hair allowing his fingers to intertwine for a moment in the soft kinky curls before wrapping his hand around the enlarged spectacular throbbing penis belonging to the man he loved most in the entire universe. He pumped his hand as fast as he was pumping his hips.

The body moaned louder and louder. Chase panted and groaned until finally he exploded into the condom deep inside his lover. In his hand he felt Brett's vein explode, and he opened his eyes just in time to see the warm 'jizz', as he called it, spurt outward across the chest and up to the neck of his lover.

13

The buzzer of the alarm went off. The boys both laughed aloud as Chase fell onto the warm sperm and kissed Brett with all the passion he could muster.

"That was wonderful!" exclaimed Brett. "And we broke the record!"

"Thank you for breakfast in bed, my dear," replied Chase in a fake English accent.

"You're welcome. Are you ready for our big adventure?"

"We just had a big adventure, didn't we?" teased Chase.

"Yep, but let's hop in the shower. Maybe we can do it again on the plane."

They began climbing out of bed and heading to the bathroom. Chase turned on the shower while removing the enlarged condom.

"Geez Honey—that looks like a packed sausage," laughed Brett.

"Are you talking about the condom or my dick?" They both laughed and jumped in the shower, and began their routine of quickly soaping and washing each other.

"Sex on the plane sounds great, as does sex in the hotel, sex on the beach, sex in the jungle…" started Chase.

"Yeah, I know, you just can't get enough of my ass," laughed Brett.

"I can't get enough of you. I love you with all my heart."

"Not as much as I love you."

Another long kiss, two new flagpoles had arisen, but they forced themselves to finish the shower and dry off.

"You dress; I'll let the dogs in. They are not going to like the fact we're going away today."

"They sensed it when we started packing. I am glad Blake is going to come by every day to take care of them. I'll miss them."

As he approached the bedroom door, he could hear their paws scratching as they jumped against the wood on the other side. The moment he opened the door, in scrambled two small miniature pinschers—one brown and one tan. Beeper and J-Henry leaped to the bed and began running in playful circles. Chase pulled on his underwear, then leaned over and started tickling and playing with them. They rolled over repeatedly before leaping and planting kisses to his chin. The boys loved these dogs, and they knew it. It was always hard to leave them, but the boys would return eagerly from vacation, fall down on the floor, and give them big hugs and rubs. The dogs delighted in leaping over them nuzzling their ears.

Brett knew Chase was a classic anal-retentive gay male. He made packing lists, which referred to other lists. He also labeled everything. They had finished packing the day before, every detail handled, and yet the final ten minutes created a frenzy of last minute items to do. He put things in a bag and after a moment of indecision, he then took them out.

Brett knew Blake would take care of the dogs, but just in case, he retrieved from the pantry two large Tupperware cake covers. He flipped the big lids over, filled each with water, and set them on the spotless kitchen floor. He also found two giant salad bowls and filled each with even more dog food than he had already placed into their doggie bowls last night. These two little dogs or puppies, as he called them, were not going to go hungry or thirsty while they were away. He knelt down and told them to come give him a hug. Quickly, they trotted across the tile with their toenails clicking, although he had them cut twice a month, and reared up, putting their front paws on his knees, and began kissing his face with gentle, tiny tongue licks. He rubbed them and held them tight as if they were his little children to whom he was saying good-bye.

"Come on. We're going to be late," said Chase as he pulled his overnight bag down the hall.

"Give the dogs a hug," said Brett as he stood up and began punching in the codes for the house alarm system.

Chase knelt down and instantly the dogs sprang to him and smothered him in kisses, which he loved. He leaned down, kissed the head of each dog, rubbed their ears, and playfully tickled them.

"This is the hardest part of leaving for a vacation."

They walked out the door and locked it behind them. Brett sighed, "Yep, I know." They crawled into the car, buckled up, started the car, rolled out of the garage, and waited to make sure the temperamental garage door went all the way down and stopped. "Give me a kiss for luck." Chase smiled, leaned over, and kissed him. The door closed on the first try.

Chase laughed. "We're going to have a great time."

"It'll be a great time if you don't chew out some flight attendant, or baggage handler, or worst yet, some cab driver in a foreign country that doesn't understand a word you're saying," teased Brett.

"What are you saying? Me? Difficult? I think not," he stated while pointing his thumb to his chest.

"Yes, you, the lovable roaring mountain lion that has to go stalking about, reminding everyone on the planet how to do their job correctly wherever we go."

"Well, somebody has to do it. Their bosses must be as slow as they are," replied Chase.

Over the past few years, airport security had tightened so they had to park the car in a special area and unload the bags. Brett stayed with the bags while Chase drove halfway to Greenville, at least that was what he thought, and parked the car in a faraway lot and jogged back to the airport.

"Enjoy your morning run, dear?" teased Brett sitting comfortably on the bags and yawning lazily as Chase came rushing up to him.

Chase playfully swatted him on the head with the plane tickets. "It's not too late for me to find a good-looking young man in the airport and give him your ticket, you know," he teased. He pretended to start looking and scouting about for such a cutie.

"You wouldn't dare because I have all your underwear in my suitcase," shot back Brett. He leaned in and despite throngs of disapproving passengers, swirling about he kissed Chase quickly on the lips.

"Let's go!"

They had begun what Chase felt was the worst part of a journey—attempting to survive the airport system, which included unloading bags, parking the car, and getting their bags in through security. Afterwards they began checking bags and making their way through ticketing and airport security. Finally, they found the gate, and plopped down in the chairs to wait for boarding. If you can survive going and returning from your vacation, then you will remember the joy of the vacation, thought Chase.

In the gate seating area, Brett pulled out a book and began reading. Chase fidgeted as usual. The only time he could sit still was after falling asleep. First, he pulled out his MP3 player and started listening to music. When he started singing aloud, forgetting he had his headsets on, Brett began to chuckle, but would not dare stop him. It was an embarrassing event much too funny to interrupt. Then bored, Chase pulled out his book to read. He did not read as fast as Brett did, and thus, his books were skinny and simple. He liked to say he was skinnier than Brett, too.

Forty-five minutes later, they each made a bathroom trip to pee, and soon walked down the ramp to board the plane. Chase, as usual, was scouting all the passengers, but on this small flight to Atlanta there was nothing worth writing home about, at least until he got to the plane and realized the flight attendant was someone he met at the bar a few weeks ago.

To Brett's chagrin, Chase and the male attendant talked and giggled about anything and everything while the entire rest of the passengers waited to board. "Chase, we'd better get to our seats so these patient folks behind us can board," pleaded Brett.

"Oh, I'm sorry," he turned and said to the waiting line. "I'm just so nervous about flying." Then turning back, he said to Brett, "This is Byron."

"Pleased to meet you," said Brett with a nod as he began pushing Chase down the aisle.

"I'll talk to you in flight," added Byron as they started down the aisle.

Brett did not recognize, Byron but was well accustomed to Chase meeting someone he either knew or wanted to meet everywhere in the world they went. They had flown all the way to Belize last year and somehow he knew the guy running the car rental agency. Brett did not care anymore and

was never jealous of these acquaintances. Chase met new friends easily while Brett remained shy at early introductions.

It took them several minutes to put their carry-on bags overhead and put the laptop computer and backpack below their legs. The laptop contained a DVD player, as well as an external eight-hour battery, and about thirty movies on disks. They rarely watched the in-flight movie, but rather picked one of their own, put on their headphones, and began watching soon after take-off.

Brett flipped through an airline magazine while Chase checked everyone out one more time as they filed in to sit down. He found everyone interesting in their own way. He teased with some children who sat across the aisle. Before long, everyone was aboard and Byron began explaining the emergency procedures on the intercom. Chase always laughed and said, "Yeah, when we're going down, I'm going to worry about putting that stupid yellow oxygen thingy on my mouth. I think not. I want Saint Peter to see me at my best."

Brett shot back without a moment's hesitation, "Yeah right. What Saint Peter would see is your head down between your legs kissing your ass goodbye!" He chuckled and added, "And come to think of it, that's the same way he would see you most any other time!" He laughed heartily.

Chase laughed, and punched Brett's arm. "You just wait. No sex for you tonight."

Brett protested, "I thought we were going to do it on the plane?"

"Oh yeah, right, but no sex tonight!"

The woman sitting with the children gave the boys a typical Sunday school pout and shook her head in disgust. The boys did not care what she thought.

It was a few more minutes until Brett noted the door of the plane closing, then Byron made his way up the aisle to be sure all of his passengers had their seat belts on and their stuff put under their seats. When he reached their seats, he reached down and pretended to check their seat buckle while bumping the back of his hand against their penises. They grinned and laughed, as did Byron. Once Byron sat down on his little jump seat just outside the cabin door and put on his seatbelt. Chase assumed it was almost time to fly. Brett knew Chase always became suddenly quiet during take off. He sat rigidly still except for the nervous tapping of his left foot resting over his right foot.

"This is the Captain," stated a booming voice over the public address speakers.

"Oh, that's good," broke in Brett as he tried to make Chase laugh. "I was afraid he was going to ask if we wanted fries with our burgers." Chase grinned, but said nothing as he began swinging his leg a bit faster.

17

The captain continued, "We're next in line for takeoff. Please remain seated, and after we are airborne, I will give you an update on our arrival time. The weather is good and we are leaving two minutes early—not a bad way to start the day. Thank you for flying…"

Chase never heard the rest of the speech, as his nervous apprehension took over his brain. Brett stopped reading, reached over, and took Chase's hand, squeezed it, and held on. "We'll be fine, honey. I saw the pilot. He's got a big dick."

"Yeah, well let's hope he grabs the right stick when it comes to flying this bird!" They both laughed, but as the pilot turned the plane down the runway, Chase's nervous foot started thumping again. The engines revved up and suddenly they took off—racing down the runway at 70, 90, 120, and finally 150 MPH. The plane lifted into the air.

Brett quickly said, "Look, we can see the Biltmore House in the early morning sunrise." He pointed out the window for Chase to see.

Chase leaned over and looked. His foot slowed down just a bit before he said, "I hope we don't crash on it. All that granite looks like it would hurt to fall on."

"You're such an optimist," said Brett sarcastically.

"I'm such a practical 'fraidy-cat," added Chase.

They had only climbed about 400 feet when suddenly they heard and felt a large explosion in the engine housing on the right side of the aircraft—the side where they sat. The plane shuddered harshly like a rag doll in a dog's mouth.

Chase dug his fingernails into Brett's leg. They both stared in shocked disbelief out the window at the huge fireball. Buzzers began ringing all over the plane, the yellow oxygen masks fell to their heads, but they were not high enough to need oxygen. The pilot and copilot struggle to hang on to the plane as it rocked left and right. They leveled out briefly. The copilot began yelling Mayday on the radio. Byron's face turned pale as he reached for the intercom to urge people to stay calm.

Boom! Another large explosion and the back part of the flaming engine blew apart. Metal shrapnel slammed into the plane. Several of the thick windows shattered. Chase nearly leaped into Brett's lap but his seatbelt held him captive. Passengers began screaming. The plane shook violently with jolts and vibration. The pilot began heading for the ground while looking for a flat area to land.

"Push the wheels back down!" he yelled at the copilot who responded as quickly as possible while continuing to yell for help over the radio.

On the Public-Address system the pilot broke in quickly, "We're going down. Stay buckled in, and put your head between your knees now!" There was no second warning.

A third and final explosion, and the fuel line feeding the burning engine exploded into a second fireball. The wing buckled and broke off and the careening propeller spun rapidly as it broke free from the engine, and in a flash, it hit the fuselage, and cut right through the aluminum skin as if it were hot butter. Four rows up, the blades instantly killed a woman sitting by the window. Then it cut through the man sitting behind her, slicing all the way through the bones and flesh before continuing right through the seats and into the floor. It slowed just slightly before killing the woman sitting in front of Brett.

Before either boy could react, the blade cut through the seats in front of them, and stopped just as it nicked Brett across the back of the head that was still between his legs as instructed. Brett never saw the blade coming. Chase had also put his head down, but terrified at hearing the second explosion, he fearfully glanced up and saw the spiraling blade coming their way. He screamed even louder and unknowingly wet his pants. When the blade hit Brett, it splattered Chase with his lover's precious blood, and bits of gray matter and hair. Chase threw up but he had no time to think of anything else. The plane continued the wild rapid descent to the ground.

The cockpit glowed with alarms and buzzers going off all over the console. "Help me hold it!" screamed the pilot to the copilot, but with the loss of a wing there was not much the pilots could do. In a flash, the plane began slowly spiraling end over end. Each turn faster and faster, and Chase screamed louder and louder. Pieces of cut up bodies including arms, legs, torsos, and heads flew about the cabin splattering everyone with blood, but they did not know it, as the terror of the moment had overwhelmed them.

Five seconds after the wing broke away the plane slammed into the ground upside down at a sharp angle and skidded across the cow pasture. It went through a barbwire fence as if it had been made of sewing thread, uprooting posts, trees, plants, and bushes and continued moving rapidly across the number five fairway of the local Hillberry Golf Course. It began slicing deeply into the turf, gradually slowing down before finally coming to an abrupt and sudden stop as it approached the raised green. The wreckage dug into the hill of a big sand trap bunker, breaking the fancy turf of the putting green apart like a hard-boiled egg.

Until that moment everything had been loud, the explosions, the searing metal, the screams, the crunching and scrapping, and even the rush of air as it flew through the disemboweled fuselage before terrifyingly sliding across the ground. However, the moment wreckage came to a stop, only the sound of something hissing remained. They said later it was the sound of the oxygen tanks leaking, and perhaps the loss of hydraulic fluid, but no one heard it. The plane remained dark and eerily quiet.

19

The pilot and copilot died instantly on impact as the nose of the plane impaled violently through their bodies. It pushed through the pilots and stopped in the back of the flight attendant jump seat killing Byron as well. The first four rows, crushed as if they had been sardines in a can, looked as if they had been run over by a freight train. Limbs and flesh, blood and guts, fuel and oil oozed from the carnage. Sparks from broken wires and batteries fell to the ground.

Many passengers died on impact. Severed heads fell onto the fairway, as did piles and piles of busted luggage and uneaten meals. The wrecked fuselage had cut through the irrigation control box. Sprinkler heads began spewing water rapidly and in just seconds, part of the plane was dripping with water as if in a huge rain shower. It was a blessed miracle they hit the golf course and set off the water sprinklers, as the water meant to keep the grass green, prevented the fuel from temporarily exploding on impact and burning the trapped and terrified survivors.

Sirens, at first heard in the distance, rapidly grew louder and louder as they drove closer to the scene. One truck had already broken through the locked entrance gate of the golf course and raced to the number five fairway.

Chase had not felt the air knocked from his lungs because when the seat ahead of him jerked back it hit him in the chin with the force of a punch delivered from the heavyweight champion of the world. Blood dripped from his nose. His tongue could feel a damaged tooth. He was too afraid to move at first. He was hanging upside down inside the twisted fuselage; still fastened in by his seat belt, which he always pulled so tight the blood would almost stop flowing to his legs. He tested his fingers and his toes, and then wiggled his wrists. "Okay so far," he thought. He slowly moved his left ankle. Instantly, a sharp pain surged up his leg to his brain. He almost passed out again.

Reluctantly, while still hoping this crash was all a dream, a nightmare, a most horrific nightmare, he finally opened his eyes. The sun was barely coming up. He could not believe all the twisted mess of seats and bodies he saw around him. He gagged at the sight of the bright red color of massive amounts of blood.

Chase had never been a hero. Oh sure, he was quick with his mouth, often too quick, nearly getting himself in a fight, but rarely did he jump into a mess to help someone. He was the small dog behind a tall fence possessing only a big bark. He preferred yelling from the sideline. Saving people just was not his nature. Brett, on the other hand, had grown up a boy scout, became a lifeguard and safety instructor, but more importantly, by nature he was always the diplomat—trying desperately to prevent a fight. He had saved numerous kids from drowning, and rushed many a screaming, bleeding kid to the emergency room for stitches. Being a hero was old hat for him.

However, this time, with the tables turned, Brett remained unconscious if alive. Blood covered the back of his head. Chase took several quick breaths to try to relax his breathing. He felt close to hyperventilating.

Carefully, he managed to get a finger or two on the safety buckle holding him. He should have thought his action through because the moment the buckle released he tumbled downward and the pain in his ankle increased as it bumped its way to the ceiling, which was now the floor in the upside down fuselage. He screamed out as the new wave of pain hit him. He cursed loudly. No one alive heard him.

He remained motionless for a full minute to catch his breath once more. Suddenly the scent of jet fuel hit his nostrils harshly. It took a few more seconds for him to realize the liquid was flammable, and the plane could explode, burning everyone. "No time for calming breaths," he said aloud. He crawled closer to Brett and leaned his face down until his nose was in front of his lover's damaged mouth. Chase then froze and waited. It was a long second but an important one. It was not huge but it was there, the gentle inhale and exhale of air. Brett was alive and he was breathing.

Chase grinned and would have jumped for joy, but remained caught like a moth in a spider web of wires, broken seats, severed seatbelts, carry on bags, and other parts of the plane. With a new determination, he whispered to Brett, "Hang on, honey! I'm going to get you out of here."

Chase set about getting his arms and then his legs removed from the mess. His ankle throbbed. He turned left and right and found the shortest way out of the plane was moving forward to a place where the fuselage had broken in half. He could see green grass through the hole in the plane. Once free of the wires, he turned to go to work on Brett. He found Brett hanging from the buckled seat belt. Now more experienced, he did not immediately release him. Though worried about the blood loss, he stayed to the course of getting the wires and luggage parts off Brett. Once performed, he braced himself, released the buckle, and prepared to catch him.

Shocked at how heavy an unconscious person was, Chase nearly fell down from the load. Brett had lain on top of him during sexual intercourse and he barely felt squished, but now Brett's limp body felt as heavy as a pro football player decked out in full gear. Chase's ankle throbbed with anguish, but slowly, he half carried and half dragged Brett to the hole in the plane. Bright red blood covered his hands. His back burned from the rash the jet fuel caused as it dripped on him, but still he dragged Brett forward.

Reaching the jagged hole, he bundled Brett up and carefully set him through the hole to the ground, which was but two feet below. He crawled out beside him, and immediately saw a steady stream of jet fuel splashing in a puddle to the ground nearby. He crawled around in front of Brett, turned the flaccid body on to his back, grabbed the back of his shirt, and began dragging him in the opposite direction from the area of the spilling fuel. It took a few minutes until they broke into the open from the wreckage. The water soon hit his face from the golf course irrigation sprinklers. It was a blessing to Chase

21

as the fuel in his hair was dripping to his eyes, causing them to burn with irritation. The rain helped to wash some of the fuel from their bodies.

Chase did not stop. He heard the sirens and saw the first truck pull up, but he fell to his knees and kept pulling Brett. They crossed the sand trap and moved up and over a small bunker outlining the sand trap. They had just made it to the other side when Chase turned back to the plane as he heard the sound of a suspiciously loud swoosh. The fuel inside the fuselage had caught on fire, and the fire went from a small flame to an explosive fireball in just a few seconds. Chase instinctively fell over Brett to protect him as the flames blew across the golf course. Luckily, the bunker they hid behind turned the flames upward. However, the heat snatched the oxygen from the air, and Chase found himself once again gasping for breath. Brett felt nothing.

The plane exploded, blowing the men from the truck to the ground, and lifting the downed planed back into the air before disintegrating into millions of pieces. No one else got out alive as the debris slammed back to the ground once more. The trees caught the flying burning bodies in their higher limbs. A mid-torso chunk flew into the windshield of the fire truck before settling on the hood.

As the next minutes ticked by Chase did not remember a whole lot. He had passed out on top of Brett. The water from the sprinklers once again washed him off, while more emergency vehicles arrived. Workers rushed about checking bodies for life, and for a few minutes, no one noticed the lovers crumpled in a heap on the back of the bunker. Finally, firefighter Robbie Jones, a ten-year veteran, found Chase. He yelled to one of his partners, and they quickly but gently lifted Chase onto a stretcher. Realizing there was a severely wounded man beneath him, he called for more help. Brett's blood loss was continuing and fearing the worst, Jones used his hands to stop the blood flow on the back of Brett's head while yelling for a paramedic.

The men rushed over with their medical kits and quickly prepared bandages to stop the bleeding, and then got IVs into the arms of both boys, and once stabilized, rushed them across the field to an undamaged EMS truck. After loading the two victims, the ambulance driver raced across the golf course. He reached the main road, but felt as if he had turned the wrong way on the track of the Daytona Raceway as hundreds of emergency vehicles and cops of all types raced towards him to the scene. He bravely continued straight ahead, forcing everyone to part like the Red Sea. His partner continued working rapidly on the patients in the back of the truck. He determined Chase was reasonably stable, though he had numerous cuts and bruises, bright red rashes from the jet fuel, and a rapidly swelling ankle. However, he feared Brett might be on the brink of death. Twice he prepared the shock paddles, ready to restart his fading pulse. Miraculously, Brett's heart would bounce back with a sudden strong pump saving his life once more.

Luckily, the nearest hospital was less than a mile away from the crash site, but you could not get there as the crow flies. The driver made it to Interstate Twenty-Six, spun the EMS vehicle east, and raced down the road to the next exit, which led to the Fletcher Hospital in a suburb of Asheville. The driver radioed ahead and an emergency team waited at the entrance for them. The professionally trained technicians immediately unloaded Brett and Chase, and rushed the gurneys into the emergency room.

Separated for the first time in the past few hours, they arrived in different examining rooms. Various doctors rushed in. They quickly cleaned Brett's wounds, applied stitches, and bandages, stripped his body by cutting away his clothes, and found additional punctures. They cleaned and dressed these wounds as well. Once stabilized, they rushed his gurney to x-ray and on for a CAT scan.

The same happened to Chase, but as they struggled to clean his face from the bits of shattered glass, his eyes suddenly opened. The bright lights made him blink several times. "Where...am...I?" he asked hoarsely.

A cheerful experienced nurse leaned in so he could see her. "You're in a hospital. You were in a..." she paused for the right word to come, "...an accident, but you're going to be fine. You have a few cuts and bruises, and we are cleaning you up, but you are fine. Just relax while we work, and then we will send you to x-ray to check your ankle. Then the doctor will give you a happy shot to help you relax and go to sleep for a while."

Chase blurted out, "No, not yet! Where's Brett?" He struggled to turn left and right to hunt for Brett, but the attendants quickly grabbed his now naked bruised and battered body and held him down.

"Be still," a doctored demanded. "Or you are going to hurt yourself. Who is Brett? Was he on the plane?" The doctor continued adding snitches to a nasty cut.

The next words in response made the actions of the emergency crew of six, stop from what they were doing. "He's my boyfriend! Is he all right?" he yelled. A deputy taking notes heard his alarming words from where he sat in the hallway.

Another long second went by before everyone went back to work. The Day of the Cross religious group owned the hospital. This religious organization did not like homosexuals. However, they were also professionals and quickly returned to their jobs.

"Was he the fellow that came in with you?" asked the doctor to Chase.

"We were together on the ground. We got out of the plane before it exploded. I do not know how I got here. Did they get him?"

The nurse leaned forward to the doctor, "He did come in with another young man. I'll see if I can find out his name."

23

Exhausted, Chase blacked out again. The nurse quickly ran from the room to the examining room next door. It was empty of people as Brett had already gone to x-ray, but in a heap in a large plastic bag were the remains of Brett's clothes. Cut from his body, they were wet with blood, water, and jet fuel and as limp as rags. She put on a pair of rubber gloves and searched through the pile, but his valuables and identification were not there.

As she left the room, she ran into a cop still holding a notepad. She asked him, "Do you know the name of the boy that was in this room?"

The cop gave her a look, like that was none of her business, but then noted she was not going to take no for an answer. He looked down at his notes and said, "I put his valuables in the security bag. His license says he is one Brett Kenneth Allen. He lives here in Asheville. He's twenty-eight."

"Thanks," she started to turn away, then turned back, and said quickly, "Is he still alive?"

"Yep, but I don't see how. He's a bloody mess."

She did not reply but rushed back to the room. Chase was still unconscious. She did not try to wake him. The crew finished their medical work, and covered him with a sheet and a blanket to keep him warm. The doctor and the nurse began pushing him out of the room and into the hospital corridor. When they entered the cooler air of the hall, Chase's eyes opened once more. He noted the light fixtures and ceiling tiles passing overhead as they wheeled him along. It reminded him of the ceiling of the plane. He trembled with fear while remaining confused about what had happen.

"Hey, honey," she said. "Welcome back. We are on the way to x-ray. Just relax." She patted his shoulder gently.

The shot they gave him made his tongue feel like rubber, but struggling he managed to say, "How about Brett? Is he alive?"

"Yes, he is. He is here, and he is ahead of you in x-ray. They are taking care of him. Now lie back and relax."

Chase heard nothing more as he passed out again.

The day began with the lovers lying side by side with strong erections, with arms and legs intertwined, and locked into wonderful lovemaking. The sun broke through the early morning clouds providing a breathtaking sunrise. It should have been a great first day, but the boys rapidly left the target of an adventurous vacation, and landed in a world of chaos and confusion. Chase had felt horrible pain, experienced fearful moments, deep despair, and occasional nervous gasps for breath, but desperately he wanted to hang on to his life. Thankfully, Brett felt no pain at all. It was not the vacation they had so carefully planned. This accident was nowhere close to what they had imagined their flight to be, and more horrifying than they could imagine.

Nevertheless, despite all, they were alive.

TWO

Chase never woke up in the imaging lab, which was just as well, as the old technician twisted the broken ankle in various painful ways to get yet another picture. Once satisfied with the x-rays, he nodded to a nurse's aide. She moved Chase to a room on the seventh floor of the hospital. There the doctor set the bone, and he received a cast on his broken ankle. Once completed, an aide took him to his room. After the orderlies lifted his exhausted body to the bed, the nurse hooked up his IV drip and gave him a second shot through the tube. This shot put him in a deep painless sleep, or so they thought. Chase dreamed deep complex dreams, but each dream always ended with him and Brett making love.

The emergency room head physician called in their best neurosurgeon to operate on Brett. They had been in surgery for six hours. His pulse remained weak, but miraculously, he was still alive. His skull, slightly sliced by the spinning propeller, remained bloody. The emergency room crew had never seen anything like it. The stainless steel blade had been so swift it cut as clean as the power surgical saw they often used to open a human skull. Thankfully, the blade had slowed as it lost momentum on its approach to Brett through the side of the plane, and through various seats and passengers before hitting the last seat ahead of Brett. Only the tip of the blade had come through the seat hitting Brett in the back of the head.

The nurse in the hall heard the surgeon say if the blade had gone another pinch of an inch, Brett's death would have been instant. Miracle one was the fact the blade had killed numerous other passengers, but somehow allowed Brett to survive. If he had crossed his arms and rested his head on them, the blade would have gone deeper, but he had used his hands to grab his ankles, and thrust his head deep beneath his legs. His head bounced up and down with the jumping and jolting of the plane, but he never let go of his ankles. At the precise moment the blade came through his seat his head had been high, but moving rapidly back down again, and thus away from the blade as it nicked him. That was miracle number two.

If a wounded passenger like Brett had flown alone, or if no one noticed he was still breathing and left him, he would have died in the big explosion following the crash. Miracle number three: the person that loved him the most was there, alive, and determined to save them both, and he did.

The surgeon's twenty-four year old son was gay, but no one in the hospital knew it. He and his wife had decided to keep the matter a secret since he loved his work in the religious hospital. They were still trying to understand how their son could be gay and though the situation remained difficult to discuss, they loved their son nonetheless. When he hurriedly

25

arrived from his home after receiving the emergency page, the surgeon's assistant spread a bit of hospital hearsay by telling him the critical boy was gay. A month before he might have joined in on the gossip, but when the nurse held up the boy's driver license picture, his heart nearly stopped. His eyes watered as he realized Brett was almost the spitting image of his own son, including his bright blue eyes.

He suffered a nightmare just last week after dreaming a bigoted man had hit his son in the back of the head with a baseball bat. He then found himself in surgery, and suddenly, discovered the patient he was working on was in fact his own son. The boy died on the table. The horrific event caused him to wake up his wife while screaming at the top of his lungs.

He sighed heavily as his mind came back to the present. "Let's go do our best work," he said to the crew as an assistant tied his surgical mask. "This boy's family is counting on us. I bet God has another miracle ready to bestow on this lad today. Remember we are God's instruments. Let's pray his love will flow through us as if we were a container of wine."

The anesthesiologist muttered through his mask as he was tying it on, "At this hour, I would prefer He was turning the water into wine." There was an odd moment of silence followed by a chuckle by all. It was the perfect comment to say to relieve the tension for the difficult job that lay ahead of them. The surgeon nodded approvingly to his team.

The gossip stopped, everyone pulled up their surgical masks and pushed through the big doors to find Brett lying naked on the table. They noted the many cuts and abrasions all over his body, and easily the surgeon guessed this man's body had already received over fifty stitches. The doctor quickly examined the head wound, and gave the anesthesiologist permission to proceed to put Brett under while he quickly began examining the rest of the boy's body. He had huge purple bruises all over his torso, and his left knee was already the size of a cantaloupe. He noted a small tattoo of a scorpion with a red tip just below the waistline, on the right side of pubic area. Astoundingly, the tattoo survived undamaged. A nurse came up and put the catheter tube into Brett's penis, and although he had seen this done many times, he still flinched, thinking no man liked having anything crammed up his penis.

After attaching various heart monitoring patches, they finally covered Brett's body up with a sheet. They placed wide straps over his body and cranked down each one tightly. An assistant stepped on a floor switch and the table began to slowly rotate 180 degrees. The surgeon sat down on a wheeled stool, and rolled over to Brett's turning head. The doctor recalled Brett's driver license picture as he stared down at Brett's shaved head. He began to examine the wound in the back of his skull. The nurse had flushed the wound of all visible debris, but when the surgeon flipped the magnifying glasses down over his eyes, he began probing with a surgical tool. He found bits of white sand now stained red and attached to the exposed brain matter.

26

"Tweezers," he suddenly barked and his assistant expertly popped them into his hand as if anticipating his every move. Gently, he removed the sand one grain at a time, and then irrigated the wound with clear fluid, and finally satisfied, he began to imagine what he would have to do to help this boy. He set about checking every section of the bruised gray matter. "We'll have to slice the skull a bit more to allow for swelling," he said to everyone.

The spinning blade of the saw easily cut into Brett's skull. He cleaned the new wound before spending more time probing and checking for any other foreign matter or broken blood vessels. Six hours later, the doctor pulled off his surgical gloves and tossed them into a container. The nurse completed bandaging Brett's head. They taped his broken nose and inserted a clear tube through his left nostril. The doctor watched sadly as the assistants wheeled Brett's gurney into the recovery room before moving on to intensive care. He knew he had done his best work, but he feared it was not going to be enough to save the lad.

He felt a bit odd because usually after surgery, while still in his green surgical clothes, he would make a brief visit with the patient's family members to give them an update about how the surgery went. The oddness was because there was no one there for him to meet with. He thought how sad a life to be gay and alone. It touched him deeply. He swallowed hard.

While changing his clothes, he stopped to thank God the gay boy he had just operated on was not his own son, and he prayed both for his own son's safety as well as for Brett's recovery. He knew the boy would need at least one more miracle to survive.

Chase suddenly woke up but he could not keep his eyes open. He tried repeatedly, but his eyelids felt too heavy. Finally, he focused on the clock on the wall. It was almost ten o'clock. A nurse came up to his bed. She was about forty years old, and blond with a nice smile. Her nametag on her blue uniform said 'Jennifer' but everyone called her Jen.

"How are you feeling? Don't try to move as you're bound to feel extremely sore," she added as she leaned forward with a cup of water putting the straw gently to his lips. "Take a sip."

"Where am I?" asked Chase through bruised lips.

"The Day of the Cross Hospital in Fletcher, seventh floor, and you were in a plane accident and…"

Chase cut her off, "…accident my ass! We were in a plane crash!"

Jen flinched at his cursing as this was a religious hospital, but her training kicked in and she answered calmly, "You're right but you survived. They say you're a miracle man."

"Where's Brett?" asked Chase after swallowing hard and searching for the strength to fuel his words. He took another sip of water. The water

soaked into his tongue and throat like water on a dry sponge. He never felt the water reaching his stomach.

"Was Brett on the plane with you?"

"Yes, he and I were heading for a vacation trip."

"After you get well, you'll be able to try that trip once again," she offered with assurance.

"Where's Brett now?" he asked with more determination.

"What is his whole name?" she asked as she looked over Chase's medical chart.

"Brett Allen," whispered Chase. The pain was overwhelming him.

"Do you know his middle name?" she asked politely as she set the cup of water down on the table next to the bed. Trained to double check and identify anyone carefully, she waited for a reply before answering or offering medical attention.

A bolt of throbbing pain shot up his leg. He grimaced in agony, and lost his temper, "How many Brett Allens do you have in this hospital? Brett, Brett Kenneth Allen!!"

She wrote the information down quickly and began heading for the door. "I will go and see if I can find out if he is here."

"They told me earlier he was here. We must have come in together. Find him and tell him I am okay. Thank you."

Jen quickly made an exit and rushed down the hall to the nurse's aid station. She typed in Brett's name and noted he was in surgery. She then came back to Chase's room and quietly opened the door.

Chase appeared to be sleeping but as the door opened he said, "Did you find him?"

"Yes, he is in surgery right now."

"Surgery? Oh my gosh! Is he all right? What happened to him?" asked Chase rapidly.

"The computer says he has a serious head wound and many contusions. That's all I know for now."

"Tell the doctors I'm his Executor, and I have Power of Attorney relating to all matters including medical. Tell them they are to do everything they can to make sure he gets well quickly." He gasped for another breath through his bruised ribs before continuing, "Please tell the staff I insist they keep me informed from now on about how he is doing and what they plan to do." Exhausted by the oral exchange, Chase sank back into the pillow and immediately passed out.

A woman in her late forties pushed through the doors to the emergency room area. She wore her bleached blond haircut short, carried a large leather pocketbook, and oddly wore white tennis shoes. She stopped in the lobby and quickly began reading all the directional signs. Confused and

frantic, she raced to the first person at the end of the long counter. "Excuse me," she said boldly and far from politely. "Where is my son?"

The clerk was a medical typist and filer, and not a nurse and answered, "I'm sorry, I wouldn't know…"

The woman cut her off, "…then find out. Where is…Brett?" Her voice broke. Tears slid down her face.

Martha had been on duty for just an hour. She heard the woman as she walked towards the counter. Quickly, she made her way to the end of the counter to the typist, and said, "Honey, I'll help this woman for you." As she turned to the lady, she smiled and asked, "Ma'am, what is your son's full name?"

"Thank you. His name is Brett Kenneth Allen, named after my father," she added without knowing why she said that. It was just something she always said whenever anyone asked his name. She had been saying it that way all his life.

Martha quickly typed his name into the computer. On finding his records, the color fell from her face. "I'm sorry; he was in that plane crash this morning. He has just come out of surgery and …"

His mom broke in again, "Surgery! What is wrong with him?"

"He has a head injury and numerous other cuts and abrasions."

"Oh, my Lord!" she exclaimed.

"Why don't you sit down over there, and I'll call someone to explain his condition to you?"

"No, I want to see him," she pleaded.

"He's in the intensive care unit. I'll see if I can arrange that. Now you just sit down, and I'll be right back." Martha gently patted the stunned Jan Allen on the forearm and smiled sweetly.

"Okay," she replied while still in shock, "I'll be right over there." She turned slowly and walked to the chairs along the wall.

While Martha was gone Henry Allen had parked the family car, and now walked in the same door his wife had just moments before. He looked up at the signs and then the counter, and found himself confused about what he should do. He was 49 years old, beginning to lose some hair, but still managed to jog three days a week, and kept himself in good shape. The last time he rushed to the hospital his wife was having a baby.

"I'm over here," Martha said on spotting him.

He quickly turned and began walking towards her. "What did you find out?" he said eagerly as he sat down beside her.

"He was in that plane crash this morning. I knew they were leaving today, but when the call came from the hospital, I thought he was in a car accident," she replied as the tears continued to flow.

Henry pulled her to his chest and let her cry. His own eyes began to water. His voice broke, but he swallowed hard and continued, "How is he?"

She looked up at him and let her fingers gently touch her husband's cheeks in a loving moment. She was unknowingly preparing him for bad news. "He has a head wound, and he has just come out of surgery. He also has various cuts and wounds about his body."

"Oh my Lord! Is he going to make it?" exclaimed his father.

"The nurse has gone to get an update. I told her I wanted to see him."

"The news report said everyone died," he replied somberly. "I hope he'll be all right. The pictures of the crash looked horrible."

Through the emergency room door came two men who were obviously brothers with similar features, hairstyles, and even clothes. Bill and Larry were Henry's only brothers. They worked on the same construction job with the same company and even drove the same brand of pickup—a Ford.

Henry spotted them and waved them over. He quickly told his brothers what they knew so far. The brothers began rapidly asking questions.

Martha spotted Jan coming towards them and suddenly she had to struggle to get another breath. "There's the nurse," she finally blurted out which shut up the three men, at least for the moment.

"Mrs. Allen, the doctor said I could take you to intensive care so you can see your son but only for a minute. He is listed as very critical at the moment. If you will follow me, I'll take you there now."

The three men followed Jan down the hallway. Henry held on to his wife's arm to give her some support. They took an elevator up to the second floor. No one said anything. When the elevator door opened, they found themselves in the way of a staff member pushing another patient just out of surgery into the elevator. They quickly got out of the way. They all stared at the patient and wondered what Brett looked like. Henry stifled a sour taste in the back of his throat.

Martha led them away from the elevators and stopped at a waiting room. "Is one of these men your husband?"

Henry spoke up, "I'm Henry Allen."

Martha gave him a good look as if sizing up whether he would be of help to his wife or not, and finally decided to take the chance. She said, "Okay, you two men should wait here. I'll take you and your wife in to see Brett."

Relieved, the two uncles sat down on a couch while the others went down a hallway, made a turn or two, and stopped where they could look through the glass door of Brett's room. Martha gently led them in where they found a doctor monitoring his vital signs. Tears began to flow down Jan's cheeks as she clenched tightly to Henry's hand. They walked around to the other side of the bed away from the doctor. Brett remained motionless. Electronic beeps and chirps came from the monitors over his bed. The big bandage engulfed his head, but they could still see the cuts and abrasions

30

causing his face to swell. They noted his scrapped bare shoulders, but his parents would have recognized him anyhow.

Jan timidly reached out, placed her fingertips on Brett's arm, and gave him a gentle caressing squeeze. Henry did not touch him. He was too busy concentrating on holding back tears. Jan did not try to hold back her tears as they bounced from her cheeks to the bed.

Martha stood back and wondered how long she should allow them to be with Brett, but forced herself to allow them a few more minutes. She broke the silence by saying, "Brett is unconscious from the surgery, but the doctor says he may also be in a coma. We just don't know yet. Some of us believe even when patients are asleep they can still hear and understand words from people who love them."

Jan nodded approvingly, "Brett, darling. We love you. We're praying for a speedy recovery. You hang in there. You're going to be fine." Then she broke down and sobbed. Henry gently pulled her away from the bed, placed his arm around her shoulders, and led her from the room. Martha sighed sadly as they began walking to the hallway. She still cared about her patients allowing scenes like this to get to her.

Martha led them back to the waiting room. "The doctor will be by to see you in a little while. It could be hours or days before Brett wakes up. The cafeteria is on the first floor and the food is good and cheap. You'll need to eat to keep your strength up so you will be ready when the time comes. If there's anything else I can do, just let me know."

"Thank you, dear," replied Jan as she smiled at Martha thankfully. Henry wondered what she meant by "when the time comes."

An hour later, a billing clerk came to the waiting room. He was a tall thin man with an earring in his left ear. He broke the worrisome silence with his deep bold voice, "Anyone here for ..." he looked at his clipboard chart, "Brett Kenneth Allen?"

"We are," replied Henry.

The clerk walked over to them and asked, "And you are of what relation?"

"We're his parents," he replied as he nodded to his wife at his side.

"I just need a little information for my records. Let's see, do you know if he is allergic to any medications?"

"No medications, but he is lactose intolerant. He can't drink or eat dairy products. That's about it," replied Jan.

"I see, and I'll need your contact phone numbers."

They gave him their home and work telephone numbers.

31

The clerk then said, "We found a donor card in his wallet. Did he tell you had agreed to let us donate his organs in the event of his death?"

The tone and nonchalant mention of death stunned them. They did not want to think about it. Jan swallowed as a tear slid down her cheek, and she said, "I knew he filled out the donor card."

"Very well," he replied, "that's a noble thing to do. Let's see…according to the chart his Executor or the person who decides what medical care he gets is …" he stopped again to read from his chart, "Chase Edward Fleming. Is that one of you two men?" he asked pointing to the uncles.

"What?" asked Bill?

"I should say the hell not!" stated Larry.

The clerk became confused at their response and tone.

"Chase is alive?" asked Jan.

Before the clerk could answer, Henry stated firmly, "I'm his father. We are his parents. You come to us with any decisions about my son's health."

The clerk began to back off, "I'll make a note of it in the chart. Thank you." He turned and left. He knew something was very wrong.

The family sat quiet for a moment before Jan spoke, "I hadn't even thought about Chase. I should have. They were going on a vacation together."

"What? Why didn't you tell me?" asked Henry.

"You know you don't like Chase. I didn't want to make you angry."

He gave her a hug as if forgiving her and recognizing he hated Chase.

Jan suddenly stood up and started walking.

"Where are you going?" asked Henry.

"I'm going to find Chase."

While the men were still cursing Chase's name, Jan headed down to the nurse's station to find out Chase's status. On learning his room number, she found an elevator and pushed the button to go up, while making a note of what floor she had just left, so she could find her way back. The hospital had all kinds of color codes and special tile inserts to guide you, but she had yet to discover what color meant what, and where the tile inserts take you.

It took her about twenty-five minutes before she found herself standing at the door to Chase's room. She took a moment to both catch her breath and clear her head before she finally pushed in. She found Chase asleep. She immediately noted a large cast on one ankle hanging in a sling attached to cable hanging from the upper rails over his bed.

Cuts and bruises covered his face and arms just like Brett. He looked peaceful sleeping there, and indeed, he was after the nurse injected his IV with more sleeping and pain medicine.

She walked to his bedside and found herself half afraid he would wake up and she would not know what to say, and yet hoping he would wake up so she could ask him about Brett. Either way, Chase slept through it all.

Jan had always been close to Brett and she thought her son was the most happy-go-lucky and adventuresome child she had ever known. When he was little, Brett had watched Tarzan swing between the trees on a vine so Brett tied a rope to a high limb in their backyard and swung over to their neighbor's tree. Once they took him to the circus, and he came home and built a circus with trapeze, rolling barrel walkers, jugglers and, of course, clowns. After watching the movie "Superman," he tied a blue towel around his neck to make a cape and jumped off their house. Thus began one of many trips for a sprained ankle, bruised rib, or minor stitches to the doctor's office. In his first ten years of life, he had been x-rayed more than she and her husband combined in their entire lifetime. Fortunately, nothing serious ever happened to him—at least not until now, she thought.

She hesitated a moment before reaching over and touching Chase's arm just as she had done to Brett less than an hour ago. "I'll be praying for your recovery, too," she whispered.

"Well, what did you find out?" asked Henry as his wife sat down next to him somberly as if in a trance.

"Is that queer alive?" asked Bill.

"Shut up, Bill," she said. "You can be so crude sometimes." She didn't say it but started to say 'no wonder your wife left you.'

"Chase did survive. I went to his room. He has a broken ankle and many cuts and bruises. He was asleep so I didn't get to talk to him. He's not in any danger though. He'll survive."

"So they were going on vacation together?" asked Larry. He pronounced each word as if they created a sour taste in his mouth.

Henry rolled his eyes as his wife answered, "Yes, they had been planning the trip for months. They had worried Chase wasn't going to be able to get off work, but last week everything came together for them. They were so excited."

"I don't know why Brett hangs around that fag," stated Bill.

Jan gave him a look he knew meant he had better shut up, and then she replied, "They have been friends for over two years now. They have the best time together. They have been everywhere and go to concerts, movies, and many parties. They seem happy."

Henry was uncomfortable with talking about Chase and quickly changed the subject. "So what's this about him being the Executor?" He didn't even use Chase's name but rather the pronoun 'him.'

33

"I don't know, but I suspect they had something drawn up in case one or the other became hurt while on their vacations. They've been to New York, San Francisco, Key West, Belize and fly somewhere about every three months."

"Well, then. That doesn't apply here. This is Brett's home and we're his parents. We'll take charge," stated Henry. "Anyone want coffee?" he asked quickly as he stood up and headed to the vending machines. No one wanted anything and so he went alone. He put his money in and waited for the machine to heat the water and give him the cup of coffee.

He walked to the window to sip his coffee and to think through what had happened today, and especially what had happened to his son. A couple of interns came in, got their coffee, and sat down at the table to drink. Henry didn't look around at them, but he knew they were there because he could hear their conversations.

"That plane crash was horrific wasn't it?" said the older one.

"Yeah, they brought about a dozen bodies in, but all of them were already dead except for those two lucky guys."

"Lucky? I would say very lucky because they crashed, managed to crawl out, the plane blew up, and yet they still survived. I would say they are way beyond lucky. I plan to get them to pick some lottery numbers for me when they are able."

The other guy laughed. "I heard they were queers. I made sure I put on two pairs of rubber gloves before cleaning them up."

"Yeah, I know what you mean. I even put on gloves to handle throwing their clothes in sanitary bags. I hope I don't catch anything from them."

"One of the guys will be okay. He just has a broken ankle, bruised ribs, and many stitches for small wounds. The other one got his head sliced open, and I heard his brain matter was falling out."

Henry lost his grip on his coffee, and it fell to the floor. He quickly grabbed some napkins to try to clean the spilled coffee off his pants. He then wiped up the floor. Anger boiling within him, he threw the paper towels in the trash. As he left the room he turned and yelled at the two men, "My son was the one with the head damage you so crudely described, and he is not a queer!" He turned and left the room.

The interns looked aghast and horrified, but could say nothing in return.

Chase woke about six hours later. It took him a moment to register where he was, while hoping it all had been a bad dream. Reality set in when the pain in his ankle surpassed the pain in his ribs. "Hello?" he called with a dry parched throat, but there was no reply. He was in the room alone. "Hello?" he called again. He studied the buttons on the side of his bed rail until he realized there was a nurse's call button. He hit the button once, then

34

again, and yet again. No one came. He assumed the button was broken and wondered what he should do next.

The door suddenly swung open and a male nurse came in. "I see you've found my favorite button," he said sarcastically. He was about twenty-seven years old and immediately displayed a take-charge attitude. Chase knew at once that he was gay and a queen to boot. He focused on the nametag before speaking. "Johnny?"

"That's my name which tells us your eyes are okay because you can read. Now why are you pressing that button? Do you think I'm your stewardess?" It was something Johnny had said so many times to his patients, trying to get them to laugh and get their minds off their illnesses. For a moment, he had forgotten Chase was in the plane crash. He wished he could snatch the spoken words back. "I'm sorry, I didn't mean that. What can I do for you in my last five minutes of this shift?"

"I'm thirsty and I need to pee," stated Chase not the least bit embarrassed. "How do I manage that while hanging by my ankle from that pipe?"

"Not a problem. He walked to the sink, filled a cup of water, brought it to the nightstand, and inserted a straw. "This will handle the thirsty problem. As to the need to pee, well …" he leaned down and pulled from the shelf under the bed and urinal bedpan. " Tah-dah, you just pee in this, and I pour it in the toilet. It's easy."

Chase rolled his eyes while trying to figure, which was worst, a broken ankle, or having to pee in a stainless steel can.

Johnny pulled the sheet up to Chase's chest revealing Chase was nude. Nudity didn't bother him at all. He gently lifted Chase's good leg out of the way, then lifted Chase's penis and inserted it in the end of the urinal tank. "Okay, baby. I've done the hard part. Now it's your turn. Let it fly."

Chase tried to start peeing but nothing would come.

"Shy are we. Let's see. Think about waterfalls, big waterfalls, thousands of gallons of water, the Niagara Falls, the Atlantic ocean for Pete's sake!" he said with a grin.

The sound of Chase's urine flow was suddenly loud and furious as his bladder finally let go.

"Whew, baby! That's the way to do it. You go boy!"

Chase squeezed, pushed, and grunted until every last drop was out of him. "Oh, that felt good."

"Now don't go getting me excited here. My uniform will look stupid if I have a large bulge in front."

Chase busted out laughing as he realized the nurse was definitely a homo just like him.

"Okay, now I have to clean you up, so just relax," he said as he took a warm washcloth and cleaned Chase's penis as well as his testicles.

"I'm Chase, and I think you and I belong to the same family."

Johnny stopped cleaning, looked up to Chase's eyes, and smiled. "I thought so. My gay radar was working overtime when I came in here. I'm Johnny, and although I'm getting off in a bit, I will be back tonight to check on you." He started moving to the door.

"Thanks. I think I will hold my pee until you get back."

"Honey, don't go doing me any favors," he laughed as he pushed out the door.

Henry returned to the waiting room to sit with his wife and sat down with a sullen look on his face. When his wife tried to ask him what was wrong, he told her nothing was wrong, and that he just needed to think for a while. He leaned back, put his head against the wall behind him, and closed his eyes. The stress of the day had gotten to him, and suddenly he felt drained. Minutes later Jan noted his breathing changed, and she knew he was asleep. She placed her head against his shoulder and did her best to sleep, but it seemed that every few minutes someone entered the waiting room and someone left, or the intercom was paging a doctor. She quickly said yet another prayer for Brett asking God to spare him. She had already forgotten her promise to pray for Chase, too.

Brett's body lay still in the intensive care ward with the only noise coming from the sounds of beeps and tones from the various vital sign equipment hooked to him. A nurse just checked his urine bag and wrote notes on his chart that the bag was finally running clear. His first bag had some blood in it, so they had monitored it carefully. She adjusted his IV bags for proper drip levels and checked his pulse manually just to confirm what she was seeing on the screen. Satisfied she had done all she could do, she left the area by pulling the curtain to give Brett some privacy although he did not know he wanted any.

The vital sign sensors attached to his naked body failed to note he had begun moving a finger a little. The anesthesia had worn off, but his brain remained wounded and bruised, and thus he remained in a deep sleep. Feeling no pain, he began to dream as if his entire life was one long videotape beginning from his earliest memory until the present.

It was Christmas Eve and though he was only five, he and his sister had tried to stay awake until Santa Claus came. Soon he left her room and settled in his own bed to rest his eyes for a while before continuing his role as the soldier on watch for old Santa. A few minutes turned into a few hours, the

next time he woke, it was seven o'clock in the morning, and his sister was rapidly tugging his arm.

"Wake up, Brett!" she whispered excitedly. "Santa has come!"

He rubbed his eyes and tried his best to get his thoughts together, and forced his brain to wake up, but the sandman had done a good job, and he just could not stay awake.

Far from satisfied, Martha Jo gave his ear a twist. "Get up or I'll open your presents for you!" she threatened.

Instantly Brett's eyes popped open, "Ow! You're hurting me. I'm up. I'm up," stated Brett as he rolled out of the covers that had somehow magically appeared on top of him during the night. He had never guessed his father had tucked him in before heading off to bed.

"Are you ready?" she asked while still holding his hand and leading him into the semi-dark living room.

"Yep," he replied taking an excited deep breath.

She flipped the light switch, and instantly the lamps on the end tables lit up as well as the lights on the Christmas tree. Suddenly there was an unexpected flash as his Dad took their picture with his old 35mm camera and then popped out the hot flashbulb into an ash tree.

"Merry Christmas," said his mother as she leaned into her husband. "Merry Christmas," said Dad.

Brett shrieked with excitement and immediately noted a bright red tractor with pedals sitting near the tree. Martha Jo saw a new life-size doll placed on the edge of the couch as well as a new sweater and dress. Brett ran to the tractor, and climbed on the seat, placing his bare feet on the black rubber peddles for the first time. He placed his hands on the steering wheel, and then looked back over his shoulder as his mother called his name. He had a huge grin on his face.

"Cheese!" she said as Dad took yet another picture.

"Yee haw!" yelled Brett as he began pushing on the pedals. He turned across the room and promptly ran over his sister's foot.

"Ow," she popped him on the shoulder. "You hit me!"

"Sorry," he said without evening flinching at the hit on his arm as he had far more important and exciting things to do. He steered down the hall to his room, then turned around and steered back. The rubber wheels kept the noise down, but it would not have mattered as Brett created his own noises by doing his best to create the sound of a real tractor. His parents laughed as he rode back and forth.

"I want to go out on the sidewalk and give it a spin," he stated as he came to halt in front of his dad.

"Sorry, pal. I thought it was cold enough to snow last night, but instead it is raining. You don't want to get your new tractor wet, do you?"

"No, sir, I sure don't." Without another thought in complaint of the rain, he spun around and went back down the hall again.

They let him ride for about an hour before finally sitting down to open his presents. There were just five but to him it looked like a huge pile. His grandparents gave him more socks, which were the same brand of socks they gave him last year just a little bit bigger. They had arrived just before time to open the presents so he quickly gave them both a hug and kiss. He loved them dearly. They were his first baby-sitters and close to being his second parents. They spoiled him and taught him manners all at the same time. No one could make homemade pancakes like his grandmother. His grandfather had a full herd of hunting dogs, and he could make a whistle the dogs could hear for miles.

Chase awoke and once again found it hard to keep his eyes open.

"Did I wake you?" said a mysterious voice.

He strained to focus and then felt a pain, "Yes, I guess. Who are you?"

"I'm Mildred, your day nurse. Sorry, I woke you, but they require me to check your blood pressure manually which I did, but I noticed you had somehow pulled your IV needle loose and leaking fluid on to the bed. I got it taped back in place and placed a few towels on the wet spot. How are you feeling?"

"I'm starved. Do they have a Burger King in this joint?" asked Chase as he tried to sit up and suddenly felt a huge surge of pain. "Yeow, that hurts!"

"Just hold still and hit that button on the side of the bed with the up arrow," she told him as she checked his chart for pain medicine prescriptions.

Chase did as told. The back third of the bed began to rise until he was almost sitting up. "Thanks, that was much easier." Another bolt of pain flew up his nerve paths from his leg to his brain. "Geez, that ankle hurts a lot."

"The doctor didn't put anything on your chart for more pain medicine. I'm going to give you some Tylenol and will call your doctor's office to see if they will give you more pain medicine."

"They'd better. Tylenol is going to be like chasing a horse with a flyswatter. It ain't going to be enough!"

She grinned. "I know what you mean. I'll order you a food tray. Maybe that will help. I'll be back in a second."

Chase did not feel like that would help, but he was hungry. He sat there thinking and all of sudden it hit him. He had forgotten to ask Mildred about Brett's condition and status. He felt immediately guilty and nervous. He was afraid she had not volunteered the information as something bad might have happen to Brett. He started to hit the call button when he noticed the phone on the nightstand. He grunted as he struggled to reach his hand to the phone, but finally he got a hold of the receiver and pulled it. The base of the

phone fell off the nightstand, but he didn't let go of the receiver, and soon reeled in the rest of the phone by pulling on the cord hand over hand.

When he finally got the phone over his bed rail and onto his lap, he dialed zero. "Hello," he said immediately.

"May I help you?" the operator asked.

"Yes, I need to know the status on Brett Allen. I don't know what room he is in, but he came in from the plane crash yesterday."

"Yes, I have him in the computer, but I'm sorry, when patients are in intensive care, we can only give medical information out to family members."

"I'm his family!" he yelled as Mildred pushed the door to his room and entered with his breakfast tray.

"Are you related to him?" asked the operator.

"No, I'm ..."

"You have to be a blood relative to get that information," she said.

Mildred set the food tray on the bed table, and began sliding it over to Chase's bed while raising it up a bit.

"I'm his boyfriend!" Chase yelled into the phone.

There was silence on the other end of the phone. Finally, the operator said, "I'm sorry, that doesn't count in this situation." She then hung up.

"I have legal authority, you bitch," he said before he realized she had hung up on him. "Damn!" he yelled as he threw up his arms in disgust, and not seeing the tray that Mildred was wheeling to him, he hit the edge of the tray and flipped it on top of him. Eggs, grits, Jell-O, milk, and orange juice splattered all over him. He became exasperated beyond words, and just sat there with the food mess all over him.

Mildred gasped as she saw the food fly up into the air and fall down on her patient. After seeing the results, she just didn't know what to say. She made eye contact with Chase, and after hearing him on the phone, she just knew he was fixing to yell at her. However, Chase knew it was his fault and not hers, and though disappointed at the results of his phone call his face broke into a grin.

He picked up a piece of bacon and took a bite, "This hospital sure has a different way of feeding their patients than I expected." His deadpan reaction made her grin as well.

"Yes, they do. I bet you can't wait to see what you'll be wearing for your lunch today!" Mildred laughed at her own joke.

Chase laughed as well. "You're right I can't. Do you have a helmet I can wear?"

They both laughed again.

Mildred began pulling the empty plate back to the tray. "Please let me get this food off your bed, and get you another tray."

Chase stopped her. "Hell no, I'm starved. I'll eat what I can from this mess, and go get me another tray, and I promise not to wave my hands again."

"Are you sure? You're a pitiful sight."

"People have been telling me that for years, but you can't eat words." He stuffed a piece of toast into his mouth. "Do you have any jelly?"

She laughed again, "I'll bring you some."

"Strawberry, and don't forget the mop!" he yelled as she was leaving the room.

THREE

"Mister Allen?" asked a hospital staff member standing just in front of him.

Henry looked up at the man in the tie, and for a brief moment was not sure where he was. He set up straight in the chair where he had been awkwardly sleeping and replied, "Yes, that's me. Has something happened?" He stretched and found his back sore from the hours in the straight chair. He swore in a whisper at the aching muscles.

Jan woke up as well, "Is Brett all right?"

"I'm sorry. His condition report hasn't changed, and they say he is definitely in a coma. Can you come down the hall to a counseling room with me?"

"Why? What's up?" asked Henry.

"Well, the press is asking for a press conference. I'm in charge of it, and I can go ahead and answer their questions, but I thought you might want to attend as well."

Henry stood and helped his wife up. "Do you have any coffee in your office?"

"Yes, yes I do," replied Bernard, the hospital public information officer. He had gotten the job right out of college after getting a degree in English, as well as corporate information and marketing. With a wife and two kids, he moved to Asheville from Clemmons, North Carolina where they had grown tired of sand, mosquitoes, bugs and hurricanes that often pounded the Carolina coast, and settled successfully into the surrounding cool mountains.

He had held the job only eight months, and in Asheville, his only experience with a live press conference was when North Carolina's famous Senator Jesse Helms arrived in an emergency after landing his plane at their airport, and rushed to the hospital complaining of chest pains. Bernard had arranged the pressroom, made sure there were plenty of phones and Internet ports available, and emceed the questions from the press to the doctors concerning the Senator's condition. He learned a lot that day from the Senator's staff and his press agent.

He led Brett's parents down the hall towards his office. The plane crash had been on the newscasts all over the country, and even though it was the day after the plane went down, the story was still a big one. Somehow, the media obtained Brett's picture as well as Chase's. The media did interviews with their local friends and co-workers.

He led Brett's parents into his office. "Please have a seat, and I'll get you some coffee." He returned moments later with the hot coffee, handed it to them, and sat down behind his desk.

41

"Thank you. I felt you would be more comfortable talking in private. The press is still covering the plane crash. He looked at his watch, "In twenty minutes, the press conference is going to begin down the hall. Your son's doctors will be there to help answer questions. I felt you might want to speak as well."

Henry looked confused, "What would we say?"

Jan spoke up as well, "What do they want to know?"

"Well, I suspect they are going to hound you wherever you go until they get to the bottom of the story. It has been my experience it is better to just be upfront and honest from the start, and soon they will be off to chase another story."

"Who will be there?" asked Henry.

"Well, of course our local TV channel reporters will be there, as well as reporters from the Citizen-Times staff, but there are also reporters and camera crews from CNN and all the network news teams."

"What?" asked Jan. "Why are they here?"

"Ma'am, this plane crash is national and maybe even global news and the fact..." he had to stop a moment and look at his notes, "Uh, Brett Allen and Chase Fleming survived is big news. They were the only survivors, and the press wants to know what happened, why the plane crashed, and how they survived."

"But we don't know the answers to those questions," rebutted Henry.

"I know, Brett is in a coma, but Chase is awake, and in fact, he ate breakfast an hour ago."

"He lived?" asked Henry.

"Yes, he did, and he will recover. Do you want to speak to him first?"

Henry answered quickly, "No, we don't. We don't approve of Chase."

Bernard became confused, "Don't approve?"

"He's a big homosexual, and our church says that, uh, that lifestyle is wrong," stated Henry reluctantly.

"I see," replied Bernard though his face turned red. "Perhaps the press just wants to know who your son was."

"Is," replied Jan quickly, "who our son Brett is? He's not dead. He's alive."

If Bernard could have crawled under his desk, he would have. "I'm sorry. You're right." Thankfully, his phone rang, giving him a break. He picked it up, "Yes? Okay, we're ready." He hung up. "The press is ready. Shall we go?" He stood and began to move around his desk.

"Hold on," said Henry, and then to his wife, "Jan, what do you think?"

"I guess if we want them to know what a good son he is, we're going to have to tell them."

42

Henry thought for a second and then looked up at Bernard. "Okay, we'll do it. Lead the way."

Bill and Larry were waiting outside Bernard's office. They followed them down the hall, and stood off to the side of the table Henry and Jan sat down to. In front of them were over fifty reporters and camera crewmembers chatting constantly as they waited for the meeting to begin. The Allen family felt overwhelmed with so many national news groups interested in this story.

Bernard stepped to the podium and began introducing the doctors and finally Henry and Jan. They politely nodded at the audience as he mentioned their names. The surgeon who had operated on Brett stood and gave a five-minute report on Brett's surgery and condition. Slow tears fell from Jan's eyes as she heard the doctor's speak solemnly of her son's status.

When he finished a reporter broke in with a question, "Did Mr. Allen ever regain consciousness?"

"No, he didn't. I suspect he is in a coma because of the swelling in his brain," replied the doctor.

Another reporter stood, "What are his chances of survival?"

Jan gasped and Henry put his arm around her. "Oh, my Lord," she whispered.

The doctor paused for a long second before replying, "I'd say he has about a 20 percent chance of survival." Jan turned her face into Henry's shirt as she struggled for a breath.

"If he survives, will Mr. Allen be able to remember anything about the plane crash?" asked a woman on the front row.

The doctor paused again, "It is too early to tell. Any brain injury is difficult to recover from." The reporter and Brett's doctor sat down.

Bernard introduced Chase's doctor who gave a report on his condition.

A reporter in the back spoke out, "It appears that Mister Fleming is in much better shape than Mr. Allen, so when can we speak to him? Can we set up an interview?"

The doctor replied, "Maybe in a few days. He remains immobilized with a broken ankle for now. He just ate his first meal since the accident. Our staff feels he needs a bit more time before moving him around."

"How about just a picture of him?" asked another reporter.

"I think we can arrange that," replied the doctor as he sat down.

Bernard returned to the podium to moderate. "Okay, now that you have the current status on the new patients, are there any questions for our staff or the parents?"

A woman leaned forward from the back row and asked, "Any truth to the story floating around that the boys are lovers?"

The crowd began to murmur and whisper to one another. Bernard turned red again. His twenty-four hour deodorant had only made it to three hours before failing. He struggled to control his composure. He took a sip of water from a glass on the table next to the podium.

"I'm afraid I have no knowledge of their private lives. We're here to answer questions about their medical condition."

Another reporter spoke to the Allen's, "Mr. and Mrs. Allen, is your son a homosexual?"

"Hell no," yelled Uncle Bill from the sidelines.

"You go to hell!" added Uncle Larry.

Henry and Jan were too stunned to reply. Jan covered her face and began sobbing. Henry stood and led her from the room. Bill and Larry continued yelling at the confused pack of reporters.

Bernard tried to announce the meeting was over, but no one heard him. The doctors and staff left the room, and the reporters began to disassemble, but they all knew there was more to the story than just a plane crash. The wolves were hungry for the truth, and the vultures were circling.

Within an hour, their high school pictures were featured on the news channels with the miraculous story of the gay lovers' survival. Tomorrow's local paper would do the same. Jan and Henry were horrified.

After his second breakfast, Chase drifted off to a deep sleep. He dreamed of meeting Brett for the first time. It had been a little over two years ago in the dressing room at Dillard's department store in the mall in Asheville. Chase had been shopping with friends and in a silly jovial mood. He and his friends often cruised the mall while making fun of ugly straight folks.

"Jimmy, look at that ugly four hundred pound guy with that tiny woman," said Chase.

Jimmy looked at where Chase had been pointing and busted out laughing. He took Chase's hand and pulled them both to their knees right there in the middle of the mall. He said solemnly with a straight face, "Let's pray that big ugly redneck is a heterosexual because there is no way in hell he could be gay, and dressed like that!"

Chase laughed aloud as he got back to his feet. Various shoppers moved around them and someone called them faggots. "I bet you can't even spell it!" shot back Chase while pulling the hysterical Jimmy to his feet.

Jimmy grabbed Chase by the arm and turned him around. "Look! It's a miracle. The ugly man disappeared! Thank you, Jesus! Thank you! Thank you! Now if you folks will get out your wallets, it's time to take an offering!" began Jimmy while mocking the infamous Evangelist Jimmy Swaggart. "The Bible says give ten percent, but little Jimmy says ten percent will only get you noticed while twenty percent will get you to the door of heaven itself! You will receive a front gate parking spot for just twenty dollars!"

Chase pulled him on down the mall while they were both laughing and giggling. People were noticing them and the boys loved it. Chase knew he was a flamer. He couldn't help himself. If there were a magic show in the mall, he would be on the front row. If they chose anyone from the audience, it had to be him. He didn't mind at all stealing someone else's fifteen minutes of fame. He was not sure why he did it, but he did.

Dillard's was having a forty percent off sale and that was all the temptation the two boys needed. They swooned through the men's section, picking out this and that and making fun of just about everything. Chase's mouth flew open wide when Jimmy pretended to feel the crotch of a nearby mannequin.

"Honey, have you ever heard of Viagra?" asked Jimmy of the mannequin.

"You're absolutely crazy," laughed Chase. "Come on, before they throw us out."

A saleslady in the corner was rapidly moving towards them to tell them to stop, but they had stopped already, and so she said way too sweetly, "May I help you?"

Jimmy shot back quickly, "No you may not, but lord knows my friend here needs all the help he can get. Do you happen to have a cute son about his 'size,' I mean 'age'?"

"What? I certainly do not," she responded as her face turned red.

"Oh, I'm sorry. I guess you have an ugly son," added Jimmy.

Chase jumped in quickly, "Sorry, ma'am. I'm looking for some slacks, and I'm a size 29."

The saleslady gathered her wits about her and pointed to an aisle near the wall, "They're over there and marked forty percent off."

"Thank you," replied Chase as he pushed Jimmy in that direction.

They looked at various slacks for about ten minutes when Jimmy became bored and walked over to the cologne section. Chase said that was fine because he wanted to try on a couple of pairs of slacks. Jimmy took off and Chase loaded his arms up with about five pairs in various styles and colors, and then turned to find a changing room. He immediately noted a tall, well-tanned, dark haired man looking through the shirts that were also on sale.

Chase whispered to himself, "Come on sweetie—just look up at me."

Brett did look up as if this scene was right out of a movie, but he only glanced up. Just as Chase was about to give up on attracting his attention, Brett looked up again, noticed Chase, and smiled at him.

Brett's big blue eyes nearly made Chase's heart skip a beat. He smiled back. Normally, Chase had never met a stranger, as he would go up and talk to anyone. He would always begin the same way, "Uh, sir, I have a question." Since Chase was blond, most everyone just assumed he was dumb,

but most of the time, he knew the answer to the question. He delighted in talking to anyone about anything, but not this time. Brett's blue eyes left him tongue-tied and drooling.

He forced himself to smile back before moving on to the changing room. He blushed when he ran into a shirt rack and quickly grabbed it before it fell over. After making his way to an outside wall, he pulled back the curtain of the nearest room, stepped in, and cussed. "Damn, who took the bench out of here?" He dropped the pile of slacks on the floor, turned, and pulled the curtain behind him. He took off his jacket, and then took his shoes off—not by untying them like most folks, but rather by pushing the heel off with the other foot's big toe. Out of habit, he took his shirt off, which was dumb as he was only trying on slacks. In his mind, he didn't want the color of slacks to clash with his shirt so he took it off and threw it on top of his jacket. He then slid out of his pants and because he had forgotten to wash clothes yesterday as he had planned, he had run out of clean underwear, so he stood there naked, except for his socks. He picked out a pair of tan corduroy pants from the pile on the floor, pulled out the plastic hook that kept the seams intact, and tossed it on the floor. He bent down, put his left leg in the pants, and pushed the foot through until it hit the carpet floor. He then began pushing the other leg through while balancing on his left foot. Apparently, Inspector Number 38 had not realized the right leg had a thread hanging in the middle of the pants leg, and it became the perfect target for Chase's toes. When he hit the thread, he tried to push his foot through, but lost his balance and in a flash, he fell backwards through the curtain onto the floor in the hallway in the dressing room area.

There he lay, naked except for one leg in the pants and his socks. Brett had just walked into the room with a pair of jeans he wanted to try on. He stopped walking to the next booth just as Chase had fallen in front of him. He looked down at Chase's naked body and grinned.

"Are you all right?" he asked politely while taking in the view.

Chase chuckled, "I have a perfectly good explanation for this situation." He did not try to cover up his groin.

"You were trying to gain my attention?" asked Brett with a sly grin.

Chase realized Brett knew he was gay. "Well, you could say that. It wasn't a planned attack, but how am I doing so far?"

Brett laughed, "I'd say you have my undivided attention."

"I am serious, I really didn't plan this. My toe became stuck on something in the other pants leg, there's no chair in the stall, and well, I lost my balance."

"What happened to your underwear?" Brett asked while studying Chase's body. Chase had been dancing all his life and recently started dancing at the local club as a go-go boy. He had the body of a gymnast but never worked out. He simply danced his ass off every weekend. While short in stature, Chase possessed a large dick. For a guy that craved attention, God had

46

given him something special to help him with his low self-esteem. It was an ego tool he carried everywhere.

Chase still did not bother to cover himself as he struggled to get to his feet. He liked having Brett look at him. Brett reached out, hooked his arm at the elbow, and pulled him up. They stood facing each other.

"I was afraid you were going to ask about my, uh, my lack of underwear. The truth is yesterday is washday, and I forgot, so today I have no underwear. I only have seven pairs and today is the eighth day." Chase didn't blush often, but this time he did. "And of course the lack of underwear could never stop me from going shopping," he added with a grin.

"With a body like yours, I guess it would be a shame to put anything over it," said Brett before he realized what he had just revealed.

Chase took him by the arm, pulled him into the stall, and then closed the curtain once more. He turned to face Brett and said, "I've never done this before in a changing room, but I have this incredible desire to kiss you." He moved in closer to Brett, and pulled Brett's hands to his bare butt. Then he looked up sweetly into Brett's blue eyes. His member grew hard.

They paused for a long moment before Brett leaned over, kissed him gently on the lips, and pulled back as if tasting him, pulled in again, and kissed him deeply. Chase's hands moved around until he could feel Brett's rapidly growing penis. They kissed for fifteen minutes. They remained passionate, suddenly forgetting the English language.

Finally, Brett pulled away, "I think I should introduce myself. My name is Brett."

"I'm Chase," he replied as he bent down and dry-mouthed Brett's penis right through his pants.

Reluctantly Brett said, "I think we'd better stop because I have this incredible wish to fuck you, but this wouldn't be the right place."

"It would be fun, but you're right. I will dress, and we'll go get something to drink and start over."

"Good idea," replied Brett as he pulled Chase to his feet and kissed him again, while playing tenderly with Chase's much-enlarged penis.

Mildred had entered his room, looked over his chart, and noted he was smiling while sleeping. She could not help but wonder what he was dreaming about. She did not know that Chase was dreaming about the most wonderful man he had ever met. Had he been awake he would have laughed aloud as he watched himself fall naked into Brett's path. He had told that story so many times to friends and new acquaintances in their travels or whenever anyone asked the couple how they met. His friends always laughed heartily at the story.

It had taken several hours for Henry and Jan to get over the confrontation at the press conference. Bernard apologized over and over, but his words were ignored. The uncles were livid and still aching for a fight as they made their way back to the waiting room down the hall from the intensive care ward where Brett remained silent and still.

After dark, Chase awoke and found himself thirsty. He had no visitors to assist and thus, he found his throat as dry and dehydrated as he had ever felt in his entire life. Not knowing what time it was, he reluctantly hit the nurse's call button, expecting Mildred, Johnny, or some other stranger to appear.

To his surprise, the door opened and in walked the second shift nurse Jeremy. "Well now, I see you're awake at…" he paused to check the watch he wore on his right arm and wrote down the time on his clipboard with his left hand, "at ten o'clock in the evening. How are you feeling? I have checked on you several times since I came on at three, but you were sleeping so soundly, I didn't have the heart to wake you."

Chase yawned and smiled, "I wasn't sleeping. I was pretending to sleep so the day nurses would leave me the hell alone. I must have dozed off while faking it." Chase grinned at himself, as he knew that sounded rather stupid.

"Oh, you're a clever lad. Are you hungry?" asked Jeremy as he came and gently squeezed Chase's arm to comfort him. He was well aware no one had come to see him. There were no flowers on the table and no cards.

"I am hungry, but I called because my throat is void of any moisture. I'm as dry as a desert."

"That I can fix," he replied as he filled the water glass in the sink and adjusted the straw so Chase could drink.

Chase felt like a camel as he sucked on the straw until drawing every drop from the glass. "More," he said promptly, like the little boy in the movie musical Oliver. "My goodness, you are thirsty. Hold on." Jeremy rushed to the sink and filled the glass again.

Chase did as before until every drop was gone.

"I suspect you're just trying to get me to hold your penis while you pee, but I think if you're up to it, I'll try to get you in a wheelchair, and we'll move you around a little bit. Perhaps get you some dinner. Would you like to get out of that bed?" Jeremy rolled the wheelchair he had parked at the end of the bed around to the side, locked the brakes, and lifted the footplates to make it easier for his patient to enter.

"I reckon I'm ready. I'm certainly bored. Let's try it."

Jeremy unhooked the strap that held Chase's leg up from the bed. Chase winched as a shot of pain flew up his leg, but gritted his teeth and fought to bear it. "Damn!" he suddenly said aloud. "That hurts like hell!"

"I know, and I'm sorry, but the sooner you're moving around the sooner you'll get well. You're going to get bedsores lying there day and night, and lord knows what is going to happen to your brains if you don't move them around a bit. Come on then—put your arms around my neck. I'm going to lift you over the edge of the bed. You then put your weight on your good leg, I'll slowly spin you around, and then carefully, you and I will slowly lower you into the wheelchair."

"Okay." That was all Chase could muster up to say. He wanted to get up and out of the bed. He grunted with all the strength he could assemble, and pulled on Jeremy's neck until he was sitting up on the bed. He put his good leg down as instructed, and with a bit of coaxing on Jeremy's part, he turned and slowly sat down in the chair.

"There you go. You're in the chair. You did it! I knew you wanted to go out for a spin," laughed Jeremy. He bent down, gently lifted first his bad leg up, closed the footplate beneath it, and lowered it down. Chase winched at the pain but said nothing. Then he put his good leg on the other plate and smiled at Chase. "But first we have to make you presentable. Your hair's a mess, and your face looks like you have been sucking on an all-day sucker. You got drool and spittle all over yourself. Let me get a hot washrag and clean you up."

"Thanks," replied Chase, nearly exhausted from the effort from the bed to the chair, and feeling a little light headed.

Jeremy returned and washed his face and ears ever so gently. He took the small free comb the hospital provided, and combed threw his hair until he thought he looked pretty good. He wheeled Chase around so he could look in the mirror on the back of the room door. "Whatyathink?" he said mimicking a comedian he had once heard who rolled his words together like a true Southern redneck.

"I looked like I fell off a horse, and the horse backed over me," stated Chase somberly with no hint of smile. Jeremy looked around until their eyes met and began forming a smile. Chase smiled back, and they both laughed aloud.

"That is a good way of putting it. If I had my choice," began Jeremy, "I guess I had rather fall off a horse than fall out of a plane. It's a miracle you're alive, but I'm glad you are." He paused and placed a hand on Chase's shoulder to squeeze it. "Okay, enough chitchat. It's late at night. Let's roll down to the cafeteria, and eat some supper together. I'm starved as well."

He waved at his partner at the counter and said he was going to supper. They rolled down the hall, took the elevator to the first floor, and then wheeled across the lobby. Chase saw a secretary at the front desk, and a few men mopping floors, but otherwise, the place looked nearly deserted. Jeremy wheeled him up to a serving line. The food smelled wonderful to Chase. A big

black woman walked up to the other side of the counter and smiled at him, "My, my," she said, "You're working late tonight. Who have you got there, Jeremy?"

"Mabel, this is Chase and he's starving and so am I"

Mabel laughed, "You're always starving, but Chase dear boy, I'm so pleased to meet you. It is late enough to be early for breakfast so what would like to eat? I've got some good old scrambled eggs, grits, toast, or would you like one of Mabel's special buttermilk biscuits?"

"Ma'am, if you don't mind, I would like all the above and some bacon, too!" replied Chase with a hungry grin. "And is that pancakes I see?"

"Why yes, it is, and I think I get the picture. You want a little bit of everything," she laughed.

"No ma'am," shot back Chase quickly, "I want a lot of everything!"

Jeremy, Mabel, and Chase all laughed together as she prepared three plates of food for Chase and then another plate for Jeremy.

Mabel got her cup of coffee, joined the boys at the table, and immediately began laughing at the teasing and carrying on that Chase and Jeremy did while eating. For almost ninety minutes, they told various tall tales, which one way or the other ended with trash talk about the other. Chase, Jeremy, and Mabel became good friends quickly. Jeremy began pushing Chase out into the hall, which Chase bluntly asked him, "Jeremy? Could you push me towards Brett's room so I can check in on him?"

Jeremy's smile fell from his face. "We're not supposed to go into intensive care." He looked at his watch. "Well, it's after eleven, and the area is probably deserted. Shoot, if they throw us out that would be about the worst that could happen. You'll have to promise to be on your best behavior and stay as quiet as possible."

Chase grinned while reaching up to squeeze Jeremy's hand resting on his shoulder. "Thanks, man. I'll owe you big time."

"All right, let's do it."

Jeremy sprinted down the hall pushing the wheelchair at times and other times riding on the back. He skidded to a halt and hit the elevator button. Surprisingly, the door opened immediately. Jeremy checked to make sure the car was empty, then pushed Chase in, and hit the floor button.

Chase sat quietly as promised. He became nervous, feeling afraid he could not stand to see Brett injured badly, or to find out he had died. When the elevator doors opened, Jeremy checked the hallway and spotted a nurse at the counter. He gently pushed Chase up to the counter.

Jeremy recognized the night nurse. "Hey, Mary, how do you stay awake on this floor? It's too quiet for me. I'd be snoozing by now," he added with a grin.

Mary laughed, "I guess I'm used to it since I've been doing it for twenty-one years."

"That was before my birth," he chuckled.

"That's it, go ahead, and make me feel old," she said.

"Mary, I've been meaning to ask you, were you a nurse to Abraham Lincoln, too?"

She stopped typing on the computer and looked up at him and laughed, "I ain't that old, you rascal. You know, you're looking a little pale. Why don't you come on around the counter, and I'll give you one of my fast acting enemas?"

They both laughed. Chase wondered what an enema was, but said nothing.

"So why are you here so late with a patient?" she said with a slight smile.

"Did I tell you how pretty you're looking today?" Jeremy said, while stretching out his words in an obvious plea for help.

"Yeah, yeah, like I said, what do you want?" she asked.

"This is Chase. He and his friend Brett were in that plane crash the other day. Chase hasn't seen Brett since the explosion. They are best friends and of course, Chase is worried about him and cannot sleep. Would you give him a few minutes with Brett?" Jeremy asked as sweetly as he possibly could.

Mary looked at Chase and his wounds, and indeed felt sympathy, but when she saw the earnest intent in Chase's eyes, her heart melted a bit. "Okay, but you can't stay long. Susan is on her break, and she'll be back soon and you need to be long gone before she gets back. We don't want any witnesses. Follow me."

Chase fought to control his breathing as he nearly gasped with excitement. As Jeremy pushed him by each of the intensive care rooms, he saw patients in bad shape. His heart began to race a bit, and decided it might be best if he did not look into the rooms until he reached Brett's room.

She stopped and opened a door, "In here."

Jeremy pushed him in and pulled him to a stop beside Brett's bed. Chase's hand slid to his face as he noted all the bruises and cuts all across Brett's body. A bit of red blood escaped around some of the stitches, but if these wounds had belonged to anyone else, Chase would have thrown up. However, every drop of blood belonged to the man he loved most in the entire world, and there was a part of him wishing he could push the blood back into his lover's body.

When his eyes reached Brett's head, he quickly noted his beautiful dark hair had been shaved off and replaced with a swami-like wrap covering almost his entire head. He noted dried spots of blood on his forehead. He saw the tube going in Brett's nose, and glimpsed at the various tubes and sensor wires hanging on poles from an assortment of machines above Brett's bed. He

51

soon spotted the heart machine monitoring Brett's pulse, and it thrilled him at the visual sight of Brett's heart beating steady and strong.

Eventually, he gazed at Brett's closed eyes and wished with all his might they would open so he could see his splendid, radiant eyes once again. On close scrutiny of Nurse Mary, Chase slowly allowed his right hand to reach forward and touch Brett's arm. He had thought it would be cold, but found it as warm as he remembered it. Tenderly, he stroked Brett's arm. Mary smiled, realizing Chase and Brett were more than friends. It did not bother her at all.

A slow tear followed yet another as they cascaded down Chase's cheeks bouncing onto Brett's arm. Mary moved in closer as she saw Brett's brow wrinkle a bit, then relax, and then did it again. He had not moved a muscle during her past two shifts. She placed an assuring hand on Chase's shoulder while putting her arm around Jeremy.

"Talk to him honey. Sometimes they can hear you. He's in a coma, and we need for him to wake up."

Chase looked up into her sweet face earnestly, and choked back tears as he began to speak softly and tenderly. "Brett? It's Chase. We made it from the plane. We're alive. I'm fine so don't you worry about me. I wish I could see your eyes. I miss those soulful eyes so much. I miss your touch. I miss your kisses in the morning." He paused before adding, "And I miss your waffles, too."

Jeremy and Mary smiled. Mary watched Brett's face and saw a muscle twitch. She was afraid to get Chase's hopes up so she said nothing. She felt confident Brett not only heard the words of his lover and partner, but deeply he would struggle to wake up. Perhaps his brain was working overtime to force his muscles to open his eyelids, but they were not ready to do so.

After a few more minutes she said, "Chase, this is enough for a visit this time, perhaps you can try again tomorrow night. I'll be working again," she said to Jeremy with a wink.

Chase turned to her, reached over, and patted her arm with his other hand, "Thank you so much."

Suddenly, the door open and a big man yelled at Chase, "You get your filthy faggot hands off my nephew!" Chase had only met Brett's uncle Bill once, but then and now, he could just see venom in his eyes. He frightfully let go of Brett's hand.

Mary stepped in front of Chase and took charge immediately, "Sir, you must keep your voice down. There are people here on the edge of death."

Bill shot back, "Yeah and one of them is Chase the homo!"

Defiantly, Chase took Brett's hand, bowed his head, and said a silent prayer. Bill's face turned a bright red. Jeremy thought the man looked like a red bull in a cartoon with steam bellowing from his nostrils.

Mary pushed a button on a small control unit she wore around her neck. "You see this? I just pushed the panic button. That means our security

police will be here in just a second, and they will haul you to jail. Now get out of here," she demanded.

Reluctantly, Bill backed out of the room while extending a middle finger gesture to Chase, but Chase was still praying. Bill cursed again, left the intensive care unit, and went to find his sibling.

Mary turned back to Jeremy, "You'd better get him out of here before the cavalry arrives." She held the door.

Chase looked up, kissed Brett's hand, and then turned and smiled at Mary. "Thank you for allowing me a few moments to be with Brett. Please keep me posted about how he is doing. I am his Executor and have authority over his Will and his Living Will."

"I will, honey, but please hurry and get out of here." She reached down and patted his shoulder.

Jeremy leaned into Mary, and whispered. "I didn't know you had a panic button for the cops."

Mary smiled slyly, "I don't. All this does is sound a buzzer at the nurse's station for someone to come help me with a patient. But since I'm the only here at the moment, there is no one coming."

Jeremy chuckled, "You're the bomb, woman. Way to go!" And then to Chase, "Hang on little dude, we're off to the races!"

Chase hung on tightly as Jeremy rounded a corner on two wheels and smartly took a service elevator. They had just entered when the main elevator opened and out walked Bill, Larry, Henry, and Jan Allen. They missed them by seconds.

Mary saw them and dialed security as they rushed up to the counter.

Henry spoke up first, "Is that faggot still up here?"

Mary ignored the slur for the moment and put her finger up indicating she was listening to the party on the phone. She was waiting on the party to pick up which they did. "Officer Sloan? Bring a few of your biggest men up here. I have a situation, and I need these folks escorted from the building immediately." She paused, "Thank you."

"Now you just hold on lady," said Henry. "Bill here says he saw Chase back there with Brett. Why on earth did you allow that faggot back there?"

"Sir, you'll watch your tongue with me. Chase is Brett's friend and partner. He's also the Executor of his Estate, his Will, and especially his Living Will. He has the right."

Larry leaned over the counter towards Mary. "That homo only has a right to cry while I punch his face in!"

Jan started to cry. Henry asked, "What do you mean his Living Will? What's an Executor?"

Mary replied, "Brett appointed his friend Chase as his Executor. It means he has sole authority over implementing his Will after death, and most importantly his Living Will while recovering. This means Brett has appointed Chase to be in charge of his medical decisions. This applies to any treatments, surgeries, and can even decide on how he dies if necessary."

"I never heard of such a thing," spout back Bill.

Mary looked at him with great dissension, "No doubt. The word Executor has eight letters—not four."

"But we're his parents," broke in Henry.

"Your son is over twenty-one years old, and by law has the right to appoint whomever he chooses to be in charge," replied Mary.

The elevator opened and two security guards and two Asheville city police officers came out. They were big men with serious looks on their faces.

Mary said to the group, "These men will escort you back to the waiting room. Don't come back up here unless I send for you. Do you understand?" She did not wait for them to reply, "Officer Jones, this man..." she pointed to Bill, "broke into an intensive care room without permission, yelled, screamed, and disturbed all the critical patients. He could have upset someone so severely they could have had yet another heart attack. I suggest you ban him from this hospital right now."

"No problem," replied Jones. He took hold of Bill's arm, twisted it behind his back, and cuffed him. Then pulled the other arm, cuffed it as well, and then walked him to the elevator.

On seeing the serious nature of these officers, Larry went with Henry and Jan and followed the officers quietly to the elevator. They returned to the waiting room where one of the officers warned the group if they did anything else to disturb the peace around here, he would personally remove them from the building.

The cops escorted Bill to the parking lot, released him from the handcuffs, and warned Bill not to return. Bill wisely did not reply and walked to his car to get another beer out of the cooler on the backseat floorboard.

"That was close," said Jeremy as he wheeled Chase into his room.

"I'll say," replied Chase. "I've got a lot of thinking to do. I don't know what I would have done without your help. I hope I didn't get you into trouble," added Chase as he touched Jeremy's arm to thank him.

"No problem. Don't worry, but let's get you back into bed before any of the staff catch us," urged Jeremy as he set the brakes on the wheelchair in preparation to help Chase into bed.

"Ouch, this hurts!" exclaimed Chase as grunted his way back into the bed. Jeremy put the light blanket over him, gave him a long drink of water, and then shut off the lights and let him return to sleep.

Soon Chase was dreaming deeply. Brett smiled at him as they sat across the table at Ruby Tuesdays. It was the evening after they met in the department store. Brett listened intently as Chase went on and on about his life and growing up. He had known he was gay from an early age, as most of the boys in school called him sissy or faggot anyhow. While he was never a great baseball player, he liked being the batboy. He could never spiral a football pass, but the title water-boy suited him just fine. Besides, everyday he saw great looking teenagers with their clothes off all the time in the locker room.

No one ever listened to Chase talk like Brett did. He laughed at the funny events that happened in Chase's life, and showed great empathy when life had been difficult. Chase accepted he was gay when he was just thirteen, and although being gay and out was not the smart thing to do in his high school, the team respected him, as no one worked harder than he did.

Somewhere in the middle of one of his stories, Chase slid his hand under the restaurant table and intertwined his fingers with Brett's. They held hands until dinner arrived, and then after dinner until it was time to leave the restaurant. Chase smiled slightly during his dream until a deep sleep allowed his battered body rest.

FOUR

Brett asked his parents repeatedly if he could campout with the neighbors in the backyard, but always received the same answer, "Not until you're six!" Rejected, he still agreed to help the boys set up their 'tent', which was a bunch of blankets, and clothespins. A few years ago, his dad had installed two iron pipes in the shapes of a capital T and planted the long end in the ground about forty feet apart. Then he ran stainless steel wire in four strands about ten inches apart from one tee and back. This became his mother's clothesline where every sunny day she hung out the washed clothes to dry. To make a tent, they threw a blanket over the top of the four strands and used clothespins to secure it. They used four blankets to create the four sides using additional pins. Finally, they pinned the corners together creating a single room or tent. They put a piece of plastic down for a ground cloth and then a quilt for their mattress. None of the boys owned a sleeping bag, so they each had a blanket and pillow tied with a belt to create a cowboy bedroll.

Late afternoon they would talk and play games in their tent, but near darkness, Brett's mother would call him in. She almost hated to, but knew soon his birthday would come. He laughed the next day when the boys told them they were telling ghost stories when suddenly a long arm extended through a crack in their blanket wall. They all screamed until his friend Brice recognized a tattoo on the arm.

"Dad," he yelled. "You can't scare me!" Brice laughed as his daddy grabbed him, and tried to tickle him as one of the blanket walls fell down.

Brett wished he had been there as it sounded superbly exciting, but he knew one day he would get to camp out as well. There were eight boys in the neighborhood, ranging in age from four to fifteen. They played army with packs, helmets, and air rifles as well as dodge ball and softball. When the snow came, they thought it sissy to build a snowman so they built a fort out of big snowballs pushed together. After completing the two forts, they split up and planned strategies for sieges. Everyone worked hard to build up their arsenal before the battle began. Brett thought he lived in the perfect neighborhood and was the luckiest kid on earth.

On his sixth birthday, he had a party in the backyard since it was too hot from the summer sun to stay inside house. Out on the picnic table he blew out candles, and all the kids in the neighborhood were soon eating cake and ice cream freshly churned by his father. His parents presented him with a wrapped present from his grandparents, which he quickly opened to find an Indian Cherokee tomahawk. All the kids whooped like Indian warriors at the sight. Years later he understood the label on the bottom of the stone that read "Made in Japan" and it made him feel sad for the Cherokees.

His last present was a box about forty-eight inches long. He gleefully ripped off the wrapping paper, and immediately saw the full color picture on

the side of the box. "It's an Army pup tent!" he yelled. His dad took his picture while his mom laughed as he held the box up for all to see.

Later that night Brett and three of his best friends sat in the new pup tent telling stories and tales too wild to believe, but great fun in the telling. Suddenly, it thundered far off in the distance. James, who was the same age as Brett, watched as the lighting bolts streaked across the sky.

"I've got to go in. A storm is coming," James announced.

"What? Are you chicken to stay out?" teased Ellis the fifteen year old.

Then just like clock work Brice would pipe in with an echo comment as he idolized Ellis. Brice was fourteen. "Your yellow stripe is showing down your back. I bet you've even got a brown streak in your underwear!" he laughed, as did the other boys.

Before James could defend himself, his mother called from her porch, "James, get in here. There's a storm coming!"

"Sorry boys, I've got to go or she'll whip me," announced James, trying to sound reluctant, but inside he felt relieved. He left before the remaining three could complain. They sat there looking at each other in silence for a few minutes, and then went back to telling a story about how Brice once saw his older sister's tits.

Soon, they felt sleepy and finally settled down in their bedrolls. They woke up about midnight with the sound of the family station wagon pulling into the driveway. Usually Brett's dad parked it alongside their house when he came home from work, but this time he pulled into the backyard and backed up to the tent. The boys peeped out to see what was going on.

"Boys," he called. "Are you awake?"

"Yeah, dad," replied Brett.

The storm is going to soak you in a few minutes. Let's put the backseat down in the station wagon, and you guys can continue your campout inside the car," he suggested. Brice wished his father were like Brett's. His father would have made him fold the tent up carefully, removing any grass, carry it to their storage room, and place it on a shelf marked with the label 'tent.' His dad was strict, demanding, and always unreasonable. Brett's dad disciplined him when he had to, but mostly he enjoyed playing ball with all the kids in their neighborhood.

The idea sounded perfect to them, as no one wanted to admit they were afraid of the lightning and rain. They threw their blankets and pillows inside, and then dad headed off to bed. Once he was gone, they locked the doors just in case Brice's dad decided to try to scare them like last time.

It was warm and cozy in the station wagon with the three boys lying side by side. The windows soon fogged up. Brett fell asleep, but about thirty minutes later, he heard his older friends whispering. Soon they pulled the

57

Brett, too confused to move, delighted in the feeling his friend gave him. It was a feeling he would never forget. It was the best birthday ever.

During Brett's dream the nurse monitoring her section of patients failed to note the change in his vital signs: pulse stronger, blood pressure went up a little, and his breathing increased. She also did not see his small erection because of the catheter but it was successful nonetheless. It all lasted less than a few minutes before returning to normal. She missed it after catching a glimpse of her supervisor arriving with questions.

"I have received a complaint from Henry Allen concerning his son's care last night. Has Mary already left for the day?"

"Yes, her shift ended at seven. She was very upset at Mr. Allen's parents and especially the uncles. She had to call security and the police as well. The uncle was yelling at the top of his lungs."

"What was he upset about exactly?"

"I heard they did not like her son's lover."

The supervisor sighed, "My goodness, what have we gotten ourselves into?"

"What do you mean? Mary said the boyfriend is the Executor of both Brett's Will and his Living Will. That would make him the person in charge would it not?"

"Yes, it would," replied the supervisor, "but I guess I need to see the paperwork to confirm as it is most unusual to have another man taking charge of a parent's child."

She left the intensive care unit and took the elevator to Chase's floor. She stopped by the nurse's station to check his chart to see how he was doing. The doctor planned to release him after lunch. Perhaps that would solve part of the problem, she hoped.

She looked through the door tentatively as she had never met a real homosexual. Her father was a minister, and she attended only private religious schools all her life. She pushed inward and found Chase staring at the ceiling with his leg still in a sling hanging from the bed rail.

"Mister Chase Fleming, I presume?" she said and immediately regretted her choice of words.

Chase looked straight at her and replied, "You presume correctly, but I had rather presume I was out of here!"

"I understand, no one ever likes to stay in the hospital, but I hope you'll appreciate the work we have done for you while your leg heals."

Chase softened his tone a bit remembering how many times Brett had told him he would get a better response from someone using his honey tone voice instead of his sharp vinegar tone. "I am sure I will, and please thank your staff. However, I'm worried about my boyfriend, Brett Allen. Is there

another specialist outside the hospital team, uh, that perhaps could help him return from his coma?"

The supervisor moved over to a chair and sat down, "I'm sorry, but we'll have to leave those decisions to the top doctors on our staff. I'm not a surgeon. I came to see you as head of the legal department."

"You have a legal department in the hospital. What for?" asked Chase naively.

"Primarily because someone is trying to get rich by suing us for something almost every month," she replied regretting the words she spoke. "We just have to make sure we cross our t's and dot our i's around here."

"Oh," he replied still confused. "So what do you want with me? I ain't planning to sue you. I don't even have a lawyer."

Inside she felt a little relief, but then she recalled why she had come for a visit. Reluctantly, she began. "I understand you're the Executor for Brett Allen especially regarding a Living Will. Is that correct?"

"Yes ma'am, it is," he replied.

"My I ask your relation to Mr. Allen."

"Do you mean am I one of his relatives?" he asked with a puzzled a look. She nodded affirmatively and he continued, "Not by blood," he paused, and then with a bit of pride he looked her straight in the eye and said, "We're boyfriends...lovers. Brett says we're married by heart."

She couldn't stop her face from blushing. She swallowed hard. "I understand, but the law doesn't recognize same sex marriages."

Chase blurted out, "Well, it should. We love each other a lot!"

"Marriage by homosexuals is illegal in the state of North Carolina."

To Chase she seemed delighted in stating something he already knew. "We wear silver commitment rings. We got them last year. In the eyes of God we feel married." He lifted his left hand to show her the ring, but she never bothered to look at it.

She sighed again deeply, "Well, we'll agree to disagree on that point. I want to make sure I'm clear though. The reason I'm here is the intensive care staff recalls you saying you were the Executor of Brett's Estate, and more particularly, the Executor of his Living Will. Is this correct?"

"Yes ma'am it is. I asked your staff to refer to me on all of Brett's medical matters and decisions. Is this a problem for you?"

"Well, no it's not, but..."

Chase cut her off, "Good. I knew I could count on you. Thank you for coming." His instincts told him to get rid of this snobby woman as soon as possible.

"I'm sorry, but I must ask to see this Living Will. Do you have it with you?"

Chase felt trapped, "You don't believe me?"

She blushed again, "I'm sure you speak the truth, but I deal in legal matters in black and white, and I must see and perhaps even make a copy of this document for our files."

Chase laughed, "Ma'am, do you know how Brett and I got here in the first place?" He did not give her a chance to answer. "We crashed in a plane, and miraculously survived when all the others didn't. The plane blew up right after we got out. I don't even have any luggage or clothes."

She answered as if she had not listened at all, "Well, in that case, you must have a copy at home, in a safe, or with your lawyer."

"I would need to ask Brett about that..." he caught himself and fought to choke back a tear, but they fell from his eyes anyhow, "but at the moment he can't speak to me. Please don't let him die." He sobbed and turned his face away from her.

She felt immediately guilty for having pressed him. "Well, I'll leave you for now. We'll talk again soon."

Chase did not reply but as the tears slowed his mind began racing. Where was the Living Will? He recalled Brett kept a copy in the laptop briefcase in a zipped compartment. He always kept the Passports, travel checks and the Wills in there, too. Before every trip Brett would ask him where they were, and what to say if needed, but how could he get it now? The fire and explosion blew everything up.

He laid back and stared at the ceiling, his mind raced for answers, but his eyes were heavy and he fell asleep. He dreamed of his first visit to Brett's house. After dinner on the night they met, Brett wanted to show him where he lived so he could find his way for future visits. They laughed and teased each other as they went from room to room. Chase recalled hearing Brett's version of the visit and it was the story he was dreaming about.

On the back of the house was a Jacuzzi. Brett installed it on a secluded deck overlooking the mountains. Brett just casually showed Chase the hot water, and then moved over to the deck to show him the view. Chase saw the view but kept thinking about the hot tub.

He interrupted Brett, "Why don't we get in?"

"Get in?" asked Brett.

"In the water, let's get in the water," urged Chase.

Brett once masturbated while thinking of different and numerous ways to get a good-looking man into his hot tub for wild sex, but never did he think of just showing someone the tub and his date volunteering to get in. "Are you sure?" asked Brett not believing what he had heard.

"Yep, let's do it. Do you have any towels?"

"Sure, I'll go get some. I'll be right back."

Brett left to obtain a couple of towels from the linen closet, and when he returned he got quite a shock. Standing beside the Jacuzzi was the beautiful and completely nude Chase.

Brett laughed, "This is twice in the same week I have caught you with your clothes off."

"Yeah, I know, but it's not fair," replied Chase slyly.

"What's not fair?"

Chase walked over to him and started unbuttoning Brett's shirt. "I haven't seen you naked even once. Come let's get these clothes off you and fall into the water."

In less than a few seconds, Brett was stepping out of his clothes. Chase knelt down and took his socks off, and brought his face to Brett's now bare genitals. He stuck out a long wet tongue and rolled the tip slowly across the bottom of his balls. Brett's penis became a large pole, which Chase quickly stuck in his mouth and sucked for a minute before sliding his tongue up Brett's bare hard tummy. He planted a deep wet kiss on his lips.

Then he broke off the kiss, "Let's get in the water. I'm getting chill bumps on my ass!"

Chase tried out all the different water jets while Brett laughed at him. Soon Chase cuddled in his arms and they continued playing with the other's penis. They made love in the tub, again in the shower, and finally on Brett's bed as they cooled down. Brett later confessed he made himself a promise to never again have sex on a first date, but Chase reminded him this wasn't a date just a visit and besides, he knew he already loved Brett.

Saying you love someone too soon was another of Brett's promises he had made. He felt anyone and everyone should wait until they had dated for at least six months before saying 'I love you,' but in reality he only made it two weeks before he was saying it to Chase.

They fell asleep in each other's arm and managed to have sex one more time before Brett had to rush off to work the next morning. He walked a little funny to his car, much like a first time cowboy might walk after riding his horse all day, but the soreness felt wonderful.

Chase suddenly awoke as an orderly brought in a lunch tray. He closed his eyes trying to get back to the dream when he realized he could remember all the times he and Brett had sex, but he could not recall where the master copy of the Living Will was. He should know, he told himself, but it had been two years since he signed his copy and besides, he thought, Brett took care of those important details. He never thought they would use them. He paid attention when Brett explained it to him, but the Living Will's importance escaped him. How could anything happen to him? He thought such things were for old people.

"Aren't you hungry?" asked Jeremy as he came in the room.

Chase turned his head towards the tray. "Hey, man. What are you doing here? I didn't think I would see you again. Your shift isn't until tonight, and the doctor is tossing me out this afternoon."

"Yeah, I heard. That's why I'm here. After the incident last night with one of Brett's uncles I felt a little worried. Do you have anyone coming to pick you up and get you home?"

Chase slowly shook his head no. "I didn't think of that. I guess I'll get a cab."

"Do you have any money?" asked Jeremy teasingly.

Chase realized everything was gone as he lost his wallet in the plane. "No, I don't," and then he smiled, "Hell, I don't have any pockets to put money in. Geez, I don't even have any pants or underwear."

Jeremy laughed, "Now don't go getting me excited." He produced a plastic shopping bag. "Here, I picked these up at Kmart. I hope I guessed the right size."

Chase found a pair of jeans and a tee shirt, a pair of socks and some underwear. "Fruit of the Loom?" he asked with a grin as he looked at the bag label.

"It is all they carry. I bet they are tearable in case you run into a hot man in the cab," laughed Jeremy.

"I doubt that but thanks. So are you going to take me home?"

"Boy, are you slow. I'm checking you out of this boring room this afternoon and getting you home. And then I'll get you some dinner while you call some of your friends to help you get going."

"You're the best. Thanks again."

Betty completed the rest of her paperwork after her visit with Chase concerning the Living Will. She came away from the meeting with two conclusions: if there was a Living Will it was not likely Chase could produce it, and two, the administration would not want her to take the word of a homosexual over a parent. After completing the paperwork, she took the file and walked down the hall to the Director's office.

Bill Furst had been the Director of the hospital for several years. He ran the hospital firmly, and managed to save the hospital thousands of dollars with his various new programs. As a result, the Board supported him on just about anything he proposed.

She knocked and pushed in on his door, "Bill, do you have a minute?"

Bill stopped reading a budget request and smiled, "Hey, Betty. How are you today?"

She returned the smile and sat down, "I'm doing very well, but I've got a bit of a problem. I'd like to show it to you and see if you agree with my conclusion."

"Okay, go for it," he replied.

"You recall the plane crash the other day? Well, the only two survivors are in the hospital right now. One is doing well with various cuts and bruises and a broken ankle. His name is Chase Fleming. The other boy is Brett Allen, and he is not doing very well. He has had surgery, but his brain is swelling, and currently he is in a coma."

"Oh, no, how much is his treatment going to cost us? Does he have insurance?" quizzed the Director with a much-worried look on his face.

"That's the good news. His baggage and clothes were destroyed in the crash, but part of his wallet survived. We went through his things and found an insurance card. I called and confirmed his account is active. I have also heard from the insurance company for the airline. They'll back up anything Brett's insurance doesn't cover."

"Whew, that's a relief," he replied with almost no concern for Brett's well being.

"The so-so news is Chase doesn't have a wallet, but his medical bills are not big and the airline will cover them. The bad news is Brett and Chase, uh, well—they're homosexuals—partners as they call it. Chase is telling everyone he is Executor of Brett's Estate and in charge of his Living Will."

"If that is true we'll have to follow the instructions of the Will," began the Director before Betty broke back in to her story.

"I know, but Chase came in without a wallet and so far, with no proof he is the Executor. He said they carry a copy of the Living Will for both of them in the pocket of their laptop computer. Unfortunately, the laptop blew up in the plane seconds after they crawled away."

"So he cannot prove he is the Executor?"

"Not yet. I suggested they probably kept the original in a safe or a file, and perhaps only took a copy with them. Chase said he signed it a few years ago and left their legal matters up to Brett."

The Director sighed, "Well, my experience, though limited, with homosexuals is they are the world's greatest liars. Unless Mister Fleming can show proof, then we'll have to follow protocol, which is his real next of kin— his parents. They are in charge of his medical care here until he regains consciousness."

"Thank you. I came to the same conclusion."

Now that he had confirmed the hospital would receive income from the insurance and airline companies, and resolved the matter of the missing Living Will, he abruptly displayed a little concern. "What is the prognosis for Mister Allen?" asked the Director.

"He has a small chance of survival."

"Make sure his account is charged very everything we do for him or administer. I want even a tissue or Q-tip on his bill. When does Chase checkout?"

"This afternoon."

"Very well, I'll be glad when we can get both of these deviants out of my hospital. If he goes home and finds the proper documents, we'll have to change our opinion and plans. Until then, inform the parents and Mister Fleming the parents are in charge for now."

"Very well, sir. Thank you for your time."

Betty left his office and went immediately to see the parents in the Intensive Care Waiting Room. "Mr. and Mrs. Allen?" she asked as he entered.

"Here," replied Henry.

Betty walked over and introduced herself. "I'm Betty Anders, with the hospital legal department. May I speak with you in a counseling room? It'll just take a moment."

Jan replied, "Of course."

Once in the room, Betty explained Chase was unable to produce the Living Will and thus, it was in the opinion of the hospital that Mr. and Mrs. Allen are in charge of Brett Allen's medical care."

"Thank God," replied Henry.

"Indeed," added Jan.

"I need for you to sign a few forms. I also have good news for you. Brett's insurance coverage is active, and the airline is willing to pick up any additional charges, so you will not have a hospital bill to pay when …" she became lost for the right words. " When, uh, Brett either gets well or expires."

Jan gasped, "What? How could you say that? He will survive! He will!"

Betty immediately regretted her statement, but she felt she was being honest. "I'm sorry. Mr. and Mrs. Allen, but I've read the doctors' reports, he has only a one in ten chance of surviving, and most likely the coma is the beginning of the end. I think you should begin making arrangements. I can ask a grief counselor to help you, if you like."

Henry gave her a hard look as his wife began crying. "No ma'am. We'll take care of, uh, arrangements ourselves."

"Very well," replied Betty. "If there's anything I can do, please don't hesitate to call on me."

"Ma'am, you can do one thing for me," stated Henry.

"Of course, what can I do?"

"My brother tells me Chase visited Brett last night in Intensive Care, and was seen holding his hand. I want you to make sure he never has a chance

65

to see Brett again. I want him barred from ever seeing Brett. Can you do that for me?"

"I understand. I'll see what I can do. Good day, Mr. and Mrs. Allen. I am sorry for your pain."

After lunch, the doctor visited Chase in his room, warned him to take it easy, and to keep his broken ankle raised for a few days. If all went well, he could then begin walking with the use of crutches. When Chase asked how long the cast would be on, he cursed when the doctor said six weeks. Jeremy flinched and grimaced because he had said it very loud. The doctor said he was sorry, but it was important he take good care of his ankle so he would be able to walk again. Chase changed his attitude and said he would.

After he left Chase turned to Jeremy and said, "Let's get the fuck out of here. Toss me the Kmart 'originals'!"

Jeremy laughed, "Let's do it!"

Chase threw off the hospital gown and stood in the middle of the room completely naked. With Jeremy laughing, they managed to get the underwear over the big white cast and on, and then a pair of shorts along one sock and shoe. Putting on a tee shirt was much easier.

"I look ridiculous," stated Chase as he looked into the mirror on the back of the door.

"Most people do when they leave the hospital, but they are so glad to get out of here they don't care," suggested Jeremy.

"I care. I wish you had bought a big hat and sunglasses," pouted Chase.

"Honey, with your smiling face, no one will notice your funny clothes. Let's go," he added as he pushed the wheelchair over to Chase."

"Yep, let's get out of here."

He sat down, left the room, and rolled down to the elevator. Jeremy pushed him out the main entrance. He failed to notice the two big men following him. He pushed Chase across the parking lot to the spot where he parked his car.

He put the wheelchair brake on, "Now you just hold on while I unlock the car and we'll figure out how we're going to get you in the backseat." He walked past Chase and took out his keys to unlock the door.

"Well looky here little brother, not one but two freaking faggots!" exclaimed Bill as they walked up.

"Yep, I could have smelled them a mile away. It must be all that fudge packing they do—whew what an awful smell. How in the hell do you guys do such awful stuff?"

Chase looked around and was about cuss out the two bigots, but his eyes caught sight of Bill and Larry, Brett's dubious uncles. His heart immediately skipped a few beats. Unfortunately, common sense did not

prevail, and Chase's quick temper flared, "You guys are two of the ugliest, mangiest rednecks I have ever seen. Now get the fuck out of my face!"

Jeremy gulped and quickly stuck the car key in the door and turned the lock. Just as he pulled the door, Bill kicked the wheelchair, and it slammed into the back of Jeremy's legs knocking him on top of Chase. He then flipped over and fell face down on the pavement.

"What the hell do you…" began Chase, but Larry interrupted him by grabbing the wheelchair, yanking it back, and then slamming it into Jeremy's car. Chase screamed at the pain as his knees hit the car. Larry pulled back and slammed him again. Chase screamed even louder.

A security guard heard the commotion, made a radio call, and then jumped in his golf cart, coming their way.

Bill grabbed the wheelchair and flipped it backwards tumbling Chase into a heap, leaving him flat on the pavement. Jeremy started to run to him, but Larry kicked him in the groin. Before Jeremy could fall down, Larry swung a fist and caught Jeremy under the chin lifting him off the ground. He landed on the back of the car parked beside his.

Chase, though winded, cussed at the two uncles again. Bill kicked Chase in the ribs to shut him up. He slammed a fist down into Chase's back, bruising a kidney. Chase screamed just as the cop got there.

"Hold up fellow. Stop that. What the hell is going on here?" he asked.

Bill yelled at him, "Just get the hell out of here. This is two freaking faggots that deserve a whipping, and we're giving it to them." He kicked Chase again. Larry punched Jeremy in the stomach knocking the wind from him. He slid off the car.

Suddenly, a police car turned the corner and flipped on the siren. Bill and Larry took a quick look and then began running away between the cars. The cop car finally stopped and two men jumped out and started chasing them. Another police car pulled in the far lot and joined in the chase.

The security guard helped Jeremy up. "Are you okay?" he asked.

"Yes, thank you," replied Jeremy. After catching his breath he ran over to Chase, "Are you all right? Oh man, I can't believe they attacked us. Chase?"

Chase grunted and managed to turn over. His nose was bleeding. "Damn. Jeremy, I'm sorry I got you mixed up in this. Can you get me in the car? Please get me out of here."

The security guard broke in, "But you're hurt, son. I need to get you back in the hospital. You need medical attention."

Chase looked at Jeremy, "Are you hurt? Do you need to go to the hospital?"

Jeremy shook his head, "No. I'm bruised and battered, but I'll be fine."

Chase looked at the cop, "Sir, I've been beaten up all my life because I'm gay. I'm used to it. Could you just help me into the car?"

The cop sighed deeply. He had never met a homosexual. His church was against homosexuality. Nevertheless, looking at what these two nice looking boys went through, he could not have turned his back on them. He bent down and by himself lifted Chase into his arms. Jeremy got the back door open to his car and they carefully put Chase on the backseat. Jeremy thanked him, and then backed out of the spot and drove away.

A few minutes later, a cop car drove up to the security guard and got out of his car. "We caught the two men. What exactly did they do?"

The guard let out a long breath and told the cops he had seen the two men come up behind Chase and Jeremy. He explained the beating and said the two boys drove off. The police said they had to talk to them to get them to press charges. The old security guard grinned, "The license tag number is DHF-3212. I've always had a habit of memorizing tag numbers."

The cop grinned, "We'll take these bastards in for assault. I think they should be horsewhipped for attacking a man in a wheelchair."

The security guard nodded in an agreement. He never mentioned the boys were gay because he wanted Bill and Larry to go to jail. He knew there was a chance the wrong cop would have let them go. He watched with a gleam in his eye as he saw the police car with Larry and Bill inside head off to jail.

FIVE

They parked in front of the house where Brett and Chase lived with Chase still lying in agony in the backseat. Jeremy got out of the car gently as the soreness and stiffness had set in on the way from the hospital. He ached all over, but he made it around the car, opened the back door, and looked in at Chase.

"Do you think you can get out of the car?" asked Jeremy.

Chase opened his eyes, looked up at Jeremy, and smiled. "You look like shit."

"You don't look so good yourself," grinned Jeremy. "Come on, let's get you out of here." Jeremy leaned into the car, took hold of Chase's hand, and pulled. Chase yelled out at the pain, but Jeremy kept pulling until he had Chase on his feet. He put one arm over his shoulder to take some weight off the leg with the cast, and slowly they made their way to the door.

"Do you have the key?" asked Jeremy.

Chase thought for a second, "Nope, I guess I lost it in the plane. Uh, wait a minute, do you see that bird feeder hanging on the porch?"

Jeremy turned around and spotted the feeder. "Yeah, what about it, are you hungry or something?"

Chase grinned, "No dingy. It has a metal bottom. Brett keeps a spare key in a magnetic box on the bottom of the feeder."

"Oh, I'll get it. Can you hold on to the railing?"

"Yeah, let's just hope a blast of wind doesn't come through, or I'll fall over."

Jeremy managed to remove the key and insert it in the lock and turned. It failed to turn the lock cylinder. He tried again. He pulled the key out, put it back in again, and still it would not turn.

"It doesn't work the lock," stated Jeremy.

"It has to; I have used it several times. Something must be wrong. Go around to the side door. The same key opens every door in the house. Brett likes to keep things simple."

Jeremy moaned as he made his way around to the side door, and the key would not open that door either. He went to the back door, the deck door, and even the basement door. The key failed every time. He returned to Chase with the bad news.

"I don't understand, but we have to get in. Uh, on the back deck you'll see a bathroom window. I always leave it cracked just a little to let fresh air in because, uh, when I have to go, uh, well, it smells pretty bad. Brett used to say when I used the potty, every toilet on our street would flush automatically out of confusion."

Jeremy laughed, "So you want me to climb onto the deck, and crawl through your bathroom window, though I'm in mortal pain."

Chase smirked and pointed to his broken ankle, "You think I can do it?"

"Nope I guess not. Boy, we're in great shape, huh?" stated Jeremy sarcastically. "Okay, I'll do it."

Jeremy took a deep breath and pushed on the bathroom window and it opened. This was the first good news he had all day. He crawled in, though every muscle in his body ached, and made his way to the front door and opened it.

"Yeah, you did it! This is a great relief. Can you help me inside?"

"Sure," replied Jeremy. He pulled the door open as far it would go and stepped on a piece of paper. "You got a note under the door." He handed it to Chase and then helped him into the house.

He set Chase down in the nearby recliner. Chase looked at the paper and realized it was an invoice from AAA Locksmith for rekeying the locks in the house. There was a note written on the bottom, "Extra keys are in the mailbox."

"This is weird. Why would someone have our locks changed?" asked Chase.

"I don't know. Should I go get the keys?"

"Yes, I guess so."

Jeremy picked up the keys, and a bundle of mail. He found Chase down the hall in the bathroom wiping his face with a washrag, rinsing the dried blood in the sink, and washing the dirt off his face and arms.

"How are you doing?" asked Jeremy as he stood in the bathroom door.

"Everything hurts, and I mean everything," stated Chase. "I hope they lock those stupid uncles away in prison for the rest of their lives."

"Yeah, I hope so, too."

"Let's heat some food. I'm starving," said Chase determined to change the subject.

"Okay, let's check out the kitchen. What do you want to eat?"

"Follow me." Chase made his way down the hall, grimacing with pain as he took a good step then dragged his cast, and then another. They opened the freezer and began sorting through the various frozen dinners until they each found something they could eat. Jeremy fetched two beers from the refrigerator so they sat on the stools at the kitchen counter and waited for the microwave to warm their meals.

They were picking at their food, occasionally taking a bite, and then several more swallows of beer, when they heard the front door open. Jeremy gave Chase a facial expression indicating 'who is here', but Chase shrugged his shoulders in reply. He then thought about the uncles and whispered, "Hand

me that big butcher knife." He was pointing at the knife block on the edge of the sink. Jeremy grabbed two knives and handed one to Chase.

They knew someone had entered the house because they heard footsteps in the living room. Then the steps stopped and they held their breath. Suddenly a man stepped into the kitchen through the dining room entry.

"What the hell are you doing here," yelled Henry.

Chase sighed, but held the knife firmly. "I live here. Why are you here? This is our house not yours. You can't come in here whenever you like."

"Says who, faggot," he replied.

"I do. Brett and I own this house. I'm calling the cops if you don't leave right now, and don't ever come back!" yelled Chase.

Henry took a step towards him, but Chase pulled the knife upwards. Henry stopped. "You think that little knife will stop me from choking the life out of you?"

Jeremy suddenly broke in, "You're right. His knife will just slow you down some, but my knife will slit your throat."

"Yeah, right," replied Henry, but he did not move any closer to them. My wife and I are now in charge of Brett's medical decisions, his legal stuff, and all his possessions. Your little faggot ass was not around when my son bought this house, which means you are not the owner—Brett is. Therefore, I am throwing you out. I had the locks changed, and apparently, you broke in. All I have to do is call the cops, and they will haul you away for breaking and entering, and threatening me with knives."

"Yeah, right, I've been living here for over two years. I'm in love with your son, and he is in love with me. Why don't you just face it and get it over with."

"That's not true..." started Henry before Chase cut him off.

"To hell it is not. We fuck ten times a week and he loves sucking my dick!"

Henry's face turned bright red, and he took a step like he was going to attack Chase, but they brought the knives up and he stepped back.

"You get your shit and get out of this house. I'll be back in the morning with my attorney and the Sheriff. If you're here, they will arrest you. I don't ever want to see you again, and my son will never see you again."

"Yeah, right, I'll have my attorney here, too. We'll have a good old time. I'm getting a hard on just thinking about it. You can join your brothers in jail for all I care "

"What?"

"Oh you didn't know. Your brothers attacked Jeremy and me as I left the hospital in a wheelchair. They beat us up but the cops caught them, and

hauled their ass to jail. I'm pressing charges big time. I plan to sue them for thousands of dollars."

Henry turned to Jeremy, "Is he telling the truth?"

"Yes he is. Just look at our faces. They beat us while I was trying to help Chase into my car."

Henry thought for a second, "Well I'm disappointed in them. They didn't do a good enough job, but I can, and if you're here tomorrow, you'll have more than one broken foot and a few bruises when I get through with you!" He turned and left the house slamming the door behind him.

Jeremy followed him to the door and locked the dead bolt. He returned to the kitchen. Chase had placed the knife on the counter and had already begun trembling in fear. Jeremy went up behind him and put his arms around him giving him a hug. "Hang in there. Things will work out. This has to have been the worst of it. It'll get better. You'll see." He made his hug a little tighter."

Chase sobbed a little. Jeremy hugged him even tighter while patting his back. Chase sobbed some more. Jeremy stroked his hair. The tears finally stopped.

"Chase? Are you all right?" asked Jeremy quietly.

"I will be when you stop squeezing my bruised ribs," grinned Chase.

"Oh, I'm sorry. I didn't think…" Jeremy quickly retrieved his arms.

"I fine, and don't worry. I guess I have some thinking to do. Would you mind staying the night? We have a guestroom all clean and ready. Brett always insisted we clean up after guests right away, as we never knew when a friend might need to stay over. I think he would like you. Can you stay?"

Jeremy hesitated for a moment wondering what he had gotten himself into by being Chase's friend, being beaten up, threatened by Brett's father, and now perhaps the cops were coming tomorrow. What should he do? Then he looked into Chase's eyes, and his fears fell away. He could not leave a wounded gay man to fight alone. "Of course I will."

"Good, let's go watch a DVD. Maybe it'll take my mind away for a while. This drama stuff is wearing me thin."

They sat on the couch watching the movie, but Chase fell asleep halfway into it. Jeremy woke him and helped him to his room. Chase rolled gingerly into the bed, pulled Brett's pillow to his face, and immediately went back to sleep. Jeremy covered him up, found the guestroom, and went to bed.

Chase's dreams recalled the first time they went to the club together. They had taken hours to get ready while Chase had laid various outfits all over the bed trying to pick out the perfect shirt and pants. Brett entered the room and started laughing, but Chase ran to him and kissed him on the mouth with just the tip of his tongue teasing him. He reached down and squeezed Brett's crotch.

72

"Now don't you get me started? I have to take a shower if we're going to be on time," replied Brett with a grin.

Chase laughed, "Oh, all right. Jump in the shower if you must." He kissed him quickly and went back to his clothes, but he watched Brett undress and delighted at seeing his cute buns. He whistled loudly, "Hang on world," he yelled, "there's a good-looking man coming through!"

Brett laughed, "You're crazy!" He tossed his boxers into Chase's face.

"Hmm…these smell good. Wait a minute! What this? These shorts have a stripe in them!" he laughed over and over until he heard the shower and the curtain slide open and back. Chase quickly stripped out of his clothes and stepped into the shower to join him. "Oh my goodness, the naked man is taking a shower," teased Chase.

"You expected a clothed man to take one?" answered Brett as he shampooed his hair.

Chase took the soap and began washing Brett's back. Soon Brett was washing Chase while caressing his body, and together, they began playing with the other's penis until they could not possibly get any harder or bigger. They kissed deeply. Brett teased Chase by running his tongue around in his ear. Chase slid a finger into Brett's butt. Brett began to tighten and loosen. Brett reached out of the shower and grabbed a condom from the basket on the back of the toilet, and tore it open. He turned around, pulled Chase's dick to him, and slid it on. Chase entered Brett with the water splashing over their heads while they continued to caresses each other.

"Faster!" yelled Brett suddenly.

"I thought you liked it slow, deep and easy," protested Chase as he picked up the pumping.

"I do, but…but…but…" he moaned with the deep thrusts, "…we're running out of hot water!"

Chase laughed heartily and instantaneously came. Brett exploded as well. Hurriedly they rewashed as the water became colder, and then quickly dried each other off.

"Are we still going out?" asked Brett, "we've already reached a climax."

"Hey, bud! That may have been your climax, but for me it was just an appetizer. After a few hours dancing with the best looking man on the face of the earth, I'll come home twice as horny!"

Mary came into Brett's room with his chart in her hand. She checked all the monitoring equipment to ensure accurate operation and recorded the various numbers. Out of habit, she placed her hand on his wrist, began checking his pulse the old fashioned way, and sighed gently at the feel of

Brett's heart in her fingertips. Coma or not, she thought, this boy's heart is strong. She stroked his arm and squeezed his hand. "Chase should be here with you," she suddenly whispered to Brett. "I know he loves you. Don't get me wrong. I go to church and they tell us homosexuality is wrong, but they could not believe it to be true if they had seen what I saw, when Chase was with you last night. His eyes reflected exactly what was in his heart. Yes, you are lucky Mister Brett Allen. You have found someone who loves you with all his heart. Now you just rest easy and let your brain heal. The swelling will go down. You will get well, and you will return to this world. Above all, soon you will return the love Chase gives to you. I know this to be true. I will pray for your recovery. I believe my God is a loving God. I do not believe He makes mistakes. He made you just as you are, and he gave you two boys the compassion and desire to love and feel love. He knows what He is doing. He knows why you're gay. He knows what you must go through. He loves you when others may curse you. He knows your pain. He loves you and I believe He will heal you. So rest, young man and that's an order," she added with a smile and a wink.

Tenderly, she bent down and kissed his hand. Suddenly, she froze as she stared at his fingers. She closed her eyes and blinked to be sure she saw what she did. She continued to stare and began counting in a whisper. Brett's index finger twitched. She had not seen any movement since he had arrived from the recovery room over forty-eight hours ago. The twitch lasted twelve seconds and then stopped.

Mary thought for a moment. "Brett, if you can hear me make your finger move again," she whispered towards him.

She waited. Nothing happen. She waited a little longer. Nothing happened. She half laughed at herself thinking she was acting too Hollywood, and this was the real world. Events like this happen only in the movies, she thought. Then she saw it. His finger began twitching once again.

She gasped bringing her hand to her face to cover her mouth. She knew she had just experienced a miracle—a real miracle. She squeezed his hand after the twitching stopped and kissed it again. Then she moved her face close to his ear.

"You did it child. You're on your way back. It'll take a bit more time so just rest easy and dream. You should dream of the mountains, dream of children playing, dream of ice-cream sundaes, dream of Christmas holidays, dream of angels singing, dream of happy times, funny times, and playful times, and dream of love and when you do, dream of Chase."

She kissed his cheek, "I will see you later. Thank you for sharing your secret with me. I will see you soon. Sweet dreams."

Brett did dream. He had reached the summer of his eighth birthday and the Korean War was all over the newspapers. His dad recently installed a forty-foot tall antenna on the top of their house and purchased a television. On

most evenings, over twenty neighbors and children crowded into the living to see the new television shows. The Milton Berle and Ed Sullivan shows drew the biggest crowds.

Brett spent weekends dressed in his army gear with his neighborhood buddies. They hiked through the woods to the swamps and walked the long huge sewer pipe to the middle of the swamp. They kept a careful eye for any sign of a snake but rarely did they see one. They had their air guns, which offered no real measure of security, but they felt safe anyhow. Brett had a new small hatchet attached in a leather case to his belt.

It had been a hot day, and they had played through most of it. In the middle of the swamp ran a river of cool water. When they reached it, they could see a sandy beach off to the right. Brice noted a tall dead oak tree about fifteen inches in diameter. He tapped it with the butt of his walking stick. "It's hollow," he announced as he turned and looked at the sandy beach. "Let's chop it down and make it fall that way so we can walk it to the beach."

"Are you crazy?" said Ellis. "We only have Brett's hatchet. It'll take forever."

"Not if we take turns swinging. Hand me the hatchet, Brett." He stuck out his hand, as if he was a surgeon preparing to make the first cut.

Brett obeyed by unsnapping the safety snaps, pulling out the hatchet, and proudly handing it over to Brice.

Brice worked out with weights, and did pushups and sit-ups every day. He had bulging muscles and a six-pack stomach. He tore off his tee shirt and handed it to Brett. Brett felt it in his fingers and nearly got an erection. "Stand back, gentlemen. A man is about to do some serious work on this old tree."

The boys laughed as they moved back a little as Brice began swinging the little hatchet at the tree. After twenty minutes, Ellis took his turn, then Brett, then James, and a new boy Eddie. When Eddie's arm gave out Brice started again. After a long ninety minutes, they heard a crack coming from within the tree.

"Stand back, boys! She's coming down," announced Brice. He took a few more swings, and then after hearing another crack he worked his way around the back of the tree and pushed. Another pop came from inside the tree followed by a steady slow cracking sound. Suddenly, Brice started running away from the trunk of the tree. The tree began falling. The boys scattered down the pipe. The tree was coming down fast. They stopped and watched in complete amazement.

The big old oak hit the limbs of the surrounding trees and took a few smaller trees with it as it slammed across the water to the sandy beach.

The boys cheered while Brice held up the hatchet in triumph. He also flexed his muscles like an Olympic Lifter. Brett couldn't take his eyes off the

75

muscles, and the sweat rolling down his chest to his crotch. He noted the little tiny black hairs growing beneath his beautiful navel.

He gave Brett the prized hatchet and began walking down the fallen tree to the beach. The rest of the boys followed like a Pied Piper leading his gang into town. When they all reached the beach Brice announced that he was too hot, and ready to go swimming. He stripped off his clothes and dove into the river. The sight of his naked body made Brett shiver, but he and the rest of the boys yanked their shorts down and dove in as well.

The boys played in the water splashing, giggling, and having a great time when suddenly Brice stood up and told the boys to shut up. Slowly, he pointed back to the big old sewer pipe. A big black man with a shotgun hung over his shoulder was walking the pipe. When he stopped at the stump, looked at the fresh chips of wood around the bottom of the trunk, and then allowed his eyes to slowly follow along the fallen tree into the swamp, on to the beach, and the river. He raised his scruffy black hat, scratched his head, and took a puff of his pipe when he saw the naked white boys swimming there.

He stared a long time while shaking his head in disbelief, and giving the crazy boys a wave before continuing his walk down the pipe. Once he was out of their sight, the boys laughed, and started splashing and wrestling one another.

Once exhausted, Brice left the river, smoothed out a section of the sand, and lay down on his back to sun himself. Ellis soon did the same. Brett stayed in the river while stealing glances at the two naked teenagers. It was a sight he would remember for a long time. Eddie fell down beside Ellis.

"Brett? Brett, come here," urged Brice.

Brett looked at him as if to say 'me' but he was the only boy still in the river. James was sitting on the sand by Eddie. He left the river and walked over to Brice. "Yeah?"

"Come on. Lie down beside me and get some sun. We need to dry off before we put our clothes back on and head home."

Brett did as he was told and felt glad to do so.

The boys told the story of the tree and the swamp, the river and the old black man on a many a campout to come. The tale of the story grew bigger and longer as the days went by, but Brett often recalled the sight of the naked Brice in the sun whenever he needed to masturbate.

Later that night, when Brice and Brett were alone he invited Brett to camp out in his backyard in his family's new fully enclosed tent. "Do you want to camp out with me tonight?"

"Sure," replied Brett, "I'll have to ask Mom, but I'm sure it will be fine. Are the other boys coming?"

"No. I thought it would be just the two of us. I have a secret to show you. Is that all right?" Brice looked into his eyes with a look that easily brought a 'yes' from Brett's lips.

Later that night, they listened to music for a while, played some card games, and then Brice showed Brett how to play poker. When he felt Brett could handle it, they started playing strip poker. Brett became naked in five hands including his socks and shoes.

Brett asked, "How do we keep playing if I'm already naked?"

"Well, on the next hand if I lose, I'll take off my next piece of clothing, but if you lose you have to massage my back for three minutes. Deal?"

"Yeah, sure," replied Brett as he would have rubbed Brice's back all night anyhow.

Brett lost again and Brice coached him as to how to massage his back.

Brett asked again, "Now what?"

"Well, if you lose this time you have to play with my dick."

Brett shrugged his shoulders indicating okay. He was beginning to think Brice was a mind reader.

Brett won a hand and then magically another. The luck continued as Brice lost a few more hands and was down to his underwear. Brett's dick became hard. They played another hand and to his surprise, Brett won again. Slowly Brice took off his underwear. Brett stared at his hardened penis. It was the biggest dick he had ever seen.

They played another hand and Brett's luck turned. He lost. Brice took Brett's hand, placed it on his dick, formed his soft fingers into a fist around his penis, and showed him how to pump it up and down. He then lay back and began moaning and sighing while enjoying the free masturbation.

They played another hand. Brett won. Brice masturbated him and it was the best and most wonderful feeling Brett had ever experienced.

"Let's take a break and go swimming," urged Brice. They had recently bought a portable pool and placed it under an oak tree near the back of their lot.

"I didn't bring a swimming suit," stated Brett dumbly.

"We'll go skinny-dipping—we're already naked."

"What if someone hears us?" asked Brett.

"It's almost midnight. We'll sneak over, slip in the water, and just float around quietly. Okay?"

Whenever Brice said 'okay', he didn't mean it as a question, but rather a nice order. Brett shook his head yes. Brice took him by the hand, together they crept to the pool while still naked, and hoping the mosquitoes didn't bite them. They slipped in the pool and swam underwater enjoying the coolness. Then Brice took Brett's hand in his, gently turned him on his back, and pulled him into his chest, wrapping his arms around him, dropping one hand to his penis to begin playing with it.

77

He took Brett's right hand and moved it behind his back to his own enlarged penis. Brett gladly began massaging it as well. Brice took his free hand, slid it under Brett's butt, and began rubbing his buns. Gently and slowly, he moved to the center and rubbed the back of Brett's genitals. Brett's penis grew larger. In time, Brice entered Brett with one finger with Brett feeling no pain. He worked the finger in and out until he found the prostate gland and began massaging it. Brett's tool grew some more.

In time, he slipped two fingers in and Brett only moaned with delight. Satisfied, he turned Brett around and kissed him seven times slowly before sliding his tongue deep into Brett's mouth. They kissed for a long time before slipping from the pool and returning to the tent. Brice had swiped a couple of towels from his momma's clothesline, and in the light of his flashlight, he gently and lovingly dried every square inch of Brett's body.

Once they were both dry, Brice led Brett to his sleeping bag and zipped down the zipper so they both could sleep in the nude together. Brett snuggled up to Brice while Brice gently stroked Brett's hair softly and tenderly. After a while, he pushed Brett's face to his chest and told him to suck his nipple. Brett did. He then pushed his head farther down and told him to kiss his bellybutton. He did. He told him to swirl his tongue around his bellybutton. He did. He then spun Brett around and on his side so his head was pointing toward Brice's feet.

Gently he guided Brett's face to his enlarged penis and told him to kiss it. He did. Then to Brett's amazement, Brice leaned over and began sucking Brett's penis. After a few moments he said, "Now Brett you suck me, and remember no biting. Suck it as gently as an ice-cream cone."

He did.

Chase's nostrils smelled something wonderful, but his far-from-awake brain could not yet decipher what it was. He rolled over and managed to open one eye and focus on the clock. 10:13AM it read. "Ugh," he moaned. He sucked in the aroma and realized it was breakfast. He struggled to his feet and made his way down the hall. He looked into the guestroom and found it empty. He yawned heavily and made it to the kitchen.

At the stove, he saw a dressed Jeremy scrambling some eggs. "Oh, you're up. About time I would say," grinned Jeremy.

"I slept well with good dreams," replied Chase.

"Are you hungry? I woke up early, and I hope you don't mind, but I rummaged around and found enough food for breakfast. Sit down and I'll bring you a plate. Juice or milk?" Jeremy began filling a plate with bacon, grits, eggs, and toast, and set it down on the table as Chase sat down.

"Milk if we have it. I have forgotten what day it is and how long ago we began our vacation trip," replied Chase as he began eating.

"This is the fourth day after the accident. The milk expires tomorrow. You might as well drink it up." He poured two glasses of milk and set them on the table.

"Oh my goodness, this food is awesome."

"Thank you, my good friend. You're just being polite because you have returned from desperately eating hospital food."

Chase laughed as Jeremy fixed another plate and sat down to eat together. "Thanks for going to all this trouble."

"No trouble. I enjoy cooking." Jeremy ate a few bites and said, "I'm glad you got up. I have to leave soon. I have to be at work by noon, and I need to go home, shower, change and get to the hospital."

"Oh, I'm sorry you have to go. Thank you for all your help," replied Chase. "I thought you worked nights."

"I do, but I promised to fill in for Pam so she could be off for her daughter's college graduation. How could I say no to that?" he added between bites. "Why don't you make a list of groceries and things you need, and I'll pick them up after work? I get off about nine."

"You don't mind?"

"It was my suggestion, and don't forget to put milk on the list and some more bread. I found some frozen corn dogs in the freezer you could eat for lunch, and another frozen dinner you could heat up for supper if you get hungry. Do you like pizza?"

Chase looked at him like he had just said something stupid. "Of course, I do. Everybody loves pizza. I like everything on it but anchovies. Those things are nasty! Brett calls 'em fish bait!"

"Good, I know a place that makes the best pizza in town. I will stop and pick up a large pizza, some salad, and be here about 9:30. Is that okay?"

"You're a freaking saint…of course it is. Thank you."

Jeremy started cleaning up the kitchen, washing the dishes and putting everything away. "What are your plans today? Jeremy asked.

"I don't know, I guess I'll take it easy and sit on the couch with my foot elevated and just try to rest some."

"Have you thought about calling a lawyer?" he asked.

Chase thought for a moment, "Do you think I need one?"

"Yes, I do I believe that man last night. I think he will be back with the cops or a lawyer or something. The look on his face is vile but determined."

Chase gulped, "I'll have to look around Brett's desk and see if I can find the number to his lawyer. I don't have one."

"Good, perhaps he has a copy of the Living Will as well and the paperwork naming you as Executor. I know you'll need it to fight the hospital for the right to protect Brett, but it'll also solve your problem with his father."

"Thanks, good advice. Are you sure you have to go?" Chase was feeling a bit lonely as Jeremy prepared to leave.

"I'm afraid so. I still need to make a living and the job does pay well, but the hours suck. Okay, I have to go. Give me a hug," Jeremy leaned into Chase who gave him a hug.

"Thanks, Jeremy. You're the best."

"I'll see you tonight. Now lock the door after I go out."

Chase did and then made his way to the office just off the kitchen. He sat in Brett's chair, looked across the desk, and saw a picture of Chase that Brett placed there over a year ago. Brett had taken the picture on a pier at the beach. Going to visit the ocean was one of their favorite destinations. They often took long walks on the beach taking in the sun and walking the dogs. "Where are our dogs?" he suddenly asked aloud.

I forgot about the dogs, he said to himself. He got up and called them, but already he knew if they were in the house, they would have been jumping at his feet. He made his way back to the kitchen and immediately noted the bowls of food Brett left for the dogs to eat appeared to be full and uneaten. His foot began to throb. He made his way to the cabinet near the sink, removed two Tylenols, and downed them with a glass of water.

Chase made his way back to the desk, deep in thought about where the dogs might be. He decided to call Blake. He dialed the number and waited for him to answer, but after a few rings he heard the answering machine pick up. He waited for the 'beep' and left a message for Blake to call him.

He opened Brett's middle drawer and began thumbing through a stack of business cards. He began sorting the cards and became surprised when he founds not one but three cards for lawyers. Which one? He wondered.

After completing the sorting, he dialed the number on the first card.

"Hello, Mister Goodlette's office. May I help you?" the secretary asked.

"Yes, my name is Chase Fleming. My partner is Brett Allen and I need to contact his lawyer, but Brett has three cards for lawyers, and I don't know which lawyer is the right one. Is Brett one of his clients?"

"I'm afraid I can't reveal Mr. Goodlette's clients to someone over the phone. May I take a message?"

Chase called her a 'bitch' under his breath, "You don't understand. Brett and I were heading out on vacation and our plane crashed. He's in the hospital and I'm home with a broken ankle. Could I speak to Mr. Goodlette?"

"I see, well no, he's not here at the moment. May I take your number, I will relay the information, and he will call you."

Chase gave her his phone number and hung up. Feeling rejected, he tossed the card to the back of the desk and dialed the second number and began the same conversation. This secretary ended the conversation the same way. The lawyer was out of the office, and thus he would have to leave a

message and number, which he did. He tossed the card to the back of the desk and into the rejected with politeness pile.

"Third times the charm," he said to himself while wishing he could reach the itch beneath the cast near his ankle. "Hello," he began earnestly as he told a nice but older woman his story. He sounded somber and sad and it worked.

"Well, son, I can't tell you if Mr. Allen is a client or not, but if you'll just hold the phone I will ask Mr. Evans if he will talk to you. Now hold on and I'll be right back," she added.

Chase grinned. "At least I get to talk to someone this time," he said to no one.

"Hello," said a deep voice through the telephone. "This is Mike Evans. May I help you?"

"Yes, sir," replied Chase quickly. "My name is Chase Fleming. My partner is Brett Allen. He and I were in a plane crash the other day while leaving on our vacation. I guess we didn't make it. He is in bad shape and in the hospital. I have a broken ankle and bunch of bruises. We need help and I'm trying to find his lawyer." Chase surprised himself at how quickly and precisely he told his story.

"I see," replied the lawyer with no conviction either way. "You've found the right man, and I'm sorry to hear about the plane crash. I hope Brett will be all right. He is a fine man. I know your name because about a year ago Brett had me put your name on a Life Insurance policy he bought naming you as the beneficiary. He asked me to read over the policy before he did it."

"He didn't tell me that. What is a beneficiary?" asked Chase innocently.

"It means in the event of Brett's death, the insurance company would pay you a large sum of money. It would be a benefit to you, hence the word beneficiary."

Chase felt stunned. He chose his reply carefully, "I would not want the money in place of Brett."

The lawyer sighed, "I'm sorry. I guess my explanation was not a good one. You're right. I would not want to replace Brett either. He's a fine young man. What can I do for you?"

"Brett told me I was his Executor. He had me sign a paper called a Living Will. He signed one as well. We carried copies of the documents in the side zipper pocket of our laptop, which burned up in the plane crash. He told me if something happened to me like a car accident, the document gave him the power to tell the doctors to fix me. If something happened to him, I was to do the same. He had me practice what to say to the hospitals."

"Very good, that's right. I gave the blank forms to him that you signed, and I answered all his questions."

81

"Well, in the hospital I told them I was the Executor, and they had to keep me informed about how he was doing and come to me with any medical decisions. That's what Brett told me to say. However, a supervisor came and said she had to see the document, but it burned up in the plane. Brett's parents are trying to take over and they even want me out of our house."

The lawyer thought for a moment before replying. "Son, let me explain. You are right on a couple of points, but if you guys signed the Living Will, you must be the Executor of that document, but Brett made me the Executor of his Estate. Please don't panic, he was just afraid," he stopped seeking the right words, "...he was just afraid if you both were in some accident and died, he would need me to carry out his final wishes. I hope you understand."

Chase nodded to no one, "I think I do. I am going to start searching the house because I think I signed four pages."

"Good thinking, lad. You're right. I know where you're going with this. The Living Wills are just one page for each of you. If you signed four, it means Brett made duplicates as copies in case he lost the originals."

"Do you have the copies?" asked Chase hopefully.

"No, I do not. I have a copy of the Will only."

"What if I can't find it?"

"Let me think about that for a while. How do I reach you?"

"I'm at our house." He gave him the telephone number. "What happens if they try to throw me out? Where would I go?"

"Is Brett conscious?"

"No, he is in the intensive care unit. They say the swelling in his brain put him in a coma. They don't know if he'll return from the coma or not, but I do. He'll come back. You'll see."

The lawyer's eyes watered a little at the heartfelt compassionate moment of positive thinking he heard Chase say. "I see. Again, I need to read up a little. If he had passed on, I could take over as Executor, but thankfully that is not the case. I can't appoint an Executor of a Living Will." He paused again, "Son, you need to find the copies. That is the most direct and simplest way to solve this problem. Call me again when you find it and I will help."

"What about them kicking me out?"

"I will read the Will. If Brett gave you the house in his Will, perhaps I can persuade the law to hold off. First things first—find the Living Will."

SIX

Late in the afternoon, Jeremy made his way to the intensive care unit on his supper break. He was thankful when he saw his friend Mary at the counter.

"Hey, Mary, you look a bit weary. Are you okay?"

She looked up into friendly eyes, "I could break down and cry or," she changed her tone, "I could spit nails right through that wall!"

He laughed, "You go girl! I bet you could. What happened?"

She sighed heavily and then decided to get it off her chest. "Poor Mister Michaels struggled all day to hang on to his life. He was a good man and about four o'clock I held his hand as he took his last breath. He had no family here, just good old Mary."

Jeremy leaned over and patted her arm, "You're a saint for caring." He looked left and right, "There ain't many in this hospital that care like you do."

"I know, but sometimes it just wears me down. I had just covered his head, walked over here to do the paperwork, and I look up and there is Mr. and Mrs. Allen here to see Brett. To my surprise, behind them stood that man we kicked out the other night. I was furious to see him and he knew it. He blew me a sarcastic kiss. I could have spit..."

"Nails!" laughed Jeremy. "I know, but I don't know how the two of them got here. They beat the shit out of me and Chase yesterday, and the cops hauled them off to jail. I thought they would be there a long time."

"Well, they were here. I told them only the parents could see Brett and they cursed me. I picked up the phone and told him if they said one more word, I would call the cops again. They shut up and moved to the chairs to sit down. I walked the parents back to see Brett."

"You were brave. I would have called the cops. How is Brett?"

Suddenly she broke into the biggest grin. "I have to tell you a secret. With the parents, he remained deep into his coma. No movement, no emotions, but I swear I thought I heard him fart when his dad walked into the room."

Jeremy laughed, "I can see why he would. He's as bad as the two uncles."

"Well, not long after I came on duty, I updated my records on his monitors and wrote down the levels. I don't know why I did it, but I started talking to him. To my surprise, his right index finger started twitching and did so for twelve seconds."

Jeremy smiled, "You know, 'hon, it was probably just a muscle reflex or something."

She shook her head, "That's what I thought, too. Therefore, I tested him. I started talking again and he did it again for exactly twelve seconds! No one twitches for the exact same length of time."

"I don't know what to make of that but it sounds like he is trying to come back, doesn't it?"

"I think so. I didn't tell his folks. His mom seems nice, but I didn't want the rest of them to know what I knew. Tomorrow I will test him again, but I told him to be cool, relax and rest, let his brain heal, and the swelling go down."

"Can I see him?" he asked.

She thought a long second or two, "Okay, but don't stay too long."

"I won't. Thanks."

Jeremy slipped around the counter and looked in through the window at Brett. Cautiously, he opened the door and went to the side of the bed. He thought about what Mary had said, and he thought about how much Chase loved this guy. He tried to imagine what Brett looked like, but the swelling and purple bruises, and the head bandage made all that a little hard. He recalled seeing a picture of Chase and Brett on the wall in their bedroom. He looked a whole lot better then, he thought.

"Hi, Brett," he whispered, "My name is Jeremy. I was Chase's nurse and we became friends. I got him home and fed him some breakfast this morning. I'm going to take him some groceries over tonight along with some pizza. Boy does he miss you. Listen, Mary is right. Your brain is a bit swollen, but it'll go back down if you just hang in there. You can do it. I'll check in on you tomorrow."

Jeremy reached over and squeezed Brett's hand. He watched the finger for a moment but nothing happened. He smiled at himself and left the room.

Jeremy gave her a hug. "Thanks Mary. Take care. I'll be back tomorrow."

"Bye, buddy, you be careful. Those two lugs are probably around somewhere."

"I will, and I will see you later."

Brett began dreaming of another campout, but this time it was in his backyard, and in a large tent his dad had bought for the whole family to use. Brice, Ellis, Eddie, and James were there. They had been laughing and cutting up for hours until they decided to play strip poker. Brett was the first one to end up naked as usual, but James was a close second with only his underwear left. Eddie would end up in third place or the third boy naked.

Brett asked what happened if he lost again because what he and Brice did when he lost was private, and Brice had told him not to tell anyone. Instead of Brice answering, it was Ellis who spoke up.

"You have to climb the big tree, broad naked."

All the boys laughed including Brett. James lost the next round. The two naked younger boys sat nervously on the edge of their sleeping bags. The bigger boys made fun of their little dicks, but they didn't care; they were having fun with their friends.

Brett lost the next round so the boys cut off their flashlights and watched as Brett stepped out of the tent into the night air. He looked left and right hoping the nearby neighbors were asleep. He looked up at the tall tree. Most boys would have been afraid to climb the tree in the daylight with their pants on, but not Brett. He had been climbing that tree since he was a little boy. He knew every limb and branch. He could swing and jump from one limb to the next like he was Tarzan or a chimpanzee. He recalled how one time when he was about seven, he climbed his tree with his air rifle slung over his shoulder, and started climbing to the top to protect the neighborhood from the Nazis. It had rained the night before and some of the bark was slick.

Brett wore his shoes until either the sole wore out or his toes stuck through the end, as money was always tight around the Allen household. He was almost to the top when his shoe slipped on the wet bark, and he fell backwards with the rifle still hanging on his shoulder. He passed through a couple of limbs and flipped head over heels to go through the next one headfirst. The rifle came off his arm, somehow the sling wrapped around his leg, and the rifle caught in the fork of a big limb. The sling moved down his leg tightening around his angle.

His rapid descent to the ground came to an abrupt halt like bungee jumping. Brett, saved from crashing to the ground, hung upside down by just one foot, but twenty feet to earth. He looked around to see if anyone had seen his fall but no one had. He yelled out but no one came. He tried to pull up but he could not get a grip on the nearest limb.

He sighed heavily, feeling the beats of his heart in the temples of his head. He started to cry because whenever he cried, his mother always came to his rescue. He cried for three minutes and no one came. There he was hanging upside down and crying, but it felt weird to him, as the tears did not run down his face. Puddles formed over his eyes making it hard for him to see.

Finally his mother heard him and came running. She did not know how to get him down, but she ran and woke up Mr. Green, a firefighter in the neighborhood, and he got a ladder and helped Brett down. She had forbidden him to climb the tree again, but the threat only lasted a week until he was climbing to the top.

Naked, he began to climb as the boys watched. He climbed all the way to the top, and stood with his chest above the top limbs, letting the night breeze flow around his bare body. He felt proud, strong, and determined he could do whatever their challenge might be.

Suddenly, a flashlight came on. Ellis had it aimed at him. Brice made him shut it off. Brett started down. The boys were giggling. Brice told them to shut up, but they laughed all the more. Brett kept coming down. They giggled again. Desperate to shut them up Brett stopped, made a quick decision, and started peeing on them.

When they realized what he had done, they dove into the tent. Brett dropped to the ground, and fell into the tent laughing. Brice tossed his hair and tickled him. They knew he was a brave kid.

Soon they were playing strip poker again, and James lost the next round. They handed him an empty seven-up bottle, and told him he had to pee until he could fill it up. He stuck his penis in the bottle and startled peeing. To their surprise, the little guy filled it up in less than a minute. Brice capped it off.

Ellis checked his watch. "It's time."

Brice grinned, "Okay boys; put your summer shorts on, but not your underwear and no shirt. Put your shoes on. We're going to visit the girls. Brett, you to need to be real friendly with the girls, and get them to take a swig of James' Seven-up with piss in it."

"Oh geez, why me?" asked Brett.

Brice looked straight at him, "Because with those big eyes of yours they'll have to believe you. Ellis, come on, get your underwear off. We're all going there with just shorts on. That'll turn the bitches on!"

The boys left the tent, crawled through the backyard fence, pushed through the bushes, and found the girls in a big dollhouse. They crept up close and listened to their gossip for a while before knocking loudly on the door, which nearly scared the piss out of the girls.

"I'm sorry," said Brice. "Did we scare you?"

Melissa replied, "No, yes, well, maybe—get in here before my parents hear you."

"I brought some friends," he said as he motioned to the rest of his gang.

"Okay, okay. Scrunch up girls, we have company."

There were three girls and they all slid to the left side leaving the right side for the boys. The boys sat down and without thinking, they crossed their legs in an Indian squat. The girls had their flashlights on, and it didn't take them long to notice the boys' exposed dicks and balls hanging loosely near the bottom of the shorts. The girls laughed, covered their mouths, and rapidly began talking and cutting up with the boys.

Melissa asked, "We have a cooler of soft drinks. Are you guys thirsty?"

"No, I'm not," said Brice, "but we did bring you one of our Seven-ups. I'm sorry I didn't realize there were more girls camping out." He turned to Brett and winked, "Do you have it Brett?"

Brett gulped, "Yeah, sure, and handed him the bottle.

Brice gave it to Melissa. "Here you go girls. Just put it in the cooler in case you get thirsty later."

Melissa took the bottle and placed it in the cooler. "We have Snickers candy bars—we'll trade you." Brett loved Snicker bars.

Brice laughed, "Trade? Trade for what?"

Melissa grinned mischievously, "Let's see, Brett, if you kiss Bonnie you can have one."

Brice and the boys laughed aloud. "That'll be easy, little dude. You can do that," urged Brice.

Brett leaned over and kissed Bonnie on the lips. Then he wiped his face on the back of his bare arm, and Melissa tossed him a candy bar. They all laughed while Brett started eating.

"Who is next? Let's see, how about Ellis kissing Janie," she suggested.

Ellis had no problem with that. He leaned over, pulled her to him, and planted a deep wet kiss to her lips, while pulling her hand to his exposed penis. Brett felt surprised when she started rapidly playing with it.

"Well, I guess they'll be busy for a while," laughed Melissa. "Okay, James, you kiss Bonnie, but use your tongue."

James nearly passed out, but Brice urged him on and so he did it. She turned to Eddie, "Don't laugh little boy, you're kissing Bonnie next." Eddie gulped.

"That leaves just us, Brice." She held up the candy bar, "If you want this candy, you're going to have to earn it."

Brice laughed as he pulled her to him, kissed her deeply, rolling their tongues over and over. She also began playing with his genitals. Brice began to get hard, and Brett began to get jealous. Brett, James, Eddie, and Bonnie just sat there while the older kids made out. Bonnie opened a candy bar for herself.

"I'm thirsty," stated Brett. "Do you have a Dr. Pepper?"

"Yeah, we do," replied Bonnie. She opened the cooler and handed it to him, and then another to James, and coke to Eddie.

"Thanks," the boys replied together.

Bonnie decided she was thirsty, too, but her choices were root beer and the Seven-Up. She hated root beer so she pulled out the bottle the boys had brought over. It had cooled in the icy water.

Brett's eyes went wide. James got the giggles. Eddie had to cover his mouth to keep from laughing. Bonnie did not catch on, popped the top, and downed a huge swig. Her face turned pale. Her eyes bulged, and then she propelled the drink outward, and all over Melissa, Janie, Ellis, and Brice.

"They gave us a bottle of piss!" she exclaimed.

Brett, Eddie, and James started laughing and began heading for the door. The girls started hitting Brice as he and Ellis made their escape while laughing their heads off. They ran back to their tent and laughed for nearly an hour before falling asleep.

Jeremy escaped the hospital without incident because he had parked in a different lot than where Bill and Larry caught him last time. He already ordered the pizza over the phone at the nurse station and picked it up after stopping for groceries. He caught the stoplight and began to think about his new friends Brett and Chase. He thought they were very lucky to have each other, and he hoped they would soon see happier days.

Chase had spent most of the day sleeping, but the rest of the time he spent rummaging through every shelf and drawer in the office. Chase thought aloud, "Where would you put it?" He tried to think like Brett, but unlike the movies, he could not do so. He plopped down on the sofa, carefully raised his ankle, placed it on a cushion, and fell fast asleep.

When the phone rang an hour later, he nearly leaped out of his skin. Reluctantly, he made his way from the couch to the end table and the phone.

"Hello."

"Chase? Is that you? Why are you home?"

"Blake! I have been trying to reach you. Brett and I never made it from Asheville. We were in a plane crash," replied Chase with a yawn.

Blake exclaimed, "Oh my! Are you guys okay?"

"Yes and no. Brett is in a coma due to a bad head cut in the crash. I managed to get us out of the plane before it blew up. I have a broken ankle, and he is in intensive care with a swollen brain. He has already had surgery, and now we just have to hope and pray he is okay."

"Oh, 'hon. I'm sorry. I didn't know. I just got back in town."

It suddenly hit him Blake picked up the dogs the afternoon after they left. "Where did you go? Where are our dogs?"

"My sister had her baby three weeks early in Boone, you know, up near the ski resort. Momma called in a panic, so I ran by your house, picked up the dogs, and took them with me. I did not know how long I would be in Boone, and could not take a chance something might happen to your dogs. By the way they're fine."

"Oh thank goodness. I was afraid Brett's family took them. I'm glad you took them with you."

"Why wouldn't you want their family to get them?"

"Because they are assholes, that's why." He told him about how they treated them in the hospital, and how they beat him and Jeremy up in the parking lot. He said Henry Allen changed the locks and was trying to take over Brett's medical stuff and the house. Chase knew they would not stop until they had thrown him out of the house.

"I'm sorry. Boy, you will need another vacation after you survive this one, won't you?" Blake had attempted to make Chase laugh.

He smiled, "You're not kidding."

"Do you want me to bring the dogs over right now?" asked Blake.

"If you don't mind, I would rather you keep them another day until we see how things develop here. I don't want the Robertsons to get our dogs."

"No, problem, but why don't I bring you some lunch over tomorrow?"

"That would be great. Thank you. Thank you for all your help."

Chase was just setting the phone down when he saw a car pull up in the driveway. He could not tell if it was Jeremy or not, so he did not move. He waited to see who it was. He got his answer all too soon. He heard two car doors slam instead of just one.

Chase had not turned on the lights, but he realized he had left the television on with the sound down while he slept. He made his way across the room to the remote and turned the television off. Brett kept a baseball bat in the hall closet. He had just removed it when he heard a fist pounding against the door.

"Come on out, you little faggot. I'm going to smash your head in one way or the other!" He jiggled the door, but found it locked.

"I will go try the back door," said Larry.

Chase moved as quickly as he could with his cast, praying he remembered to lock the back door after putting the trash out. He heard Larry jump over the chain length fence surrounding the backyard. Bill slammed his fist against the front door and yelled even louder. Chase flinched at the sound. He made it to the kitchen. In the shadows of the windows, he saw Larry coming towards the door.

Chase rushed across the room to the door and just managed to slide the dead bolt across as Larry turned the knob. He found the knob in the lock position but easy to break in with just a credit card. This is why Brett always told Chase to check the back door dead bolt before leaving the house. Chase stepped back a step or two as Larry put a shoulder to the door but it held.

Just as Chase moved to the kitchen table, the doggie door swung open and a boot pushed in. Chase covered his mouth with his hand as he almost screamed out. Then Larry yelled as he removed his foot, "Chase, if you are in there, we're going to kill you." Chase was glad the door was too small for Larry to crawl through.

Frightened, Chase began scanning the room. He had the bat, but he grabbed a knife. Then he remembered the phone, so he started moving to the living room. As he turned from the kitchen, his eyes caught sight of a little green L.E.D light on the wall.

"The alarm system," whispered Chase to no one but himself. "I can hit the panic code." He set the baseball bat and knife down, and dragged his foot over to the wall. The house was dark, but the keypad on the alarm was the same as a telephone pad. He closed his eyes to think of the code for panic. He had never done it, but Brett had showed it to him when training him how to set and unset the alarm system.

Larry and Bill began to kick and pound the doors. A light went on in the house across the street. The next-door neighbor's porch light came on. Chase was thinking as fast he could. "123 sets it, 423 unsets it," he whispered aloud, and then suddenly his face broke into a grin. "Star and pound key at the same times is the panic code!"

Quickly, he felt the keypad and slid his fingers down the buttons until his index and ring fingers stopped over the star and pound.

"I'm going to bust this door down you freaking faggot!" yelled Bill.

Chase shook with fear, but managed to place his fingers over the keys and pushed. Instantly, a loud siren went off inside the house. Chase covered his ears. Two sirens on the outside of the house, mounted way up high where no one could reach them, also went off. More neighbor lights came on. Larry left the door and scrambled over the fence.

"Come on, Bill; let's get out of here before the cops come."

Bill kicked the door again, "Damn. Don't worry, Chase. I'll be back. Your days are running out, faggot!" He spit on the door and ran to his car. Chase slid down the wall crying. The uncles backed out of the driveway in their car and turned up the street nearly running head on into the car coming in.

Jeremy recognized the uncles, so he slid his hand up to cover part of his face. They did not slow down, but ran the stop sign on the corner and kept on going. Jeremy pulled into the driveway and stepped out of his car as Mr. and Mrs. Alvin Smith crossed the street.

"There were two men trying to break into Brett's house," exclaimed Alvin.

"I called the police," added Liz.

"Is Chase still in there?" asked Jeremy.

"I was home all day," she replied. "I haven't seen him or Brett."

"Brett's in the hospital. He and Chase were in that plane crash."

"Is he all right?" asked Alvin.

"He is in a coma. Chase has a broken foot with a cast on it. I'm going to see if he is okay. Will you stand here and watch in case someone is still there?"

"Of course we will. Go ahead," replied Liz.

Jeremy crossed the lawn and immediately saw the marks on the door. The sirens were waking the entire neighborhood. He knocked on the door. Chase heard the knock, but started shaking out of control.

"Chase! It's Jeremy. Let me in. They're gone. You're safe!"

Chase heard his voice and turned his head towards the door. Jeremy called again. Slowly he stood up and punched 423 on the burglar alarm. Abruptly the sirens stopped. He turned and slowly walked to the front door. He peeped through the window and saw Jeremy's face in the moonlight. He turned the dead bolt and pulled the door.

"Jeremy?"

"Chase, are you okay?"

"Yes, they didn't get in."

Jeremy turned to the Smiths still watching. "He's okay. They didn't get in. Thank you. I'll take care of him."

"Okay, you call us if you need us. Please give our best to Brett. I'll pray for him," replied Liz.

"Thank you, I will."

Jeremy stepped into the house, closed the door, and took the trembling Chase in his arms. "They are gone. You're safe. I'm so sorry I wasn't here."

"I am glad you weren't. They would have killed you, too."

Jeremy grinned, "You don't know how fast I can run when I have to."

Chase smiled. "I think I have to pee now!" He broke the embrace. "I'll be back in a minute." He turned to limp down the hall.

Jeremy called after him, "I'm going to get the groceries and the pizza out of the car."

It took a long twenty seconds before he could urinate, but to Chase it was one of the best experiences of his life. He had somehow escaped death for the fourth time this week. He survived the crash, the plane blowing up, the uncles in the parking lot, and the attack on the house. How much more would he have to endure? He wondered.

Chase started down the hall when the doorbell rang. He picked up the bat leaning against the wall and stopped in the hall across from the front door.

"Sir, it is the police. Can you open the door please?"

Jeremy met him coming from the kitchen. Jeremy turned on more lights and opened the door.

"Are you Brett Roberson?" asked the dark haired police officer.

"No, I'm a friend. My name is Jeremy Booker."

"May we come in?" he asked politely.

Jeremy nodded, "Of course, I'm glad you came. You just missed them."

The officer looked over at Chase, "And who are you?"

"I'm Chase Fleming. Uh, Brett and I are roommates. I've lived here for two years."

"I see," replied the officer as he wrote Chase's name down on his notepad. "Well, what happened here?"

"I had just awoken from a nap when I heard someone drive up. Yesterday these two men beat us in the hospital parking lot so I grabbed this bat for protection. I had the dead bolt on the front door. I recognized the men coming to my door."

"Beat up? Were the police involved?" he asked.

"Yes, they hauled them off to jail. I guess they got out."

He turned to his partner, "Call this in and get an update on that arrest."

"10 4," replied the officer as he stepped back out into the yard for a bit of privacy.

"Go on, son. Tell me what happened," urged the police officer.

"They started yelling and kicking the door trying to break in. I saw Larry start for the back door so I hurriedly got there before he did and slipped the bolt. Then he stuck his foot through the doggie door."

"Did he get in?"

"No, he yelled, threatening to kill me several times. I managed to get to the alarm system and set off the panic sirens."

"That's probably when your neighbors called us. Where did they go?"

"I don't know. I felt terrified and stayed hidden in the house."

Jeremy spoke up, "They passed me driving fast when I was coming down this street."

"This street is a dead end, isn't it?" asked the officer.

"Yes, it is."

"So that means they were heading south." He turned to Jeremy, "Can you describe the car?"

"Yes, light blue Malibu, probably four or five years old, white top with a cracked windshield."

"That-a-boy, must folks don't remember any details. Was the crack running vertical or horizontal?"

"Horizontal. It caught my eye because they were heading straight for me so I got over to the side off the road as far as I could. They flew past but I recognized them from yesterday. I covered my face so they couldn't see me."

"You believed they would harm you as well."

"After the beating they gave us yesterday, I'm sure of it. I was pushing Chase in a wheelchair to my car when they attacked."

"They hit a man in a wheelchair?"

"Yes. They knocked us both down and continued kicking and hitting us until the security guard stopped them, and they took off running when they saw the cop cars. Whoops, sorry, I meant police cars." Jeremy blushed.

"That's all right, son. I like the word cops."

"Can you put them back in jail?"

92

"Maybe—if they had gotten in this would be easy, but so far it appears to be a threat."

"Al? Can you come here a second?" called the officer in the yard.

"Excuse me," he said to Chase and Jeremy as went out into the yard.

The men talked for several minutes, learning of the one-sided fight in the hospital parking lot and why it began. He thinks the gay boys deserved what they got. He also learned Brett and Chase were lovers, and Brett was in a coma. He returned to the house.

"Okay, boys, I have the report. Keep your doors locked, and if they come back call us."

"Aren't you going to arrest them?" asked Jeremy.

"I have to speak to my Lieutenant first. I'll be in touch." He turned and left.

Jeremy shut the door and locked it. "Sure you will. They found out we are gay, and they are not going to do anything to help us."

Chase sighed, "You're probably right. I think I need some more Tylenol." He began walking to the kitchen.

"You sit down at the table, and I'll bring you something to drink, some Tylenol, and the best pizza in town."

Jeremy had tried hard to cheer Chase up, but it only helped a little.

After dinner, they moved to the living room and began to watch a movie. It was a comedy, but Chase did not laugh where perhaps he should. He sat in a trance. Jeremy kept the movie running for about an hour, but finally hit pause on the remote control.

"Not into watching a movie tonight, huh?" he said.

"No. I've replayed the events of the past few days over and over in my mind. Today, I tried to find a copy of the Living Will. I did talk to Brett's attorney, but he doesn't have a copy and can't make a new one because it requires Brett's signature, which he can't do. Tomorrow, I'll take on searching the bedroom and see if I can find it."

"Are you sleepy? Do you want to go to bed?"

"I slept a good bit today so no, I'm wide awake, but if you're tired, please stay over in the guest room again."

"I will, but I'm okay."

"Jeremy, I want to go back to the hospital," said Chase.

"Why? Does your leg hurt?"

"No, I want to see Brett again. Can you get me in?"

"It'll be risky, but if Mary is working, I might be able to pull it off. I saw her before I left, and I went in to see Brett."

"You did? How was he?" asked Chase with enthusiasm.

"He is fine, and nothing has changed. I just told him you were okay, and soon you both would be together again."

Chase smiled, "Thanks, that was sweet of you. Can you call and see what time Mary gets off?"

"Okay, I'll be right back."

Jeremy made the call and found out Mary gets off at midnight. He had to beg her to allow them in, but after he told her about the earlier attack, she agreed.

Chase got up immediately and went to the bathroom to clean up. He stripped out of his clothes, took a hot washcloth, and bathed in the sink. He brushed his hair, gargled, and then began dressing. Jeremy sat on his bed and helped when he needed it, but wisely let Chase do as much as he could. They both laughed when Chase got one leg of his boxer underpants caught on the cast. Chase nearly fell over before he finally got them up.

Jeremy drove around to the back of the hospital to the employee entrance. He waited until he saw several other staff members approaching the door, then he drove up to the door, and let Chase out. Chase made his way inside the door and waited for Jeremy to park the car.

He led him into the men's locker room where he normally changed his clothes. This time he just put a green medical shirt over his regular clothes, before putting Chase in a nearby wheelchair, and pushed him to the service elevator. They avoided any public hallways or waiting rooms.

Together, they silently watched the floors tick by until they stopped and the door opened. Jeremy leaned into the hallway and saw no one. Carefully, he pushed Chase to the corner of the hall. He checked the hall once again, and saw a distraught family pacing back and forth at the waiting area entrance. He did not recognize them.

He was just about to push Chase to the nursing station when Jan Allen came from the Intensive Care Unit after obviously seeing Brett. He jumped back and told Chase to remain quiet. Jeremy watched, as she got on the elevator alone. He decided it was too risky to push Chase to the counter.

"Chase, stay quiet and remain here. I'm going to make sure no one else is in Brett's room or the area. I'll be right back."

He left before Chase could reply, but his heart began pounding in his chest. Jeremy checked out the waiting room first, and then stepped around the counter to the Intensive Care Unit. He did see a man, but he was in a room next door to Brett. He spotted Mary changing an IV bottle in another room.

"Hi," he whispered as he poked his head in the door.

"Hi, Brett's mother was just here," she replied.

"Yeah, I know, I saw her. I have Chase hiding around the corner. We came up the service elevator. I checked the waiting room. There are no other family members waiting, and the mother took the elevator down."

"They are going to fire me over this," she said as she took off her rubber gloves and tossed them in the trash.

94

"Just keep working with your patients, we'll just sneak in and out, you can honestly say you never saw Chase."

"Okay, be careful. I'm going to room eight," she said as she turned and walked down the hall.

Jeremy quickly ran back to Chase, wheeled him around the corner, and into Brett's room. He then pulled a curtain across the window so no one could see in. He then stood guard at the door peering out the edge of the curtain, hoping to see no one and certainly not any of the Allen clan.

Chase reached over and took Brett's hand, "Hey. It's Chase. I've missed you," he leaned over and gently kissed his hand. "I hope you're doing okay in there behind all those bandages. They say your vital signs are perfect so that is good. Jeremy is taking care of getting me to and from the hospital to see you. I'm sorry I can't see you every day or stay long. Your folks are being a pain in the ass. Whoops, sorry, didn't mean to cuss about your family, but they are giving me a hard time.

"I called your lawyer today to see if he had a copy of the Living Will but he didn't. So I've looked everywhere in the office at home, and so far I haven't found it. I know if you could talk you would tell me exactly where to find it, but I guess I will have to keep trying to remember where you said it was hidden.

"Soon your swelling will go down, and then like the rest of us you'll have to eat hospital food instead of having it pushed through a tube to you." He paused for a moment and said matter of fatly, "I bet if they would let me suck your dick you'd wake up!"

He smiled at the thought and kissed Brett's hand. "Well, I guess I had better go. Jeremy made me promise to stay just a few minutes, or your parents are liable to catch me. I know when you wake up you're going to tell your family to get the hell out of here—lord knows I will, and I will use only four letter words.

"You keep resting and doing your best to get well soon. I miss you so much it hurts inside. We survived the plane crash and we will survive this, too. You'll see. Sleep tight. I love you. I love you with all my heart."

Chase pulled himself up from the wheelchair, stumbled over, and kissed Brett on the mouth tenderly. Jeremy quickly held the chair as Chase sat down again. He checked the curtain, opened the door, and nearly ran into Mary.

"Shh, his father is waiting at the counter!" she whispered.

Jeremy exclaimed, "Oh my gosh!"

"Shh," she said again.

"What do we do?" asked Chase.

Jeremy spotted a gurney. "I know. Chase hop on the gurney, and I'll cover you with a sheet like you're dead."

95

"Are you crazy?" asked Mary.

"Do you have a better idea?" asked Jeremy with a grin.

"No, I do not. I must have been a nut for getting involved." She turned to Chase. "That boy in there loves you. I don't know how I know that, but when I see you with him, I know you love him and he loves you. I can't honestly see why God would have a problem with that."

"Thanks for your help, Mary," replied Chase as he squeezed her hand.

"I will go tell the father to have a seat because I'm changing his son's soiled linens. As he walks into the waiting area you roll Chase out of here."

Chase got up, climbed on the table, and Jeremy covered him head to toe in a sheet. With the cast, one foot was much taller than the other. He did not know how to solve the problem, but quickly turned the gurney in preparation for their escape.

He could see Mary talking to Mr. Allen in the reflection in the windows. When Mr. Allen started for the waiting room, he started pushing Chase. Just as he passed the corner of the nurse station, Mr. Allen did a u-turn. "Nurse, has he had any movements?" he asked.

Startled, Mary slowly turned around to face him, "No, I don't believe so. Sometimes coma patients have spasms, but your son has been still. He doesn't even respond when I have to stick him for a blood sample."

"Oh," Mr. Allen said. He stopped talking as the gurney passed in front of him. He should have recognized Jeremy. He did not look at the person pushing, but rather at the odd hidden lump at the other end. It appeared the body had two heads at each end. He wrinkled his face and started to ask another question, but decided not to and turned back to the waiting room.

Once alone in the elevator, Jeremy lifted the sheet. "He didn't see either one of us. I think we'll just continue this ruse until we get to the locker room. Down you go," he said as he recovered Chase and the doors opened.

They made it to his car and quickly drove away. Chase did not say much on the way home. Jeremy sensed his mind might be replaying the events of the day. He stayed quiet, letting Chase think. He could not imagine how he would feel if the man he loved most was in a coma. How he handled the entire one-sided, conversation was remarkable. He began to realize Brett handled all the financial and legal issues, while Chase handled, well, Chase.

He assumed Chase always helped, but rarely took the lead in any project, but Brett must have been keen on making sure Chase felt like many things were his ideas. They each complemented the other, and their love made it all happen. He became envious of the couple.

He put Chase to bed and made his way to his room. It had been a long day, and they felt exhausted. Chase closed his eyes hoping to dream of Brett once more. Instead, his brain kept replaying the attack on the house, and how frightened he was. It was more than hour before he finally drifted off.

SEVEN

Hearing Chase's voice stirred something deep in Brett. No one could tell it by staring at him, but if they checked the monitors on the shelf above his head, they would see the rise in the number of heart beats per minute, his lungs filled a little deeper, and his temperature up one degree. However, Mary was busy with another patient, while pretending she had not seen Chase enter the room. She hoped no one would ask if she did, as she hated to lie. Chase's mind and heart focused on communicating with Brett and not on checking the machines.

When Chase kissed him, his index finger twitched, but Chase had already let go, so he could lean over for the kiss. Brett's body desperately tried to communicate with Chase, but there were too many obstacles in his way.

He wanted to wake up. He wished to wake up, but after every deep sleep and dream cycle, he tried to open his eyes, and each time he could not make his muscles react, as they should. His attempt to control his nerves would only last a few seconds, and off he went to another dream.

The moments came more often but the results were still the same. Twice today, Brett could see light for a few seconds through his eyelids, but never at the same time. He did not know this occurred when Mary checked his eyes with her penlight.

Once he felt his fingertips, and he quickly tapped the bed linens, but no one saw him do it. He also had the ability to tune out, and he did so when his dad came in his room. If they allowed his uncles in to see him, he would have tuned them out as well. Thankfully, the hospital banned the uncles from the Intensive Care Unit, and put them on the do-not-allow list.

His mom brought about a contradiction. He cared a lot about his mom, but spent less and less time with her, as she had not yet accepted he was gay, and because she did not like the man, he loved. He knew Chase could come on a little strong, act a little too gay, be a bit flippant, but what people often missed is behind his sometimes silly voice was a deeply compassionate heart. Beneath his little boy looks and childlike antics, grew the love of his life. No one knew what it was like to wake up next to Chase, and to feel him cuddle in your arms. Brett loved feeling like he was taking care of Chase, and especially loved the way Chase counted on him to take charge and lead them. He accepted the responsibility with great pride.

Chase and Brett were learning how to be a loving couple and how to build their relationship. The vacation trip was to be a celebration of another year together. It could have been a great time, but in a flash, everything changed. If he understood, what had happened to him he would know he was fighting for his life, but his mind had wiped away the crash and thankfully, the

awful pain. It was as if he had fallen in a deep dark cave, and way up at the top he could see just a little sky and the face of Chase. With no rope to climb out of the hole, he had to find another way to get back to the man he loved and the life he lived. If he could feel or see a flicker of light, he felt he had accomplished another step up to the top of the hole. A minute later, his mind drifted into a dream of his past.

It was confusing time for Brett. He loved hanging out with Brice, especially when they were alone. He often dreamed of Brice and thought about him when he masturbated, but Brice had started spending more time talking with the girls in the neighborhood and less time playing with the boys. However, at least once a week and sometimes three times a week, he and Brice would camp out.

Brett also camped out alone with James, the only boy in the neighborhood that was his age. They, too, played strip poker, made up their own rules, but the results were always the same. They would spend time kissing and sucking, but never discuss it the following day.

Those times were fun as his penis had begun to grow, but his time with Brice was always mesmerizing because Brice was growing, too. Sure, he was taller, stronger, possessed more muscles, and was easily the best looking guy in the neighborhood, but his penis became the envy of the other boys as well.

Brice and Brett no longer played poker, but just sat around listening to music and talking until Brice was sure, his parents had gone to bed. From time to time, he would peek out the tent rear window waiting and watching for all the houselights to go out. Once he felt secure, the routine now followed a pattern.

Brice would dim the light, and zip down the door so if anyone did surprise them they would have time to separate and cover up before they could get the stubborn zipper up. In addition, they would not be able to see well because of the diminished light.

Brice would slowly strip off his shirt, which always excited Brett, making his member firm and hard, and then Brett would stand facing Brice. Brice would reach down, pull Brett's shirt over his head, and then softly rub his hands down Brett's bare chest. They both loved the feel of each other's skin, and always spent a lot of time caressing the other. Brice would pull Brett to him, and place tender kisses to Brett's softy tummy. He liked to undress Brett, one piece of clothing at a time.

After another minute or so, he would undo Brett's pants and slide them down slowly until Brett could step out of them. Brice would begin feeling Brett's buns through his white cotton briefs. He would gently squeeze his genitals, hook a finger inside the waistband, slide his hands around to his back, and slowly pull his underwear down and off. Brett was always fully hard by the time his underwear hit the floor of the tent.

Brice would continue to play with Brett's butt while pulling him to him. He would take Brett's smaller dick in his mouth and suck it carefully, getting tighter with each stroke. Brett would place his hands on the back of Brice's hair rubbing it tenderly while covering his ears with his warm hands.

After a while, and with no words spoken, Brice would release Brett's penis, pull him to his face, and kiss him deeply. Then he would stand and Brett would undo Brice's pants and pull them down and off followed by his underwear. For the first few years, Brice always wore briefs, but recently had switched to boxers The sight of his long loose penis and big hanging balls always sent a chill of excitement and anticipation up Brett's naked spine.

Brice remained standing as he pushed Brett's face to his groin. Brett knew exactly what he was supposed to do. He began by licking the bottom of Brice's genitals. Over and over, he rolled his warm wet tongue, and grinned when he saw the hair on Brice's legs stand up. Brice would put his hands behind Brett's hair and rub his soft hair and ears. Before long, he would lift Brett's head just a little and Brett would take his cue to begin licking the shaft of Brice's hardening penis. He licked it up and down like a long dripping ice-cream cone. He loved doing it and Brice loved the feeling as well.

Brice instructed him to begin sucking only the head of Brice's dick. Months ago Brice told him to suck it like a Tootsie Roll Pop and with great determination to get to the candy inside. Brett always thought about the candy when he started sucking. He knew he was good by the quiet moans he heard above his head. Brice would nearly go into a trance during this preliminary stage of their lovemaking.

Barbara had been on her shift in the intensive care unit for about two hours when it was time to log the monitor numbers from her patients. When she got to Brett's room, she began writing down the numbers and after recording a few and looking at his previous reading, she realized almost everything was up a little. It puzzled her, so she felt his face and noted it felt warm. She leaned down to the number of units of urine in his bag. Brett suddenly urinated with a strong stream while most patients just dripped. She thought it was a bit odd, but waited for him to finish, and then recorded the number on his chart.

She looked again at his heart monitor and down to her chart. It had been the first number she had written down and it was already ten beats a minute higher. She stood back and thought a second and decided to move on, but mentally made a note to check on him in an hour instead of the usual two hours.

Brett usually lost track of time at this point, but when Brice thought he was about to explode his load, he would pull out of Brett's beautiful warm

long roster of women for the same ecstasy he felt with his young friend. He tried hard, but never again felt such devotion.

Brice brought along a washcloth or two and always gently, tenderly, and lovingly cleaned Brett up. He would then break out a snack to replenish the energy after heavy sex. They would eat and lie around naked to cool down. One time when they were laughing afterwards, Brice worked his big toe into Brett's butt. "Good grief," he exclaimed, "I could drive my car in there!"

They laughed heartily and Brett loved every minute of it. When they became sleepy, Brice would pull Brett in a spooning position in his sleeping bag where they remained until dawn. Brett never slept as well than after the sex with Brice, and he loved the feeling of Brice's penis resting against his bare buttocks.

Chase heard a noise and almost woke up. He rolled to the side of the bed, and found himself staring at pair of plaid flannel boxers hiding a left over hard on. He knew Brett loved to wear boxers, but only those from either LL Bean or Eddie Bauer, and only flannel ones—even in the summertime. Brett always liked the soft feel of the flannel and did not care at all what others thought of his style of boxers.

For a moment, Chase forgot about the plane crash, his broken ankle, or even the uncles. He thought he was staring at Brett. He reached upwards through the loose leg of the shorts, grabbed the genitals, and began playing with them. The penis began to swell.

He wanted sex with Brett. He wanted it badly. He tested his eyes and opened the lids just a little, but it was enough. He opened them wide and realized he had a big hold on Jeremy.

"Boy, you sure have a funny way of saying good morning. Do you do that with all your guests!" teased Jeremy.

Chased laughed, "I'm sorry. Brett wears flannel boxers, and I thought it was he. Wow, I have zoomed back to reality." He left his hand holding Jeremy's penis. "You do have a stout dick though."

"Thanks, but that is NOT what we're having for breakfast. Come on, it's time to get up. I have waffles and sausage for breakfast, and I don't mean mine."

Jeremy bent down and Chase grabbed him around the neck. Jeremy pulled upward until he had Chase on his feet beside the bed. He had his hands around Chase's back as he steadied him.

"What happened to your underwear?" asked Jeremy noting Chase was nude.

"Whoops, I forgot them. I usually sleep in the nude, and they just kept getting in my way, so I got my good leg out of them, but they're stuck on my cast."

102

Jeremy bent down, untangled the shorts, allowed Chase to put his good leg back in, and then he pulled up. His hair tickled Chase's genitals. He snapped the waistband, "Now I feel safer. Come on, let's eat."

Jeremy helped him down the hall, sat him down in a chair, and brought him a hot plate of food. "Eat before it gets cold."

"Wow, this is g…" stated Chase with a mouth full of food.

"You were trying to say good I assume. You're just starved but thank you," laughed Jeremy. He sat down beside him to begin eating as well. He took a big spoonful and prepared to stuff it in his own mouth, "Here, let me chew this and talk at the same time so you can understand me, too!"

Chase laughed and swung his good knee into Jeremy's and laughed again.

Later Chase stood in the hall outside the guest room door. "What are you going to do today?" asked Jeremy as he continued dressing.

"Try to find that damn Living Will. I just don't recall where Brett told me he was going to put it. I should have paid better attention. I never thought I would need it. If I ever find it and I will, I'm going to have that darn thing framed!" exclaimed Chase.

"Here's the plan today. I work twelve to eight again. Tomorrow I have off—yeah!! I'll call you on my breaks to make sure you're okay, and I hope you will report there are no bad guys visiting today. Keep the doors locked. Keep the cordless phone handy in case you need to call the police, and so I can reach you without you hopping to the phone. You're liable to fall and break something else!" he teased.

Chase laughed and held up his right hand as if taking an oath, "Yes, mother dear. I promise."

"All right, here I go. Give me a hug," urged Jeremy. Chase gladly did.

"I'm getting used to having you around. Especially breakfast. It was yummy. Thanks," grinned Chase as he kissed Jeremy on his forehead.

"You're welcome. Why not take a bath today? You could leave your cast on the edge of the tub so it doesn't get wet."

"Are you saying I need a bath?"

Jeremy leaned into Chase's ear, "Yes, you need a bath!"

Chase playfully punched him.

Chase spent the day rummaging through the chest of drawers, the dresser, and in the nightstand in their rooms, but could not find the Living Will. He searched through the closet sliding apart every single shirt and pants hanging there, but found nothing. He started going through the stacks of t-

103

shirts, shorts, and when he got to the sweaters, he pushed his hand beneath each sweater one at a time. On the fourth sweater, his hand bumped an envelope. He also felt a box. He gingerly pulled both out, and realized the envelope was the size of a card. He flipped it over and read his name carefully printed across the front. He recognized the handwriting immediately—it was Brett's. His lover's handwriting had always been poor, so often he printed the words when he wanted to make a good impression.

He found the envelope sealed and for a brief moment, Chase contemplated not opening it, but realizing he had to find the Living Will, he decided it outweighed any thoughts of invading Brett's privacy. Gently, he pulled out a card and turned it over.

On the front of the card was a picture of a gorgeous nude hunk and the words, "I was thinking of you when I picked out this card but…"

Chase grinned as he opened the card and continued reading, "After seeing the good-looking man on the front of this card, I had to stop and masturbate!" Chase laughed aloud.

He then noted the handwritten note Brett added to the bottom of the card, "Happy Third Anniversary! I hope you like the card, and I hope you love me as much as I love you. I have never been happier in my life than the minutes, hours, and days I spend with you. My love for you is as pure and everlasting as gold itself. Love, Brett."

Chase started to cry. His tears hit the card as he laid it aside, and slowly opened the box. The box was from Creasmans, Brett's favorite jeweler. Inside he found a beautiful Figaro bracelet; the loops identical with the one Brett wore; the one Chase often rolled his fingers over while lying together on the couch watching a movie. Brett did not usually wear jewelry, but he loved this bracelet.

Chase held it up and watched as the light sparkled off it. He kissed the bracelet, and then put it back in the box. He returned the card and the box back to their hiding place.

He sat down on the bed, fell back across the bedspread, and began to recall their adventure to New York where they stopped in the Village in a little gay card shop. Chase, enthralled with all the pink triangles and rainbow trinkets for sale, giggled loudly. He thought he had landed in a gay utopia. Together, they read cards, bumper stickers, and refrigerator magnets and laughed. He could not imagine how Brett managed to buy an anniversary card in the store without Chase knowing it or catching him.

As they walked down the street, they stopped in clothing store where they immediately noted the staff to be gay friendly and some gay themselves. The clerks were far from shy and in seconds, they had Chase and Brett trying on jackets. They brought out various shirts, matching colors in the jackets, but Brett declined saying they did not need to buy a jacket.

The clerk responded instantly, "Need? Honey, no one buys anything they need here. This store is all about 'want'! And honey, my gay boys love the clothes I find them, and they all want 'em!" They all laughed heartily.

Chase picked out a pair of slacks he liked. "Try them on, honey," urged the clerk.

"Where's the changing room?" asked Chase.

The staff laughed at both his question and his Southern accent. "Honey, there are no changing rooms here. All our shoppers just strip down in the aisle and try anything on they want." He gave Chase a wink, "Now you know why the entire staff is standing just over there. They're waiting for YOU to undress!"

Chase and Brett busted out laughing. Chase looked at Brett for assurance. Brett responded, "You've never been shy before—why start now? Take your pants off, and perhaps you'll get a tip!" he urged while laughing.

Chase giggled and unbuckled his pants. To his surprise, the clerk fell to his knees and began pulling Chase's pants off while casually bumping the back of his hand against Chase's penis. Chase loved the attention.

Once the pants were down the clerk turned to his staff, "And your scores are?"

The row of clerks each held up ten fingers.

"Ah, yes, our first all ten winner of the week!" he yelled. The entire store turned to see Chase standing there in his underwear. The clerk helped him on with his pants, pushed him to a mirror, and showed him how wonderful he looked. Then he spun him around and pulled off his shirt showing his bare chest. "Judges, if you please!" he yelled.

Once again, four out of the five clerks gave him ten fingers but one gave him a nine. "Uh oh, looks like we lost an all ten score. Hernando, why did you give him a nine when everyone else gave him a ten?"

Hernando grinned as he began walking over to Chase. "I need a closer look. The light is reflecting off his beautiful chest. He turned his head left and right, and then turned Chase around, "Whoops, I have to change my vote." He took Chase's right hand and held it up, folding in his fingers leaving two pointing to the ceiling. He then held up his ten fingers alongside Chase's. "I give him a twelve!!" he exclaimed.

The entire store guffawed with raucous laughter and cat whistles. Chase blushed, but Brett knew he loved every minute of the attention. Brett winked at him, and Chase instantly gave him one back. Another clerk walked over carrying a tiny pair of briefs with a seam down the center of the back from the waistband to the crotch.

"The pants would look a whole lot better if he was wearing the right underwear," stated Robbie. "These lift and shape your buns into beautiful melons. Now get those slacks and shorts off, and I'll show you."

Before Chase could respond, the two clerks pulled down the slacks, then his boxer shorts, and suddenly, they stopped leaving Chase standing there naked.

The clerk held his hand out to the side as if presenting Chase to a panel of beauty queen judges at a pageant. "Well, gentlemen, and I use that word loosely, what is your score now?"

The remaining four judges quickly huddled for a second as the whole store waited for an answer. Then astonishingly, they quickly kicked off their shoes, removed their socks, fell into a line facing them. On a quick count of three, they all jumped backward onto the table filled with stacks of slacks and held up ten fingers. They raised their feet while wiggling their toes and screamed in unison, "He gets a twenty!"

Again the whole store laughed, but Chase nearly fell down he was giggling so hard. The clerk quickly helped him into the 'buns' underwear, turned him around and around showing them off, and then put a beautiful shirt on him followed by the slacks. He did a few quick modeling turns. The staff and customers applauded the results.

They bought the clothes and gave everyone a big hug. It was a shopping experience of a lifetime, and the two lovers talked about it repeatedly for more than a year. If Brett ever felt like Chase might be feeling sad over something, he would tell the shopping story once again, but always adding more to it.

The results were always the same with both laughing heartily.

Not long after dark, Chase forced himself to wake up, and slowly made his way to the bathroom. He ran the water until warm enough, and put the stopper in the drain. Slowly, he slid out of his clothes and tried to figure out how he was going to sit in the tub leaving a leg hanging out. He placed a bath towel on the closed toilet seat, turned around, and sat on the edge of the tub. He leaned back and placed his hands on the opposite wall, lifted his butt before slowly lowering himself into the water. He swung his good leg around and let it submerge.

The hot water felt wonderful so he leaned back and placed his back against the edge and snuggled down into the water. He snatched a bottle of bubble bath in the shape of Garfield the Cat, and squirted it into the stream of water flowing into the tub. Soon the tub filled with bubbles covering all but his face. He turned off the water and began playing with his penis, but mostly just let the water soothe his muscles.

He almost drifted off to sleep when the doorbell suddenly rang. His mind raced for answers as to who might be at the door. He thought of Girl Scouts selling cookies, a salesman, Mormon Missionaries, or Brett's uncles. The latter gave him a scare, as he would be defenseless against them. He did not have any money in his pocket, so he could not buy cookies, and he was not in the mood for a vacuum cleaner demonstration. He thought a little

longer about the Mormons because sometimes those young college boys were just too cute to resist.

The bell rang again. Chase sat in the water in silence. Suddenly, he heard the lock turn in the door and push open. Chase held his breath.

"Chase? Chase? Where are you?" asked Jeremy loudly from the living room.

Chase let out a huge sigh. "In the tub!" he yelled. He heard Jeremy setting something down in the kitchen, as well as the clicks of light switches as Jeremy lit up the house. Chase knew Jeremy would come into the bedroom, but when he leaned around the bathroom doorframe and said 'boo', he still jumped.

"Don't do that!" laughed Chase.

"Or what?" teased Jeremy.

Chase threw a handful of bubbles at him. "Or I will drown you in bubble bath."

"Yeah, right—hey, it is good to see you. You look better, or maybe you just got some of the dirt off."

"Yeah, I feel better. The hot water felt wonderful. I just can't figure out how to do my hair."

"Hold on, I have an idea. I'll be right back," stated Jeremy as he left the room, and returned carrying a plastic tea pitcher. "Okay, I think you'd better sit up, or you'll get bubbles in your nose. Let me help you," urged Jeremy as he Chase took his hand and pulled him into a sitting position. "Close your eyes," he said.

Jeremy bent down, dunked the tea pitcher, and slowly poured the water over Chase hair.

"Oh, that feels good," said Chase.

Jeremy did it several times, then set the pitcher down, and snatched up a bottle of shampoo on the shelf in the corner of the tub. He squirted a daub onto Chase's hair and then began massaging it into his scalp.

"Okay, you're hired. Can you come by and do this everyday?" begged Chase.

"Until you get well, of course I can. Shut your eyes, I'm going to rinse." He filled the pitcher with clean water out of the tap and poured it over his head. He put a daub of conditioner on his hair, rubbed it through the wet hair, and rinsed it as well.

"Boy, you smell a whole lot better," teased Jeremy.

"I know. I had a little trouble getting in, and I'm not sure how to get out."

Jeremy pulled the plug out of the drain. Once all the water drained, he took numerous pitchers of water, and washed the bubbles off Chase.

"Okay, let's get you up." Jeremy put his hands under Chase's arms and pulled him up, and out of the tub like a child.

Jeremy paused after Chase stabilized on his good leg noting Chase's beautiful body. "You're giving me a hard on, but it does look like your wounds are healing nicely."

"I can't wait to get this freaking cast cut off me."

Jeremy took a towel and started on drying Chase's hair, then slowly toweled Chase all the way down to his toes, his back, and his buns and between his legs. Chase loved the feel of the soft towel and the attention, and his penis began to harden. Jeremy noted it as he felt stiffness in his pants as well.

"Oh, my I'm getting excited. We'd better dress you quickly," stated Jeremy grinning as he put the towel on the sink.

Chase put his arms on Jeremy's back and pulled him to him. "Thanks, now lead me into my room."

Together, they managed to dress Chase.

"Did you bring anything to eat? I'm starved," asked Chase.

"Nope, nothing, well, I did bring some more groceries. I thought we would go out to eat."

"Do you think I can?"

"I think you'd better start getting out of here, or you are going to go nuts. I brought home a pair of crutches for you to try. Hang on, I'll get them."

Jeremy returned to the living room, picked up the aluminum crutches, and returned to the bedroom. He held a crutch up measuring Chase, adjusted the extensions, tightened the bolts, and placed them under Chase's arms.

"Now use your good leg and lean forward one step. Now move the crutches forward and do it again. Do not put any weight on the cast."

Chase did as instructed and soon he was moving down the hall. Satisfied, Jeremy grabbed his car keys and helped Chase out the door, locked it, and then on to his car. Once inside, Chase said, "I didn't know you had a key."

"Remember, when we had to come in through the window, and I found the keys in the mailbox. Well, this morning I took one off the ring, tested it, and then locked the door as I left. I did not want the boogie man to get you."

"Good thinking. Just hang on to it and remind me to change the key on my ring." He thought a second and added, "Whoops, I don't have a key ring. I guess it burned up on the plane. I had put it in a zipper side pocket of my carry on bag."

"We'll get you a new one," replied Jeremy as he patted his leg. "Okay, what would you like to eat?"

"Mexican," said Chase emphatically. "I want some Chimichanga. Do you know the Mexican restaurant on Patton?"

108

"Yes, of course, but I have never been there."
"Trust me you'll like it. It is one of Brett's favorites."
"Okay, let's go."

Dinner had been fun with Chase drinking his first beer in a long time. He had not relaxed since arriving at the airport to begin their vacation and of course, his nerves remained in frenzy in the immediate days following the plane crash. They laughed and talked for almost two hours about happier times as Chase related various events in their life. However, there were sad moments as Chase told him of their tender times. Chase left no doubt in Jeremy's mind of his love for Brett, and from hearing all the lovely things Brett did for Chase he knew the passion for each other was the same.

They paid the bill with Chase insisting he pay after all Jeremy had done to help him. They pushed through the door with a euphoric attitude. Chase slipped his arm around Jeremy, gave him a hug, and kissed him on the cheek. "Thank you for helping me. It was not intentional, but Brett and I made so many plans, often our friends fell by the wayside. We soon realized most of our friends were only bar friends and not real friends. However, I should call some of my close friends, and tell them I am doing better and ask them to pray Brett survives as well."

Jeremy gave him a good hug and returned the kiss to Chase's cheek as they reached Jeremy's car parked in the last spot next to Patton Avenue. They failed to notice a group of boys watching them. A car full of teenagers pulled out of the Burger King across the street, made a sharp u-turn, and slowed down near them and started calling them names.

Chase got angry quickly, cursed, and made a hand gesture. The boys responded by throwing empty beer bottles at them before speeding off. Chase called after them repeating the same words as he could think of nothing more to say. Shaken, but okay, they got in Jeremy's car and pulled out in the opposite direction.

"Are you ready to go home?" asked Jeremy.

"No, I feel like I have been in a cage for a month. I cannot wait to break this cast open and free myself. I feel like a prisoner with this ball and chain on my ankle. The crutches help, but boy do they hurt my armpits," complained Chase.

"It is because you're such a tender baby," teased Jeremy.

Chase looked at him mischievously as he punched Jeremy's knee, "Like you're some Olympic wrestler yourself. I will be fine. Let's just drive around a little and let me see the stars for a while."

"Okay, but lock your door in case the hooligans come back," he warned.

"Yes, mother dear," replied Chase sarcastically.

EIGHT

Two months later...

The orderly pushed Chase down the hall and into an examining room. Carefully, he leaned forward to help Chase up on the table, but Chase had adapted to his cast and stubbornly stood up on his own and hopped onto the table.

"Looks like you're doing well. The doctor will be in to check out the x-rays we took to determine if you get to wear this cast another month or so," stated the orderly.

"No way, dude. This sucker is coming off today if I have to cut it off myself."

The orderly grinned, "Well, if you do it yourself try not to cut your leg off, too."

Chase smiled. "I have been wondering, exactly how do you get this hard thing off my ankle without cutting my foot?"

The orderly walked over to a rolling cart and lifted a stainless steel open blade power saw. "We cut it off you and I'm sorry, but occasionally we cut off the foot, too, and have to glue it back on," he teased.

Chase gulped. "Ouch! I think I had better be going." He faked getting ready to leap off the table.

The orderly laughed, "No way. My job is to keep you here, and I am good at my job!"

Chase dropped his shoulders. "Is it going to hurt?"

The orderly softened his teasing, "Not yet." He paused, "Okay, no the cutting doesn't hurt, and we do this all the time. However, it will hurt when you first start moving your ankle, but soon you will be as good as new. Just keep flexing it no matter how sore it is."

"Will I still have to use the crutches?"

The orderly smiled, "Don't worry, only for a few more days. The more you're able to move and stretch your ankle, though it is as stiff as a board, the sooner you will be able to walk again."

The door opened and the doctor walked in. He nodded at Chase, and went to the wall and flipped on a light switch for the wall panel. He began putting the big x-rays of Chase's foot on the wall. He studied the various views for several minutes before turning around and facing Chase. "Your ankle has healed correctly. Are you ready to get this cast off your leg?"

"Yes," replied Chase timidly, "but don't you go cutting my foot off, too."

The doctor laughed, "I promise, I haven't cut a single leg off...uh...this week—so far."

Chase replied, "How many casts have you taken off this week?"

The doctor sighed with a slight grin, "You're my first."

Chase rolled his eyes, "I was hoping you had practiced on someone else first."

The doctor padded him on the shoulder. "I promise. You'll be fine. Are you ready?" The orderly rolled the cart over. He arranged a pillow and helped Chase lie down. The doctor said, "Now you just lie down and be still, and I'll have this off in a jiffy."

Chase gulped. He gripped the side of the table so tightly his knuckles were white. The doctor tested the saw with a zip-zip motion in the air. Chase nearly passed out. The orderly put his hands on Chase's shoulders to make sure he did not move. The grinding began. Five minutes later, the cast came away like peeling an orange. The doctor put the saw down.

"You're free of the cast. Now the orderly is going to clean your foot up a bit, and I'll be back in a moment to examine it. You were very brave," he added as he patted Chase's thigh.

"Thanks," was all Chase could mutter as he let the blood begin flowing back to his fingers.

Jeremy had to work that day so Chase had taken a cab to the hospital to have his cast removed. The doctor did the final examination of his ankle and presented him with good news. He urged Chase to move his ankle as much as possible, and to try to walk a little farther each day. He would see him again in six weeks to see how he was progressing. Chase thanked the doctor and began making his way down the hall to the main exit to catch a cab home.

He took one step at a time using his crutches for support. His foot felt like it had been asleep for a long time, giving him the feeling he had stepped on a porcupine, but he was so eager to walk he would grimace or say a curse word and keep going. He stopped for a breather and soon spotted Mary coming his way.

"Hey, boy, look at you! You have that old cast off the foot. How you doing?" she asked as she gave him a hug.

Chase was glad to see her and began bragging right away, "They just cut it off a little while ago. I told 'em I was tired of that darn thing on my ankle. They understood and cut it off."

Mary knew better, but she played along, "I'm sure you were. Have you been to see Brett today?"

"No, Jeremy has been working hard, and I've been afraid to since that last close call we had."

Mary laughed, "Yep, but you fooled them."

"How's he doing?" asked Chase in a quieter tone.

"You know they moved him from Intensive Care?" she asked and Chase nodded.

111

"Once I can walk I hope to stop in every day or so. What room is in?" asked Chase.

"824," she replied, "but you better be careful. His parents don't come by often, but they do come. Those two uncles are a piece of work," she warned.

"Mary, I think I will go ahead and try to see him now, but what do I say to him? It's been so long since I heard his voice," said Chase.

Mary gave him another hug, "Honey, you just talk to him about anything. He needs to hear your voice." She looked around to see if anyone was listening before continuing. "Now, Chase, don't get your hopes up, but sometimes when I talk to him he moves his fingers. I've also noted his heart rate increases as does his blood pressure and even his temperature when I talk to him. If he'll do that for me, I'm sure he'll do even more for you. Inside, behind the darkness of that coma, is Brett, and he is anxious to get back to normal. Don't you dare give up on him." She leaned over and kissed Chase on the forehead.

Chase smiled, "I won't give up. I'm just feeling a little lost without him. Thank you for telling me. I will see him more often."

"Okay, well, I have to get back to work. Are you going to be okay?"

"Yes, ma'am, I will. See you later."

Chase waved good-bye and made his way up the hall to the elevator. Worn out when he hit the button for the eighth floor, he felt thankful he could rest during the ride up. When the elevator door opened, he again used the crutches to make his way out. He read the signs until he found the directions to room 824. He began making his way down the hall, and unlike the Intensive Care Unit, no one cared he was there. He went down the hall, made a turn, and made his way halfway down the next hallway. He reached the door, but could not see inside.

Suddenly, he stopped. He listened to see if he could hear any voices. He heard none. He sighed heavily as he did not think today he could handle running into the Allen clan. He pushed the door open just a little, and seeing no one there, he moved into the room. He stopped when he saw Brett lying in the bed on his back perfectly still. He looked better with far fewer tubes in him, a smaller bandage on his head, and he could tell his hair had grown. However, the tubes still bothered him, which Chase assumed was how they fed him and kept him alive. He saw a heart monitor to the right of bed on the wall with a steady eighty beats a minute. Now and then, another machine automatically checked his blood pressure. Chase could not remember what the two numbers meant, but Brett's skin color was good. His other scrapes and wounds had healed. Thankfully, the stitches, long ago removed, healed quickly, too. Four weeks ago, a second surgery closed up his skull after the swelling in his brain receded. Jeremy had told him physically Brett was in good shape—he just needed to wake up.

112

Chase moved around to the bed and sat down in the chair beside the bed exhausted. He sat there several minutes catching his breath then reached up and took hold of Brett's hand. He intertwined their fingers and then placed his other hand over them. Tears swelled up in his eyes as he began to speak aloud.

"Hey, Brett, it is Chase. I'm back. I'm sorry it has been a while since I've been here, but soon I'll be able to drive, and I'll see you every day. I have to figure out when your folks come around so I don't meet them, but I will come, I promise you. They took my cast off today, so although it hurts a little, I will start walking a little more each day. They used a power saw…"

Chase continued telling Brett about today's adventure, but Brett's brain did not process the words to the point where he could respond, but his heart knew the sound of Chase's voice. His heart picked up to ninety beats a minute, but not enough to set off an alarm, so Chase never knew his voice created this reaction. Brett's brow wrinkled as if he had a cramp or gas, but Chase continued talking.

"I've been looking all over the house for the Living Will. I sure wish I knew where you put it. Jeremy told me to try to think like you, and I tried, but I don't think I can think like you because you have more brains than I do. I wish you could just wake up for five seconds and tell me where it is," he stated and then grinned at himself. "Okay, I know that was dumb because if you could wake up, I would not need to find the darn Living Will.

"Jeremy has been a big help, and I can't wait for you to meet him. I know you'll like him. He is like you. You know dependable, responsible, caring, loving…" he stopped for a moment thinking hard before continuing, "but he is not you. You are special. No one has ever loved me the way you do."

Tears began rolling down his face, "I need for you to hold me again. I need for you kiss me. I need to hear your voice. I wish I had a recording of your voice. I have pictures of you I keep by my bed, but I don't have your voice. Please come back," he dropped his head to Brett's arm and sobbed.

A nurse came into the room carrying a tray. She set the tray on the table over the bed. She h heard Chase's last few comments, and caught on quickly that Chase was not a brother or a friend but rather Brett's lover. She came around, put her arm over his shoulder, and patted his back gently. "Don't worry little one. He's going to be fine. One of these days he will just wake up and wonder what all the fuss about him is for."

Chase wiped the tears away and turned to see an older black woman with the prettiest smile he had ever seen. He tried to smile back at her. "Thank you. My name is Chase."

"You can call me Janie," she replied. "I'm pleased to meet you."

"Me, too," he said. "How's he doing?"

113

"Fine, let me record his numbers and we'll see." She picked up the clipboard and began looking at the monitors. She looked over the rim of her glasses as if not sure she was seeing correctly before writing. "Well now, it looks like his blood pressure is up a little and so his heart rate. You must be good for him. You must come back to see him. I believe he can hear you."

"I will, but I am worried."

"Why are you worried, child? The good Lord is going to take care of him one way or the other."

"I know that. His parents have been trying to take control of him. We both filled out Living Wills because he was afraid of something like this, but the copies burned up in the plane crash, and I cannot find the originals."

"Oh, I see."

Chase asked, "Listen, have you noted a particular time the Robertsons come to visit?"

"Hmm, let me see, I believe his mother comes Monday, Wednesday, and Friday and always in the mornings as that is my shift. I had to work a Sunday a few weeks ago, and his dad and uncles came with the mother to see him that afternoon."

"I was afraid of that. They don't like me very much. The uncles have threatened to kill me. They even tried to lock me out of our house. If they caught me in here, I am sure they would break both my legs, and I just got the cast off this one. I guess they are no longer barred from the hospital."

"That's too bad. Relatives can act so stupid sometimes."

"Yes they can—may I ask a favor?" he asked while rolling soft forlorn eyes at her.

She laughed, "What can I do, my dear?"

"Don't tell them I was here. If they find out, they are liable to post a guard or something. I want to come see him every day."

"No problem, but you be careful. We don't need the both of you hurt." She picked up her tray to leave. "I will see you later, and nice to meet you." She moved to the door.

"Thank you and nice to meet you, too," added Chase with a smile.

After she left, Chase began saying goodbye to Brett, and then leaned over, kissed him on the lips, as well as several times on his cheeks. Brett's heartbeat went up again.

Sadly, he let go of Brett's fingers and noted how sweaty their hands were. He kissed Brett's hand, and put it beneath the sheet. He made his way to the door and turned to look at Brett one last time, "I love you," he said sincerely, and added with a bit of flair, "now hurry up and get your ass out of that bed!" Chase laughed at himself and pushed out the door.

Brett's heartbeat and blood pressure continued upward a bit more.

It had been a couple of weeks since the removal of his cast, and Chase finally managed to start driving his car. He pushed himself to walk several times a day, and now made his way down the street and back without his crutches or even a cane. He had felt so good he crossed the street and continued into the next block before turning around.

He glanced at his watch, "Shit! I'm late!" He began making his way back to the house as quickly as he could and arrived exhausted. He undressed and walked to the shower.

"Hello," a voice from the hall said.

"I'm in the shower," replied Chase as he enjoyed the shower so much now that his cast was off.

"You're always in the tub or the shower when I come," replied Jeremy.

Chase reluctantly turned off the water, reached through the curtain for the towel, and then swung open the curtain.

"Boy, you sure know how to make an entrance!" laughed Jeremy.

Chase stood there broad naked, drying his hair with the towel, "Huh?"

He turned around and found Jeremy standing before him, whom he had expected, but not the other man standing beside him. "Whoops, I'm sorry. I didn't know we had company." He quickly covered himself with the towel.

Jeremy laughed, "Chase, this is my new boyfriend Paul that I have been telling you about." He turned to Paul and put his arm around his waist, "Paul, this is my crazy part time nudist friend Chase."

Paul was a bit taller than Jeremy with blond hair and blue eyes, and he possessed beautiful white teeth. Chase was a mesmerized for a second or two, "Oh, wonderful, uh, nice to meet you, Paul. Jeremy has told me so much about you. But don't worry, I never believed him."

"Yeah, right," laughed Jeremy. "You're looking good, but we're starved. Do you think you could wear clothes to the restaurant this time? I hate it when people stare at us the entire meal," teased Jeremy again.

"All right, if you insist. Why don't you guys go get a beer in the refrigerator, and I'll dress."

"There is no beer in the refrigerator. I haven't bought groceries since last Friday."

"You're right, you didn't, but I bought them today. I drove my car today, and I walked in and out of the store today!" Chase grinned from ear to ear.

"Way to go, Sport! I knew you could do it. Okay, we'll go get the beer and you put some clothes on."

All during the meal Chase could tell Jeremy and Paul had fallen hard for each other. They laughed, held hands, and whispered to each other, and Chase could not help himself, he was feeling a little jealous and a little left out.

"Well, I guess I had better get back. I had a big day, but I'm exhausted, and you two lovebirds must be dying to get in the sack. Thank you for dinner. It was great."

"Are you sure?" asked Jeremy, half-agreeing and half-worried Chase was okay.

"Yes, mother dear, I am fine. Just drop me off and try to obey the speed limit while heading to your love shack." He turned to Paul, "Oh, Paul, I should tell you, Jeremy likes to have his ear fucked."

Paul became confused, "What"?

Chase continued with a straight face, "Yep, in the ear. You see every boy he has ever dated has managed to fuck every other orifice in his body, but his ear. So do me a favor, as I'm tired of hearing him pout about not getting any in the ear, and give it lots of attention."

Paul grinned, "You're kidding, right?"

"Yes, I am," replied Chase without smiling.

Paul looked at Jeremy, and then Jeremy made eye contact with Chase. Suddenly they all three busted out laughing.

Chase had kept them laughing all the way home, but now that he was inside, he felt lonely. He knew Brett could live alone, but he was not sure he could. The walls seem to close in on him. Sometimes noises in the house scared him. He decided to ask Blake to bring the dogs over to keep him company and to walk with him. He stopped in the hall and called him, and he agreed to bring the dogs tomorrow.

He sat down on the couch and turned on the television. He had watched fewer than twenty minutes before falling asleep. He stayed there all night.

The dogs arrived early the next morning and immediately swooned over him with numerous kisses. Chase laughed at how rapidly their tails were moving back and forth. He thanked Blake several times for taking such good care of them. He made a mental note to stop and pick up dog food on the way, but thankfully, Blake had brought along a partial bag as well as their doggie toys.

After Blake left, Chase hooked up their leashes and took the dogs for a long walk. He felt spirited, energized by the dogs, and walked farther than ever before. He and the dogs took a nap when he got back home, then he showered and prepared for an afternoon visit at the hospital.

He was walking down the hospital hall when Janie came up behind him. "Hey, good-looking—what you got cooking," she said with a grin.

"Oh, nothing much, how are you doing?" he grinned in return.

"I need to talk to you."

Chase stopped and faced her, "Okay, what's up?"

"Yesterday Mrs. Allen arrived to see Brett."

"Yeah, so what?"

"Yesterday was Tuesday. She usually comes on Monday, Wednesday, and Friday."

"Yeah, okay, I remember."

"She didn't come alone. Her husband and an attorney came with them."

"An attorney? What did he want?"

"They told me they were planning on moving him to a nursing home."

"Why would they do that? He is getting great care here because you're looking after him."

"Thanks, and you're right he is, but his dad thinks they should stop feeding him and let him die. Our hospital does not allow such a thing. They could move him to a nursing home willing to carry out his wishes."

Chase started hyperventilating. Between struggling for a breath, "They...can't...I...love him. He's...coming...back! I know it!" he finished in a huff.

Janie hugged him, "I know you do and you're right, but they are in control of Brett's health."

"What do I do?"

"Do you have an attorney?" she asked.

"Yes, Brett does. I have spoken to him about the Living Will, but he did not have a copy, and he can't make up a new one without Brett signing it."

Janie sighed and hugged him again, "Call him anyhow. Maybe he has an idea. You go on ahead. I've got to get back to work."

Chase squeezed her hand, "Thank you for telling me. Thank you so much."

When Chase returned home, he called the attorney and left a message. It was an hour later before he received the call. Chase related the situation and the attorney reminded him once more he had to find the Living Will. He said if they moved Brett, he would petition the court to make him aware of any plans to allow Brett to die. He would also file an injunction to slow them down. He warned him eventually they could win—only the Living Will could save Brett.

117

Chase picked at his supper and wished Jeremy was coming over, but he and Paul had gone to the beach for the week so he felt alone in his thoughts. He leashed up the dogs and took another long walk.

After returning home he spent the evening going through Brett's desk and closet looking for the Will, but found nothing more than he had seen the first time. He then got an idea it might be in storage so he climbed the rickety ladder into the attic and carefully looked over the boxes labeled there. Brett was so organized every single box told him what was inside. He opened each box anyhow. He tore through things but found nothing of the Will. He picked up several photo albums and brought them down the steps with him.

After getting something to drink and a bowl of ice cream, he sat at the table and began looking at pictures of Brett's early childhood. He laughed at seeing Brett dressed like a cowboy at age two, and Superman at age five. He saw pictures of a birthday party, and a picture of him receiving a pup tent. He saw a picture of some friends camping out including a guy named Ellis who appeared taller and older, and a good-looking guy named Brice

He saw a picture of Brett climbing in a tree, and another picture floating on a raft at the beach. He loved all the pictures and left the books so he could look again tomorrow. He gave the dogs a hug and all three headed for bed.

He dreamed of a trip he and Brett made to Washington just last year. They had spent the day sightseeing a four-block section Brett had drawn on the District of Columbia map. Exhausted from the day's adventure, they enjoyed a great dinner, and then took what they called a bar nap. It usually took Brett about ten minutes or so to drift off to sleep, but not Chase. He could lie down, close his eyes, and drift off all in the same minute. Brett was forever envious of this unique talent.

They awoke about ten, took a shower together, dressed, and headed off to town to try out a couple of gay dance bars. They stumbled into a club called Woody's. The sign outside advertised the best dance bar in town. Jokingly, Chase counted aloud the patrons dancing.

"I count seven," he laughed.

"I think you can officially call this club dead on arrival," shouted Brett over the loud music. "Let's get something to drink. Maybe it'll pick up."

They both turned to each other and said simultaneously, "Not!"

However, they did get a beer and after a few minutes this older man made his way to them. Although Brett was not in the mood to fend off a creeper, Chase was so bored, that he would have talked to the wall. Brett nodded hello to the old-timer, but allowed Chase to do all the talking.

After a few minutes, Chase promptly set his beer on the bar and yelled over the loud music into Brett's ear, "Come on, we're getting out of here!"

"Why we're having so much fun?" teased Brett sarcastically.

118

"Come on, this guy told me where a strip club is. I want to see naked men!"

"Why didn't you say so? Here hold my beer, and I'll strip down right now and save you some time."

Chase took the beer and set it on the counter, grabbed Brett's hand and dragged him out of the bar. As they passed the bored doorman, Brett said with a straight face, "I told him to wait at least thirty minutes but lord! He just has to fuck at the top of every hour. What's a guy to do?" He shrugged his shoulders as if sincere. The doorman laughed at them.

They crossed the street, went down a half block, and spotted a sign with two words on it...Nude Men!

"Yahoo!" exclaimed Chase as he continued pulling Brett towards it.

"Are you sure? They are probably old and former Senators."

"No they are not. The man said they are young and cute."

"But you already have me," teased Brett.

"Yep, but your skinny butt may not be enough tonight!"

Brett replied as he tried to turn and see his ass. "What skinny butt?"

"Come on!"

There was a charming fat man at the door. They paid him ten bucks, and the guy told them the regular dancers were on the bar, but in an hour, they would be an amateur stripper contest. He suggested they enter.

Brett laughed, "I'm not taking my clothes off for all these men to gawk at."

"I would, now come on," urged a pleading Chase as he dragged Brett into the big room.

The club appeared to be like a former dance club, but now a single bar in a big U shape extended from the rear wall. They spotted five naked men dancing on the bar and swinging around fire poles positioned every ten feet. Each man was completely bare except for a pair of white socks. They got Brett's attention. Chase pulled him to the bar. They ordered beers and soon one at a time, the dancers stopped in front of them, and Chase put a dollar in their socks.

After a while, the strippers spent more and more time with them because Chase and Brett were fun to talk to, and they were cute. A red-haired fellow finished his run, went through the door, and in a few minutes came out dressed in a pair of shorts and cut-off tee shirt. He immediately came up to Chase and introduced himself. Chase introduced Brett as his boyfriend. The boy's name was Will. He was fairly good looking, but one particular part of his anatomy was outstanding, and thus he had a job as a stripper.

He told Chase about the contest and urged him to enter. Chase leaned into Brett and asked, "Well, should I?"

Brett knew the answer so there was no point in saying no. Besides, he spent a lot of time teaching Chase how to make his own decisions. They had yet to cover how to handle requests from a stripper with a big dick. He leaned in and said, "Give me your wallet, watch, and ring, and go have fun."

"Are you sure?" asked Chase as he began handing stuff to Brett, and then leaned over and French kissed Brett long and deep. The patrons around them stared and clapped. Brett blushed and Chase sprinted off with Will to the backroom to get ready.

Chase got a shock when he entered the dimly lit room. Will quickly closed and locked the door. "We do not allow guests back here as we have to get ready for our turn on the bar. Come on."

Chase's eyes went wide as he saw two of the strippers masturbating each other, and another boy on his knees sucking away on another stripper. Will pulled him to a corner, fished through his sports bag, and found a G-string about Chase's size.

"This should do," stated Will as he handed it to Chase.

"Is this all of it?" asked Chase with a laugh as he held up the skinny garment.

"It doesn't matter. After you make your entrance, you're going to take it off anyhow. The contest is fewer than forty-five minutes away, and the winner will get a thousand dollars. If you give me a hundred dollars of your winnings, I will tell you how to win. Or if you will let me suck you and get you ready, you can keep the whole thousand."

Chase thought he said it with such confidence he could not resist. Will did not wait for an answer. He began undoing Chase's shirt buttons while Chase worked the zipper on his pants. In fifteen seconds, he stood before Will naked. Will immediately dropped all his clothes off, too.

"Damn, I was wrong. I don't need to tell you a single thing. You're going to win this contest easily. You're freaking gorgeous, and I suspect that sausage you're carrying is going to be huge. Now listen to me, you have to go out there with a G-string on, but you must get and keep a hard-on to win. The men want to see the biggest dick in the bar, but you must also make them want you as well. I doubt you'll have a problem with the last part."

Chase bent down and pulled up the G-string. "Does it fit?"

"Yep, perfectly—now we just need to get you hard. Do you like porno?"

"Huh?"

Will laughed and threw him a Hot Male magazine. Chase began looking through the pages of nude pictures. Will knelt down, pulled the G-string down to Chase's ankles, and began sucking his balls feverously. He soon worked his way up to Chase's rapidly growing penis with a mouth so warm and wonderful Chase had to sigh, but he kept looking at the magazine. He was hard in sixty seconds.

120

Will pulled off, "Well that didn't take long. Stay here and play with it, and I'll be right back. I have to get your name on the amateur stripper list." Will pulled up his shorts and took off.

Chase sat down on the bench and slowly played with himself while flipping through the magazine. He noted there were about five guys onstage, and at least five more making out in the back. Not a bad job, he thought.

Will soon returned, "I got you on the list. The boss was in a pissy mood, so I have to sleep with him again tonight, but who cares, you're going to win!" He leaned over and kissed Chase right on the mouth.

Brett sat out front watching the dancers. He did not notice a couple had sat down beside him. When he turned their way, he nodded and smiled. They were in their sixties, but still laughed and carried on, and Brett soon noted how in love they were with each other. He saw little touches and pats, and occasional kisses. They soon struck up a conversation.

"Why are you alone, dear?" one of the men asked Brett.

"I'm not. My partner is dancing in the amateur show."

"Is he hung?" asked the other.

Brett blushed, "Well, yes."

"He'll win and we'll make sure of it. Just point him out."

Chase had sized up the other three contestants for the amateur contest and felt sure he could beat them, but ten minutes before time for the event to begin in walked eight guys some of which looked like bodybuilders. They stripped naked in thirty seconds, began playing with each other, and soon had tight hard packages. Their g-strings barely covered their merchandise. Chase gulped and suddenly felt inadequate.

Will made his way around the big guys and playfully pulled on Chase's penis, "Don't worry, big boy. All those guys come in every week to win the cash. Most of them are not even gay. You're fresh meat, and although these guys bring along friends to yell for them, the judges are going to love you."

"Thanks, I hope so," replied a worried Chase.

"Work the crowd. Hold on to the pole and lean out into the crowd. Give them quick kisses, and flirt like crazy. You're going to make a ton of money. You'll love it. Can you dance?" asked Will as he placed Chase's hand on his own dick.

"Yeah, sure."

"Well, swing your ass, and they'll love you even more."

At the bar the lights went down a big spotlight came on. The Master of Ceremonies introduced the three judges and announced they had twelve

121

contestants tonight. He introduced the first one who stepped through the door. They played good dance music, and the crowd cheered as a big muscle guy made his way around the bar, but even Brett could tell the guy could not dance. He just moved a little and smiled.

After he moved about fifteen feet down the bar working the crowd, they introduced the second one. This guy could dance a little and was cute, but Brett felt he had a small package for a naked competition, and reminded himself to never enter one of these contests.

One by one, the men came out, posed a little and then yanked off their G-string, and began working their way around the bar. Various patrons would tip them by putting a dollar in their socks. Brett could not believe how much money they were making.

Chase was last. The Master of Ceremonies announced he was in town visiting and a newcomer to stripping, and pleaded with folks to be nice.

Will pinched his butt and pushed him through the door. The spotlight hit him in the eye and people applauded a little, but soon they realized how naturally handsome and cute Chase was. He spun around a little, and then began to dance.

The guy next to Brett said, "Wow, he's a cutie and boy can he dance. Is this one yours?"

Brett nodded yes and smiled.

Chase undid his G-string and took it off with great flair. The crowd loved it, but their mouths fell open when they saw his penis. He had it firm and hard, and it responded to the attention. He began dancing down the bar, swinging around the pole, doing various gymnastic moves, leaned out into the crowed, smiled enthusiastically, and everyone could see he loved doing it. He began to get cheers and applause, and they overloaded his socks with dollars.

Near the end of the bar was Brett. Chase put on a show for him, swinging around his neck, flirting like crazy, and to everyone's surprise he finally leaned down and gave Brett a huge wet kiss. Brett tipped him while winking at him.

Chase joined the line of contestants and waited for the results. He did not have to wait long. The judges unanimously selected him, and the whole bar stood and clapped. They gave Chase the cash, and announced he would be back out to work the crowd in a few minutes.

Backstage some of the losers called him a fag and even pushed him, but Will grabbed him and brought him over to his bench. Together, they unfolded all the cash. Chase gave Will a hundred bucks for his help. Chase put on his shorts, and quickly slipped out the door and brought the cash to Brett.

"Hold all this money. I'm going back for more!" yelled Chase.

Brett put all the cash in his pockets. Chase reached in and squeezed Brett's balls a little and kissed him again. "Good luck and keep your socks on!" laughed Brett.

Chase hurried backstage and soon was working his way around the bar. By the close of the club, he had made over two thousand dollars in one night, a night they would laugh about for years to come. They got back to their hotel about four in the morning. After dancing his ass off, they stopped and picked up doughnuts and milk. They ate, drank, and headed for the shower to wash all the smoke and bar smell off them. They made out in the shower, and fell in the bed hot and ready for real sex.

Brett could not remember a time when Chase was so voracious, and he loved every minute of it. There was at least one tourist on the streets of Washington the next day walking like he had ridden a horse last night.

NINE

Now that Chase could drive, he knew he had to go back to work. The airline's insurance company had paid all the medical bills and doctor appointments, and gave him enough cash to live on these past few months. He needed to work for some money for personal things, but also to keep busy.

He played with the dogs for a while, as this was the first time he was going to be away for more than a few hours. After exhausting the dogs, he dressed and changed, and then changed clothes again, until satisfied he looked his best. The new job in the kiosk in the center of the mall excited him. He had worked for a clothing store in the mall last year, but he only saw the people visiting his store. This time he would see everybody walking up and down the big halls in the mall.

He arrived early, a habit he made years ago, but he also kept his watch and alarm clocks set ten minutes ahead just in case. Because he already knew how to run a cash register and the credit card machine, the manager trained him in a few hours.

He liked showing customers the sunglasses, and soon realized the folks buying the higher price sunglasses did so because they wanted to look good, and not just for enhancing their vision. They wanted other folks to see how cool they looked. Therefore, he quickly rattled off the facts about the glasses as they were UV coated, shatter resistant, polarized, spring-load hinges and bendable frames, and moved on to how good they looked in them.

On his breaks, he flipped through fashion magazines and even a Sports Illustrated. He memorized the pages where he saw athletes or models wearing the glasses he sold. Chase began telling customers he had seen the glasses in this or that magazine, and his sales began going up.

In his first week, he broke all rookie sales awards and got a free lunch from the district manager. Saturday night he was off at nine, stopped at Taco Bell for takeout, and drove home. He was feeling good and excited about the new job, and how well it was going. He had seen several old acquaintances and even some high school friends in the mall. They laughed and told stories while he managed to sell a pair of glasses to just about everyone. He took pride in acting and selling as professional as possible.

He pulled in the garage, and walked to the kitchen door. Immediately noted his key would not go in the lock. He walked around to the front door, and the key would not go in that door either. He set his food down on the porch, and went to the mailbox to see if new keys were in the box like last time, but they were not there.

He went around to the back porch and found every window locked. He could hear the dogs inside. He knew Brett's Dad had probably changed the locks again, but he had no idea why he chose tonight. Reluctantly, he broke the guest bedroom window and climbed in. He quickly stepped into the hall and shut the door so the dogs would not step on the glass. He came down the

hall and found the dogs safe in the kitchen. He knelt down and received many doggie kisses. He fed the dogs, checked their water bowl, and went to the front porch to get his food he had left there, flipping light switches on as he went.

A car moved down the road quickly, and skidded to a halt in his front yard. The sudden maneuver bewildered Chase until he saw Brett's uncles get out of the car.

"What the hell are you doing in that house?" yelled Bill walking towards him.

"I live here you big dope," replied Chase as he stepped back into the house.

"No you don't," shot back Larry as he came around the car. "The law says we own the house."

"Brett's lawyer drew up the Will. As long as Brett's alive it is his house, and if he passes away, he has willed it to me," yelled Chase.

"That's a lie, you faggot. My dad had the locks changed because he owns the house. He's going to let Brett die in a nursing home, and your ass is mine." Bill pulled a baseball bat from the backseat floorboard.

Chase saw the bat and yelled, "Get the hell off my property!" Quickly, he ducked inside, set his food down, and locked the deadbolt on the door. He saw the cordless phone on the coffee table, grabbed it, and dialed 911 for the emergency operator.

"Ma'am, help! Two men are trying to break in my house with baseball bats. They said they would kill me!" He gave her the address, and she told him she would radio a nearby patrol car.

Chase hung up and ran to the kitchen, got a chair, and brought it back and placed it against the front doorknob to give the door a little more support. He then ran back to the kitchen, sat down on the floor, and began stroking the dogs to calm them down a bit. He then decided to call Jeremy, urged him to come quickly, but to be careful as the uncles were still at the door.

The uncles yelled and screamed obscenities while attempting to kick the door in. Other neighboring lights went on, as they came out to see what all the fuss was about. One neighbor called the Sheriff. Chase laid the phone down and huddled tightly with his dogs—his face white with fear.

A police car turned down their street with the blue light flashing, and screeched to a halt in front of Chase's house. A moment later a deputy showed up, and then another police car.

The first officer saw the baseball bat in Bill's hand and drew his weapon, "All right, big fellow! That's enough!" he yelled as he threw the beam of his flashlight on them.

Reluctantly, the uncles stopped and turned around. Their faces were bright red and sweat soaked their shirts. Bill dropped the bat.

"Don't shoot," he said.

"Step away from the porch," commanded the officer as the deputy and the other officer joined him. "Lie down on the ground face first. Spread your legs, and put your hands on the back of your head. Now hold still, or I will put a bullet in your head."

The other two cops quickly handcuffed them, and felt the uncles down for other weapons, but found none. They stood them up.

"Now what in the hell is going on here? Why are you attacking this house?"

Bill spoke up first, "This is my brother's house, and there's a guy in there. He broke in."

"How do you know he broke in?"

"Because my dad had the locks changed this afternoon, and all the keys are in my pocket," replied Larry.

"You should have called us first before taking the law in your own hands. Get those keys," he told his partner.

The cop fished through Larry's pocket until he found two keys on a small ring. "Got 'em," he said as he held them up.

"Go unlock the door and bring the fellow out here. Do you guys know his name?"

Bill replied, "His name is Chase."

The officers unlocked the door and it moved a little, but the chair held the door. "Sir, this is Officer Bevans. I need for you to come out. Everything is all right now. You're safe, but I need for you to come to the door right now."

Chase heard the policeman's voice and sighed with relief. He stood up, told the dogs to stay, and made his way to the door. He moved the chair, cut on the front porch and living room lights. He opened the door.

"Are you armed?" asked the officer.

"No, I'm not," he replied quietly, still shaken from the thought of certain death should Bill and Larry hit him with that bat.

"Step on out here," said the officer moving his hand from the butt of his pistol to his side. "Come over here a moment and tell me what is going on here."

Chase moved way around the uncles and then faced them while standing with the officers. "Brett and I live here. We were in a plane crash a few months ago, and Brett is in a coma in the hospital. These two jerks are his uncles…"

Bill and Larry started calling him names, "He's a freaking faggot, and we're going to bust his ass…"

The cops took a strong hold of their cuffed arms. "Hold still or I'll put you in the back of the cruiser," he ordered.

Chase continued, "Today they had the locks changed on my house. This is the second time they have done this, but last time we found the keys. I

126

could not find the keys, and the dogs were going crazy inside. I had to get in to make sure they had food and water, so I broke a window to get in."

"So this is your house?" asked the officer.

"Yes, Brett's, and mine" he replied.

"No it is not. This was Brett's house long before he met this bastard," yelled Bill.

"Hold on a minute," the cop placed his pistol in his holster and clicked his walkie-talkie button clipped to his shirt.

Chase could hear him calling headquarters and reading out their street address. After a few minutes, he turned back to the group, "Sir this house is registered to one Brett Allen and no one else."

"Brett is in the hospital. We are partners. I live here, too. All my stuff is in there," protested Chase.

"You're a couple?" the officer said with great distaste and sarcasm.

"Yes, we are," stated Chase proudly.

"Well, that's just great," the officer said to the other cops. "Well, do you have any proof of joint ownership?"

"No, I do not. Brett has a Will and his attorney has it. He told me Brett left the house to me in case he passed away..." Chase could not finish the sentence.

"Well, in that case, the law is not on your side," said the officer almost proudly.

Chase replied, "But I live here!"

"I suggest you get an attorney. I'll give you two days to get your stuff out of there. If you come back after that, I'll have to arrest you for trespassing."

"What about them? They tried to kill me!"

The officer thought for a moment, "I am going to take them to the jail for the night to give them time to cool off, and I'll release them in the morning."

"What if I press charges?" asked Chase.

"What charges? They were trying to protect their brother's home," he said with a smirk, and then turned to the officers, "Load these boys up. I will call a wrecker to pick up their car." He turned towards the street leaving Chase standing there.

Larry spit in Chase's face as he passed by. The cop quickly pushed him on by. Chase took his shirt off and wiped the spit from his face. He stood there and watched as the cops loaded the uncles up and drove away. There in the yard he had never felt so alone. After a while, he walked into the house and returned to the kitchen, sat down, and cried.

He was picking at his food when Jeremy and Paul arrived. "Oh my gosh! Are you okay?" asked Jeremy.

"Yeah, they didn't get to me this time," replied Chase.

"Those big apes—they should lock them up and throw away the key."

"Yeah, well, the law is on their side. They received a get out of jail free card good for in the morning. They'll probably come straight here."

"Oh no, what are you going to do?"

"I don't know. I will call the lawyer again in the morning. I have to be out by Friday, and I still haven't found the Living Will."

"Well, the three of us have to find it. Paul doesn't know the habits of either one of you, so he will look in the places you and I didn't think of. Come on, we have to find the Living Will."

Though exhausted from the confrontation, Chase got himself up and they started in the living room that doubled as an office for Brett. They opened every book, every drawer, and every cabinet and so far, the Will remained elusive.

At the hospital, Brett continued to experience moments of white light through his eyelids, but he could not command them to open. Beneath the sheet, he occasionally moved his toes and flexed his ankles, and he moved his fingers, but there was no one there to see him. The only evidence was the recorded reading of his heart monitor. His brain concentrated heavily on trying to lift his arm, but just could not will his muscles to work. Exhausted from the effort, he fell into a deep sleep.

Brett's birthday had been fun, and he hoped he and Brice would be spending the night together in the tent, but sadly, his birthday had been on a Saturday, and Brice was going out on a date. His dating was happening more often than Brett wanted it to. At first, he would tell Brett to camp out, and he would join him later.

Brett would just about drift off to sleep when Brice would suddenly appear. He would step into the tent, immediately strip out of his clothes and rapidly pull Brett's clothes off. Instead of the tender foreplay he had grown to love, he placed Brett on his back, inserted a lotion coated finger or two in Brett's butt to loosen him up, and then promptly fucked him.

While Brett missed the sexual foreplay they used to do, he could not understand how voracious and forceful Brice had become after going out on a date. He pumped him harder and faster than ever before. Most of the time, Brice left early in the morning, but sometimes after pulling out, he would leave and go home.

As the months went by that summer, Brice and Brett met less often until they no longer met at all. Brett felt crushed because he had fallen in love with Brice, even though he was only twelve years old.

He and James camped out a few times and they played strip poker, masturbated each other, and kissed a little, but there just was no love there. His dreams were always of Brice.

The following spring, Brett signed up to join a group of students from his school for a train trip to Washington, D.C. Excited about going, he sat next to a pretty blond girl who flirted with him quite often. He joined the boys in a pillow fight or other horseplay, but by midnight, he returned to his seat to sleep. The girl leaned her head on his shoulder, and soon they were both asleep.

About three in the morning he awoke feeling weird, and he thought he might be sick. He looked around and everyone in the railcar was fast asleep. He gently pushed the girl away from him and made his way to the bathroom. He stood at a urinal, unzipped his pants, and when he reached in to pull his penis out, his hand felt a gooey substance. He pulled his hand away quickly, bent over, and looked at his dick. He found it covered in a white creamy glob much like the stuff his mom put on hot cinnamon rolls. He moved into a toilet stall and shut the door. Carefully, he rolled his shirt up and held it under his chin, and pushed down his shorts and underwear.

It was then he suddenly realized it was sperm. Had it not been for Brice, he would never have known what had happened, but he had masturbated Brice enough to know what it looked like. He used toilet paper to clean himself up. He felt like he was now on the road to becoming a man at two months shy of his thirteenth birthday. He stood in the toilet and began pumping himself to see if he could do it again. It took a while, but he closed his eyes and thought of Brice, and sure enough he felt the thrill of ejaculation.

Feeling elated he cleaned himself up, peed quickly, dressed, and headed down the aisle to his seat. He knew he would never tell his parents he had reached this right of manhood because of what happened to James.

Just a few months ago, James awoke to find his penis covered in the white stuff as well. After dressing for breakfast, he joined the rest of his family at the Sunday morning breakfast table. After he had eaten a little, he just sat there silently while deep in thought. His mother asked him, "Honey, are you feeling all right?"

James just blurted it out, "I don't know, Mom. I'm a little scared."

"Why honey, everything is fine here. What's troubling you?" she asked tenderly.

James hesitated so his father spoke up, "What is it James?" His voice made James skip a breath.

"Well, uh, sir, I woke up this morning and this white, gooey stuff covered my penis, and I think I might have cancer or something worst!"

His wife looked at him and the father turned green, "Uh, uh, son, nothing to worry about. You and I will talk about it after breakfast. Now you just eat up."

His mother winked at her husband and turned back to the kitchen stifling a chuckle. His dad pulled his paper up to cover his face, and he almost broke out laughing.

Every time James told the story the boys in the neighborhood would bust out laughing, so Brett was positive when his turn came, he was not going to say anything to anybody.

He masturbated so many times that weekend in Washington his penis turned red and sore. He did not care, as it was the best feeling he had done alone, but it paled in comparison to the feeling he had when he had made love to Brice. He knew that feeling was gone forever, and he had no clues how to meet another boy who enjoyed sex with boys as much as he did. It left him feeling sad and lonely for a long time.

Chase, Jeremy, and Paul searched until after midnight and found nothing. Paul had looked through all the books noting quite a few on the Civil War. "He likes this war stuff?" he asked Chase.

"He loves the Civil War and everything about it. He read about uniforms and musical instruments as well as muskets and cannons. It fascinated him. He has dragged me through many Civil War Museums and across battlefields. I did not like it until he took me to Gettysburg and we did the tour. The intelligent but witty guides made the historic battle come alive for me. He took me to houses with musket balls still stuck in the walls. He showed me a barn where a cannonball when through one side and out the other. He took me up on Cemetery Ridge. I stood on the very rocks the Yankees did when they fired down over and over at the advancing Confederate soldiers. He showed me where Captain Chamberlain desperately led a bayonet charge down the hill winning the skirmish, which led to the Yankee victory. I saw monuments and gravestones of so many men, I soon had to feel great pride in what our country went through and survived.

"Brett told me to feel lucky because if we had been born a little over a hundred years earlier, we would have been in a gray uniform and fighting for our lives, too. It made me think and soon I was walking through the museums and looking at their weapons and tools. I do not know how the soldiers stayed alive in the cold snowy winters or hot humidity of the summers. I cannot imagine wearing those itching gray wool uniforms. Those soldiers were sure tougher than I am."

Paul listened to Chase talk as he continued opening the final stack of books. On the edge of the big bookcase was a large calendar. Each month featured a full color picture of a realistic Civil War battle scene.

"That was Brett's favorite calendar," stated Chase as he came over to look at it with Paul.

"I can see why. The pictures are incredible," replied Paul as he turned the pages.

"When he bought it, he flipped through each month telling me about the battle and its significance, and the part it played in the war. I used to wonder how life would be now if the South would have won." Chase returned to the desk he was searching through.

Jeremy grinned, "Me, too. Instead of old Paul here, I might have had me a nice young buck to fuck!"

Paul closed the calendar and playfully swatted Jeremy with it, "Who are you calling old? Your birthday is before mine, and I fuck very well, thank you!"

As he drew the calendar back, he flipped the closed calendar over, and there was some white paper taped to the back. "What's this?"

Chase looked up from a drawer he was going through. His eyes went wide, "Oh my gosh! I remember. That's the Living Will!"

Paul brought it to him and laid it on the desk. Gently, Chase pulled at the tape holding it face down to the calendar and turned it over. The three of them quickly leaned in to read it as if reading a valuable treasure map.

Chase did not read as fast as they did because the tears were flowing from his eyes. "That's Brett's," stated Jeremy. "What is the second page?"

Chase slid the top away, "It's mine. They're both here!"

"Oh my gosh. We found it!" yelled Jeremy.

"Yeah!" screamed Chase. "We just saved Brett's life. I have to get this to the attorney in the morning."

"Yeah, but let's get some beer. It's time to celebrate!" urged Jeremy.

The three sat in the kitchen drinking beers while reading the Living Will again until exhausted, and Chase headed for bed. He begged Jeremy and Paul to stay overnight, which they did. Soon the house was quiet once again. The two dogs slept on the edge of Chase's bed as he drifted off to sleep and dream.

In his sleep, Chase smiled. He recalled a trip to Fort Sumter almost two years ago. The journey to Charleston was one of their first trips together, and they stayed in a gay bed and breakfast on the beach. They went out to dance the first night but the club was DOA as Chase called it—"Dead On Arrival." The next day Brett led Chase through the historic sites downtown. They loved the old homes and felt sadness at the Slave Market and the Museum. By noon, they were on a ferry heading to Fort Sumter, which still guarded the entrance to Charleston Harbor as it had for centuries. Brett explained the importance of the Yankee blockade, which prevented Charleston from receiving all the fine goods from all around the world, especially the weapons and gunpowder they needed to win the war. The

Yankees robbed the city of the ability to ship their cotton to Europe to produce the money they needed to fund the war. Brett had said it was a crucial hinge pin of the war. Chase just nodded in agreement, as he had no clue what a hinge pin was.

On the ferry ride to the island of Fort Sumter, Chase thought it was funny two fairies were riding on a ferry. Brett made him howl when he said that was what they called a three-way.

As they toured the island and took many photos, they stopped in front of a big cannon. Chase could not resist climbing onto the cannon and straddling it. He placed a hand on each side of it as if it was his penis. Brett laughed and took the picture. Later, they found a smaller one and Chase went around to the front and pushed his butt to it and bent over, smiled and said, "Ah, that feels good!" Brett snapped the picture, and they both laughed heartily.

In one of the underground caverns, Brett ran his fingers over the carved names he found in the brick walls. He felt like he was touching the men who had served there. Chase took another approach and started singing and dancing in the big room while enjoying the echo off the walls.

They had a great dinner over in Mount Pleasant where the day's catch and the shrimp came in to the dock right beside the restaurant. They both walked out of the restaurant stuffed to the brim with the great dishes at the seafood buffet. They found the car in the big lot, drove to the Battery in downtown Charleston, and parked the car.

"Let's walk a bit of this supper off," urged Brett as walked up the steps.

Chase was feeling happy, silly, and leaped up the steps, and did a couple of quick dance moves before leaning in for a hug from Brett. They did not care who was looking, but began walking along the walkway boarding the harbor. The sun was heading for sunset and the seagulls were gracefully flying into the wind and appeared to be gliding backwards. Chase spotted a dolphin about a hundred yards out and whistled to him as if he was calling their dogs.

"Look at that two mast sailboat. Isn't she awesome?" Brett pointed as the boat parallel the walkway.

Chase glanced away from his dolphin and started waving to the people onboard the boat that quickly returned his wave with a tip of their wineglass.

"We have to take sailing lessons one day. I want to learn to sail a boat like that, and take my honey to some secluded island paradise and make love to him on the beach," stated Brett.

Chase thought for a second, "Wouldn't we get eaten alive by crabs and sand fleas?"

"I wouldn't, because I would be on top!" replied Brett as he half slapped Chase's butt and took a couple of quick steps to avoid Chase's swipe at him.

132

They laughed and carried on all the way down sidewalk. Brett would remind him how the Battery Park filled up with the Charleston social elite eating barbecue and cucumber sandwiches and watching Fort Sumter, knowing eventually something was going to happen to those blooming Yankees camping out there during the blockade. They turned and looked at the park behind them. A bandstand still stood in the center and as Brett talked, Chase could just imagine rich folks walking under white umbrellas sipping tea and strolling along. In his mind he saw the ladies walking softly in their long multilayered dresses with pearls around their necks, and the men in formal white suits trying not to break a sweat.

When the sun went down, they left the park and drove to a downtown parking lot just off King Street. They went around the corner and quickly found the famous Duffy's—a gay bar with a little dancing in the back, but a whole lot of drinking and tall tales up front. Stepping into the bar was like stepping from the straight world through a magic curtain into the gay world. Gay posters of pin-up boys covered the walls, and Chase studied each one's penis like he was taking an art class. He also enjoyed the decorations in rainbow colors and pink triangles.

They got a drink at the bar and sat at a little table not far away. Every few minutes another customer would come in and wave to his friends, and in an hour, they packed the bar. Chase and Brett met several locals, and learned the pitiful club they went to last night, changed hands like the seasons in a year. They learned there was a big gay crowd in the community most likely because of the colleges in the area: College of Charleston, Charleston Southern, and even the Medical College. To their surprise, they even met several Citadel Cadets from the military college. They showed the boys their school rings, but they came in dressed in pressed khakis and pale blue shirts while trying to do their best not to look like they went to the Citadel. However, the one thing they could not change was their military haircut. The sides of their heads looked sharp and straight as if sliced by a big watermelon knife.

Chase thought they were both cute and soon the four of them sat together swapping stories. One of the boys was from North Carolina, so they had a good time chatting together. They told them of a gay section at the south end of Folly Beach. They quickly decided to meet there, and then shifted the conversation to their adventures on Fort Sumter. After many laughs and many drinks, the cadets felt like it was time for them to go.

Chase and Brett stood to give them a hug, but the boys promptly invited them over to the house they were staying in for the weekend for a drink. Brett was a bit tired but Chase was already on his second wind, so they agreed to follow their car to the house. They turned towards the harbor on

King Street and to their surprise, the cadets parked in front of one of the big houses across from Battery Park. Chase and Brett climbed out of their car.

Chase asked hesitantly, "You live here?"

Steve answered, "Well, for the weekend. My uncle is a big banker in Charlotte and his family has owned the house for two centuries and change. They don't get down here often, so he gave me a key so I could check up on it. Come on inside. I think you'll like it."

Chase elbowed Brett with a silly grin on his face, and together they held hands as they walked up the eighteen steps to the front door. In case a hurricane drove the ocean over the harbor walls, the builders placed the house on tall pillars. He said it did not happen often, but it did happen. He turned them around on the porch, and before their eyes was a picturesque scenic view of the entire harbor. He opened the door with his key, reached in, and flipped on the lights and turned off the alarm system.

With great flair, he bent over like a servant and invited them inside. Chase eyed a staircase leading upwards from the foyer like the one in the movie "Gone with the Wind." Steve walked the young couple from room to room while telling stories about his ancestors and their roles in Charleston's history. He had relatives who were mayors, governors, and even a few generals. My great, great, great grandfather was a slave ship captain, and the other an explorer who had sailed around the world twice. They also owned summer plantation homes in Summerville where they spent the summer to avoid the heat and the stench of hot Charleston. The Johnson plantation in Summerville has remained in his family ever since. Chase had to pull Brett along as he studied the magnificent paintings covering the walls, the leather bound books in the bookcases, and glass cases displaying guns made over two hundred years ago.

They settled on the veranda in the back of the house and sipped Long Island Teas until all felt buzzed and silly. Steve insisted they stay for the night and Brett quickly agreed, as he was too drunk to drive.

"Time to white-whale!" laughed Robert.

"Yeah, boys, you're going to like this!" exclaimed Steve as he jumped up and started taking his clothes off. Robert began doing the same.

"Hey, what are you guys doing?" asked Brett feeling a little alarmed.

"We're going skinny-dipping and you're coming with us. Now get those clothes off!" laughed Steve.

Chase nodded yes to Brett and so they began stripping as well. Shoes, socks, and clothes were flying everywhere. Robert snatched the plastic pitcher of Long Island Iced Tea, and the boys followed the cadets through a beautiful manicured arbor covered in the purple flowers of a Clematis vine. They pushed through a white gate and discovered a lighted swimming pool. Steve jumped in creating a big splash. Robert set the picture of alcohol on the table, and did a back flip off the side of the pool into the water. Brett and Chase laughed and dove in.

The water felt wonderful as they played and splashed each other before settling down to floating on some rafts.

"I thought we were going white-whaling?" asked Chase.

Steve and Robert looked at each other and laughed. "Hold on Chase, we'll show you what white-whaling is." They left the raft and swam slowly towards the deep end of the pool. In a synchronized fashion, they both suddenly did a surface dive, but hung their white butts on the surface in limbo for a few seconds before descending to the bottom.

"Oh, I get it!" laughed Chase. "Come on, Brett. We can do that." Together they joined the other couple in the deep end. They, too, came up laughing.

"Come on boys, I'm getting cold. Let's get in the Jacuzzi," urged Robert.

"You have a Jacuzzi, too?" asked Chase.

Robert leaned over the ladder and helped Chase up. "Come on, cutie pie, I'm going to show you the world!"

They all laughed as they walked down the path to the right of the pool and Steve flipped on a light. The lights came on in the swirling blue waters. They all got in with each couple cuddling. Steve leaned back and looked up into the sky. Above them, Brett and Chase saw a canopy of dark green vines intertwined with trellis and sticks overhead which created a big circle in the center. Through the center, they could see the stars above very bright and clear.

Steve and Robert became quiet as they continued making out. Chase faced Brett in the water and made out as well. Soon Steve showed the boys their rooms, and they went down the hall to theirs. The old house creaked and squeaked with the rhythm of intense lovemaking in each room. The evening ended magnificently, and the sex was spectacular. From then on, Charleston remained one of their favorite cities, and they returned as often as they could.

TEN

When morning came, Jeremy and Paul said their goodbyes as they watched Chase drive off with the treasured Living Will on the front seat. They both crossed their fingers, while mouthing prayers to the sky, hoping the simple but important document would save Brett's life. Chase surprisingly slept well, despite the fear the Living Will would not give him the power he hoped was his. He parked a block away from the attorney's office. He walked briskly up the steps holding the Will tightly. He saw the brass sign on the door to Michael Evans office and pushed in.

"May I help you?" asked the receptionist as she took another sip of her morning coffee.

"Yes, ma'am," replied Chase politely feeling a bit nervous. "I'm here to see Michael."

"I see," she replied as she set down the coffee cup, and picked up the black appointment book and pen. "Do you have an appointment?" she asked when she could not find his name on the appointment book.

"No ma'am, but Michael told me to call him the moment I found the Living Will. We finally found it last night. I thought it best to bring it to him right away."

"I see," she said hesitantly. "Well, he is not here just yet, but should be here any moment. I'm not sure he can see you, as he has a trial at nine in the courthouse across the street."

"I'll wait," replied Chase, indicating he was not leaving until he saw Michael.

He sat on the couch in the waiting area, and flipped page after page in the boring magazines on the coffee table while wishing they had some comic books he could read. Suddenly, the door opened and Chase looked up to see Michael coming in. It took Michael a moment to recognize him, but his face broke into a grin.

"Did you find it?" he asked in anticipation.

Chase dropped the magazine back to the table, picked up the Will, and held it up in front of his chest as he stood up proudly, "Yes, sir. I did."

"Great Scott!" exclaimed Michael. "I had just about given up hope. Come on in. I have a trial soon so let's handle this quickly." He led Chase to his office. Mary followed him with a cup of coffee and closed the door as she left. Chase handed him the Living Will. Michael pulled on a pair of reading glasses, and read the Will from top to bottom even though he had written the form almost a year ago. He noted the two signatures. He recognized Brett's inscription. "Is this your signature?" he asked. Chase nodded yes. "You signed it in front of Brett and this notary?" he asked as if crossing his t's and dotting his i's.

136

"Yes, sir, we did. We used the woman at the bank. That's her signature and seal below it. I had never seen that done before so I will never forget it."

"Good boy," replied Michael. "I just want to make sure everything is correct. I am assuming you're still having trouble with Brett's relatives."

"Yes, I am. How did you know?" asked Chase.

"Their attorney gave me a call a month ago. I told him I had drawn up the Living Will, and you and Brett signed it. He asked me to fax him a copy, and I had to tell him I did not have a copy. He said he was preparing papers to obtain a judge's approval to put the Allen family permanently in charge of Brett. I told him while he might have the legal right to do so, I feared for Brett's life. I told him you were desperately trying to find it. He agreed to move slowly, which is probably why they did not serve you with papers."

"What happens now?" asked Chase.

Michael grinned as he hit his intercom button, "Mary, bring your notary seal, and a pad please." He turned back to Chase. "Son, you just hold on a second. We're going to make a few copies of this Living Will, notarize them, and send a copy to the Allen clan and their attorney. I am going to put the original in my files, and make you two more notarized copies.

"The copies to Henry Allen will make them mad, but when they call their attorney he will tell them they have no case whatsoever. I suspect they'll take us to court anyhow. I am going to give you two copies. You will take one copy, and put it in a safe place where you can find it when you need it. You should take the other copy to the hospital and straighten them out a bit," he grinned again when he said this. "If they give you any lip…" he picked up one of his business cards, "you give them my card and tell them to call me while you're standing there. They'll back down, or I'll sue them for a ton of money and enjoy doing it!" he laughed.

Chase smiled. He was already feeling much better. Mary took care of the copies, the notary seals, the faxing, and the copies.

"Michael? There are some problems I need to ask you about," began Chase quietly.

Michael looked up from his paperwork, set down his pen, and looked at Chase with warm sympathetic eyes. "What is it, son?"

"The Robertsons wanted to move Brett to a nursing home so they could order the staff to stop feeding him so he would…die."

"That's horrible."

"Does this Living Will prevent them from doing that?"

"Yes, it does, however, they might be able to persuade the hospital to release Brett to them and in turn, persuade a nursing home director into taking

him in. They probably would use the gay thing as a religious excuse to do this."

"I see. Then I want to take him home so I can protect him. I know he is coming back. He is getting better. The nurse has seen movement in his fingers. I know he hears me when I talk to him," added Chase as tears filled his eyes. "I can't let them kill him."

"Can you take care of him at home?"

"Yes, I can and I have a friend who is a nurse and another friend is a therapist. The airline is paying the hospital bill. Maybe they will give me some money to take care of him at home."

Michael thought a second, "Wait a minute. I think I get the picture now. I forgot about the airlines. They probably want to avoid a big legal suit costing them millions for the plane crash. I bet one of their associates has paid the father a visit, and told him Brett was going to die soon anyhow. If he would let Brett go ahead and die, he would pay the family a large sum of cash."

"Can they do that?" asked Chase.

"Unfortunately, the world is full of unscrupulous, greedy folks. Which airline was it?"

Chase told him. Michael began rapidly scribbling notes. "Chase, with your permission, I'm going to call the airline, and I'll send them a copy of the Living Will, too. I will warn them they are not to pay a single dime to anyone else but you. I will tell them you need ten thousand dollars a month to take care of Brett at home, or they could possibly pay the nursing home for years at a much higher rate, and we'll sue them for millions. I think they will agree with our plan."

"There's one more problem. They locked me out of the house again. The cops came when the two uncles tried to beat in the door with a baseball bat. They said they were going to kill me. The cops called someone on the radio that told them the house is in Brett's name and not our names. They said I have to move out by Friday, or they'll throw me out."

Michael shook his head in disbelief, "That's not going to happen. Legally, they have you. You're not on the deed, and that is a mistake we will correct when we get Brett up and around. However, you're not entitled to stay in the house for now."

"Oh no, what do I do?"

"Hold on, we have two choices: You could use some of the ten thousand to get a new place, or you could move Brett home. The Living Will puts you in charge of his health, and we can prove we have two medical technicians to take care of him. We're simply taking him home and providing the care Brett needs including your help as a housekeeper."

Chase grinned, "You've never seen me clean house."

Michael laughed, "It is just a figure of speech. Your job will be to oversee his health treatment. I know you can do that, and I am here to help

you. Don't you worry, we'll beat these bastards, but I'm worried about those uncles. I have a friend at the police station. I'll make a call to him. I'll also send papers threatening to sue the uncles if any harm comes to you."

Chase smiled and said softly, "Thank you, Michael. This is the best news I have had in months."

"Okay, Bud, I have to go to court. By this afternoon, I will have everything done, and I will call you this evening for an update."

Chase stood, clutching the copies in his hand. "I'm going to the hospital right now."

Michael stood and shook his hand. "Chase, you're very brave. I will tell you one personal note about me. My wife and I had a gay son. We did not find out until after he died. He committed suicide. It broke our heart. We need to find a way to prevent these needless gay suicides as soon as possible. You're among friends here. Now run along and tell that hospital a thing or two!" He laughed again as he bade Chase goodbye.

Chase parked his car in the lot next to the hospital. He took a breath while doing his best to remember all Michael had told him. With the copies of the Living Will in his hand, he strode confidently into the hospital foyer, and asked the information clerk at the front desk for directions to the administration offices. He walked down a hallway and took the elevator to the second floor. He approached the receptionist at the counter.

"Excuse me, I need to speak to Betty," he said sweetly but unable to recall her last name.

The receptionist smiled, "Betty Anders. May I tell her who is here?"

"Yes, you may," replied a nervous Chase. There was a pause why she waited. He blurted out, "I'm sorry, I am a little frazzled today. Chase Fleming," he blushed.

"Okay, Mr. Fleming, just one moment," replied the receptionist, displaying a comforting smile. She buzzed Betty's office and in a moment, she stepped into the hallway.

"Good morning, Mr. Fleming. If you will come this way I'll show you to my office," she said clearly and politely. Chase was sure she did not recall his face, but as she rounded her desk and sat down, she realized exactly who Chase was. "I remember you. You were in the plane crash. What can I do for you?" Her smile disappeared.

He caught that she did not ask how he was doing in his recovery or even ask about Brett. Chase smiled as he handed her a copy of the Living Will, "This is a notarized copy of the Living Will that Brett and I signed together. My attorney notarized this copy for you this morning."

She took the paper and read the document from beginning to end. She saw similar versions from time to time and recognized immediately the

power of this simple but important legal page. "I see you were telling me the truth after all."

Chase shot back quickly, "Exactly what did I do to make you mistrust my words?" He knew the answer.

She flushed a little, "I'm sure nothing, but my job is to make sure we handle every patient in a clear and legal manner."

"Did you know Brett's parents were planning on moving him from your hospital so they can let him die in a nursing home?"

"No, I'm sorry that would never happen here."

"From this moment on, you are to notify everyone on your staff I'm in charge of Brett's complete medical treatment. Print out his complete medical history and his billing statement for me. I need you to mail one copy to my attorney's address on the bottom of the Living Will. I'm going up to visit Brett, and I'll expect you to have my copy ready for me when I return."

"But..."she started to protest but Chase cut her off.

"You realize, of course, my attorney and I have discussed the possibility of suing your hospital for failing to recognize me as Brett's lawful partner, and perhaps for helping the parents with plans to let him die?"

"That's not true," she said.

"I should hope not, but it would make a sensational news story, don't you think?"

She swallowed hard, "I'm sure we can rectify this as soon as possible."

"How much is the airline paying you for Brett's care?"

"I do not know."

"I'll expect a clear accounting of all payments and charges in the copies of the bills you are preparing for us. One last thing: from now on, no one is to see Brett except his mother and myself. No one is to secure any knowledge of his condition except me. Is that clear enough for you to understand?" he said with great flair.

"Yes it is. I will make the arrangements and calls right away."

"Thank you."

"What are your plans for Brett?"

"Don't worry, as we'll soon be out of your hospital. I plan to move him home as soon as possible. My attorney is arranging health and therapy care for Brett, as well as taking care to make sure the airline's money starts flowing our way."

She stood, "I wish him a speedy recovery, and I'm happy to have had a part in both of your medical treatments."

Chase sensed this was a statement she said to any patient or family members visiting her office. "Why thank you, Betty. I appreciate your concern," he said sarcastically. "Now if you will excuse me, I will go see Brett and will return in an hour for my paperwork. I would appreciate if you would inform the staff on Brett's floor of my wishes immediately."

"I will take care of it," she reached out to shake his hand.

Chase looked at her and then brought his gaze up to her face, and held his eyes there long enough to make her feel uncomfortable before turning to leave.

Once in the elevator, he let out a yell. The adrenalin was flying through his veins, he felt step one had gone well, and he enjoyed every minute of it. When he reached Brett's floor, he immediately caught sight of Brett's dad and his uncles arguing with the nurse at the station. He stepped across the hall into the edge of an open office out of sight, but he could easily hear their arguments.

The nurse told them only Brett's mother could see Brett. She told them the dad and uncles were permanently barred from seeing him. His mother had gone back to see Brett. The men continued to argue. She suggested they go to the administration office, as she had to follow orders. When they refused, she threatened to call security so they backed down and punched the elevator button.

Chase waited until they were out of sight and walked up to the nurse. "You handled those lug heads very well," he said with a smile.

"Thank you," she smiled. "May I help you?"

"Yes, you may. My name is Chase Fleming. No doubt Betty has called you about me?"

"So you're the one to thank for the hot tempers?" she teased with a grin.

"Indeed I am. Did you know those three wanted to transfer Brett to a nursing home and let him die?"

Her face went pale, "No, I didn't, but I'm not surprised. I always dread when they show up."

"You understand, from now on, only I and his mother are to see him."

"Yes, I do and I thank you for that," she replied. "I will type a note and tape it to the top of his file so the other staff will know as well."

"No one else is to make any medical decisions for him."

"Not a problem. Mrs. Allen is back there with him now. Do you want to go ahead and see him?"

"Yes. Is he in the same room?"

She replied yes, and he turned to walk down the hall while still feeling euphoric. Thank God for the Civil War calendar, he thought while half feeling he had just won a modern day war himself.

He reached Brett's door, took a deep breath, and pushed in. He found Jan Allen sitting at her son's side reading her Bible to Brett. She looked up and stared at Chase until she could focus on his face.

Chase smiled as he moved to the other side of Brett's bed, pulled up a chair, and sat down. "Jan, how are you?"

She hesitated before replying, "I'm fine but tired."

"I understand," Chase replied, while imagining living with the rest of her family must be an exhaustive nightmare. "Did they explain to you I found the Living Will and I'm now in charge of Brett's medical healing?"

"Yes, but what do you plan to do?"

"I don't plan to kill him."

"I beg your pardon," she asked quickly.

"Did you know your husband planned to transfer Brett to a nursing home because the hospital would not agree to his wishes to stop feeding Brett so he could go ahead and die?"

"That's not true!" she exclaimed.

"I'm afraid it is, but don't worry, I don't intend for that to happen."

"I can't believe Henry would harm Brett. Why would they do such a thing?"

"It's all about greed, because the airline wants to cut their losses, and save some cash. They offered Henry a substantial sum of cash if he did as I described, saving them thousands on medical bills."

She did not reply, but closed her eyes remembering phone calls she had overhead, as well as whispered phrases from Henry to his brothers. He recalled appointments made without her, and the new big screen television Henry just up and bought, and moved in yesterday. She knew in her heart Chase could be telling the truth.

Chase continued after she opened her eyes. "After consulting with his doctors, if they agree, I plan to move Brett home. I have a nurse and medical therapist ready to take over. The airline will continue to pay his recovery bills. We will work with him twenty-four hours a day. I know he is ready to come out of this coma, and I know in my heart he wants to live!"

Neither Jan nor Chase noted Brett's heartbeat had increased on the monitor but it had. They also did not see his toes move, but they had as well. Nevertheless, they did feel him suddenly breathe deeply, and they both turned their head to see his chest rise much higher than before and descend.

Chase lowered his voice to a whisper as if telling her a secret, "He hears us, Mrs. Allen. He wants to come back. I just know it!" exclaimed Chase once more.

Tears slid down her face as she nodded agreeing. "I believe you. I can tell you love him. What do you want me to do?"

"Two things," replied Chase surprisingly quick, "I want you to come to our house every day and read to him. Tell him stories about his growing up. Stir his memories and recharge his storage banks. Paul says folks who have suffered brain trauma sometimes lose their memory and become confused. We should help refresh his memory by telling him all about his life."

"Paul in the Bible spoke to you?" she asked incredibly.

142

Chase giggled, "No, I'm sorry. My friend Paul, the therapist, but I believe him to be right. Will you come to our house and help me with his memory?"

"Of course, I will."

"But please remember, I am not going to allow anyone else in your family on our property until Brett can take control again."

"I understand. What was the other thing you wanted me to do?"

Chase fell silent for a long minute. "I want you to tell me about his childhood, too. I have loved him for over two years. I have been with him when he is awake and when he is asleep. I have heard occasional stories of something in his past, but after the crash, I realized I don't know a lot about how he grew up, and what his life was like. I want to know everything." He paused as she nodded yes. "I know you don't approve of us, but you should know Brett loves me very much. This Living Will, putting me in charge of his life and health, should tell you he trusted me. However, what it doesn't say is I love your son Brett more than anything or anybody in the entire world. I have not told many people about what happened in the crash, but after the plane stopped moving, I found Brett bleeding about the head and lying unconscious. Though my ankle was broken, I somehow managed to drag the both of us out of the plane and behind a hill before the plane blew up. I would give my life for him, and he would do the same for me. If you know Brett, you will know our love to be true."

Jan reached across Brett's chest and took Chase's hand in hers. "I will do all you have asked and more. I love my son Brett, and I believe you love him as well. We will work together to get him well, and I pray daily we will succeed."

He squeezed her hand back, "So tell us about Brett as a baby. Did he start out as cute as he is now?"

She let out a huge sigh of pride, "An absolutely gorgeous baby!"

Chase listened intently as she described highlights of his first years. Brett's fingers moved from time to time as he listened to his mother talk, and the occasional chuckles from the man he loved.

After walking Jan to the lobby and saying goodbye, Chase returned to the administration office. Betty had left a thick folder at the counter for him containing all the documents and printouts he requested. He also found a business card she had placed there from someone in the legal affairs office for the airline. He made a mental note to get this information to his lawyer.

He came out of the office feeling elated and almost skipped to the curb. He took a step to cross the street and his ears picked up the screech of tires. He glanced to his left to see a car racing towards him. He froze like a

deer in headlights for a long second or two, before finally leaping back to the sidewalk.

Undaunted, the car jumped the curb and continued racing down the sidewalk at him. Chase got to his knees and leaped over the hedge as the car roared by. The folder he had dropped on the sidewalk flew open and the pages filled the air. He rolled over and stood up in time to see part of the tag, but he knew who it was—the infamous uncles. He shot them a finger, and yelled at them as they sped off.

A security guard came running across the lawn and helped Chase up. "My goodness, I thought you were a goner!" he exclaimed.

"Me, too," he replied. Chase started to pick up the papers and the guard began helping him.

"Are you hurt?"

"No, just a scrape on my forearm, I'll live I guess," replied Chase.

Together, they gathered all the paperwork before Chase continued to his car to head home. It had been an amazing morning, but he found himself starved, and immediately pulled into a Burger King to eat. It was the closest thing to a celebration he had allowed himself to enjoy since the plane crash, but he ate with great pride, enjoying every bite of success.

Later in the day, Brett began to dream of turning thirteen. It was the first birthday in his short life in which he was not home to celebrate. It saddened him a little to be away but not for long. Earlier in the spring, one of his best friends in school had invited him to join him in attending a summer camp for boys in the mountains of North Carolina. He went home with the catalog, deliriously excited about the opportunity to learn to canoe, sail, rock climb, backpack, and more. The euphoric joyful feeling lasted only a few hours when his dad sat him down and explained they could not possibly afford the $550 registration fee.

He knew his family had everything they needed, and he never went hungry, but it never dawned on him they were just average middle class hardworking folks. He knew kids at school that walked around with cash in their pockets, rode better bicycles, and dressed nicer. His jeans often had patches on the knees, and his belt had cracks in the leather. He had gone to spend the night at parties at his rich friends' houses, and found himself amazed how large and enormous the rooms were. His home was a mere eleven hundred square feet, and for one of his friends, their triple car garage was just about the same size.

He realized he had hurt his parents' feelings by asking to go to this camp, so he quickly changed the subject by asking if they were going to his grandparents this weekend. He said grandpa asked him to go foxhunting with his hounds. He loved playing with the hunting dogs that jumped all around him and licked his face. He delighted in running around and around the house while they chased him.

144

He never mentioned the camp the rich again, until one day his mother told him the church was sending a dozen boys to a church camp for a whole week. She handed him a slip of paper with his name on the invitation. His parents sighed with a chuckle as he jumped around excited about attending camp. At the time, no one realized he would be away for his birthday.

He sat in his cabin with fifteen other boys waiting for rest hour to get over with so he could get back to fun and adventure. The camp did not have horses, sailboats, or even canoes, but they played field games, and hiked in the mountains, and swam twice a day in the pool. They had skit nights by the staff and later in the week, the cabins presented their own skits. The camp split up his church group two by two to different cabins so they would have a chance to get to know other boys. The counselor was a handsome college boy with blond hair, blue eyes, and a body ripped with muscles. Roger was a quarterback on his high school football team, but not big enough for college ball. He teased the boys repeatedly and they loved it. He grabbed them in headlocks and bear hugs, and tickled them whenever he could. Brett adored him, and late in the night, he made his juice with the image of his counselor's body on the inside of his eyelids.

Brett became popular at camp and all the staff liked him. So did many of the boys, but especially a guy from Gaffney. Josh had a dark skin for a white boy, with jet-black hair, and dark mischievous eyes. When he smiled, his teeth were whiter than any in the camp or so thought Brett. They became friends after trying to out swim the other in the camp's swimming contest. Brett won and Josh congratulated him by giving him a hug. The touch of his skin almost embarrassed Brett in his loose fitting bathing suit. He knew some of the boys wore athletic supporters under their suits, but he did not have one.

When all the events were over, Brett and Josh played in the water and swam down to the bottom of the deep end, and just sat there touching each other until their lungs were about to burst. They would jet back to the surface for air. While resting above the water, they pushed and pulled the other. Josh caught his hand in Brett's waistband and gave a pull. Brett dropped beneath the water as Josh held on to his trunks, pulling him to the bottom. They tried to talk underwater before giggling their way to the surface.

After swimming they walked down to the bathhouse, stripped off their wet bathing suits and stood under the hot showers where they began lathering up with the cheap soap they found there. Josh started playing with his penis with the soap, and after glancing to see if anyone else was in the bathhouse, Brett did the same. They both laughed at their growth, but had to quit when they heard a counselor singing his way to the shower. They dried off quickly while staring at each other's body.

ELEVEN

Jeremy and Paul spent their weekend preparing the house for Brett's expected arrival. They moved the master bed closer to the wall to make room for the hospital bed by putting it closer to the big windows on the backside of the house. Paul told them when patients lay in bed all day it helps the days go by if they can see outside. Chase knew Brett loved the mountains, and agreed the view of the Western North Carolina Mountains might inspire him once he woke up.

They also filled the wall across from the bed with large pictures. Chase went to work on his computer, scanning numerous favorite pictures of the two of them on their travels. He also made a Welcome Home banner and hung it from the ceiling.

They went out to eat and celebrate after becoming exhausted with their preparations. Paul began telling him what he would have to do to maintain Brett at home: monitoring his IV and heart, and the blood pressure machine. He would also change his urine drip while keeping it germfree and clean, and take care of the feeding tube.

On Monday, Chase went to see attorney Michael Evans again. As usual, Chase was waiting on the couch when Michael arrived.

Michael grinned when he saw him, "Good morning, Chase. I heard you made quite an impression on the hospital administrator."

"She called?" asked Chase as he stood to shake Michael's hand.

"Yes she did. I think she felt concerned we might sue them. I assured her there is no current plans to do so as long as her staff carried out your wishes. I reminded her Brett must remain alive."

"What did she say about taking Brett home?"

"I don't think the hospital will be a problem. They were making good money from the airline, but they were having a time with Brett's father and uncles. They tend to shun from controversies."

"Jeremy, Paul, and I worked all weekend rearranging the house to prepare for Brett." Chase followed Michael into his office and sat down. Michael's secretary brought him a cup of coffee. Chase handed Michael the list Paul prepared. "Paul is a licensed physical therapist and works at the hospital. Jeremy is a licensed nurse and also works at the hospital. They have listed all the items we need to manage Brett at home. How do I get some money from the airlines to pay for this? I have a new job but I only make $7.55 an hour, and I have missed a lot of work, so they are giving me fewer hours. I can barely buy food, and the bills are stacking up everywhere: electricity, gas, phone, cable, insurance, and more. Brett pays most of these bills electronically from his checking account. I don't know how much we have left, but surely it is close to running out."

Michael looked over the list, not the least surprised at the costs to care for Brett. "I'll call the airline this morning and arrange a transfer of funds

148

to me by courier this afternoon. I'll open a new checking account for you at my bank. I'll have my secretary obtain a debit card for you. Here take this pad and pen. I want you to make some notes.

"As Brett's attorney, I am officially hiring you as Brett's housekeeper. Your salary, hmm, let's see, how about five hundred a week?"

"Five hundred dollars! I've never made that much in my life," exclaimed Chase.

"Well, don't get too excited. I need for you to use that money for all the little things you'll need. Here's the plan: Use the debit card to purchase all these medical supplies, rent a hospital bed, and get a good one to make it easier for you to care for Brett. The motorized ones will help you a lot. Purchase a refrigerator to put in his room to keep all his food and medicines. Keep all the bills and bring them to me, as I will have to account for every penny to the airlines.

"The five hundred dollars a week will cover incidentals the airline might fuss about. I will take over Brett's account and bills, and write you a check out of Brett's account for your salary every week. This will give us a receipt for your work." He stopped working and called his secretary on the intercom and began relaying instructions for the bank account, debit card, and asked her to write Chase a check for him to take home in a few minutes.

"I suspect no one has any idea how long this is going to take, so we'll just keep the money situation like this for a month or so, and then reevaluate. Make a journal of any progress you note from Brett. Write down the date and time of any movements: fingers, toes, arms, and mouth. We may need this later to buy us more time if they take us to court."

"Yes, sir, no problem, I can keep it all on my computer so it is easier to read. My handwriting is not so hot," he said with a hint of embarrassment. Chase knew his handwriting could sometimes be illegible, and his spelling ability shamed him, too. The computer helped with spelling the big words, and correcting his mistakes.

"Chase, this is a huge job and it is going to take a lot of your time. You may need to hire more help. Call me if you get to this point. We'll figure something out. Let me warn you, you will also need to take some mental time off. If you have to, hire a baby-sitter, but don't let yourself become exhausted, because you never know when the day will come when Brett wakes up. When that happens, you'll need a ton of energy."

Chase smiled at Michael's positive thought. "Okay. I will. I'm still worried about the house legal mess. The cops did not show up Friday as I thought they might."

"If they do, just call me. I am hoping the information I sent over to Henry Allen will slow him down a bit. I also talked with his attorney, but

people often do things in a hateful way. We'll just handle it when we have to. Okay?

"Now, my secretary has a check for you, so pick it up and if you can come by after lunch we'll have your debit card ready. Call me if you need me." Michael stood and walked around his desk to shake Chase's hand.

Chase stood and shook his hand, and then to Michael's surprise Chase gave him a big hug. Michael stood there for a second, completely caught off guard as few clients embraced their attorney. Nevertheless, he wrapped his long arms around Chase and hugged him back. He smelled the shampoo scent in Chase's hair and immediately thought of the son he had lost forever.

Chase thanked him again and left the office.

He cashed the check at the grocery store and returned home with eight bags of groceries as they were out of just about everything from food to cleaning supplies. He fed the dogs and went out the front door to get the mail. The box was full, as he had forgotten to check it since last Thursday. As he made his way across the street, he spotted a Sheriff's car coming down the street towards him. He sighed heavily, knowing trouble was on the way. He stopped in his driveway and waited for the Sheriff's deputy to get out of his car.

"Are you Chase Fleming?" he asked as he got out of the car with a blue folded paper in his hand.

"Yes, I am. May I help you?" replied Chase timidly.

"Henry Allen has charged you with trespassing," stated the officer.

Chase shot back, "How can he charge me with trespassing in my own home? He does not own this house."

"You live here?"

"Yes, for over two years now."

"Does anyone else live here?" asked the officer.

"Yes, my roommate, Brett Allen."

"Is he Mister Allen's son?"

"Yes, he is. Brett is in a coma in the hospital, but I have been getting the house ready because they are going to bring him home to continue his recovery here," replied Chase.

The officer took his hat off and scratched the back of his head. "This sounds like a big can of worms to me."

"I think you should talk to my lawyer Michael Evans. I can get his number for you," said Chase.

"No, I'm sorry, that's not my job. I have to give you this summons to appear in court. I'm not going to arrest you. It'll be up to a judge as to what happens next." He handed the papers to Chase.

Chase took the paper and out of habit said 'thank you' although he did not feel like thanking anyone for bringing him more trouble.

"Good luck to you, son," said the officer as he returned to his car and backed out of the driveway.

Michael was in court when Chase dropped by his office to pick up the bankcard, so he left the court summons and the stack of bills with his secretary. She said Michael would call him. He picked Paul up at Jeremy's house, and immediately drove to a rental store for medical equipment. Chase made sure the bed they rented was the best one they had, and he told the clerk to send the bill to his attorney. They also rented a heart and blood pressure monitoring system, an oxygen tank, and valve assembly. Chase arranged for delivery for the equipment.

They left there and drove to a medical supply store. Paul gave them a copy of his medical license and once satisfied, they ordered everything from IV supplies to bedpans and rubber sheets to adult diapers. They spent thirty minutes picking various things to keep as many germs away from Brett as possible. Paul explained it was vital Brett not catch a cold or a virus while in their care. They put down a case of rubber gloves and even surgical masks.

Paul said if anyone came to see Brett that he did know, they had to wear the masks.

"Even his mother?" asked Chase.

"Probably not, as long as she does not have a cold, but please remind her to warn you if she picks up anything. We cannot take a chance on him getting sick."

He also picked out a stethoscope. Chase held it up. "What is this for?"

"It's for you. Jeremy and I will check his lungs when we are there, but every four hours I want you to listen to him breathe. If he gets any sign of pneumonia we must start treatment immediately."

Chase gulped, "What does pneumonia sound like?"

"A gurgling sound and sometimes a wheezing tone. Don't worry, I'll show you how." Paul smiled and gave Chase a slight assuring hug before moving over to a display of catheter equipment. We'll need several urine bags, tubes, and a couple of inserts," he told the clerk.

Chase started to ask but Paul beat him to it, "Brett cannot control when he pees so we have to take care of his urine ourselves." He held up an insert so Chase could see it in the plastic sterile bag. "This goes into his penis, the tube attached drips into a urine bag. You must write down how much he pees every four hours. Oh, that reminds me, we need to order some charts, and a medical clipboard."

"Won't that insert thing hurt?"

Paul grinned, "Well, we put a little lubricant on the insert, and it just slides in. I don't think Brett can feel it."

"Yeah right, when he wakes up, I bet that is the first thing he yanks out!"

The clerk and Paul laughed. They also ordered Brett's liquid food and created a standing order for more food delivered on Mondays. They finally finished their shopping with the clerk promising to deliver everything in the morning.

Chase dropped Paul off who told him not to worry. He and Jeremy would come over tomorrow and get all the supplies organized and ready. Chase thanked him numerous times for his help and expertise. Paul gave him a big reassuring hug, which Chase needed, as he feared taking care of Brett might be more than he could handle.

He arrived home with the phone ringing. He quickly unlocked the door, turned off the alarm, reached down and petted the dogs, and ran to the phone. "Hello?"

"Chase, this is Michael Evans. How are you?"

"I have just come in. We got the hospital bed and medical supplies ordered," he replied.

"Good. When will you be ready to bring Brett home?"

"The last of the stuff comes tomorrow morning," replied Chase. "Why? What is the hurry?"

"I read the summons, and I talked with Henry Allen's attorney. He cannot convince the old man to drop the trespassing charge. We'll have to go to court."

"Are they going to arrest me? Will I have to go to jail? What happens to Brett if I do..." began Chase rapidly.

"Hold on, let's don't panic. I have a plan. If we can get Brett out of the hospital and into your house, it would be difficult for them to throw Brett's housekeeper out. If he is not there, Henry is pushing to have you removed because you're gay, and manipulating his son as well as taking advantage of him."

"That's not true. We love each other. We're partners. If we could marry, we would have."

"I know, but let's concentrate on getting Brett home quickly. The hearing is on Friday at ten. You have to be there. Why don't we meet in my office at 9:30 and we'll walk over to the courthouse together?"

"Okay, so I should go tell the hospital I want to take him now?"

"Yes, I will fax a letter to the administrator right now. You get everything ready at home and try to get him moved on Wednesday so he is there and settled before Friday."

"Okay, I will. Thanks, Michael. I will see you on Friday."

"Chase, you can do this. I've already seen how strong you are for Brett. He is counting on you. Don't let anyone stop you. If you need me you call me."

Chase thanked him again, got a glass of juice out of the refrigerator, sat down, and called Jeremy and Paul relaying what the lawyer told him. They both said they would see him tomorrow, and not to worry so much.

At four, the doorbell rang and Chase hesitantly looked through the peephole before opening the door. He felt relieved to see the uniform for the medical rental company. Chase began helping him haul in the hospital bed in various sections. By five, quitting time for their employee, they had assembled the bed so the occupant could see out the window. The man also installed the oxygen tank and the backup tank, and the monitoring equipment for Brett's heart and blood pressure. He showed Chase how to pull up the IV poles from the corners of the bed, and how to manage the multifunction bed. He even programmed the panel on the inside of the bed's frame so the patient could change the channels on the television. He also showed him the small screen for the mini-computer that inflated various sections of the bed at odd times to help prevent bedsores.

Chase became impressed and listened intently as the person told him he might want to get a television stand to put the television high on the wall. He showed him how to plug an extension cord to a lamp underneath the bed so Brett could turn the light on and off. He also showed him how the patient could push a button, which sounded a buzzer to summon for help.

After the installer left, Chase fed the dogs and played with them for a while, ate a frozen dinner, sorted through the mail, and in his mind he tried to remember all Michael and Paul had told him he must do. He cleaned up the kitchen, locked the front door, and walked down the hall to the bedroom. He stopped in the doorway realizing how different the room already looked. He tried to imagine Brett lying in the bed waiting for him. Slowly, he walked over to the bed and turned around to see what Brett would see when he woke up. He arranged some pictures keeping a favorite one in his hands. He climbed up on the bed, put the picture beside him, and began playing with all the buttons on the sidewall of the bed.

He raised the head of the bed up and then the feet. He turned the television on and off again before picking the framed picture of Brett back up and kissing the picture. He closed his eyes while lowering the picture to his chest. Exhausted from the stress of the day, Chase drifted immediately asleep though it was still daylight.

At first, his dreams were of happy times with Brett, especially their first Christmas together. Chase absolutely loved Christmas and carefully picked out a gift he thought Brett would love. He wrapped it with perfection and showed their guests his gift under the tree.

153

Brett purchased a leather jacket a few months before Christmas. He managed to keep it hidden from Chase's curious nature. However, he did not place it under the tree. Instead, he wrapped over a dozen smaller presents in various unusually sized boxes, and placed each one under the tree. Inquisitiveness just about drove Chase crazy, so he began begging Brett to open their presents early, but Brett held firm to waiting until Christmas morning. Chase feared he could not wait that long, but Brett gave him various stupid clues driving Chase wild with anticipation.

When Christmas came, Chase woke Brett up like a seven-year-old at four in the morning. Brett protested while slyly grinning at Chase and his childlike awe-inspiring nature. He loved teasing Chase almost as much as he just loved him. Reluctantly he got up and dressed, grabbed the camera and found Chase sitting by the tree with all twelve packages arranged in the order of biggest to smallest.

"Sorry, pal. Look at the cards. They are each one numbered in the order you must open them," stated Brett.

"What?" Chase began rearranging the packages by numbers on the nametags. "Now can I?"

"You didn't say 'mother may I', but yes you can," laughed Brett.

Chase's face broke into a huge grin as his dimples fell in, and Brett snapped the first of many pictures. Box number one was a new pair of Calvin Klein white briefs.

"Thank you. I just love Calvin," he exclaimed as he started on box two.

He opened a second pair of Calvins. "Hey wait a minute, are all these boxes Calvins?" asked Chase.

Brett laughed, "You said you loved them!" He paused, "But no they are not. Go ahead and open box three."

Chase tore off the wrapping and discovered a beautiful bottle of cologne. "Ooo, this smells good. Thank you."

"You're welcome. Let's just hope it works on you!"

Chase looked up to give him a smirk and in anticipation of the reaction, Brett snapped another picture. Chase tore open another box and found yet another pair of underwear. They both laughed as the game continued.

The last box was bigger than all the rest. Chase took a deep breath and tore open the box. He went through all the paper inside, but did not find anything until his hand discovered an index card. The card said: this box is big enough to hold my heart, which I gladly give to you, but not nearly big enough to hold all the love I have for you. I love you, Chase, Merry Christmas!"

Chase grinned, "Aw, that's so sweet. I love you, too." He started to put the card down, before noting that at the very bottom of the card, it said

154

'turn over'. He did and read aloud, "PS. Your last gift is behind the couch. Love, Brett."

Chase took a long second to read the note again before leaping up and onto the couch scattering the dogs. Behind the couch, he found a much bigger box. "Has this been here all this time?" he asked and he sat down and began tearing at the paper wrap.

"Maybe yes, maybe no, open it," urged Brett as he held up the camera.

Chase removed the big lid and discovered the beautiful brown leather jacket. The aroma of the fine leather hit his nostrils. "Oh my gosh! This is gorgeous." He lifted it out of the box carefully. Brett snapped another picture.

"Try it on, it is just like mine," encouraged Brett.

Chase stood up and put the jacket on while running his hands over the leather. Brett snapped another picture with the camera.

"Where did you get it?" asked Chase.

"I ordered it from the same store in Toronto where I found mine. I hope you like it."

Chase locked up at Brett as he snapped yet another picture. He walked quickly over to Brett as Brett pressed the button again. Later they would laugh as the last picture was only of Chase's nose just inches from the camera. Brett lowered the camera as Chase bear hugged him, and they kissed long and deep.

Brett opened his present and together they laughed and kissed again as they began their Christmas day. It was a special memory Chase wished he had on videotape, so he could see Brett's smile. He spent the rest of the night asleep in Brett's new bed.

Tuesday afternoon the three boys filled shelves with the supplies and put many items in the refrigerator. They stripped the bed and washed the linens using bleach to kill any germs. They also began training Chase in emergency procedures. They showed him how to do CPR, and to keep doing it until help arrived. Jeremy used an extension cord and moved the phone to the side of the new bed. Paul played patient while Jeremy showed Chase how to listen to his lungs.

"Oh, that is cold," stated Paul as Chase touched his bare skin with the stethoscope.

"They always are," replied Jeremy while taking his hand and moving the receiver up and down Paul's chest. "Don't breathe hot air on it as you'll put germs on Brett's body. Any time you have to change his IV, clean him up, or change his linens, you must wear the rubber gloves. We must not take a chance of him catching any viruses."

They taught him how to check the monitoring equipment, and record the numbers and notes on the medical charts. By evening, they decided to go out to eat, as it may be the last time in a long time the three of them can eat out together, as most likely one of the three would always have to be with Brett.

While waiting for their food, Chase told them about the summons and court appearance, and how worried he was. They tried to assure him and did their best to move on to another topic.

"How did the hospital react to you taking Brett home?" asked Jeremy.

"Surprisingly, well. Of course, Michael had spoken to Miss Betty before I got there, but I think they were glad to get rid of him or us."

"So let's toast tomorrow. Brett finally comes home, and I hope soon, he'll come alive again!" exclaimed Jeremy as he held his glass to the center of the table. Paul and Chase raised theirs before touching the glasses lightly together and downing another celebratory swallow.

Chase met Jan at the hospital at ten the next morning. He told her they were moving Brett today and she felt thrilled. She showed Chase a new cell phone she had bought secretly and gave Chase the number on a card she prepared for him. He promised to call her if anything happened. She wondered when it would be possible for her to come see Brett. He told her tomorrow afternoon would be good, and together they took the elevator up to see Brett in the hospital room for the last time.

Chase listened as she told Brett how much she loved him, and Chase grinned with delight as she told him another funny story of Brett as a child. Brett's pulse picked up a bit. Soon, Mary, the intensive care nurse who had helped Chase early on with seeing Brett, interrupted them.

"How are you, Chase? You look so much better," she said as she hugged him.

"I am," he replied as he stood to give her a hug. "Mary, this is Brett's mom, Jan."

"We've met, but I'm sorry I had forgotten your name," replied Jan as she shook her hand.

Mary smiled, "I hear you are taking this handsome boy home today."

"Yes we are," replied Chase. "I hope with the work we do with him at home, we can wake this dude up. I was thinking about buying a set of cymbals," stated Chase with a serious look.

Both women looked at him dubiously. "I don't think..." began Mary before Chase cut her off.

"Gotcha," he quickly said with a big grin. "Don't worry. No cymbals, but maybe a bass drum," he teased again.

"You're terrible. You'd better take good care of this boy, or I'm going to bring over one of my super long hip shots for you!"

156

Chase's face looked terrified, "Okay, I promise. I'll be good."

They all laughed for a moment. Then Mary leaned in close to them. "Chase, I haven't seen you in a long while, but I have something to tell you. When Brett was in my charge, after you left his room, the hospital requires me to go in and make sure the patient is okay. Sometimes, I would go in and immediately discover Brett's pulse would be quicker, his breathing more labored, and blood pressure would rise a bit."

"What are you saying? Is there a problem?" asked Chase.

Mary smiled, "Oh, no, not a problem at all. What I am saying is after you spent time with him his monitoring numbers went up. It means he can hear you!" she exclaimed. "I know I'm not supposed to say such things about a patient, but I believe it to be true. Sometimes I would discover him moving his fingers. When I asked him to move his finger, it would take about sixty seconds for his brain to send the correct signals to his finger, but if I waited patiently, he would move it."

"Oh my gosh! I knew he would come back to us!" exclaimed Chase.

"Be sure to watch his fingers, toes, arms, and legs for movements, and even his mouth and eyes when you're with him at home. I know you believe he can hear so you read to him, talk to him, pray with him, and tell him you love him. He has to fight to come back to you. Help him do so," she urged.

Jan began to cry with elation. Chase hugged Mary gleefully, "I will! I will! I will!" He also surprised Jan with a jubilant hug, bringing a big smile to her face as well.

Chase followed the ambulance home where he found Jeremy and Paul waiting for him. Jeremy recognized one of the EMS technicians as a gay friend from the club. They smiled and winked at each other. Chase showed them where they were taking Brett. They returned to the ambulance and brought Brett out on a gurney. Neighbors watched through their windows while children sat on the curb to watch. To Chase, time seemed to stop, but it only took a few minutes to move him from the truck to the house. Jeremy, Paul, and the technicians easily lifted Brett's much lighter body to the bed. Chase signed their paperwork and they left.

Jeremy and Paul went immediately to work rearranging Brett's tubes hanging from the bed poles, and teaching Chase all they could. Chase nearly fainted when they lifted the sheet to check on the catheter. Chase knew Brett's penis from top to bottom, but what he saw today was a small, limp, dark colored piece of flesh.

Jeremy realized Chase had frozen in disbelief. He smiled, "Chase, don't worry, Brett's penis will return to normal once he is awake and can

control his bladder so we can remove the tube. You might have to help him, but I suspect you're good at making erections," he teased.

Still shocked, Chase just slowly nodded yes. With Brett secured, they began checking the monitoring equipment and allowed Chase to write the numbers on the chart. Jeremy bought a new wall clock and put it over Brett's bed as Chase had to record the time of everything he did.

They stopped and went to the kitchen to eat while Paul explained he was going to begin Brett's therapy after lunch. He promised to show Chase what to do. Jeremy gave Chase the telephone number for a nursing service. He urged Chase to call them and set up a shift so they can come in to give him some time off and relief. They knew if he stayed with Brett twenty-four hours a day, he would become physically and mentally exhausted.

Returning to the bedroom after lunch, Paul began by massaging the muscles in Brett's right leg. Chase followed his example on the left leg. Gently they worked the muscles all the way down to his toes. Then he moved his toes forward and back numerous times, and began moving his feet up and down and around.

"If Brett was awake, this would hurt a bit because he hasn't used them in a while. Since he is in a coma, we'll get him past the pain as soon as we can." He began bending his knee forwards and back, and then moving his hip. Chase asked a few questions, but mostly concentrated on taking care of Brett.

They worked his upper body in a similar fashion and when they finished, drops of perspiration covered Chase's forehead.

Paul patted him on the back after snapping off his rubber gloves, "You did well for your first lesson. We are going to do this about four times a day," he announced as he stepped on the lid to the trashcan, tossing the gloves into the trash liner. He held the lid open signaling Chase should do the same.

"Isn't that a lot? They only do it once a day at the hospital," Jeremy stated.

"That's because that is all the insurance will pay for. We can't hurt him by exercising his muscles," replied Paul, "but we can speed up his muscle toning by doing more workouts."

Jeremy came up and put an arm around Chase. He picked up Brett's arm, "Chase, just be careful with this shunt. You do not want to knock it out as it holds the needle in Brett's veins. This is how the IV gets into his circulation system. If you accidentally do it, please do not panic. Just tape the wound with one of these bandages just over his head on the shelf and then call for help. We'll come back and put it in. Do not try to put it in yourself as you might get an air bubble in it or miss sticking the vein. We'll give him his shots through these other ports attached to the shunt. We must also be careful with the feeding tube."

Chase gulped, "Okay, I got it."

158

Chase got a phone call on Thursday morning from Michael, "How's it going so far?"

"We're doing great. We're exercising Brett's muscles and trying to get him loose and fit."

"Anything change in his condition?"

"No, everything is normal including is pulse, breathing, and blood pressure."

"I need you in my office at nine thirty tomorrow, and we'll walk over to the courthouse together. I'm sending a photographer over there in an hour to take some pictures of Brett, and the set up just in case I need them in court. Did you experience any problems renting the equipment and getting supplies?"

"No, everyone was nice. I told them to send the bills to you."

"Very good, the airline responded quickly, so financially we are in good shape. They are sending a representative to testify to the fact they would prefer Brett stay at home instead of the hospital. Of course, they'll say that because it is cheaper for them."

"Are we going to win?"

"It depends on the judge. Judge Hawkins is a bit of a pain in the ass, a real hard-line guy. Did I say that nicely? He is also homophobic. Anyhow, there is no need for you to panic. Just try not to show any emotion if the Allen group calls you any names. It is important we show maturity and control, okay."

"I get the picture. No problem," Chase promised.

"Wear a coat and tie tomorrow. I need for you to look like a grown up, at least for one day," teased Michael.

Chase grinned, "All right. I'll even shave."

"You shave?" laughed Michael.

Chase grinned and blushed, "At least once a week or so."

"Okay, buddy. Be tough. We are going to make this work. See you tomorrow."

TWELVE

Paul and Jeremy came over as often as they could, but the realization Chase would be alone with Brett much of the time began to set in. However, it was a thought he did not allow his mind to dwell on because he was too busy reading Jeremy's notes and following his instructions. He knew most folks felt he would fail in taking care of Brett, or he would start off well, then become bored and quit. Chase knew such a pattern had followed him all his life, but this time, he must change course and complete an important and life threatening task. He would fight to keep Brett alive, and awake again. For the first time in his life, he would not allow himself to just give up and quit when things got tough.

He spoke to Brett constantly—even reading the medical instructions aloud in case Brett wanted to know what he was doing. If he went to the bathroom, he kept talking to Brett. He yelled down the hall when he went to the kitchen. He did not want Brett to think he had left him. The dogs began to think Chase had indeed gone crazy.

He sponge bathed Brett as lovingly as he possibly could. It felt so good to be able to touch his skin again. He brushed Brett's hair to prepare for the attorney's photographer. He checked the measure line on the urine bag, recorded the number, and then emptied the bag.

"Geez, Brett. You're peeing like a camel. I cannot believe I am emptying your pee bottle. You're going to owe me big time when you wake up!" he teased.

He changed his gloves and began rubbing a daub of antiseptic lotion into his palms to warm the cool lotion up. He lifted the sheet covering Brett's legs and began massaging Brett's muscles. "Dow, you've been in a plane crash, lain around on your ass for months, and you still have gorgeous legs. I'm going to work on your muscles and joints a bit, and rub them with this lotion. Yep, I know I'm spoiling you, but I love you."

Chase was concentrating so hard he failed to note the pick up in the beat of Brett's heart. He rubbed his thighs deeply, squeezing, pulling, and rubbing as Brett had done to him so many times when they had sex. Chase had been nervous at first, but now he felt relaxed and easy with Brett. As he worked his way down to his feet, he wondered if Brett might be ticklish.

Chase was incredibility ticklish, and Brett often tortured him by grabbing a foot and lightly rubbing the bottom of his feet with a light feather or just a finger. It did not matter what he used, it resulted in Chase jumping about trying to escape while laughing uncontrollably. How Chase wished the same could be true for Brett. He tested the bottom of his feet but there was no response. No movement in the toes, no twitching in the face, and no bending of his legs to try to get away.

Disappointed, Chase rubbed the feet a bit more, including the muscles and joints of his ankles and each individual toe. He had just put the left foot down and picked up the right foot when he saw the toes flinch on the left foot all by themselves. He grinned, "That's my boy, you just keep trying to move those toes, and you will get well."

The photographer took pictures of Brett in the bed, of the shelves of medical supplies, the monitoring systems, and even the refrigerator. Jeremy arrived in his green nurse uniform for the pictures, as he made changes to the IV drip controller. He took a picture of Chase bending Brett's knee joints over and over again, and another with Chase writing the monitoring numbers on the medical chart.

Once finished the photographer bade goodbye, while Chase and Jeremy returned to Brett's room. Chase could not hold back any longer, "He moved his toes on his left foot this morning."

"He did. Wow, that's great," replied Jeremy.

"Yes, I had just finished massaging and working the ankle joint, and set the foot down. A minute or two after I started on the other foot, he flinched his toes."

"You realize it could have been just a twitch, but talk to him while you are doing his therapy, and see if you can get him to do things on command." Jeremy checked all his vital signs and then gave Chase a hug. "I am sorry I have to hurry on to the hospital. You are doing very well on your procedures and recordings. Keep up the good work. I have arranged to work a double shift today so I can be with you in court tomorrow."

Chase felt touched. "I cannot thank you enough for doing that for me."

"I'll be coming on a run, so don't panic if you don't see me there early, but I will be there." He hugged Chase again and kissed him on the cheek.

"Thank you," replied Chase as he kissed Jeremy on his cheek as well.

Later that afternoon Jan Allen arrived at precisely two o'clock and Chase was glad to see her. She had not been to their house in a long time, so Chase showed her around. Surprised to discover how clean and organized the house was, she smiled approvingly. After finding the Living Will, Chase spent days restoring the house to normal, and doing a bit of interior decorating in the process. It kept him busy, and though he could be lazy at times, once Chase started cleaning, it was usually best to get out of his way.

She knelt down to play with the dogs before Chase escorted her to Brett's room. She did not tell Chase, but she worried about the condition of Brett's health in an at-home situation, but on entering the room and seeing all the work they had done, she immediately regained her confidence. After she washed her hands with the sterilizing soap, Chase led her to Brett's bedside

where he had placed a chair. She turned to see all the pictures on the wall, and instantly realized this room was far better than the room in the hospital. He lowered Brett's bed rail with the push of a button so she could easily hold Brett's hand and see his face. He sat down on the other side of the bed.

"My, my, Chase, you have done a wonderful job. Brett looks fantastic," she said.

Chase smiled, "I had a lot of help and training by Jeremy the nurse, and Paul the physical therapist. In the hospital they only did his therapy once a day, but here we do it four times a day."

"Excellent. I read where it is important to keep a coma patient's muscles in great shape which improves the blood flow to the brain, and prepares their bodies for when they awake."

Chase smiled, "Tell us one of your stories about Brett. I have been talking nonstop to Brett, and I know this is unbelievable, but I have exhausted my mouth. I'll just sit and listen, if that is okay with you."

She reached across Brett's chest, squeezed Chase's hand, and smiled. "Did I tell you about his sixth birthday when he got a pup tent for his big gift? It was a big party with all the children in the neighborhood attending including my parents. His dad churned ice cream and each of the kids got a cup. I think it was either banana or strawberry but it was so good. Brett was so excited..."

Chase placed his chin on the bed and listened intently as she continued talking for almost an hour. When finished, she leaned over and gave Brett a little kiss on his cheek. His heartbeat picked up a little. Chase thanked her over and over again for coming, and she hoped to return tomorrow after the trial.

She hugged Chase, "I know my husband is fighting to take Brett to a nursing home, and kick you out of this house, but I am praying you win and he loses." She gave him a wink, a smile, and another hug.

Chase felt elated as he watched her drive away. It had been a good first visit, and he enjoyed hearing about Brett's sixth birthday.

An hour later, a friend of Jeremy's arrived. He met him at the door. "Hi, I'm Chase." He held the door open and extended his hand.

"I'm Jack," he replied as he shook Chase's hand firmly.

Chase noted Jack was not what he was expecting in a substitute nurse. He was handsome, tall, and obviously lifted weights. His skin was smooth with a dark tan and a tattoo on his forearm. He also had braces on his teeth, and Chase guessed he was about thirty-five or so. His voice was as deep as a broadcaster, but he seemed friendly and charming.

"Jeremy said you and Brett were lovers. How long have you been together?" he asked as Chase gave him the house tour before heading to Brett's room.

"A little over two years I think. I have sort of lost time since the plane crash."

162

"I have never met a plane crash survivor. You look pretty good," stated Jack with a wink. "Are you in good health?"

"Yes, I'm fine, but unfortunately, Brett was not as lucky. The propeller sliced through the cabin and stopped just as it nicked Brett. Thankfully, his head was between his legs like a scared dog."

"Were you scared?" asked Jack.

"Shoot, my head was so far between my legs I could read the tag on my underwear!" They both laughed.

Chase went over the chart with Jack, and showed him all the stored supplies. Jack, of course, was familiar with everything, but he allowed Chase to show him anyhow.

"Does Brett have any injuries other than being in a coma?" He took out his stethoscope and listened to Brett's heart, his lungs, his stomach, and his intestines.

"No, his body healed from all the cuts, scrapes, and stitches, and I am doing physical therapy on him four times a day."

"Good," replied Jack as he checked the monitoring equipment and the IV drip. "He looks great. You are doing a very good job. Jeremy tells me you have a court appearance at ten tomorrow. I can get here at nine. Is that okay?"

"Yes, of course. That is perfect. Thank you so much."

Jack retrieved a business card from his wallet and handed it to Chase. "My phone numbers are on the card. I'll send you a bill for my services, but if you have any questions, now or in the future, please call me. Any time you need for me to fill in for you, just call. If you can plan a little, I can usually work it out, but I help about a dozen home patients. In case you're wondering, I am gay, too. I hope you win tomorrow."

Chase smiled as he took the card, "Thank you. I am just handling everything one day at a time."

"I'll be going, and I'll see you in the morning." Jack shook his hand and Chase led him to the front door, and waved goodbye. Chase felt lucky to have such a good new strong support group around him. His confidence soared, and yet the trial still worried him.

Chase heated up some frozen spaghetti sauce Brett had made a few months ago. While the noodles were cooking, he ate a salad. The kitchen was too quiet, so after fixing his plate of spaghetti, he grabbed his glass of iced tea and made his way to Brett's room. He placed the food on the table at the end of Brett's bed, slid it over to the right, lowered it down, and started eating after turning the television on.

The aroma of the familiar spaghetti sauce hit Brett's nostrils and they moved a little. Chase was watching the history channel and enjoying his dinner. Bite after bite he devoured the wonderful sauce. Brett's toes flinched several

163

times. His pulsed picked up. Chase finished the plate, and set it on the floor so the eager dogs could lick the plate clean.

He stood up and his eyes caught sight of the numbers on the heart monitor. Brett's pulse was up ten points. He wrote it down on the chart. Suddenly, the automatic blood pressure machine activated so Chase waited for the report, and it showed his pressure increased a little as well.

The event puzzled him because he had not touched Brett, massaged his legs, or given him a kiss, and the only sounds were of the History Channel. He thought about it for a few minutes as the dogs finished the plate, and he picked it up. He held the plate and slowly turned to face Brett.

The idea hit him like a strong slap to his face. He ran down the hall to the kitchen, put a spoonful of Brett's sauce on the plate, and ran back to Brett's room. He put the plate on the table, slid it back to the bed, and right up to Brett's chin. He adjusted the plate to the edge closest to Brett's face, and picked up a brochure on the shelf by the bed. He thought for a second, looked at the pulse monitor, and then slowly began gently fanning the aroma of the sauce into Brett's nostrils. He reached down and removed the sheet exposing Brett's toes. He placed a hand on his stomach so he could see and feel both at the same time. He continued fanning the sauce.

His efforts continued for a full two minutes. Slowly, Brett's pulse began to rise. Chase nearly jumped out of his shoes he was so excited, but he kept fanning. The pulse went up another ten beats. In Chase's mind, he had achieved an amazing victory, and stopped fanning. He put the brochure down and just as he started to move the table, he saw Brett's index finger on his right hand move three times. He looked down at his feet and his left foot moved.

"Wahoo!" he yelled. "Way to go, Brett. You're coming back, and I'm going to save some of this sauce for when you wake up."

He set the plate down again, and the dogs went back to work licking the sauce once again. Hours later, Chase cut out the lights, turned off the television, gave Brett a kiss, a nuzzle to his ear, and fell in his own bed, and immediately went to sleep feeling elated and exhausted.

The light that Brett's brain noted behind his eyelids suddenly disappeared. He relaxed as his pulse returned to a resting state. Soon he was dreaming of the summer of his thirteenth year. He had signed up for a Red Cross Junior Lifeguard Course the first two weeks of June. He passed with flying-colors, outshining everyone in the class. He felt thrilled when the handsome instructor presented him his certificate, his patch, and his wallet certification card. He would have to wait until he was sixteen to take the next course, but was overjoyed with his success. Jan took a picture of him with the instructor, and he framed the picture and put it on his wall.

One of his friends in the class was Bobby Sheffield, a curly redhead with bright green eyes and an incredible body. Brett could easily have fallen in love with him, but Bobby had a girlfriend. Together the boys had great fun

164

swimming every day at the pool. Bobby planned to be a lifeguard at a summer camp immediately after passing the test. However, when the school mailed out the report cards, Bobby had failed math, and his dad forced him to attend summer school.

The camp director had a senior lifeguard, but desperately needed a junior lifeguard to assist. Bobby apologized to the director several times for having to cancel due to summer school. When the camp director asked if he knew of any guards not already working an idea clicked in Bobby's brain. He mentioned Brett and gave the director his phone number. The director immediately made the call and got Brett on the phone. He offered Brett the job with free room and board and fifteen dollars a week. The camp was the same religious camp he had attended last year.

Though excited, he told the director he wanted the job, but he would need to talk to his parents. The director asked to speak to his dad. They chatted for a few minutes before he put the director on hold while they explained everything to mom, and when they agreed, Brett nearly passed out he was so wound up. He would now have a chance to work Monday through Saturday while earning some extra cash, and have something to do all summer. His days of mowing grass for cash were over. He reported for duty the following Monday morning.

The camp's training was simple—only two hours long. He met a tall young woman who was the senior guard. He was the only other lifeguard. She went over the rules of the pool, and showed him how to add chlorine to the water. She then put him to work sweeping the deck and pulling frogs from the pool. After lunch, the campers began arriving, one carload after another, which began seven weeks of weekly camps for girls followed by three weeks of boys' camp.

The girls, from ages nine to sixteen, fell immediately in love with the only male lifeguard who happened to be deeply tanned and very good-looking. They flirted with him constantly, but he took his guarding job seriously, keeping his eyes on the pool. He saved a little girl on the first afternoon that had fallen in the deep end of the pool, earning the respect of the other guard as well as the camp director.

He lived in a cabin set back away from the rest of the camp. He had a bunk bed in his room, and there were two bunk beds in the other room, as well as a bathroom. Three male dishwashers bunked in the same cabin. One of the boys, Robbie Williams moved into the room with Brett, and quickly made friends with him. Brett found Robbie to be funny, and darkly tanned, with the whitest teeth, which contrasted with his dark chocolate eyes. He was two years older than Brett, but Brett was taller.

Many a night, Robbie created a gentle rocking to the lower bunk as he masturbated on his top bunk. Brett secretly joined him, trying to keep the same

165

rhythm. As the summer heated up, one or two nights a week Robbie and Brett would skip evening chapel and sneak to the pool. They did not want to wear bathing suits through the camp so they planned to swim in the nude. Once inside, Brett carefully locked the gate in case anyone came along. Secured behind the fence, they stripped out of their clothes and dove into the water. The nightly skinny-dipping allowed them to play while checking out each other's body. They often tried to beat the other in a swimming race, and especially the 'who could swim the farthest underwater in one breath' event. Brett won by ten yards.

Robbie told him one of the senior dishwashers held the underwater record. His name was Lug Bolt. Brett laughed at the name, which Robbie explained was a nickname. His real name was Lawrence Bolt. Lug hated the name Lawrence so he picked Lug. Everyone loved his nickname, and the dishwashers still teased him by calling him Lawrence-baby. However, he could swim underwater two full laps in one breath, and for that he had their respect.

"I bet you can beat that record before the end of the summer," said Robbie as he held on to the edge of the pool while resting.

"I hope so. I guess I will just have to keep trying to learn how to hold my breath longer."

"Yeah, but you also need to learn to pull and kick harder," stated Robbie.

"How do I do that?"

Robbie thought for a second and then grinned, "Let's make the swim again, but this time I'll put my arms around your neck like I was riding a big sea turtle. This means you'll be pulling both of us. The more you do it, the stronger you will be."

Brett said sure, so he turned his back to Robbie, and started hyperventilating like he learned in his lifeguard class by taking several deep breaths. He gave Robbie the thumbs up sign, and they both descended and pushed off. Brett struggled as hard as he could and made it to the other end of the pool before coming up.

"Wahoo!" yelled Robbie with a big grin. "You did it. Let's do it again."

"Let me catch my breath," replied Brett.

"You wimp," teased Robbie. "I'll help you." He began massaging Brett's shoulder while his naked body floated into Brett's back. His penis bumped against Brett's beautiful butt and began to slowly grow hard. The touch of Robbie's hands to his shoulders and the erection to his back created a stir in him as well.

"Okay, let's go," said Brett as he took a big breath, Robbie climbed on his back, and he pushed off.

With each stroke, Robbie moved back as Brett pulled, and then Robbie would glide forward as Brett prepared his next stroke. After a few strokes, Robbie's hardened penis touched Brett's anus as he spread his legs for another frog kick. This excited Brett all the more, and he stroked even harder. They

166

reached the other end of the pool, but instead of stopping, Brett turned and pushed off, and made it halfway back before coming up.

"Yes!" Robbie exclaimed as Brett turned to face him. Robbie gave him a hug. Their dicks touched each other. "Way to go."

"Thanks," replied a puffing Brett as he hugged him back, letting a tired hand float down to Robbie's white butt.

Robbie stopped talking and stared into Brett's eyes. Brett's chest was still rising and falling hard, but he kept his gaze on Bobby's eyes. Bobby slowly ran a hand down Brett's chest feeling his muscles, his belly button, and finally he gripped Brett's erection and his own, and began playing with them. Brett put another hand on Robbie's buns and squeezed them. They felt wonderful.

They kissed long and deep, and then suddenly, Robbie pulled away, "Okay, dude, enough for now. Let's do the swim again." He spun Brett around, and together they swam to the deep end to start again.

Brett leaned backwards into Robbie as the older boy clung to his back. He could feel his penis bumping his backside. He grabbed a good breath, and once again delighted at the attention to his rear, as he took stroke after stroke making the two full lengths possible.

"I thought I was going to bust for air," laughed Robbie after they finally surfaced.

"Why? I'm the one doing all the work," shot back Brett.

"Yeah, I know. I'll make it up to you, but listen we must keep the two links of the pool a secret, or Lug will start practicing, too."

"I think that is enough underwater swimming for tonight. Let's go float in the shallow end."

They slowly swam to the point where they could stand up. Robbie rubbed his muscles, played with his penis, and then swam between Brett's legs while exhaling slowly so thousands of tiny bubbles would tickle his genitals. Soon Brett did the same for him. Robbie pulled up behind him and carefully glided the tip of his dick into Brett. He thought Brett might pull away, but Brett pushed back instead. He only went far enough for just the tip to hold when Robbie pulled out.

"Geez, I just about shot!"

"Come on," urged Brett. "Follow me."

They swam to the edge of the pool, stole some towels off the clothesline, and spread them on the grass. Brett ran to his lifeguard chair and returned with a plastic bottle of baby oil he daily used to make his tan even darker. They fell down on the towels and began making out, and masturbating. Brett put Robbie on his back, poured some of the baby oil into his hand, and wrapped his fingers around Robbie's swollen cock. It was the first penis he had ever seen with a slight twist to it. He teased Robbie for having worn it out by masturbating all the time.

167

Once lubricated, Brett laid the capped bottle aside, scooted closer toward Robbie's chest while straddling him, lifted his butt while guiding Robbie's erection towards his hole, and easily slid downward on the shaft. The feeling made Robbie's eyes swell widely with excitement. Brett grinned, leaned over and kissed him, and then took Robbie's right hand and placed it on his own erection. Brett began to move his hips up and down, while constantly tightening his anus muscles. With each stroke, Robbie's heart pushed more blood causing his erection to swell. Expertly, Brett kept the rhythm slow and steady while enjoying the ride. When he felt like Robbie could not stand the wait any longer he picked up his speed to double time. When he obtained triple speed he thought Robbie was having a stroke, as he contorted, twitched, then finally gave up, and exploded inside Brett.

Sweating and exhausted, Brett fell into Robbie's waiting arms where they kissed over and over again. "That was amazing! Can you teach me to do that?" he asked.

"Of course, but not tonight, as I am whipped," said Brett.

"Oh no you don't—lie on your back," ordered Robbie.

He grinned as he slid down, took Brett's erection in his mouth, and worked it until he was sure Brett had no more juice to produce. They dove in the water exhausted.

They skinny-dipped about forty times the rest of the summer before Brett lost count. Some nights, horny Robbie would sneak out of bed at midnight into Brett's bed, where they would silently make out with deep French kisses. Robbie showed Brett how to suck his tongue, which drove Brett wild with anticipation, and of course, they would finish by sucking each other off, before falling asleep wrapped in each other's arms.

Brett thought this summer was by far the best in his life. He forgot about his broken love for Brice, and thought only of Robbie. Life was good. He has to be at camp all summer, play with Robbie at night, and to his amazement, he earned fifteen dollars a week for something he would gladly have done for free.

Chase, freshly shaved with just a bit of cologne he had borrowed from Brett's dresser, dressed in a dark blue suit with his hair combed. He was nervous as he stood outside the courtroom with Michael Evans his attorney. Michael reminded him to keep his cool because losing his temper could mean losing the case. Chase said he would, and began mentally preparing himself by saying over and over in his head all the vile things the uncles might say about him.

He pulled Michael's arm and nodded towards the parking lot as Jan and Henry with the two uncles crossed the lot with their attorney.

"Let me guess," said Michael. "The two guys in the ill fitting golf shirts are the uncles?"

"That's the tag team," replied Chase.

168

"Well, they are not going to hurt you here, or the bailiff will lock them up. Let's go ahead and take our seat at the table so you don't have to face them."

Chase turned to follow Michael and spotted Jeremy rushing to him. "You made it," stated Chase as he gave Jeremy a hug.

"Traffic was bad, my hair is still wet from the shower, but I am here. I'll sit right behind you, so just let me know if there is anything I can do."

"Thanks. Jeremy, this is Michael Evans, my attorney. Michael, this is Jeremy Booker, the nurse helping me with Brett's care."

"I'm most pleased to meet you, Jeremy," stated Michael as he shook Jeremy's hand. "I haven't met many male nurses. Do they tease you a lot?"

"Yes, but most of my friends are in retail or a boring corporate jobs. My job pays well, though the hours suck a little, but it is never boring. I also feel like I am helping people."

Michael smiled, "Good for you. Okay, fellows, let's go in."

Out of the corner of his eye, Chase saw Henry and Jan sit at the other table with Larry and Bill right behind them. He also spotted several of Brett's relatives all sitting on their side of the aisle. Behind Chase, Jeremy sat alone, but just as the bailiff called the court to order and told them to stand, Mary came in, sat down beside Jeremy, and winked at Chase. He smiled and whispered 'thank you' to her.

Everyone stood as the door opened for Judge Hawkins to enter. To Michael's surprise, Judge Mildred Clemmons walked in and took her seat. Everyone then set down as she pounded the gavel calling the court in session.

"Judge Hawkins is a lady?" whispered Chase.

"No, far from it—she's not even a gentleman. Mildred Clemmons is new to our county, and I know nothing about her. I do not know if this is a good thing or a bad thing, we'll just have to proceed."

"Would the two attorneys approach the bench?" Mildred said firmly.

They stood before her as she turned off her microphone. She leaned over so only the two men could hear her. "Judge Hawkins is, well, let's see, how do I tactfully put this, uh, Judge Hawkins has the shits!" Both attorneys fought hard to stifle a chuckle. "It seems he ate at his daughter's new house last night, has been throwing up all night, and now has a severe case of diarrhea. He has asked me to substitute for him. I trust neither one of you have any objection to my handling this case?" It was the kind of a question even a fool knew better than to answer negatively.

Michael returned to the table and just smiled at Chase. The bailiff read the summons, and the Allen's attorney, Jim Stevenson, began a speech on the situation, "Your honor, Henry and Jan Allen's son was in the plane crash out at the golf course a few months ago and sadly, her son, Brett Allen, lies in a coma in the hospital."

169

"Objection!" exclaimed Michael so quickly Chase nearly jumped out of his seat.

Their attorney replied, "How could you object to my statement?"

"Because it is incorrect—Brett Allen is NOT in the hospital. He is at his home."

Chase looked over at Jan as he realized she had not told her husband or his attorney where she visited Brett the day before. The father and the uncles remained barred from seeing Brett in the hospital, and no one told them of the move. Jan glanced in his direction, so Chase winked at her. She smiled. She had kept the secret.

"I see," replied the attorney, and seemed a bit confused as he gave a shrug to Henry as if to say, 'what is this?' "Well, as I was saying, the parents feel they are the lawful ones to take charge of their son's recovery since he is not married. We have also discovered Chase Fleming broke into Brett's home twice after Henry had the locks changed, and thus he is trespassing on Brett's property. The parents feel this is a gross abuse and clear case of someone taking advantage of a friend in a helpless coma. We ask the court to uphold the family values of our community, and the Christian ethics our founding fathers created.

"The government does not guarantee a gay roommate the rights of any kind, and certainly not the right to control another's health. Some say these people live a deviant lifestyle by choice, and exhibiting no spiritual servant of God's values. He is trying to act like a surviving spouse. Chase Fleming verbally abused this fine set of parents who have done nothing to him. His actions and sex life are an abomination of God's law. The parents believe he has overwhelmingly confused their son, abused him, and poured his despicable propaganda into Brett's mind. They have seen him touch Brett while he lies helpless in a hospital bed—unfortunately unable to defend himself. The parents should remain the rightful guardians of Brett's medical care, and wish Chase removed from their son's home.

"We beg the court to give these wonderful parents the justice they deserve, so they can protect their son from this homosexual!" He sat down.

Michael shook his head in disbelief at such a horrible display of bigoted hateful comments. He looked over at Chase who was shaking as if he was freezing. Chase fought to hold back his tongue, and his anger, while inside he was boiling with rage. He had chill bumps up and down his legs. He rolled his eyes and chewed his lip as he looked up at Michael.

Michael leaned into him and whispered, "I think it is time we kick some ass—don't you think?" He gave Chase a smile and a wink. Chase quickly smiled back, immediately feeling better.

Mildred, pushing fifty with a few gray hairs, and a couple of small wrinkles, looked over her wire rim glasses and smiled at Michael. "I assume you have another viewpoint on this matter?"

"Yes, your Honor, I most certainly do," replied Michael.

170

"You may proceed." Mildred implied nothing in her tone, and revealed nothing in her facial expressions, but silently she hoped Michael would say what she could not.

Michael stood and smiled at the judge. "Your Honor, let's get this fact over with quickly. I represent both Brett Allen as Executor of his Estate, and the preparer of Living Wills for both he and his life partner Chase Fleming. I also represent Chase. Brett and Chase are not roommates, but partners who live together. They have lived together for over two years, taking many vacations together, eating hundreds of meals together, sharing their holidays, their happy times, and even a few sad times together. They even asked me if the state of North Carolina would one day allow them to marry each other. Sadly, I told them North Carolina would be one of the last states to remove their prejudice against homosexuals.

"They deeply loved, I'm sorry, let me say that again. They love each other as much or more than my loving wife and I do. They complete each other's sentences, read the other's mind, and share a joyous feeling of happiness and love that is inspiring.

"They were leaving on a spectacular exotic vacation when their plane tragically crashed on take-off. Chase is afraid of flying, but he would have gladly gone to the moon if Brett wanted him to.

"As the engine exploded on their side of the plane, the rapidly spinning propeller broke loose from the shaft, and seared through the fuselage like a hot knife cutting through butter. The blade of the propeller began to slow as it chewed seats and passengers alike before finally stopping at Brett's head. The slice to his head knocked him unconscious when the plane came to a grinding, sliding halt in the edge of a bunker on the golf course.

"Your Honor, this is a picture of Brett and Chase." He held up a picture they had made the previous Christmas. Michael had it enlarged, showed it to the Allen table, and then handed it to the judge. "You may note, Brett is much taller, and at least thirty-five pounds heavier than Chase.

"When the plane stopped moving, Chase found himself cut and bleeding in numerous places, and hanging upside down, still strapped by his seat belt. Though terrified, he managed to unbuckle himself and fell to the upended ceiling of the plane. The pain of his broken ankle nearly made him pass out. He wiped his face on his shirt and gagged at the sight of his blood, Brett's blood, as well as the blood and brain matter from other passengers. The scene he sat in was horrifying. His nostrils also smelled the overpowering stench of jet fuel. Completely alone, he got his wits about him, struggled to his feet, and unbuckled Brett letting his limp body fall on top of him to cushion the blow.

"Despite the broken ankle, as well as being battered, bruised, and bleeding, Chase dragged Brett from the plane, across the bunker and over and behind a sand trap. He thought the worst was over, but he was wrong. His ears

heard the unmistakable swoosh sound of fuel igniting. In terrifying horror, he saw the jet fuel turn into a flame, and in seconds, the entire plane exploded. Chase did not run away from this horrifying carnage, but instead he used his own body to cover and protect the man he loved.

"This young lad saved Brett Allen, his partner and friend. He risked his own life though terrified, and though no one would have blamed him if he had ejected from his seat and ran from the plane alone. He stayed, helped his friend from his entrapment, and heroically rescued him.

"He deserves a badge of honor, a commendation, his picture in the paper, and perhaps a photo opportunity with the President of the United States." He paused, as the courtroom remained silent. In a softer voice he would soon build on, he continued, "But that is not the treatment this hero received. Bill and Larry Allen, and Henry Allen, Brett's father, called him vile names in public. The hospital did not honor his Living Will when he told them the signed copies were lost in the fire and explosion of the plane. In fact, the hospital considered his relationship worthless in the eyes of their religion, completely forgetting the love their Bible so emphatically demands of them.

"Chase had to sneak in to see Brett when the parents refused to allow him to see his wounded lover. The hospital never considered his status of being in charge, and though he lay in a hospital bed recovering from his own wounds, they told him he would have to produce the Living Will, or they would exclude him permanently. That is what happened to this hero.

"When he recovered enough to go home, the medical nurse sitting behind him in this courtroom pushed him in his wheelchair to his auto. Bill and Larry Allen attacked them, pushed Chase from the wheelchair to the ground and the two thugs continued to beat and kick them. That is what happened to this hero.

"When the police broke up the melee and he finally gets home, he found the locks changed without his permission, and yet he had lived there for almost two years. He broke into his own house. They planned to block him out of Brett's life, his health, his future, and even the house. That is what happened to this hero.

"Not long ago, Bill and Larry Allen paid him another visit. They attacked the home, kicking and beating the front door with baseball bats. The police came to break up the ruckus, and the police told Chase he would have to move out, as his name was not on the deed. He and Brett shared a bedroom. His clothes still hang in their closet, his stereo and compact discs are in the den, and his car is parked in the carport. None of this proof of his residence mattered to anyone." He paused before saying slowly, "That is what happened to this hero.

"He did not receive credit for his service, respect for their home, a medal for his bravery, privacy for his love, and compassion for his predicament. He deserves far more than what he has received from Henry Allen, Bill and Larry Allen, the hospital administration, and the local police.

"Your Honor, this is Exhibit A—Brett's Will naming me as Executor of his estate. I have been his attorney for over five years. While his Legal Will should remain private until his death, I am taking the liberty of allowing Your Honor to view it in confidence. Please note the beneficiary of Brett's house upon his death. I trust my opponent has no objection."

Michael did not wait for Jim Stevenson to speak up, but quickly continued as he brought Exhibit A to the bench. He held up his next document. "I also have Exhibit B—Brett's Living Will which clearly names Chase Fleming as the sole person in charge of all of Brett's medical decisions, including surgery and medication as required. If Brett could not regain his health, Chase and only Chase have the right to terminate his life. He also has the power to donate Brett's organs should such a tragic event occur. Brett trusted Chase with his life in sickness and in health, and in good times or bad. He demonstrated this trust by signing in front of a Notary this Living Will."

Michael turned back to the bench with a copy of the Living Will. Judge Clemons had just finished scanning the Legal Will and immediately began reading the Living Will.

"Chase is not trespassing in Brett's home because he was invited by Brett to move in. Brett Allen invited him to live there. He has lived there for two years, and all his belonging are there with their two dogs." Michael brought to the bench a picture of their yard and house, their two dogs, kitchen and living room, as well as pictures on the wall of Brett and Chase on vacations all around the world.

"He DID have to break into his own house because Henry Allen unlawfully had the locks changed…twice! In addition, I might add, without Chase's consent to do so. He also received an attack on his house by Bill and Larry Allen, Brett's uncles, where they threatened to kill him with a baseball bat. Let me repeat, on the day of Chase's release from the hospital with a cast on his broken foot, these two uncles attacked him while nurse Jeremy Booker pushed him in a wheelchair. The security guard and the deputies helped break up the fight and hauled the uncles to jail on that occasion as well.

"Now we'll get to the current situation. We discovered the airlines had promised Henry Allen a rather large sum of money if he would remove his comatose son from the hospital and move him to a nursing home. They promised to pay all his expenses in doing so. They did this because the religious hospital has a policy against removing life support from a comatose patient so they can die. Therefore, Henry Allen planned to have their son moved to a nursing home willing to allow Brett to starve to death by removing his feeding tube.

"Since Chase Fleming is in charge of Brett's Living Will, and his medical health and safety, we felt it prudent to move Brett to his home, so he could not only be taking care of Brett medically, but also for his own safety. As

Executor, I have instructed the airline to make their payments for Brett's medical bills to my office. I have made copies of his bills and disbursements to pay these bills, and I give those to you now, Your Honor.

"Brett cannot live at home alone, so I have appointed his partner, Chase Fleming, to serve as his housekeeper, since he must be there to take care of Brett's medical needs per the Living Will. I have also hired Nurse Jeremy Booker, and physical therapist, Paul Renker to take care of Brett's medical needs.

"Your Honor, I bring to your bench a folder of pictures of the room we have prepared for Brett and the equipment obtained." Michael paused as the judge went through the pictures, stopping when she saw the picture of Brett in his hospital bed. She bit her lip, and slowly flipped to the next one.

"He daily receives his medicine and nourishment as well as multiple sessions of physical therapy to keep his body in shape for his return. Therefore, Your Honor, I submit the summons is false, since Chase cannot trespass in his own home, but further, he is now housekeeper of that home, so he can take good care of Brett during his recovery. Your Honor, I thank you for you time." Michael sat down.

"What is his expectant recovery?" Mildred asked.

Henry's attorney spoke up first, "He's been out for several months, Your Honor, after suffering a severe gash to his head in the plane crash. He has not opened his eyes, or spoken since that event. His brain swelled during surgery and though it has receded, after discussion with doctors, he could very well be totally brain dead."

Chase wanted to jump up and dispute their proclamation, but he bit his tongue to remind him not to say anything. Mary shocked him when she stood up.

"Your Honor, I'm Mary Templeton. I was Brett's intensive care nurse, and looked in on him many times while he stayed in the hospital. I have seen Brett's pulse and blood pressure go up when Chase talks to him, and I have asked him to move his fingers and he did so. I believe he is trying to find his way back, and he is far from being a vegetable as this lawyer suggests."

"Thank you. You may sit back down," replied Mildred.

"Do the attorneys have anything else to add?" No one moved. "Does anyone else have anything to say?"

Henry spoke up, "Ma'am, there is no way I'm going to let the control of my son's health fall to that...that...homosexual Chase Fleming. He is evil, Your Honor, as all those types are. That gay disease crap probably runs through his veins. Please let us take care of our only son."

Bill Allen shot off his mouth next, "That Chase Fleming is a freaking faggot...uh, Your Honor!" he said laughing as he elbowed his brother.

Larry added, "Yeah, that's right. He's a 'fudge-packer.' His kind doesn't belong around here."

Mildred hit her gavel, "Gentlemen, and I use the word loosely, you will say nothing more in my courtroom, or I will have you thrown in jail." She stared at them intently over the rims of her glasses before continuing. "We'll take a recess before I return with my decision."

"All rise," said the bailiff.

THIRTEEN

"Did it go well? It seemed like it did. You were thorough and to the point," said Chase nervously.

Michael smiled and patted his knee, "It did go well. We have the law of the Living Will on our side, but I have seen many a judge rule against the law in favor of morality. That is why I hit them first with the fact that you and Brett are gay and partners. The rest of my speech was about the facts. I do not know this judge, but I pray she looked hard at the picture of Brett and you in his room. You should feel proud Brett insisted on the Living Wills. I am afraid many gay people remain completely left out when it comes to their partner's care because they failed to create these special documents."

"So what do we do now?" asked Chase.

"We wait. I don't think it will be too long, because if she felt she needed more time, she would have told us how long to wait. I suspect she wanted to check the facts against the law, or just to clear her head after the outburst of the two uncles."

"I am not surprised at their name-calling. Every time they have attacked me, they have called me names. You did not mention the time they nearly ran me over, why not?"

"Because you could not see the driver's face and identify them, nor could you get the license tag number. If I had used it, and they proved we were wrong, the judge might think the rest of the things I mentioned were false, too. Better to present only strong evidence, and show no weaknesses in our case."

"Oh," replied Chase solemnly. "You know, Michael, you are a whole lot smarter than you look." Chase grinned slyly. He had stolen the comment from Brett, as he had used it on him many a time.

Michael grinned and slapped his knee, "Gee thanks. That means a lot." He let out a laugh.

Moments later, the bailiff entered the courtroom, walked over to Attorney Jim Stevenson, and whispered something. Jim spoke briefly to Henry Allen and then stood.

He then made his way to Michael and whispered to him, "Judge Mildred Clemmons wishes to speak with you and Mr. Chase Fleming and Attorney Jim Stevenson in her chambers."

Michael nodded, whispered to Chase, and they all followed the bailiff to the judge's office. Quietly they filed in.

"Gentlemen, thank you for coming. Please have a seat. Because of the outburst by your rude clients," she nodded at Jim Stevenson, who turned a shade of pink, "I have decided to ask my final questions in private. Mr. Stevenson, I trust you will make smarter choices the next time you appear in my courtroom by avoiding the 'quality' of this type of clients in the future."

Jim replied sheepishly, "Yes, I do try but unfortunately, everyone is entitled to an attorney." After the look she gave him, he deeply wished he could recover his last comment.

"Yes, how fortunate we are," she replied sarcastically. "Now to the point, Chase, I want to ask you a few questions. Do you believe Brett can recover? I don't just mean open his eyes, I mean, do you believe he can have a life of value?"

Chase looked at Michael as if seeking permission to speak. Michael nodded with a slight smile and worried look on his face.

Chase turned back to the judge. "Your Honor, Brett's childhood was a good one, but without much money. He earned his money by cutting an acre of his neighbor's grass every week for one whole dollar. It would take him three hours in the hot summer sun to do so. He worked while in high school and still graduated with honors. He paid his own way through college, and paid off his loan in just three years. He saved for the down payment on his house by working two jobs. He is his own man.

"He never starts anything without finishing it. Do you know how annoying that is?" He smiled and Mildred returned his smile. "He sometimes picks up my clothes, takes away my plate, and always offers me the last piece of chicken, steak, or pie. He is completely selfless. He taught me: it is the little things that demonstrate the love someone has for another, and if we forget the little things, we're bound to stumble over the big things.

"Once we were hiking in the Great Smoky Mountains and somehow took a wrong turn. I was the navigator, but he never blamed me. Later, when we discovered our mistake, we had to retrace over three miles of rugged hiking, and then do a climb of four miles to get to our next campsite. I did not find out until later he did the hike with twenty more pounds of food in his pack than mine, and he had a bleeding blister the size of a silver dollar on his right heel. When we stopped to rest he got a violent cramp in his thigh and fell to the ground in pain, but he massaged and worked it out, and insisted we finish the hike.

"He is not a quitter, he has taught me to remain confidant and positive, to keep my eye on any goal, and if I do that, anything and everything is possible.

"Your Honor, this may sound silly to you, but have you ever sat beside someone you truly love, and somehow, you can feel what they are thinking? Brett and I do that all the time. We laugh without saying aloud what we are laughing at. I feel him trying to talk to me when I am with him. He is moving his muscles a little bit more almost every day. He is going to come back. I just know it."

Mildred pulled her glasses off and replied, "Chase, how long can you afford to wait for him to return? When is it too long? When is the cost too much?"

Chase sighed heavily. An undisturbed tear slid down his cheek. "Ma'am, I can wait forever if I have to. If we run out of money, I will get second job, a third job, a fourth—whatever it takes. He has only been home for two nights. We certainly deserve the time to help him make it back.

"He loves me. He will not give up. He will climb over any obstacle, work through any pain, fight any challenge, but Your Honor, I promise you— Brett will come back to life!" He fell back in his seat breathing rapidly as more tears fell to his suit.

Mildred smiled at Chase, allowing a quiet moment, before responding, "Thank you, Chase. I think you have answered my questions very well. Gentlemen, you may return to the courtroom."

They stood and followed the bailiff to their waiting chairs.

Michael began looking over his notes, while Chase turned around and began talking with Jeremy. Not long after, the bailiff entered the room.

"All rise!"

The judge reentered the room, opened a case folder, arranged her paperwork, took off her glasses, and took a breath. The courtroom fell quiet of all whispers and murmurs. Chase fidgeted nervously, but looked straight at her.

"This is a most unusual case, and to reach my decision I had to break it down into simple elements. On the matter of the Living Will, the court must uphold the decision made by Brett Allen, and legally signed in front of a Notary long before the accident. Therefore, he could not have been under any duress, as he had plenty of time to change his mind, and he did not. Further, I see Chase Fleming as solely responsible for the medical condition, treatment, and outcome of Brett Allen.

"I also find Mr. Michael Evans to be the Executor of his Estate as well as his attorney of record. Brett Allen gave him this right in his Will, and did so without duress, since he legally signed the Will more than a year ago. The Will states in the event of Brett Allen's passing, the house, along with all his assets, belong entirely to Chase Fleming.

"Now the juggling act begins. Since Chase Fleming is in charge of Brett Allen's health, etc., he has a right to be with Brett at all times. As Executor, Michael Evans has the right to hire a housekeeper to take care of Brett, and provide twenty-four hour care, including the living quarters for a housekeeper.

"As Brett Allen's Attorney, he has the right, on Brett's behalf and absence, to seek the best interest of Brett Allen, therefore he has the right to seek payments from the airline for Brett Allen's care and disburse such proceeds as he sees fit.

"The laws of our land do not permit gay couples to marry, or have the rights a married couple has. However, Chase has the right to be there as housekeeper, and he lived there, as a roommate for more than two years, thus accusing him of trespassing is ridiculous. To do so would be splitting hairs because if Brett Allen lives, based on the Will, he intends to keep Chase

Fleming a part of his life. If he should die, and we pray not, then the house would go to Chase Fleming anyhow. There is no point in arguing trespassing. I will instruct the police to drop any record of Chase trespassing.

"In summary, I suspect Henry Allen, as well as Bill and Larry Allen are overgrown bigots, who have taken the law in their own hands by changing the locks. They have attacked Chase Fleming on more than one occasion, and they best not return to my courtroom with any future altercations on Chase Fleming, or they will be spending a very long decade or two in prison. I hope I have made this final point very clear.

"Is there anything else you two attorneys need to bring before this court today?" She said the question once again in such a way neither attorney offered to say anything. "Very well," she paused and then turned to Chase, "Son, I wish you Godspeed, and truly hope and pray you are able to help Brett recover from this most tragic accident. Please keep me informed on his condition. I would like to meet him someday."

She turned to the Allen family and said. "I understand your worry over your son. It played hard on my decision, as I have three children myself. However, giving how you conducted yourselves so far in this matter, I would rather have my three children taken care of by young Chase, than any of you. Let this be a lesson to you. This court stands adjourned."

"All rise!" said the bailiff with a grin.

After she left, Chase leaped into Michael's arms as he stood. "You did it! Thank you. Thank you!" Then he turned and gave Jeremy a hug. The judge caught his actions out of the corner of her eye, and smiled as she left the courtroom.

The two brothers passed by and called them names as usual, but the bailiff wisely anticipated a problem, and stepped between them and Chase, and expertly escorted the uncles out of the courtroom with his nightstick in his hand. Henry strode out defiantly behind them. Jan lingered, winked at Chase, and leaned over and gave him a hug. "Way to go, son. Way to go!"

Jack wrote the top of the hour monitor readings on the medical chart, then lifted Brett's wrist to take his pulse the old-fashioned way, just to be sure—a habit he maintained throughout his career. He had just about finished his silent count, when suddenly Brett turned his wrist. Jack nearly jumped out of his shoes as he fell back letting go of his wrist. To his disbelief, he watched as Brett held the wrist in the air for a few seconds before slowly letting it fall back to the bed. Jack shook his head wondering if he was dreaming. He had just set the clipboard down when the phone suddenly rang startling him once again. His heart leaped again.

"Uh, hello. My I help you?" asked Jack while putting his right hand over his heart to calm himself.

179

"We won!" shouted Chase.

He pulled the phone away from his ear. "That's great. I'm happy for you."

"How is Brett?"

Jack turned around and looked at Brett. He remained lifeless and still, but with a little color to his face. He thought for a second about telling Chase about the incident, but decided not to. "Uh, he is fine. Monitoring levels are very good."

"We're going out to celebrate a little. I will be home about three, if that is okay. Can you stay until three?"

"Yes, of course, I work eight hour shifts, so as long as you're back by five, I'm fine."

"Very well, if you need me you can reach me on my cell phone as I just turned it back on now that I'm out of the courtroom."

"Okay, I'm sure we'll be fine."

"Thank you, Jack. I appreciate your help immensely."

Michael invited Chase and Jeremy to join him for lunch so off they went. Michael was being a bit protective, feeling it was unlikely Bill and Larry would attempt to harm them with a lawyer for a witness around. He was right as he spotted the uncles driving out of the parking lot. He smiled, but said nothing. He wanted to enjoy the happiness of the moment, but he feared they had many long months ahead taking care of Brett.

The winter had been one of the first Brett had spent in many years without having sex with another person. His right hand had grown stronger than the left as a result. He counted the days of the week until summer, like a little kid marking the days off until Christmas. Now he was a tall fourteen years old, as he had grown just over three inches since last year. He started working on his tan by lying in the backyard, and he continued cutting grass for cash until the day before leaving for another summer as a lifeguard at camp.

He was not quite old enough for a driver's license, so he had to wait until his dad woke up from working late to drop him off. He was due at the camp before one or just after lunch for orientation. He told his dad he had to be there by ten to get the pool ready. It was a white lie. No one asked him to get the pool clean, but he knew it would need to have the bottom swept of dead bugs and filters emptied of live ones.

He really wanted to arrive at the camp where he could be free and act grown up. He knew Robbie's dad had enrolled him in military school and could not attend camp this year. Brett felt sad at the news, but laughed when Robbie said it was the best thing his dad had ever done for him, as the school was an all-male institution with big open shower rooms for boys his age. Robbie laughed, and said he felt like a kid in a candy store. Brett smiled at the thought, though he knew his family could never afford to send him to such a school.

After settling into the staff hut, with his clothes put away and his bed made, he stripped down, lay on the bed, and defiantly masturbated. It was an exhilarating moment of freedom, and he squeezed every drop of independence from his spent penis. He pulled on his swimsuit, swung a towel over his shoulder, and decided to test his new purple flip-flops. He felt sure no one would make a mistake and walk away with his flats this summer. You could see these purple ones for miles, he thought.

He oiled up to continue working on his tan, cleaned out the bugs as planned, checked the water clarity with the test kit, adjusted the gas valve on the chlorine cylinder, and still had two hours before orientation. He looked back down the trail leading to camp and saw no one. The donations for the pool came years after constructing the cabins, so they built it about a quarter mile from the nearest camp building. Seeing no one, he dove in, stripped off his trunks, and laid them across the floating rope separating the deep end from the shallow end. He swam along the bottom feeling the water rushing all over his naked body, especially between his legs.

He took a deep breath, and did a lazy underwater stroke to the far end. He would work on his endurance when someone else was around to watch in case he blacked out, but for now, he was just relaxing. He made a couple of more laps, and then decided to practice his backstroke, the weaker stroke for him. He discovered swimming on your back while naked had added benefits as the water rushed around his shoulders, along his side and across his genitals.

While he pulled at the water, the water pulled at his penis. The result was a half-done erection. He laughed at the view but kept stroking. It was if he was a submarine with his periscope up. When he reached the deep end, he looked back over his head to prepare for a flip turn, and realized there was a boy sitting on the diving board watching him.

Brett quickly dropped his legs descending his naked body below the waterline. "Hello, I did not hear you come in."

"I found the gate unlocked, and thought I would check out the pool."

"And you are?" asked Brett, obviously caught red faced and embarrassed at being caught skinny-dipping.

"My name is Ryan. Ryan Culkin. I'm one of the dishwashers."

"Oh, I'm Brett Allen. It's nice to meet you."

"Same here," he replied.

"I'm sorry I embarrassed you by swimming in the nude. Once the staff and the kids arrive. I practically have to glue my swimming suit on. It would surprise you how many girls try to pull it off when I go in the water. I have to always keep moving," he added with a grin.

"There's nothing you should be embarrassed for as I love to go skinny-dipping, too. I can see why the girls want to pull your suit off. You are very good looking. I wish I was."

Brett's face became a deep red at Ryan's bold statement, but he hoped his suntan hid it. "Oh, the girls are going to love you, too. They always love a blond, especially with blue eyes like yours."

"Do you mind if I join you?" asked Ryan.

Brett hesitated, as he was not sure where this was heading, but also he was afraid the rest of the staff would catch them. "What time is it?"

"12:15," he replied.

"Hmm, we only have about fifteen minutes to swim before we better dry off so our hair will be dry when we see the rest of the staff."

"Great," Ryan replied as he leaped off the diving board to the cement deck, kicked his tennis shoes off while pulling his tee shirt over his head. Then he unbuckled his pants and yanked them down with his underwear over his ankles and off his feet. He took off his watch and laid it on his shorts, ran to the edge of the pool and dove in.

Brett loved the view, as he thought Ryan was very cute.

Ryan came to the surface grinning, "Oh my, this feels wonderful."

"You forgot something," said Brett slyly.

Ryan turned around in the water, and then gave him a sheepish look, "What? What did I forget?"

Brett laughed, "Your socks. They are still on your feet!"

Ryan quickly looked down and laughed. He removed the wet socks and hung them on the diving board. Together, they swam around the deep end for a while stealing looks at each other's crotch before swimming to the shallow water to stand and talk some more before climbing out of the pool.

As they dried off, they took turns drying the other's back. It was a simple gesture, and the beginning of a new summer romance. They laughed at each other's jokes, and Ryan became thrilled when Brett asked him to be his roommate. He would be more than a roommate before the first week was out. Brett always did love blonds with blue eyes.

Chase had tried to stay awake watching a movie on the DVD player, but his emotional stress-filled day in court left him spent and fatigued. He finished what he called his med-check of Brett, which included writing the numbers down from the monitoring equipment, and checking IV drips and his urine tube and bag. The sight of Brett's nude body caused him to pause, as he wished the body would wake up and hug him tightly.

He cut off the lights and fell into his bed scattering the dogs to their favorite corners. He managed to pull the covers over his body before immediately drifting off to sleep. For a brief moment, his brain rewound the day, but he was so exhausted he soon fell into a deep sleep.

Just after four in the morning, lightning streaked across the skies following distant booms. Every three or four minutes another bolt would etch the blackened sky, getting a bit closer with each episode. Fifteen minutes later,

182

Brett's eyelids moved in reaction to the quick changes of light. Suddenly, he began moving a finger and his right foot.

Chase's breaths had been shallow throughout the night. Neither the lightning nor the never-ending booms afterwards brought him back from his deep sleep. In his brain, it was as if someone had flipped on a remote control device activating his dream channel. He thought he was too tired to dream. He dreamed of Brett in hodgepodge events of their life. Though still asleep, his brow wrinkled trying to figure out a sequence. He did not know why he was not reliving a complete and wonderful event like lovemaking. The scenes changed quickly as if the channel up button remained held down by a mysterious finger.

Suddenly, a closer bolt of lighting streaked across the backside of the house. Brett reacted by shaking his hand. Chase's brain suddenly stopped the revolving pictures, leaving a black picture that soon developed into a faraway movement of something way off in the distance. It was as if he was looking through the wrong end of his telescope. His eyebrows fluttered briefly, as he tried to focus on the picture. The picture suddenly began zooming closer and closer. Click, click, and click with each picture doubling the previous one.

His ears heard a boom and presto—the picture suddenly filled his dream screen. The figure was white with his back to Chase. Slowly, he began turning while removing a hat, revealing bit by bit a beautiful full color picture of Brett beginning at his chin, and slowly illuminating his entire face. He dropped the white cape off and before Chase stood Brett strong and healthy, bare-chested, and wearing white shorts. He smiled at Chase and blew him a kiss.

Chase's legs began moving back and forth wishing he could run to Brett in his dream and embrace him. The dogs lifted their heads as the bed moved a little. In the dream, he stretched out his hand as far as he could, and Brett began reaching for him as well. Closer and closer, the distance between them narrowed.

Just as their fingers touched another huge streak of lighting hit a big oak tree, just forty yards behind their house. Instead of the faraway delayed boom, this strike was so close the thunder shook the doors, windows, picture frames and even rattled the dishes in the cabinets.

In a flash, Brett's colorful and beautiful face fell apart into thousands of tiny pixels that began circling his head like a small cyclone before spiraling high above and out in to space. Chase screamed to call Brett back, and then again, even louder. The dogs' ears stood up. He screamed a third time. In the hospital, bed Brett moved his hand.

Chase abruptly sat up and looked about the room. He saw another bolt of lighting in the sky. He got out of bed and walked over to Brett, just to make sure he was there and still breathing. He noted the monitor. Brett's pulse was up, his breathing slightly labored. He flicked on a light and swore he saw Brett's eyelids react to the sudden flash of light.

183

He grabbed the clipboard to write down the accelerated numbers. Still sleepy, he sat down in the chair by the bed. While holding the clipboard in his left hand, he laid it down on the bed over Brett's left arm. He began writing the numbers. He opened and closed his eyes several times to fight off the sleep. He stifled a yawn. He had just recorded his pulse numbers when unexpectedly Brett's hand moved and touched him.

Chase leaped back overturning the chair. He stared at the hand as it moved a few inches left and right. He felt like he was seeing Frankenstein come alive, but then he quickly moved back to the bed, and placed his hand in Brett's pale hand. The hand stopped moving and slowly his hand closed over Chase's fingers.

"Hooray!" shouted Chase. "You did it. Come on, Brett. Squeeze me again," he urged. Brett's fingers relaxed just slightly and paused.

"You can do it, Brett. I know you can. Come on pal. Squeeze once more. I have to know it was not a reflex but willful. I love you, damn it. Squeeze!" pleaded Chase.

Perhaps at the speed the space shuttle creeps to the launch pad, Brett's fingers moved until they could touch Chase's skin. "That's it. You did it. I love you!"

Tears slid down Chase's face as alone he sat there for the rest of night, half-afraid to let go, fearing Brett was saying goodbye, but also jubilant in hopes Brett was saying hello. He slept leaning his head onto the side of the bed with hair touching Brett's chest, so he could feel him breathe, and hear his heartbeat. He slept deeply, like a new puppy cuddled tightly against his mom, listening to the slow but deliberate beats of Brett's heart.

Brett enjoyed the attention that the two hundred new girl campers gave him every week. They pawed over him, pinched his butt if they were brave, or pulled his toes while he sat on the lifeguard chair on duty. They flirted every way they could, while dreaming of his tan bare chest and cute butt in their cabins at night.

Now and then, he would signal the head guard he was hot and needed to cool off. Getting an approving nod, he would take his guard helmet off, which he thought made him look like Jungle Jim on a safari, remove the lanyard holding his whistle, stand up on the seat, and begin a beautiful swan dive to the deep end.

The entire female group would stop their splashing, playing, or tanning, look up, and watch him fly through the air. Some would note the muscles in his long slender legs. Other would see his shoulder muscles, or his bulging abs, the result of daily sit-ups. Some of the older girls would note his beautiful tight buns, as well as the bulge on the front of his suit.

The scene always happened too fast for the girls, but not fast enough for Brett. The cool water felt wonderful as he dove to the bottom, swam back and forth in the deep end for a few strokes while adjusting his itching balls, and

184

then finally swam up to the ladder. Sometimes he came up in the shallow end, immediately surrounded by fifty girls like a movie star at a premier. Girls would try to talk to him. Some would touch him, and to his amazement, some girls felt his butt. No one could see their strayed hand, as they were all moving back and forth like a frenzy of fish feeding on tossed breadcrumbs. Occasionally, an older girl would touch his genitals, squeezing gently.

He always refrained from reacting at this personal touch, while hoping they were not going to pull his suit off. He did his best not to make eye contact with the culprit. He would let it last for a few seconds before swimming back to the deep end, and climbing out of the pool to head back to his guard station.

All this was great fun and the girls' attention certainly increased his confidence, but nothing excited him more than the approaching weeks when the girls would disappear, and the boys would return.

The boys' staff arrived during the last week of girls' camp for their training for the arrival of the male campers the following week. Most of the counselors were former campers now grown, but most likely seniors in high school or in college. Brett knew most of them from the previous summer, but enjoyed meeting the new boys, especially Jimmy and Timmy, twins from Gaffney. These two boys were incredible athletes, and had the bodies of Olympic champions. They were also very funny, and enjoyed all the various jokes Brett polished over the summer.

Brett was the camp's ping-pong champion, and every camper enjoyed challenging him to a game. Wisely, he played his game to the level of his opponent. In one game against an eight-year-old, he purposely missed easy shots, and when he did return the ball, he placed it in an easy spot. He would still win, but he told the group watching how tough it was to beat this youngster. With each point the child won, his excitement would grow. Brett made the game fun, and the outcome of a winner unimportant.

However, when he played Jimmy or Timmy, he had to work his ass off, and remained unbeaten for the rest of the summer. From time to time, the twins would stick around after the pool closing for the day, and help Brett clean up the area. They hung lost wet towels on the rail, cleaned out the debris traps, and hosed down the entry deck, washing away the sand from the children's flip-flops.

One hot day, they decided to swim some after their chores. They did cannonballs off the diving board followed by Brett's famous watermelon dive, which sent a huge plume of water fifteen feet in the air. They played tag or just wrestled in the water, with the twins in a team against Brett. Brett always won, but it was great fun for the gang.

One day, they decided to play Marco Polo, a game in which one person had to keep his eyes closed while dipping below the water, and as he would surface, he would say 'Marco.' The other players immediately called back

'Polo.' He would then swim towards the sound, and try to touch them while keeping his eyes closed.

Timmy had been Marco for a few minutes, while Jimmy and Brett remained in the deep end. Back and forth, they swam around or under Timmy, laughing as he just missed catching them. Growing tired, Jimmy and Brett crept to the corner of the pool with their heads just above the surface, while Timmy moved about trying to find them.

Jimmy slipped around to Brett's back and put his hands on his shoulders to hold on. Now and then Brett would sink beneath the waters, and swim to the opposite corner with Jimmy still hanging onto his back. While resting on the other side, Jimmy shocked Brett by sliding his right hand down, under Brett's arm, and began feeling Brett's chest. Brett did not remove his hand, so Jimmy slid it down farther, while playing with the little sun bleached blond hairs around his navel.

Brett kept a sharp eye in case Timmy turned in their direction, while Jimmy began squeezing Brett's penis creating an instant reaction. Seconds later, he had his hand inside Brett's swimming trunks, while Brett slipped a hand behind him, playing with Jimmy's privates.

When it was time to get out of the pool, Brett had to linger a little longer, while counting backwards from a hundred, so his stiff erection would go down. He climbed the ladder and grabbed a towel to cover his groin. Jimmy laughed and winked at him. Brett smiled and winked back in return.

Very few people in the camp could tell the twins apart, but Brett could. He had studied the way they walked, their voice, and all their facial features until he could identify either twin every time. The boys' camp occurred in August, which in the Carolinas was the hottest time of the year. There was no air-conditioning in the camp. After chapel, the camp opened the canteen so the kids could buy a little candy and a cold soft drink. Jimmy leaned into Brett and whispered they should go skinny-dipping after taps. Brett agreed, so Jimmy settled his kids down and got the campers in bed just in time for taps. The rest of the boys' staff was going to the Program Director's house to watch a movie. Brett told them he had already seen it, and was going to read a book. Brett read every day during rest hour and before he went to bed at night, so no one doubted him.

He waited for the staff to hike the trail to go watch the movie, and then crept around the outside edge of the campground leading to the pool to avoid the few remaining lights. He had done this a hundred times and could have done it in his sleep, but he always worried about stepping on a snake. When he reached the pool, Jimmy was already inside the gate. He walked over to Jimmy who stood by the lifeguard stand naked, and playing with his penis. Thankfully, the sky, covered with partial clouds, gave them just a hint of moonlight so they could see. Brett could see Jimmy's white butt. He smiled and walked over to him. Jimmy reached down and slid Brett's shorts off, while Brett pulled his tee shirt over his head, and placed his clothes on the lifeguard chair.

186

Jimmy immediately reached over and began playing with Brett's penis, which had already begun to grow, then leaned in and gave Brett a huge swirling hot tongue kiss. Brett reacted quickly with an erection strong enough to hang the camp flag on. Too hot for sex, they quickly forgot about swimming. Brett grabbed a couple of towels off the towel fence, and together, they moved to the far corner of the pool deck away from the camp. He took their clothes with them just in case someone came to the pool, so they could slip on their shorts and step into the pool.

He made a blanket of the towels and together, they lay down and began making out. Jimmy was an incredible kisser, and from time to time, he pulled away from the kiss and slid his glistening tongue across Brett's cheek until he reached his ear. He would tease Brett by barely touching the outer rim of his ear, but slowly he moved in the center with a flicker of his tongue. Brett had never experienced this, but loved it, and practically purred like a kitten when the warm wet tip of Jimmy's tongue began moving end and out of his ear.

Soon they were sucking each other while Jimmy slipped a finger inside Brett's anus to massage the pulsing, throbbing prostate gland. After a childhood of being a bottom, he thought he had become a top, but not tonight. Jimmy's multitalented throat abilities, combined with his finger plunges, brought Brett to a new height of ecstasy.

Brett had some lubricant in his pocket so he reached around and thoroughly lubed Jimmy's swollen member. He lied down and spread his legs. Jimmy easily slid in, while kissing his way across Brett's chest to his mouth. Brett closed his eyes while enjoying the ride. Jimmy managed to kiss him, slide to an ear, and back again to his mouth keeping Brett mystified and horny. Jimmy picked up the speed of his pump a little and dragged his tongue towards Brett's other ear.

"Yes, yes, this is wonderful!" exclaimed Brett with his eyes closed and delirious.

"I can make it twice as good if you want me to," said Jimmy between swirling his tongue in Brett's right ear.

"I don't see how, but if you can, go for it!" replied an ecstatic Brett.

Moments later, Brett felt a warm tongue in his left ear. Wait a minute, thought Brett. How can he have a tongue in both ears?

Brett opened his eyes, looked to his left, and discovered Timmy joining the party. "Where did you come from?" he asked alarmed. His eyes fell to Timmy's hard on and his beautiful naked body.

Timmy leaned up and replied, "I have been here all along. I just could not sit on the sidelines any longer!"

He kissed his way to Brett's hot inviting mouth as Jimmy continued to pump him. The experienced twins obviously held no secrets between them. Minutes later, Timmy straddled his face and fed his wonderful erection to Brett.

187

Timmy then spun around, leaned down, and began sucking Brett, while Brett began licking and lightly sucking Timmy's balls.

After a while, Timmy rose and began French kissing Jimmy while masturbating Brett. This made Jimmy pump faster. Without a word said, Timmy broke the kiss, bent over and placed his penis in Brett's mouth, then went down on Brett at a much faster pace.

Brett was sure he could feel three heart beats as the group continued their final position sucking and pumping until finally Jimmy exploded into Brett. This set off a chain reaction causing Brett to explode into Timmy, followed by Timmy ejaculating into Brett.

Spent and exhausted, the three boys fell into one another, slowly rubbing their hands over their hot steaming bodies.

"I need a swim," whispered Brett.

"Come on, let's go," replied Timmy.

They slid into the water, and continued to play and touch one another until Brett felt it was time for them to slip back into camp. Boys' camp only lasted three weeks, but the twins and Brett managed to make as much use of the opportunities as possible.

FOURTEEN

Everyone warned him, but Chase still hoped Brett would wake sooner than later. It had been several days since he last moved, but on the advice of Jeremy, Chase returned to his job in the mall, as the holiday season had kicked in and they needed his help. For weeks, he had spent days and nights with Brett, massaging his legs, moving his joints, and changing bags and bottles. Jeremy and Paul gave him much praise, but together they felt soon Chase was going to collapse from physical and mental fatigue.

Michael arranged for a nurse to come in every day for an eight-hour shift to give Chase some relief. He also arranged for a counselor to spend some time with Chase, giving him a chance to air his feelings. Chase no longer slept all night, but rather just took naps, as the stress began to affect him. Sometimes when he was beat down, Brett would suddenly move, and when Chase asked him he would move again, and the jubilation carried Chase for a few more days.

The nurse arrived just as Chase finished dressing. He went over the chart, told the lady to make herself at home, wrote down his cell phone number and his work number, gave Brett a kiss, and drove out of the driveway. As he drove away, he immediately felt the stress falling from his shoulders. For eight hours, someone else would be in charge, he thought.

His manager showed him a few changes in procedure, introduced him to the new employees, and showed him the brochures on the new products. Customers started coming by immediately with shopping bags full of holiday presents. Chase had completely forgotten about fall shopping in the mall for Christmas. He was not even sure what month or day it was.

After lunch, three gay friends stopped to chat and catch up on the local gossip. A bit later, Jeremy called on his cell phone to see how he was doing. He smiled at the sound of his voice.

"I'm fine. It feels pretty good to be out of the house for a while," replied Chase.

"Excellent. Unbelievably, it will help Brett when you come home and tell him about your day. You'll have something new each day to tell him. I have to run, but don't plan anything for dinner. Paul is at home cooking and we're bringing dinner over about six."

"What's he cooking?" asked Chase out of curiosity.

"I don't know. He wouldn't tell me, but he never disappoints when he cooks. See you soon," replied Jeremy.

Jeremy and Paul came in the front door with bags of food, and set them on the kitchen counter. They heard nothing in the house, although the dogs were jumping up and down at the smell of the food.

189

"Chase?" asked Jeremy as he began heading to the back of the house and Brett's room. He heard nothing in reply. He leaned in the doorway and found Chase asleep while sitting in the chair next to Brett's bed, with his face against Brett's side, and his hand holding Brett's. A few strands of Chase's hair had fallen across Brett's stomach, and Brett's right hand was touching Chase's hair.

Suddenly, it dawned on him Brett's right hand was not at his side as he had seen so many times, but actually moved across his chest to Chase's hair. How did it get there, he wondered.

He looked at the monitoring equipment and found everything normal. He stepped around the bed, leaned over, and began massaging Chase's shoulders. Chase stirred. "Are you hungry, big boy?" asked Jeremy.

Chase turned around trying to focus, until he realized it was Jeremy. "Oh, hi, I guess I fell asleep."

"Look at Brett's right hand," said Jeremy.

"What?" asked Chase, but then his head turned back to Brett afraid something was wrong. "Oh my gosh—it is on his chest!"

"Did you move it there?" asked Jeremy.

"No, I wrote down the chart numbers, and sat down to tell him about my day. I fell asleep at some point," replied Chase.

"Amazing, I guess old Brett moved it by himself. This is very exciting," said Jeremy.

"That's the first time he moved his arm across the chest, but he has moved his arm several times before," replied Chase as he stood up.

Jeremy gave him a hug. "I think you're making a pretty good nurse and physical therapist all rolled into one."

"Thanks. I'm starved. Is Paul here?"

Paul leaned in the door. "Dinner is served!" He walked over and gave Chase a hug, picked up the chart, and then added, "You're doing very well, but come on, let's eat while it is hot. You're losing weight, and your skinny ass can't afford to lose much more!"

"Was there a compliment in there?" asked Chase with a grin.

"Yep," replied Paul with a smile as he hugged Chase again.

Three weeks later, Chase woke with a start as the phone continued ringing. The room was dark, but the displays on the monitoring equipment produced a light green glow across the room. He shook the sleep from his eyes and picked up the phone. "Hello?"

"Chase, I'm sorry to wake you," began Jeremy, "but Brett's mother just arrived in the emergency room."

"Oh my gosh! Is she okay?" asked Chase now wide-awake.

"She has chest pains. Could be anything, but we'll know more in an hour or so. I thought you would want to know."

"Thanks. I appreciate you calling. What should I do? Should I come down there?"

"No, don't. The father and the uncles are in the waiting room. I don't think they recognized me when I came by. I will call you when I know more. Go back to sleep."

"Okay, please call me when you know how she is."

"I will."

Chase fell back asleep, but not long after he began to dream of the trip he and Brett took to Key West. He had never been on a plane, and could hardly sleep the night before. Brett kept reassuring him all would be fine as he had flown over a hundred times in North America, once to Hawaii, and twice to Europe with no problems.

They found their luggage on the huge baggage carousel, and hauled it to their rental car. Chase acted as navigator as they found the right expressway and began heading south. Once they reached US 1, Chase put the map down and began watching the view. When they left the mainland and started crossing the numerous long, two-lane bridges his excitement increased.

"We should have gotten a convertible," he complained.

"Next time," replied Brett, recalling his first trip to Miami when he did rent a convertible and thought he was going to die in a hailstorm. He felt like his head was in a bass drum.

The trip took about three hours, but after they reached the bed and breakfast where they had reservations, they immediately felt at home. The gay bed and breakfast boasted twenty rooms, a pool, ten men Jacuzzi, exercise room, and a video sex room. A cute gay boy helped them with their luggage to the room. Brett tipped him, but instead of leaving, the boy insisted they join him on a tour of the place.

Chase nodded okay and so they dropped everything in the room and followed their guide around. They found many guests lying by the pool, some of which were nude, so Chase got a big kick out of that. The video room was playing a porno, and two men were jacking each other off in the corner. Chase made a note to visit the room later that night.

The guide ended the tour at the bar by the pool, which also served lunch. They were starving and quickly ordered cheeseburgers and curly fries. A cute black guy, who did drag on Friday nights, brought their lunch to the table. He set down their plates and drinks, and a platter filled with a variety of freshly cut fruit.

"I'm sorry," began Brett, "we didn't order the fruit."

The waiter grinned, "It's complimentary on your first night. Besides, we have lots of fruits around here."

"Oh, that was bad," laughed Chase.

191

The waiter laughed with him, and asked, "Where are you boys from?"

"Asheville," replied Chase quickly. "In North Carolina," he added.

"I know where it is. Just because I wear dresses once a week, doesn't make me a dummy. You're in the western part, east of Knoxville. Am I right?"

"Yes, you are," replied Brett as Chase started eating. "Have you been there?"

"Oh yes, I grew up in Hendersonville, but once I graduated high school, I decided to get out of that town."

"Too many hooters for you?" asked Chase slyly, recalling the nickname for folks from Hendersonville.

"Too many damn rednecks, so I traveled south spending time in Jacksonville at a club, a huge one, but I wanted to see more, so I made my way to Fort Lauderdale, and found a sea of gay friends. Two years later, I visited Key West on a vacation trip and loved it. I went home, got my stuff, and moved here. Okay, enough about me. When you're done with dinner, step over to the bar, and I'll make you an awesome fruit drink. Later tonight, you can see my show at the Bender. The show is at midnight. Enjoy your lunch."

They spent the afternoon sightseeing, and then returned to the inn, changed clothes and fell in the pool. It did not take long for the other guests to notice the two new strangers, both of whom were good looking. Chase, being two years younger, got the most attention. They swam back and forth, and then settled with Chase hugging Brett from the back while letting his legs drift in the water.

He whispered in to Brett's ear, "Let's go skinny-dipping."

Brett laughed, "Why?"

"I don't know, I guess because we can. It looks like it is legal around here."

"You know I'm shy," began Brett. "You're the one with the killer body."

Brett turned around and kissed Chase for three or four seconds, and just as he broke the kiss, he yanked down Chase's swim shorts until he had them off. Chase had fallen beneath the water and when he came up, he was grinning.

"I'll get you!" he exclaimed, as he swam after Brett who had already dove to the deep end still carrying Chase's shorts. Chase caught him and yanked his swim trunks off as well. They kissed underwater and then surfaced, and left their clothing on the side of the pool. Almost immediately, the entire lounge chairs around the pool filled with the guests, and they were all gaping at the two young men.

However, Brett ignored them and kept his eyes on Chase, teasing and splashing him, and when he could, he pinched his butt. Chase loved it, but he also loved the audience. The day was a good start of their vacation. They ate seafood for dinner, hit a few bars, and found the Bender about forty minutes prior to show time. The place was packed, but somehow they found a small table close to the stage.

The show featured about six drag queens with each lady introducing the following act. Halfway through, they asked for a volunteer from the audience. It did not surprise Brett when Chase was chosen, as he always liked the spotlight. They asked him where he was from, and the audience loved his Southern accent. The drag queen told him they would need his help during the next song. He was supposed to hold a hoop curtain up so the singer-dancer could make changes to her outfit while continuing the song.

Chase stood in the middle of the stage holding the curtain up high over his head. The curtain parted at each end, but Chase had not noticed the second seam where he stood. The drag queen began her song and after a minute, she stepped through the curtain urging Chase to hold it higher, and removed part of the costume, and returned to the stage wearing a skimpy outfit with a huge green boa. She tickled Chase's nose with it, and he faked a huge sneeze. The crowd loved him.

Minutes later, she returned to the curtain, urged him to keep his hands high so she could change. As she began changing, she threw the green boa around his neck. Chase kept the curtain high as instructed. He never felt the drag queen's hand as he cleverly reached through the other end of the curtain, and undid Chase's belt, zipper, and snap. Then in a flash she dropped his pants and underwear to the floor exposing Chase's beautiful white butt below his t-shirt. She then stood up, parted the curtains completely, and with the microphone she said, "Honey, I know you love my act, but you can wait until I am finished to drop your pants!"

The crowded roared, but Chase did not catch on, as he was too busy holding the curtain up high. The drag queen winked at the crowd and said, "Honey, are you feeling a draft? I think I'm getting a chill."

Chase gave her a funny look, and then she pointed to her eyes with a V shape to her fingers indicating he should watch her. She pointed to his eyes, and then he followed her finger down and around to his naked butt.

Instantly, he dropped the curtain and yanked up his pants. The crowd stood and cheered as she helped him take a bow and planted a big red smooch kiss to his cheek. The crowd gave him a big hand, and he returned to his seat. Brett was howling, and Chase's face remained a bright red for the rest of the evening.

Afterwards, Chase insisted they race back to the inn where they stripped out of their clothes and made their way to the Jacuzzi. Once they were hot enough, they dried off, wrapped the big towels around their waist, and made their way into the video porn room. They were surprised to see about eight couples around the room on various carpeted levels all making out and naked. Chase and Brett watched the video a little, and the crowd a little more.

Chase whispered to Brett, "Let's make love here and now."

Brett gave him a worried look, "Are you sure?"

"Yep," he whispered slyly as he knelt down in front of Brett, pulled his towel away, and began taking Brett's penis in his mouth. Once he achieved an erection, Chase pulled his towel away and stood up so Brett could suck him. The crowd began watching them, as they were the youngest in the room, and the best looking, too.

There were baskets around the room so Chase pulled out of Brett's mouth, placed a condom on his penis, and pushed Brett on to his back, spread his legs like he was a cop ready to frisk him, moved forward on his knees, and expertly entered Brett. They pumped, kissed, and somehow Chase managed to masturbate Brett until they both came.

Brett had been so aroused he covered his chest with lots of white cream. Wickedly, Chase took his hand and spread it all over Brett's chest. He licked some of it off to the delight of the men, before tenderly cleaning Brett with a towel.

They laughed and went back to the shower near the Jacuzzi to wash up. The outdoor shower became a favorite of theirs. There were no private stalls, just an open room with a railing around the edge, and filled with every kind of shampoo and body wash available on the planet. They took turns washing the other, dried off, and returned to their room to sleep.

They loved Key West, especially the freedom they had to hold hands, kiss, cuddle, or just cut up in the stores. The rainbow flags at the entrance to every store gave the boys a great feeling of pride.

Jeremy met Chase at the employee entrance and brought him up the back elevator of the hospital.

"How's she doing?" Chase asked nervously, afraid of bad news.

"It's her gall bladder. She had an attack, at least that is what they call it, but what happens is gallstones fell into the bile duct and blocked it. It hurts like hell, and you feel like you are having a heart attack."

Chase thought for a second, and then asked shyly, "I know this is dumb, but is she going to die"

Jeremy put his arm around him, "No, she is having surgery at ten. If she does well, she could actually go home tonight."

"Don't they have to cut her open to get it out?"

"Sometimes, but mostly they cut about three holes, put a small camera in with a light and the surgeon brings his small tools in through the other holes. In no time at all, he sews it off, cuts it loose, and sucks it out one of the holes."

"Ouch! I hope I never have to do that. Can she live without her gall bladder?"

"Yes, she can. She will need to eat a lighter diet with less fat, but she will be fine. She had thought she was having a heart attack, and her husband called for the ambulance. I think I can sneak you in if you want to see her before surgery."

"Sure, but what do I say?" asked Chase as the elevator stopped.

"Just tell her you are praying for her, and you are confident she will be fine."

Jeremy checked the hall before leading Chase into an empty room. "Wait here and I will go see if the coast is clear, so to speak," he added with a wink.

Jeremy saw the father leaving the room while talking to the doctor who told him to go to the second floor waiting room, and he would send word out during the surgery as to how she was doing. Afterwards, he promised to come see Henry for an update. Henry nodded okay and punched the elevator button. Jeremy waited until Henry entered the car and the doors closed. He walked briskly to her pre-op room.

"Hey, Sally! How you doing, girl?" asked Jeremy with a sly grin as he went over to high five a pretty little black woman standing near Mrs. Allen.

"What are you up to you rascal? I haven't seen you in ages," she replied.

"Just being good, and it is so hard for me to do," he said with a grin.

"So why are you up here may I ask?" she asked tilting her head to the side and looking at the edge of her eyes anticipating something unusual.

"A friend of mine is a very good friend of Mrs. Allen. He just got here and wanted to pop in, and say a prayer with her. Would this be cool with you?"

She looked up at the wall clock and smiled sweetly, "Of course, we always have time for one more prayer. Send him on back."

Jeremy thanked her, took off down the hall, and returned with Chase. "Sally, this is Chase Fleming."

"I'm pleased to meet you. I need to go to my station for a moment. Chase, would you watch her for me?" She left the room as he nodded okay.

Jeremy walked over to the window and stared out below.

"Mrs. Allen?" asked Chase softly.

Though mildly sedated for the pain, she opened her eyes, focused, and smiled. "My goodness, Chase, how in the world did you know I was here?"

"I have a lot of friends in the hospital," he replied pointing at Jeremy at the window. Jeremy turned and gave her a little salute.

"I'm so glad to see you, but I do not feel so good," she replied nervously.

"Jeremy says they do this procedure all the time, and by nightfall you will be up and around. It's the modern world, you know," he blabbed on trying to think of what Brett would say.

"The pain started after midnight, and just became so painful I could hardly walk."

"Are you in pain now?" asked Chase as he took her hand.

"No, the medicine they gave me helped a lot. I'm just sore."

195

No words passed between them for a long twenty seconds. Jeremy turned from the windows thinking something must be wrong. Chase pulled a chair over to the bed and sat down. He looked back at the door and then to Mrs. Allen. "I have some news for you. Good news!" he said with a grin.

"Well, Chase, after the night I had last night, I would say I am ready for some good news. Tell me, please."

Chase's eyes filled with color as his mouth formed a tight smile. "Brett moved last night. I fell asleep next to his bed with my head rolled against his side. Jeremy and Paul came over, and they found me asleep, but Brett's right hand had moved across his chest to my head. He felt my hair," he added with a gleam to his eye.

"Oh, my, this is so wonderful. You must have been excited."

"Yes, but it is not the first time he has moved. From time to time, I can get him to close his fingers on my hand, or move his foot."

"He is telling us he is coming back!" she said excitedly.

"I believe so, too. It is so wonderful when he moves. I am still talking to him and holding his hand. His therapy is going well. I cannot wait for the day when he is really back."

"Me, too," she replied in a whisper.

"Am I staying too long?" he asked.

"Oh no, I have forty-five minutes until surgery. Please stay with me. They threw Henry out, and I was glad to get rid of him. He is upset because he missed breakfast, and here I lie fixing to get my gallbladder taken out. He is a pain in the you-know-what!" she laughed as did Chase.

"Tell me something about Brett I don't know," he begged.

Jan thought for a long moment, "I will tell you something funny since I feel like I need a laugh, too. When Brett was about seven, one of the teachers at the summer Vacation Bible School asked him if he would like to march in the next day carrying the American flag. She told him it was a great honor to carry the flag, and only a strong boy like Brett could do it. He was thrilled to accept the challenge.

"He wanted to pick out his clothes by himself, so I let him. It was hot day in early June, so he laid out a clean tee shirt, socks, underwear, his belt, and a new pair of khaki shorts I had bought him. They had zippers on all the pockets to hold everything inside a little boy might carry.

"He set the alarm clock, but must have knocked off the button and did not get up immediately. I had to knock on his door to wake him. When he realized he was behind his schedule he leaped out of bed, and quickly dressed. I could barely get him to eat some breakfast before he darted out the door, running all the way to the church.

"There were about one hundred and fifty kids already there. They lined up behind Brett as the teacher brought out the flagpole. She told him to put the bottom tip in his belt buckle, and hold the flag up and away from him. He was to march slowly into the church and walk to the podium. There would be a brass

196

stand, and he was to go there, and when she told him he was to put the flag in the stand and go sit down with his friends.

"Brett was so proud he actually saluted her as if he was in the army or something. He was so cute. The kids marched in behind him as he followed her instructions. The teacher waited at the podium next to Brett until the last child entered. She led them in a short prayer. Then she led the children in the Pledge of Allegiance. Brett held the flag smartly, with the bottom tip still touching his belt, or so he thought.

"With the pledge over, she whispered to Brett to put the flag in the brass stand and go sit down. He politely said he would. He looked down and found the stand, put the tip of the flag in it as the kids sat down. All eyes were still on the stage as to what the teacher was going to say next.

"Brett took a step backward to begin his way off the stage, and to his surprise the flag in the stand came with him. Puzzled, he took another step back, and the stand slid across the floor again as if he was a magnet and the flag metal. He moved a step left, then right, and the flag came with him. The kids began to giggle. The teacher told him to sit down. He whispered, "I can't!"

"The teacher snatched the edge of the unfurled flag, and pulled it aside so she could see if Brett had his foot on the stand. He didn't, but when her eyes followed the pole upwards, she grinned when she realized Brett had probably dressed so fast he forgot the most important zipper—his fly!

"He had left his main zipper down, and when he moved the butt of the pole from his belt downward, it went through his zipper and out the left pants leg of his shorts. She pulled the flagpole out as the kids laughed. Brett blushed, zipped up his pants, and walked to the back of the church and sat down alone.

"It took a few years before Brett could laugh, too, but it was one of the most beautiful child-like funny moments of his life. At least once a year I tell someone Brett's magnetic flag story."

Chase laughed as did Jeremy still standing by the window. Sally entered the room.

"Well, for a lady about to have her gall bladder removed, you certainly seem happy about it."

Jan squeezed Chase's hand, "Sally will take good care of me, and so you go home, and take good care of my son. I love you, Chase."

"I love you, too," he replied as bent down and kissed her hand.

Chase rode the elevator down laughing and grinning with Jeremy all the way. When they reached the main floor, the door opened, and just twenty feet across from the elevator stood Bill and Larry, the uncles. Chase and Jeremy exited the car without looking in their direction, but out of the corner of Chase's eye, he caught sight of the uncles.

"Shit!" he said interrupting Jeremy. "The uncles are here. Quick, get me out of here."

Jeremy glanced around. The uncles spotted them. "This way," he said.

Bill and Larry set their coffee cups down and started following them. Jeremy ran down a hall, made a quick turn, spotted a mop bucket, instantly turned over the bucket of water, and spread it with the mop.

"Run!" Jeremy said to Chase as they rushed to next exit.

Bill and Larry came down the hall sprinting. They reached the corner, hit the water, skidded as if they were on ice, and then tumbled on top of the other. Nurses ran to their aid.

Jeremy laughed as he watched Chase sprint to his car, now able to run faster than the uncles could. Chase grinned, too, when he pulled out of the parking lot with the uncles standing on the sidewalk shooting him the bird finger.

Chase pulled towards the main entrance of the hospital, and there he found a tall flagpole. He stopped, leaned out the window, and followed the pole with his eyes to the top. There he saw a beautiful gigantic American Flag. He started laughing as he recalled Jan's story of Brett and the magnetic flag. He laughed all the way home.

Later, he told Brett the story. He almost cried when Brett responded with the movement in the fingers on both his hands. When Jeremy called and said the surgery went well, Chase told Brett his mother was okay, and she would be fine. With great energy, Chase worked on Brett's therapy diligently. He knew in his heart Brett was making his way back to him.

Early the next morning, Chase slipped into the hospital again. Jeremy laughs and tells him if they keep these shenanigans up, he is going to have to get Chase an employee identification card. Chase had stopped at the market and brought in a vase of flowers. Jan was awake when he got there. Surgery had gone well.

"How are you this morning?" he said cheerfully as he pushed in on the door.

"Oh Chase, I'm fine. How are you?"

"Good. Did the surgery go well?"

"Oh yes, and during it I dreamed of Brett as a child the whole time. It was the most wonderful experience, except for removing my gall bladder."

"Do you hurt?"

"Not much, but if I'm good, they'll let me go home this afternoon. My heart rate was up a little during surgery so they kept me overnight. It is fine now, but I have to walk down the hall and back three times, and pee before they'll let me go."

"You look great. You're a tough old bird, Mrs. Allen."

"Chase, you are so funny, and you make me feel so good."

198

"My pleasure," he said as he leaned in and kissed her forehead. "You just do what the doctor said and get well."

"I will, but as much as I would like for you to stay, Henry is on the way up. You'd better get out of here. I will call you tomorrow after Henry goes to work."

"Okay. You take good care. See you soon."

Chase winked as he turned to go out the door. He spotted Henry and quickly turned the other way. Henry looked up, but only saw the back of Chase's head. He gave him an odd look of familiarity as he pushed the door into Jan's room.

"Hey, hon. How you feeling?" he asked.

"I'm good. I just have to pass some gas and walk some," she replied.

"Well, now. Who sent you these flowers?" he asked suspiciously as recalled the figure in the hall.

She did not reply.

"He was here, wasn't he? Bill and Larry told me they spotted him. Why in the hell was he here?" he yelled.

"He told me Brett was doing better," she said proudly.

"Yeah, right, how good could he be, living with that fruitcake?"

Before she could reply, Henry snatched up the vase, walked to the door, and threw them across the hall, smashing the vase and flowers into pieces. He then turned back to Jan. "If you ever talk to Chase again I'll hurt you!" He stomped out of the room and down the hall as Jan began to cry. Sally quickly came to her to make sure she was okay. Henry kicked the flowers as he walked down the hall, angrier than he had ever been in his life. He also stomped on the buds as if they were Chase's face.

FIFTEEN

Chase flipped off the alarm, yawned, and turned on the television. He felt his erection, but felt too sleepy and tired to do anything about it. He rolled out of bed with a groan, but needed to get in the shower quickly, or he was sure he would fall back into bed. He stumbled to the wall, and flipped on the overhead light out of habit. The sudden bright light made Brett's eyelids rapidly twitch. Chase stretched, petted the sleepy dogs on the end of the bed, and walked into the bathroom to turn the shower on and pee, missing the movement of Brett's eyes.

Brett's face wrinkled for several seconds and then relaxed. His heartbeat pulsed strongly just under the skin of his temples. Perspiration formed on his upper lip. He desperately wanted to open his eyes. He wanted to make a noise, move his legs, raise a hand, but his brain struggled to send the right signals to his nervous and muscular systems. He soon tired after reluctantly letting go of the effort, and drifted off. Moments later, he began dreaming.

Summer had finally arrived, he was sixteen, and head lifeguard at the camp. It felt good to be the boss, and Ryan Culkin surprised him by taking his Red Cross Junior Lifeguard training over the winter, applied, and received the job from the camp director. As usual, Brett arrived early to camp on the first day, and headed to the pool. Culkin also arrived early, put his things in the staff cabin, changed his clothes to his bathing suit, and headed to the pool as well.

Brett was retrieving some leaves from the bottom of the pool by diving down, and picking up about a dozen leaves at a time. He did not see Ryan dive in the water and swim up behind him. Just as Brett pushed off the bottom towards the surface and the ladder, Ryan reached out, grabbed Brett's Speedos, and yanked them down and off.

Still holding the leaves, Brett looked down to see what happened to his suit. Ryan spun him around, grabbed his penis, and pretended to masturbate him. Brett let go of the leaves, swam to surface, grabbed a breath of air, and dove underwater. Ryan, still clutching Brett's member, looked up and grinned. Brett laughed as tiny bubbles floated out of Ryan's teeth.

Ryan pulled him down so they were face-to-face, leaned in and kissed him. Brett kissed him back, but managed to yank Ryan's suit down and off as well. Together, they swam to the rope so they could stand up.

"You are a dirty dog!" laughed Brett.

"I had been thinking about an entrance like this all winter. My hand almost wore out from all the self-pumping I had to do. You look great as usual. Damn, you are so good looking," replied Ryan.

"Thanks. I cannot believe how big you are. You must be a foot taller since last summer. And you're almost as good looking as me!" laughed Brett as he splashed Ryan.

"I wish. You are awesome," replied Ryan as he reached over, grabbed Brett's penis, and gently pulled him into a long wet kiss. When they broke the kiss, Ryan smiled and said, "Brett, I've dreamed about you forever. I kept hoping you would call me. Come on, I need to do it right now!"

He anxiously pulled Brett from the water. They grabbed towels, moved over behind the storage shed, and fell down on the pile of hastily thrown towels. Ryan produced a condom and placed it on Brett's still growing erection. Moments later, he entered Ryan, scooted up until his knees were just under Ryan genitals, leaned over, and began French kissing him, as his hips began to pump.

When completed, Brett masturbated Ryan as they continued kissing. As they showered off with the water hose, Brett asked Ryan if he wanted to be his roommate.

"I'm sorry, dude, I already have a roommate," replied Ryan.

Brett look disappointed as his daydreams of night dreams with Ryan began fading away.

Ryan laughed, "Don't look so disappointed. I have already put all my stuff in your room. You really did not have a choice. I wanted to be with you and no one else."

"You're cruel," grinned Brett as he kissed him again.

The rest of the summer, they carefully plotted midnight rendezvous while doing their best to act convincingly straight during the day. Brett occasionally remembered two unusual events from that summer. The first one troubled him deeply.

During the final boys' week of the summer, a fourteen-year-old camper hit on him. At first, it was a buddy thing with Dane leaning into him, jumping on his back for a piggyback ride, or just talking as they walked through camp. From time to time, they wrestled in the water at the pool, and that is when Brett realized Dane wanted more than just being a friend, because he boldly slid his hand down and inside the front of Brett's swimsuit.

Brett quickly pulled his hand out, gave him a stern look, and then swam to the ladder and climbed out. He had gone in the water to cool off, so he put a towel over his lap and spent the rest of the day behind his dark sunglasses thinking.

Dane was easily the cutest camper of the summer with a flawless body. Brett surmised if he was a camper close to Dane's age they would be meeting every night for hot sex, but he was not a camper. He took the job of head lifeguard seriously and thus, he felt he was in a leadership role. He knew all the campers looked up to him—boys and girls alike. He also knew they often made him into a hero, but he knew better. He always felt the praise he received was only temporary for the week, and assumed that after the kids left the camp they soon forgot about him. Dane apparently had not forgotten.

201

Brett treated him coldly for the next few days until Dane confronted him. "What's wrong? I thought we were friends."

"We are friends. All the campers are my friends, but I cannot play favorites. I must be a good staffer to all," began Brett, feeling boringly stupid.

"Yeah, but I know better. I know you like me."

Brett sighed, "You're right, I like all the campers. You are a great guy, but you crossed the line in the pool. I am not that kind of guy. You could have gotten me fired. The staff might have tarred and feathered me, and whipped my butt right out of camp. I need this job. I want to go to college." Brett thought for a second and tried to sound sympathetic, "You need to be friends with boys your own age."

Dane said, "Your loss. You could have had me any way you wanted me."

"Pa-pardon?" stuttered Brett.

Dane winked at him, "You heard me. Don't worry, your secret is safe with me, but when I become a staffer, you and I are going to tango."

Dane blew him a kiss and walked off. Brett stood there shaken, and filled with worry. How did Dane know? Did he do the right thing by saying no to a boy who desperately wanted sex? Brett wondered, but in his heart, he knew it was okay with boys his age, but still he worried Dane would tell on him. He felt relieved when Dane went home on Saturday. He spent the weekend looking in the mirror wondering how Dane knew he was gay. He came away with no clues, but spent the next few days trying to walk like John Wayne while doing his best to be as butch as possible. He finally gave up feeling it made him look gay for sure.

At the end of the boys' camp, all the counselor staff went home, but the dishwashers and the lifeguards remained as a large church in Hendersonville rented out the camp for a week for their youth group. They placed the girls at one end of the camp with college students for counselors, and did the same on the other end of the camp for the boys. The only duty required was lifeguarding at the pool. His job was too easy compared to what he had been doing all summer. An hour of guarding in the morning, and only two hours in the afternoon left him bored.

Most of the boy campers were fifteen to eighteen years old and the staff twenty to twenty three. Though Brett was just sixteen, he liked this group of boys, as they were bigger—especially between the legs. He had to keep a towel over his Speedo to keep from showing his enlarged penis. Ryan just laughed at him as he was enjoying the view, too.

On the second night after their evening Bible classes, the staff hung out at the canteen eating and drinking sodas for a while. A handsome overseas student, sat down beside Brett. His name was George and he told Brett where he was from.

"You're from where?" asked Brett, not quite sure of the accent.

"Norway. It's in Europe?" George replied slyly.

"I know where it is, thank you very much."

"Just kidding, where are you from?" George asked.

"From here in North Carolina," said Brett. "Do you know where that is?"

Catching on to Brett's teasing he responded, "Do all the folks here talk so funny?"

Brett started to reply but stopped and grinned, "You're pulling my leg aren't you?"

George laughed, leaned in to Brett, and whispered, "I wish."

Brett almost fell off the bench he was sitting on. Brett gave him a practiced dumb look. "What?"

George winked at him. "You know what I mean."

Brett's smile fell from his face. "I'm afraid I'm tired, and I have to head to bed."

"Suit yourself," replied George matter-of-factly.

Brett did walk to his cabin, fell down on his bed, and tried to read a chapter in the novel he had been reading. So far, he had read the first page thirty times, and still could not recall a word of it. His mind kept replaying meeting George. He wondered how George knew about him, and feared others might know. Frightened, he tossed and turned all night.

The following night Brett was walking over to the canteen from the basketball court, but before he got there, George came up behind him.

"Hey good looking, what you got cooking?" asked George.

Brett faked a laugh. "Not much. How are you?"

"Bored, I am a Christian, but they are overtaxing my brain with all these religious seminars. All work and no play are just about to kill me," he replied with a laugh. "Listen, I need a favor. I was reading at the pool today and left my book. Could we go get it?"

"Sure." Brett hated himself for replying so quickly without thinking. His natural tendency to help the staff and campers, and so his answer just popped out.

"Great, let's go," replied George before Brett could stop him.

They walked up the path to the pool while the entire rest of the camp went to the canteen in the opposite direction. Brett knew they were alone, and wondered what George might have planned. He unlocked the gate and walked in with George.

"It should be over there on the other side," stated George as began walking around the pool.

Out of habit, Brett followed him, and wondered why he did. He already knew George could swim. George found the book on the bench, and turned back to Brett. Suddenly, he put his arms around him.

"Brett, you are the most gorgeous American I have ever met."

Shocked, Brett replied, "Uh, well thanks." He wished he could have said more, but his brain must have taken a lunch break.

George smiled but held him. Brett thought it felt great to be in the arms of an older man, at least a few years older. He smelled great and his arms felt warm and smooth against his skin.

George bravely but slowly moved his face closer to Brett's until he could kiss him. He kissed with a quick touch of his lips as if testing the waters. Brett's feet had also gone on break, too. Running away was no longer at option. George kissed him four more times, each time a bit longer. On the last one, he parted his mouth and pushed his tongue into Brett's mouth.

George's actions mesmerized Brett. He was so manly, strong, and handsome. Brett could feel George's penis swelling as did his own. George had him. He did not know how he knew, but he did. George suddenly broke the embrace, and pulled his shirt over his head revealing his muscular abs. Brett reached over and touched his chest. He played with George's hardened nipples. George reached down and felt Brett's genitals.

He leaned in and kissed Brett again, and then pulled his shirt over his head, unbuckled his pants, and in a flash Brett stood naked before him in the moonlight. George scrambled out of his clothes, and together they knelt down on the pile of clothes. Brett suddenly realized George's penis looked different from his. He thought about it a second while his brain went into overdrive. He soon figured it out. George was uncircumcised. He had never seen a penis like this before. It looked a bit funny to him, but as he played with it, the erection grew pushing the head out of the extra skin. Soon he held tightly to one of the biggest dicks he had ever seen. Brett easily succumbed to a bottom role, letting George lead the way. George began by spending quality time on Brett's erection and genitals. Gently he sucked first one ball, and then the other in his mouth, while slipping a finger into Brett's butt.

Then he straddled Brett and fed him his own genitals before leaning over him so Brett could take him in his mouth. After a while, he turned Brett over into a doggy position. Brett had rarely done it this way, as he preferred looking at the person he was making love to, but this time he went along with George's lead.

Brett knew George was even larger than Brice was—much larger. George slid back and retrieved a condom from his wallet. He used one hand to stroke Brett's genitals while he put a finger deep inside Brett, pressing his prostate. Brett's eyes lit up with excitement. Soon he added a second finger, and he told Brett to tighten and loosen his butt repeatedly. Brett just learned an easier way to relax, and he hoped it worked for the big tool approaching him.

Gently George pushed in a little, Brett repeated the tightening, and then George suddenly pushed in deeper, and then a bit more. No one had ever been so far inside him. His throbbing prostate protested under the pressure with great excitement. His penis instantly became larger than ever before. Even the hair on his neck stood up as if charged with static. He groaned with pleasure as George

204

placed his warms hands on the sides of Brett's hips. Slowly and steadily, George went to work. Brett could feel him deep inside, and the pleasure was so great he prayed it would never stop.

By the time George exploded, Brett felt drenched with George's sweat, and he loved the smell of him. George rolled him over and feverously went to work on Brett's erection until he managed to squirt every last drop out of Brett.

Later that night, Ryan wanted sex, but Brett said no, but he did allow Ryan to cuddle up with him. In his arms was Ryan, but his mind and heart wished he were with George. He had fallen in love with Bryce as a boy, but as a young man, he just experienced his first grownup love with a real man.

Unlike the previous week when he could not wait for Dane to leave, he never wanted George to leave, but the end of the week and the summer came all too soon. Saying good-bye to George became difficult, because later that day he was flying back to Norway, and Brett would never see him again.

George became one of his favorite dreams for the rest of his life, and his butt ached and twitched just to think about him.

Two weeks after recovering from her gallbladder surgery, Jan told Henry she was going grocery shopping. Her plan was to see her son again. Henry did not think much of it until he got up to get another beer from the refrigerator and spotted her grocery list on the table. He snatched it up, grabbed his truck keys, and sped off after her. He knew she drove slow and was only a few blocks ahead of him.

His tires spun rocks as he turned onto McDowell Street. He crested the top of the hill, and saw her blue car just at the top of the next hill waiting on the red light. The light turned green, and she should have turned right to the grocery store, but she turned left. He was about fifty yards back and let off the gas to avoid getting too close as he, too, made the left turn. He followed her for several miles, realizing she was going to see Brett.

When she turned onto Brett's street, he stopped at the intersection, and watched her turn into Brett's driveway. He was angry she lied to him, but he held his anger for now, as he turned his truck around and went back to the house.

Chase was waiting for her at the door as she came up the sidewalk to the front steps. "My goodness, you're looking good today. Mrs. Allen has recovered very well from surgery," he added with a big smile as if telling the whole neighborhood.

"Yep, they cannot keep a good old broad down," she replied with a grin. He held the door open, and she stepped in and gave him a hug. "I missed your hugs, Chase. I missed talking to you."

"I missed you, too. Come on in. I have something to show you," said Chase as he led her down the hall to Brett's room.

She went immediately to her son, leaned over, and kissed him on the cheek. "He looks good," she stated with tearful eyes. "It has been so long since I have seen him. How is he doing?"

"Great. Come sit down by his bed, and hold his hand for a second." Chase led her around to the far side of the bed, and held her chair for her.

"How are you doing?" she asked Chase. "Is taking care of Brett getting too hard for you?"

"No, well, sometimes," he replied. "I do not mind at all taking care of him, but sometimes when I am alone with him for an entire weekend, I get a little lonely, but being back at work has helped. My sales are up, and I won the award for salesperson of the month a few weeks ago. I have never won anything in my life, and it was a thrill."

"Way to go, I am very proud of you," she replied with wink.

"Okay, watch this," Chase removed the sheet covering Brett's bare feet. "Do you remember how the doctor could touch his feet and he would not move?"

"Yes, of course, but as a young boy, Brett was very ticklish, especially his feet," she replied.

Chase grinned and picked up a small feather at the foot of the bed and stroked the tip of it back and forth across Brett's foot. Suddenly, Brett's toes flexed and the knuckle of a toe popped.

Jan gasped, "Oh my goodness, he moved!" She put her hands to her chest as if the sudden breath hurt.

Chase looked up at her and winked. "There's more. This time, watch his fingers when I tickle his foot."

Jan quickly looked down at Brett's left hand as Chase waved the feather back and forth. Brett's toes moved a few times, and so did the fingers on his hand. "Oh, this is so exciting. Chase, you have done so well with him. It just shows you that medicine and doctors are important, but there is nothing more powerful than the healing power of love."

Chase stopped torturing Brett with the feather, and replaced the sheet over Brett's feet. "I better not do it anymore or he is liable to slap me!"

She laughed suddenly, "You are so funny."

"I have one more for you," replied Chase as he pulled the sheet down from Brett's chest, exposing his soft tender tummy. Chase hesitated for a second, then leaned over and tenderly kissed Brett's belly button. Brett's fingers in the left hand moved.

"You are like a magician, commanding him to move!" she exclaimed.

"Shh," he whispered as he kissed Brett's belly several more times, and then laid his head down along Brett's left side. Chase looked up at her face, and put a finger to his lips indicating for her to be quiet.

206

Moments later Chase pointed to the other side of his head. Curious, Jan slowly rose and abruptly caught her breath as she saw Brett's right hand move to Chase's hair as it lay gently on his head. Tears slowly descended her cheeks. She reached out and held on to Chase's hand and hesitantly, but with brave determination, she reached over and put her fingers in Brett's hand. Moments later Brett closed his hand. Her heart leaped with joy and excitement.

"He is coming back, isn't he?" she asked with confidence.

"Yes ma'am, he is. I just know it. His heart is strong, his breathing is good, and I am exercising his joints and muscles four times a day and they, too, are getting stronger He now has bulging arm and leg muscles."

Chase pulled away, stood up, and put his arm around Jan giving her a little hug as she stood there with her son holding her hand. Chase encouraged her to sit back down.

"Jan, tell Brett and I another story about him growing up. I always love to hear your stories, and I am sure Brett does, too."

"Well, to be honest I have been thinking of this next story while I was recuperating. I couldn't wait to tell it to you." She paused and smiled, "In the sixth grade, Brett became a school patrol boy. Along with about fifteen boys, they were in charge of making sure the school children crossed the intersections on the way to school safely. Soon he became a sergeant, then a lieutenant, and in just under ninety days, he had impressed the safety leader so much she made him captain over all the boys.

"There were two policewomen who each handled two big intersections. One of the women had to take maternity leave as she came close to the birth of her first child. The school could not find anyone to take her place, and so the safety leader put Brett in charge of this adult job. This important task excited Brett. I admit I worried for his safety, but I did not let on. I told him I was sure he would do a good job. He had to get up a little earlier for over two months while he covered for her.

"On the first day of every month, the children brought all the newspapers they saved for the library paper drive. They would sell the recycled newspapers for cash to buy books. By this time, Brett was growing like a weed. He grew almost an inch a month for three straight months. Sadly, our money was tight, so his pants legs just kept creeping up his legs. Some of the kids called him 'high-water,' and that was a little cruel. However, he never complained, as he knew the family had little extra cash for new pants.

"One day as the kids brought the papers in, it started to rain. Brett put on his bright yellow patrol raincoat, and bravely stood in the intersection stopping traffic so the kids could hurriedly make their way to school and out of the rain. One of the last kids to cross was a girl named Wanda. She had about fourteen-inch stack of papers in her arms. She crossed the walk lane, and

accidentally spilled the papers in the middle of the road. Brett quickly bent over to help her, and immediately heard the sound of a big rip.

"He helped her up, grabbed the newspapers, and together, they hurried across the street so the traffic could keep moving. After she moved on a little, Brett reached inside his raincoat and felt the back of his pants. They had split from his belt all the way to his crotch.

"When his duty time was over, he went to the principal's office and told the secretary what had happen. She had him show her, thinking she might be able to mend them but the hole was so big she could not. She suggested he call his parents to come to his rescue with another pair of jeans.

"Brett knew his dad would be asleep, as he worked nights, so he reluctantly called him. Henry grumbled but dressed, found a pair of jeans, and brought them to the school. Brett quickly changed and headed off to class.

"At recess, Brett was swinging on the jungle gym bars while playing with his friends. He liked to swing upside down while hanging with his legs bent over the bar. He would dismount by swinging quickly doing a slow back flip, spinning in the air and landing perfectly. It always scared me to death, but he did it with the flair of an Olympic gymnast. I have a picture of him in the air in the scrapbook.

"When he heard the teacher blow the whistle sounding the end of recess, Brett quickly took a couple of practice swings, and must have swung pretty hard as the teacher said he went higher than ever before. As he rotated, he realized he was not going to score a ten on this landing, so he swung his arms to slow his rotation, and landed with his legs spread a bit wide and bent to cushion his fall.

"I am sure you have guessed. The moment his feet hit the ground, his pants split again! Brett felt his behind, and found another big rip in his pants, making it twice in the same day. He had reached a new level of embarrassment. He whispered to the teacher his predicament, so she sent him on to the principal's office.

"The secretary laughed heartily when he walked in, guessing the problem. He spun around so she could see. His white underwear was hanging through the big crack in his pants. She fell back in her chair laughing as she handed him the phone.

"Brett called his dad again. Henry grumbled, but got out of bed once more and took him another pair of jeans. Brett quickly changed and went to class. At just after 1:00 P.M., the bell rang and first graders left early to go home. Brett also left class early, and quickly road his bike to his intersection to help the first graders across the street. It was still raining, so when he jumped on his bike to head back to school, his right foot slipped off the wet bike peddles. Instantly, he heard the unmistakable sound of his pants ripping—again!

"He had his raincoat on and once more reached in and felt the big rip. He walked into the Principal's office, and this time the secretary became

208

unglued as she tried to cover her mouth to keep from laughing and just handed him the phone.

"Brett waited for his dad to answer, but Henry took a little longer before picking up the phone. He told Brett he had no more pants to bring him, and he would just have to tough it out. Sadly, Brett hung up the phone and returned to his last two classes of the day still wearing his raincoat so the kids could not see the big rip in his pants!

"When he got home at three o'clock, Henry was waiting for him. Brett assumed he was going to get a big beating for destroying three pairs of jeans, but Henry took one look at the pants legs, which were at least six inches higher than his tennis shoes and realized the problem. He led Brett to the car, and they drove to the Belk Department Store. Henry brought Brett five new pairs of jeans, and he made sure they not only fit, but he would have room to grow in the butt as well as the legs."

Chase laughed, "That must have been a sight—busting his pants three times in the same day. I wish I would have been there and seen that!"

"Brett never thought it was funny, but I did. I reminded him of this story a few years ago, and I caught him laughing as well. At the end of the school year, the city awarded Brett the Patrol Boy of the Year Award. He got his picture in the newspaper, and they allowed him to keep his badge. He was on the top of the world, and to my knowledge he has never, ever, split his pants again!"

They both laughed repeatedly, but reluctantly, Jan looked at her watch and realized it was time for her to go. She bent over the bed and kissed Brett's cheek, brushed his hair with her fingers, squeezed his hand one more time, walked around the bed gently touching his feet through the sheet, and then gave Chase a big hug. "I enjoyed my visit so much today. You are doing a great job. I will look forward to seeing what new magical trick you come up with next time. I love the both of you very much. I will sneak away again tomorrow," she said with a bit of sadness in her eyes.

"We both look forward to your visits, so you come any time. If I am at work, I have left instructions with the nurse to allow you in."

He watched in the doorway as she drove away. He tried to imagine Brett as a child, and wished he had more pictures of him from his childhood. He walked down the hall to Brett's dresser. He kept a fancy box on the top of it where he kept cuff links, watches, and rings. Chase opened it and in the bottom, he pulled out the short stack of pictures Brett kept there. He found a few old pictures, and one he had never noticed before—the picture of Brett accepting his school patrol boy award. He smiled warmly before returning the pictures, and grabbing the clipboard to write down the monitoring numbers, and log in Jan's visit, just in case Brett became sick with a cold or something.

209

Jan entered the house carrying a few bags of groceries and set them on the table. The house was quiet and no sign of Henry though his truck was in the drive. Just as she began to put the food away, Henry came up behind her carrying the grocery list.

"You left the list on the table!" he said suddenly.

She flinched not realizing he was there, "Oh, I wondered what happen to it. I thought it was in my purse. I tried to recall everything on the list."

"I followed you trying to catch up with you to give you the list, but you did not go to the store, at least not first. Where did you go?" he asked in an accusatory tone.

Jan sensed he knew the answer, so she boldly replied, "I went to see our son."

"You went over to Brett's house where that filthy faggot is trespassing! How dare you!" he yelled as slapped her hard across the face, knocking her to the floor.

"Get up! Get up I say!" he screamed.

Jan struggled to her feet while holding the burning red mark on her face. The moment she turned to face him, he hit her again. She fell to her knees once more. Still weak from her recent surgery it took her a moment to catch her breath. Her eyes searched the counter for something to stop him with.

"Get up, bitch!" he yelled.

Slowly, Jan got up. This time she did not face him, but spotted the knife rack on the counter by the sink. She snatched the largest knife, and spun around. "If you touch me again, I'll cut you," she said quickly.

Henry looked at the knife, and laughed mockingly, "Yeah, and if you do I'll slice you up like deer meat." He took a step in her direction, but she swung the blade warning him to stay away.

"Okay, okay," he said as he stepped back.

Jan still held the knife in front of her. "Stay away from me," she warned, as tears fell from her eyes.

"Okay, you're right, I'm sorry," he replied as he faked turning away, and then in a flash, he spun around grabbing the hand holding knife. They struggled, he slapped her with his free hand, she stumbled, and together they fell to the floor with a huge thud.

The house fell silent until Henry heard the sound of Jan's last breath leaving her body. He rolled off her, immediately saw her blouse covered in blood. He looked at his own body and found no wounds, but his hands were bloody. The knife had entered Jan's body below her stomach in an upward position. He guessed the tip of the knife had pierced her heart. She was dead with her eyes locked open staring at the ceiling.

It had happened so fast Henry could hardly believe the scene across from him. He had not heard his neighbors Sally and Tom enter the front door coming to the aid of Jan's screams. Henry turned his head as Sally covered her mouth and gasped.

210

"You killed her!" she exclaimed.

Tom turned his wife away from the scene, "Call 911, honey."

Sally looked up at her husband's reassuring face, and instantly felt thankful nothing like this would ever happen between her and Tom. She walked to the phone by the television and dialed the number.

Tom felt Jan's neck for a pulse though she bled out quickly. Henry sat in the growing pool of blood in disbelief. He started to cry. He covered his tears with his bloody hands and sobbed. Tom returned to his wife and held her as she nervously shook with fear, while they agonizingly waited for the police and ambulance.

Chase enjoyed the visit from Jan so much he found himself full of energy. He turned up the radio and began cleaning the house. He threw out old newspapers recalling the story of the split pants and the paper drive at Brett's old elementary school, and mopped the floors. He then vacuumed the carpet, took out the trash, dusted the furniture, and put some dirty clothes in the laundry, while singing and dancing to the various hits playing on the radio.

By suppertime, he found himself starved and went to the refrigerator to find something to eat. He spotted the pot of baked spaghetti Jeremy brought over. He spooned out a plate full, set it in the microwave, and hit the buttons to warm it up. He fed the dogs, and then fixed some sweet tea, turned on the television, and walked out the door to the mailbox to retrieve the mail.

He returned to the house while thumbing through the mail. He set the mail down and brought his warmed food to the table. He sat down and took his first bite as the commercial ended. The news reporter began telling the story of a man arrested today for killing his wife. Chase took a second bite as the video of the murder scene began to play.

Suddenly, he dropped his fork to the table missing the plate and scattering food onto the white table he had just cleaned. He watched in horror as the deputies led Henry away in handcuffs, and then the television screened filled with a picture of Jan taken from a frame in Brett's old room in her house. Chase covered his mouth. He could not believe what he was hearing and seeing.

More video began to play showing the coroner pushing a gurney with a body completely covered with a sheet. He could see some blood as the video ran out, and the reporter said the neighbors heard Henry yelling at his wife, and they found him in a pool of blood by the side of her spent body.

Suddenly, the phone rang causing Chase to flinch. Slowly he got up, walked to the phone, and picked it up. "Hello?"

"Did you see the news?" asked Jeremy.

"Yes, I just did."

"I'm so sorry, Chase. She was a wonderful woman, married to a bitch of a man. I am at work. Paul is on the way to your house, and I'll be there in an hour."

"Okay, thank you," was all Chase could mumble.

"Hang in there, buddy. Brett needs you now more than ever. You are his only family. You are his partner. You are his lover. Keep focused on the goal. You are doing a great job with Brett. I will see you soon. I love you," added Jeremy, desperately trying to find the right words to say.

"I love you, too," Chase whispered before returning the receiver to the phone. He turned around with his back to the side of the refrigerator. Slowly, he slid down to the floors, pulled his knees to his chest, and sobbed uncontrollably until Paul arrived.

He told Paul about the afternoon visit by Jan, and what a wonderful time they had. He sobbed again. Jeremy and Paul stayed through the night. He prayed Jan would be safe and happy in heaven, and he begged her to help him with Brett. He knew she would. He took comfort in knowing she would never have to see Henry again, but still, he knew he would miss her, and the wonderful stories she told him of her son Brett.

SIXTEEN

It had been several weeks since Jan's death. After discussing it with Jeremy and Paul, Chase decided not to tell Brett about her passing. His first priority was to continue to help Brett on his journey back, and he wouldn't take a chance on anything that might cause him a setback. Sometimes, days passed with no movement at all, but just when Chase was about to give up, Brett would move a foot or a hand, returning Chase's optimism.

Brett reacted to the bright light in the early mornings as Chase dressed for work. The day nurse would check Brett's vitals, and then open the blinds for the day. Once she turned the overhead light off, leaving only the reading lamp on, she began reading her book in the corner. In the still of the morning, Brett would begin to dream.

Brett loved high school. He knew everybody and everybody knew him, but no one knew he was gay. At this stage of his life, he knew nothing about the word gay or homosexual. For now, he knew he felt different, but he expected to change once he had sex with a woman. He did not believe he was queer, just very horny, and felt one day he would grow out of his male sexual tendencies. He never dated in high school, using the excuse he had to work and had no money to do so, both of which were true. He did not attend his prom for the same reasons.

During lunch one day in the cafeteria, a new student asked if he could sit at Brett's table. Brett said yes without looking up, but as Terry sat down, Brett began studying his features. Terry was about five feet ten inches while Brett was well over six feet. He had dark brown hair with deep chocolate eyes. His eyes stood out because of his eyebrows. Brett had never known a boy to have such perfectly straight eyebrows, far better than most of the best looking girls in his school. At least once a week, Terry's older sister plucked his eyebrows.

His naturally tanned, yet smooth as silk skin made Terry's white teeth simply sparkle like a toothpaste television commercial. Brett thought Terry could easily have passed as an Italian or Spaniard. He watched Terry carefully, while noting his soft hands and perfect nails. Brett thought Terry was easily the most beautiful boy in high school.

"My name is Terry Robinson. I'm pleased to meet you," he added as he reached over and shook Brett's hand.

"I'm Brett Allen," began Brett, "are you new here?"

"Yes, just moved in from Miami. My Dad works at the air base. He is in the Air Force, so I guess I'm in the military as well," he added with a grin.

Brett asked, "How so?"

213

"Well, every few years we up and move to a new base somewhere in the world."

"Oh, that sounds like fun," added Brett.

"Well, it can be, but you have to say goodbye to old friends and start finding new ones. I don't have a single friend left from my early years."

Brett grinned, "Our last names sound like an attorney firm, don't you think? You know, Allen and Robinson."

Terry laughed. Brett was smitten. "Yes, I guess so. Do they have a tennis team at this school?"

"Yes, we do, but I don't know much about them. The players' families are all members of the Country Club. That is a little too rich for me."

"Probably me, too, but I played a lot at my last school in Florida. Would you like to play a game after school?" he asked hopefully.

"Me? Are you kidding? You could whip my butt even if I used two tennis rackets!" laughed Brett.

"Come on, you can't be that bad," pleaded Terry.

"Oh yes I can, but yes, I will play you, but you cannot tell anyone you beat me a hundred to one."

Terry laughed, "They don't keep score that way, but I promise." They stopped as they heard the school bell ring. "Whoops got to run. My next class is on the freaking fourth floor. I will see you after school," said Terry as he quickly stood up, grabbed his tray, and left for class.

"See you later," replied Brett as he got up as well. Brett watched Terry's butt all the way out of the cafeteria. Later that night, he would recall the memory as needed between the sheets.

Brett waited nervously for Terry to arrive at the court. So far, no one else was playing, and he was hoping it would stay that way. He turned around and saw Terry waving at him as he came across the far court to the bench where Brett sat. Terry was dressed in an all white tennis shirt and shorts. He even had white tennis shoes on.

Brett looked down at his clothes as if he had forgotten what he had worn all day: a light blue button-down collar oxford shirt, navy blue slacks, and black tennis shoes. He had taken gym last year and in his high school, you only had to take it once. He had no gym clothes at school.

"Hey, dude," said Terry as he came up to him. "Are you ready to play?"

Brett stood up, "Well, when I said yes I forgot I had no gym clothes at school. This is all I have."

Terry set his racket bag down, and zipped open his large sports bag. "No problem, I have everything you need." He pulled out a pair of shorts and a shirt. "Here put these on," he said as he handed the clothes to Brett.

"Out here?"

Terry turned and looked around. A fifteen-foot fence along with eight-foot tall boxwood hedges surrounded the entire tennis courts. They were alone. "I think you are safe here. Come on, strip!" exclaimed Terry as he reached over and began undoing Brett's shirt.

Brett chuckled and blushed, "Okay, but if we get arrested for indecent exposure I am going to give you a noogie!" With his shirt off, Brett dropped his pants, hoping he had no sign of a beginning erection as he stood before Terry wearing only his tight cotton briefs.

"Put these shorts on before we get arrested, and what the hell is a noogie?" asked Terry.

Brett stepped into the shorts and pulled them up. They were a perfect fit because though he was tall he was still skinny. "You don't know what a noogie is? Well, you grab your friend in a head lock, and pretend to rub your knuckles hard into their scalp until they give up!" He pulled the tennis shirt over his head and looked over at Terry. The bottom of the shirt was too short for his tall frame. He looked like he was wearing a girl's midriff blouse.

Terry laughed, "Well, the shirt is short a little. Who cares? I think you look cute," Terry bellowed.

Brett grabbed him and gave him a noogie. "Now you know what a noogie is!"

"Ouch, come on, let's play," said Terry as he broke away laughing and grabbed two rackets, handing Brett his.

They warmed up by volleying back and forth a few times. Brett was amazed at how good Terry was. He smacked the ball forehand, backhand, and overhead with great precision. He never hit it out of bounds. His serves just missed the tip of the net, and always fell in the right square. Brett, on the other hand, felt amazed when his ball went over the net and stayed in bounds.

Terry was patient, showing Brett how to hold the racket correctly. He showed him how to use the strings to hit the ball with a top or bottom spin, and even a curved ball. He wisely decided not to play a single game, but together they had a fun afternoon as Terry continued coaching Brett.

For the next few weeks, they saw each other before and after school, during lunch, and even at the morning break. During the second month of their new friendship, it rained every day for a week. Brett soon discovered Terry could play chess as well. Brett brought his miniature set to school so they could play whenever they had a chance. Brett could beat Terry in chess, but he knew he would never be a match for Terry in tennis.

Brett talked Terry into joining the chess club because all the rest of the members he declared boring compared to Terry. Two weeks later, they traveled to Raleigh for a chess match. Brett and Terry roomed together in the motel. The cheap hotel only had one double bed, but they stripped down to their underwear

and settled down to sleep. Terry went right to sleep, but Brett could not. His mind replayed his view of Terry undressing over and over again.

His nostrils inhaled Terry's wonderful masculine scent. He rolled on his side looking at Terry's back. The curtains allowed a little bit of the streetlight into the room. Brett could see the soft brown strands of Terry's hair. He moved his face slightly closer until he could smell the Pantene shampoo that Terry's used. His erection began growing a bit larger and poking at his waistband.

Terry felt warm and pushed the cover off his upper torso. Brett studied his back, almost drooling over his beautiful tanned skin. He felt Terry was by far the cleanest friend he had ever met. His body seemed to shine even in the darken room.

Brett wished he could reach out and feel the warm skin of his friend, but way too afraid to do so. He never had a hint Terry might be like him, but he was always friendly to Brett, tousling his hair, punching his arm, leaning into him when they found something funny, bear hugging him, and even slapping his butt from time to time. Terry talked mostly about girls and their knockers, and Brett joined in the trash talk, though he did not feel the same way.

Brett slipped his hand into his underwear and quietly began playing with his penis. His erection grew until it reached way beyond his waistband. He wanted to pick up speed, but with Terry in bed with him, he decided he best not.

Suddenly, turned from laying on his left side, to rolling first on his back and then on over to his right side, and placing the side of his face on Brett's bare shoulder before finishing by bringing his left arm over Brett's bare chest.

Brett laid there frozen in both delight and fear. His best friend, his good-looking friend, continued to sleep with his warm tender lips just inches from his, and he didn't know what he should do. Terry moved his hand until the open palm lay tightly against Brett's ribs. Brett's hand was still inside his underwear. He tested his new situation by playing with his penis just a little to see if Terry would move or wake up.

Terry continued to sleep. Brett noticed Terry's tiny nostrils moved in and out with each breath. He turned his face until Terry's soft strands of hair touched his face. Brett's erection continued to grow.

Terry suddenly set up and looked down at Brett. He pulled the sheet back as he sat up, saw Brett's penis sticking out the top of his white briefs, and Brett's hand slowly masturbating it.

"I take it you're horny, too? I cannot sleep either. Let's race!" exclaimed Terry.

"What?"

"You heard me, strip, and let's pound the sausage!" laughed Terry.

To Brett's delight, Terry hooked his thumbs into his waistband, lifted his butt, and jerked his underwear all the way off. Brett had seen his penis from time to time in the shower, but this time Terry's tool was rapidly growing. Brett remained frozen wondering what to do next.

216

"Get 'em off!" he demanded as he straddled Brett's legs, reached up, and practically tore Brett's underwear down. Terry leaned over, pulled the briefs over Brett's toes, and threw them against the curtain. He then lay down beside Brett with his left arm against Brett's chest and wrapped his fingers around his erection.

"Loser has to go get the tissues," stated Terry. "On your mark, get set, go!"

Terry began pumping himself rapidly. Brett did not move as the shock of his best friend's erection overwhelmed him.

"What are you pee shy?" asked Terry. "Whoops, I mean pounding the sausage shy?" laughed Terry.

"Oh, no, I can beat you," said Brett as he picked up his speed as well.

Together, they made the bed vibrate as they pumped faster and faster. Terry laid his free hand on Brett's soft tummy. Brett stared at Terry's penis, and he hoped Terry was staring at his. Terry's legs began to jump around until he put his leg over Brett's leg.

Brett felt Terry just made a big mistake because the touch of Terry's hot vibrating leg on his own caused Brett to explode all over his chest.

"Damn," grunted Terry as he closed his eyes and concentrated on his work until Brett saw and felt Terry's toes flex first downward and then up as he, too, exploded.

Brett loved watching the hot sperm leap out like a lava flow explosion. It went way up his chest. When he finished, Terry turned his face towards Brett. "You won. I will get the tissues."

"No," replied Brett, "I won, but don't move. You have a glob of sperm on your face. I will get tissues." Brett started laughing.

"Do I? Oh my, that was so much fun! Okay, hurry up. I don't want to taste my sperm. It is so hot and warm on your skin. The walls in our rental house are so thin I can never beat off when I want to."

Brett quickly cleaned his chest free of the sperm, and then brought a handful of tissues to the bed. He took a couple and wiped Terry's face clean. "That's better. I don't think I could look at you with a glob of jizz on your face," he said with a laugh.

Terry took the rest of the tissues and wiped himself up.

"I've got to pee," said Brett as he returned to the bathroom.

"Me, too, I have to pee badly," replied Terry as he jumped up, tossing the tissues in the trashcan.

Brett had started peeing into the toilet with a slight erection. "Move over," demanded Terry with a slight elbow to Brett's ribs. Terry began peeing beside him and finished before Brett did.

"Okay, now we can sleep," declared Terry as he headed back to bed in the nude.

217

Brett drank a glass of water, wondering if anything else would happen. If not, he knew he could replay the masturbating video in his head repeatedly for the rest of the night or even his entire life. He, too, remained naked and slid in the bed. They were too hot for covers for a while, but later, Brett reluctantly covered Terry's beautiful nude body with the sheet.

The next night Brett felt great disappointment when Terry went promptly to sleep after a long day of the tournament. He played with himself for a while, but feeling tired he soon drifted off to sleep. Brett began to dream of the previous night as well as other episodes of sex during his life. Terry remained asleep on his back.

Brett's erection pushed up through his waistband as he turned towards Terry sliding an arm across Terry's lower belly. Together, they remained a sleep. Later, Brett felt a little chill and moved closer to Terry with his body touching his, especially the tip of his penis, which instantly grew harder. His arm pulled back until his open palm lay on top of Terry's penis beneath the white briefs.

Though asleep, Brett loved to cuddle and drifted deeper into his sleep. The boys remained this way for over an hour when Terry's eyes suddenly opened. He looked to his right and smelled Brett's hair, and then he looked down his side and saw Brett's erection touching his bare side.

Instantly, he pushed Brett over and rolled out of bed. "Get off me, man!"

Brett rolled onto his back, "What?"

"You heard me. You were fondling me. I ain't a woman you fool. I ain't no queer either!" yelled Terry.

"I'm sorry. I was asleep," replied Brett thinking as fast as he could. Then he lied, "I was dreaming about Jennifer Fallon. Sorry, dude."

"You slept with Jennifer?" asked Terry.

Brett knew he was testing him, "Yes, but it was in the ninth grade. Her teats are much nicer now," he added hoping to convince Terry.

"Oh, well, go back to sleep. I'll sleep on the floor," stated Terry as he snatched his pillow and pulled the bedspread to the floor.

Brett remained in shock and did not know what else to say. He hoped he had convinced Terry of his innocence. He slept little for the rest of the night.

The next day the school group traveled home after the morning final matches. His school won, but Brett felt no elation. He received the verdict on his innocence all too soon, as Terry gave him the cold-shoulder treatment all day. Brett sat in the back of the van while Terry sat in the front. They ate at McDonalds, but Terry sat with the girls while Brett ate alone.

Brett hoped things would return to normal the following week, but they did not. Brett tried a few times to talk to Terry, but Terry instantly gave him a mean 'get lost' look that stunned him. He became so depressed his grades began to suffer. He wondered if Terry told any of his friends, knowing that if he did, he would now become the school's official faggot. He had seen what some of the

school's bullies did to sissy boys by tripping them as they walked by, knocking their books down, and one boy had his head stuffed in a toilet. The school staff did nothing to help these poor boys.

Since reaching high school, Brett usually walked home alone to save his family the bus fare. One section of the road home ran along an undeveloped small forest. Many high school boys met in the woods to smoke or drink beer, but Brett did his best to stay out of the forest. There was one boy, Mark Sexton, who had failed at least two grades, and quickly became the biggest bully of this group. They were not the same as the upper income bullies in school, but rather closer to being an organized gang of rednecks. Brett was sixteen while Mark was closer to nineteen.

Brett had seen Mark grab and intimidate other walkers into giving up their lunch money. He had seen Mark put his hand down the front of a girl's blouse, and watched as he put his probing fingers under a girl's dress. Everybody talked about him, and did their best to stay away from him. Brett always picked up his pace to just under a sprint as he passed by the forest. More than once, he heard Mark call at him to stop, but he always pretended not to hear and rushed on.

Mark began watching Brett when he passed by in the hall at school. Once he blew Brett a mocking kiss, causing Brett to fear Mark pinned him for being queer. On another occasion when the entire student body was pushing their way into the school's gym for a pep rally, Brett felt someone place a hand on his buttocks and squeeze. He was not sure who it was, so he kept moving, but a second later, they did it again. He turned and found Mark immediately behind him as the crowd Chinese shuffle-stepped their way into the gym. Because they were so crowded, no one could see his hands. When he turned around, Mark allowed his hands to squeeze Brett's genitals.

Alarmed, Brett quickly turned back around and tried to hurry through the crowd. He could hear Mark laughing as he moved away. He prayed no one saw Mark touched his privates, and more importantly, that Brett failed to push Mark away.

He had stayed late at school finishing an article for the school paper. The buses were gone, and the roads empty of students as he made his way down the road. When he reached the forest, he picked up speed as usual, but Mark waited for him behind a tree. Just as Brett neared the final fifty-feet, Mark leaped out from the tree and faced him. Brett froze in his tracks.

"Hey," began Mark. Brett noted he was at least four inches taller, and possessed huge bulging biceps. Compared to Mark's, Brett felt his bicep muscles looked like bad mosquito bites.

"Uh, hey," replied Brett fearfully.

"Did you like my squeeze the other day?" asked Mark sarcastically.

"No," replied Brett quietly.

219

"Man, you have some big balls. Is everything else big down there?"

Brett felt stunned by the question and did not know what to say, "I don't know."

"I'm betting they are. Come on, I want to show you something," ordered Mark as he put his strong arm around Brett's neck and pulled him to the forest.

They walked down a small trail about a hundred feet from the road. Mark stopped walking and turned Brett to face him. He helped Brett set down his book bag. He stared into Brett's eyes, which were darting in many directions to keep from looking at Mark. Mark was not good looking, in Brett's view, and he had an ugly scar down one side of his face. Rumors around school told the story of a knife fight he won, but received a slice from a knife by a guy he later killed.

"You are the cutest thing in this school," said Mark.

Brett nearly wet his pants. In his wildest fits of imagination, he would never have guessed Mark liked guys.

"Your ass is round like small melons. I just loved squeezing them. Where did you get those big balls?"

"I don't know," replied Brett nervously. "At the big ball store I guess."

Mark smiled as he began unbuttoning Brett's shirt. Once opened he began running his hands over Brett's soft and tender flesh. He slightly pinched one of his nipples until it grew hard. He then pulled Brett's shirt off and unbuckled his jeans. He reached in and tenderly fondled his balls.

"Hmmm, boy, these feel good. See I told you they were huge," said Mark with a grin.

Brett remained frozen. He never feared becoming naked, but he did fear Mark might hurt him. Mark slid Brett's pants down, and told Brett to kick off his shoes and step out of them. Brett did. Mark unbuckled his pants, pulled his penis out, and began playing with himself. Brett only glanced at it, but it was a big penis. Mark knelt down and began sucking Brett's balls right through his white briefs. Brett began an erection much to Mark's delight.

Soon Mark hooked a single finger in the back of Brett's underwear and pulled them down. Brett stepped out of them without direction. Mark placed his hands on Brett's bare waist, and for a minute or two, just stared at the bare skin standing before him.

"You are gorgeous. You are so good looking. I just want to eat you up," teased Mark.

Brett thought he might be serious, chop him up into small bits, and pop the morsels down his wicked face like eating popcorn at a movie. Mark began playing with Brett's penis before pulling Brett to him and taking his whole erection in his mouth. As he sucked, his hands roamed Brett's back and settled onto his butt.

He tried not to feel anything, but Mark appeared to be an expert, so he closed his eyes and replayed the masturbating race with Terry in the hotel.

220

"I want all your juice, little man, so when you shoot—keep squeezing until I get every drop out," ordered Mark.

Brett nodded downward at the grinning face before closing his eyes and returning to the dream. He felt Mark's finger probe his anus. Mark pulled off briefly to wet his middle finger. He continued his work on the front while his finger easily slid in and began massaging Brett's prostate gland.

A few minutes later, Brett expelled his load deep into Mark's throat. It shocked him when Mark swallowed every drop and yet kept sucking.

"There's no more," protested Brett, hoping to dress and leave.

"Push the remains of the jizz out with a little pee," ordered Mark.

"What?" Brett asked astonishingly.

"You heard me. Pee!" he said harshly.

Brett began to grunt as Mark kept working. He felt Mark's saliva dripping down his genitals. He tried again until finally, his bladder let loose, and he filled Mark with a big squirt of urine. Mark squeezed his penis as if he was squeezing the teat on a cow stopping the flow. Mark swallowed, put his mouth over the penis head, let go of his grip, and swallowed another big squirt. Then he turned Brett to his left, and let go as Brett shot his stream all the way to a nearby tree.

"Awesome, little man, you had a good load for me. Way to go!" exclaimed Mark as he licked his lips. Brett prayed he would not have to kiss Mark.

Mark took off his shirt, and lay down on their clothes pushing his pants and underwear down to his knees. Brett thought he was fixing to fuck him. "Straddle me," he ordered.

Brett gave him a puzzled look, but Mark had him turn around, straddle him and then urged him down to his knees. They were now in a sixty-nine sex position, but Mark placed his hands on Brett's hips and pulled him over his face. He spread Brett's buttocks and to Brett's bewilderment, Mark began probing the rim of his anus with his tongue while masturbating himself. Thankfully, Brett did not have to do anything but allow it to happen, and he gladly did. The hot tongue felt wonderful. No one ever did that to him before.

Mark shot a big load onto his chest, took a rag out of his pocket, and wiped himself up. He got up and told Brett to dress. Brett quickly did so.

Once dressed, Mark pulled him into a hug. "That was good, little man." He put his mouth to Brett's ear and blew hot breath inside his head slowly. "If you tell anyone about this, I'll cut you so no one will ever recognize you. Do you understand me?"

Brett began to shake in fear.

"Do you?" asked Mark again.

Brett shook his head affirmatively.

"Very good, your ass is mine. If anyone tells me you told, you are dead meat, but if you do not tell, you will be safe from now on. If anyone tries to harm you, just point them out, and I will take care of them for you."

Mark stuck his tongue in Brett's ear. "You taste so sweet. Don't ever change." He broke the embrace, squeezed Brett's genitals, and smiled. "Now you can take those big balls on home, little man. Start making me some more jizz!"

Brett grabbed his book bag and followed the trail back to the road. He ran most of the way home and immediately took a long hot shower, scrubbing his body clean several times. He never dreamed of sex with Mark and he never tried to.

Mark winked at him when they saw each other at school. One day a big football player came running around the hallway, dodging students left and right, as if running for a touchdown. Brett did not see him coming as he closed his locker and turned to head to class. The football player hit him broadside and knocked him down. The player stopped and looked back.

"Sorry man, are you okay?"

"Yeah," replied Brett as he got to his feet.

The player laughed, "Darn, I was hoping I broke something!" He laughed heartily and continued his run down the hall.

Brett watched him. When he reached the corner, an arm suddenly reached out knocking the player to his feet. Puzzled, Brett moved into the middle of the hall to see what happen. It was then he saw Mark standing over the player. The player got up to one knee and made the mistake of opening his mouth.

"What the hell do you think you are doing?" began the player.

Mark rapidly hit him across the chin with his fist. The player fell back to the floor unconscious. Mark looked up the hall to Brett, brought his hand up to an invisible hat, gave Brett a nod, and walked off.

Brett felt shock and dismay, but as he turned to walk to class, he walked a little taller and little braver. He never knew when Mark wanted him. Sometimes once a week and other times twice, but Mark never hurt him, but in his own way, he felt he was making love to Brett.

Brett felt thankful Mark's routine was always the same, never venturing to other sexual acts. He never talked much with Mark and still avoided him at school, but Brett never said no when he wanted sex.

One Friday night, Brett saw Mark with a girl at the football game. His hands were all over her as he gave her deep wet kisses while keeping one hand in her crotch. It puzzled Brett greatly. He had gone out with some friends to a drive-in restaurant and walked home from there. He had walked only a few blocks when Mark pulled up beside him.

"Come on, little man, I'll give you a ride home," he ordered nicely.

Brett looked at the girl. He noted her smeared lipstick, and her missing blouse buttons, but he climbed into the backseat anyhow. They drove a few

blocks before Mark stopped. He French kissed the girl deeply, and then she got out, and began straightening her clothes while walking briskly to her house in the next block. She waved goodbye, and Mark waited until she entered her house.

"Get in the front seat, little man," ordered Mark with a grin. "Don't worry about her. Her Dad is a preacher, and she has to be home by ten. She really gets my motor burning, but I am trying to be nice." He laughed and hit the gas. Brett sank deep in the seat and then slid against the door on the first turn and into Mark on the second.

"Well, now—that's feels nice," Mark laughed as he placed his right hand in Brett's lap and began squeezing his genitals.

Three blocks later, he pulled into a driveway, and cut off the lights and the engine. "Come on," he said.

Reluctantly, he got out of the car and followed Mark into the house. "Hey Mom," he said to the woman on the couch. Brett saw her, but could not have counted all the empty beer cans on the coffee table. "This is little man. We are going upstairs for a while. Night, Mom." She saw him with her eyes, but never said anything.

When they reached Mark's room, Brett received quite a shock. He knew Mark was a thug, but his room displayed a neat and clean appearance that did not fit Mark's character. "I know, everyone is shocked, I am a neat freak, what can I say," he said with a laugh. "Get your clothes off," he added with hardly a pause.

Brett did as told while Mark began as usual, but Brett sensed this night would be different. Mark was horny for his girlfriend, and Brett would have to satisfy his craving. After Brett filled Mark's throat with jizz, Mark slipped on a condom, laid Brett on his back, pulled his legs up to his shoulders, and rolled Brett back to his shoulders like a mother changing a baby's diaper. Mark leaned over and stuck a wet tongue in Brett's butt. Brett's dick leaped with excitement.

Gently, Mark lowered his butt down to the mattress, spread his legs, leaned over, and gently entered Brett. Brett remembered the encounter with George, and gave Mark a wonderful ride. He was thankful Brice taught him how to be a comfortable bottom. He didn't fear a big penis, remaining relaxed, making entry painless, and overwhelmingly satisfying. Mark sighed, "Your ass is better than any pussy in this town!" When finished, Mark gave him a twenty dollar bill and said, "Kid, buy some more underwear. I'm keeping these." Mark held up Brett's underwear, smelled the crotch, and bit them. "Hmm, boy, these smell and taste good!" Brett thought he was an absolutely crazy man with big muscles and scars, but somehow he could also be a gentle giant. He never hurt Brett, but Brett always felt he could.

Mark used him for about two months, but during the holidays, he heard Mark had been killed while drag racing down the old airport road. Mark blew a tire, lost control of his car, and flipped as he went down a steep embankment.

Brett felt sad he had died. He knew he did not love Mark, nor was he attracted to him, but Mark helped him get over the loss of Terry's friendship. Oddly, when he returned to school, he felt alone again. He closed his locker and turned to walk down the hall. He saw the same football player coming his way, but this time he moved to the far side of the hall, giving Brett plenty of space.

Brett smiled at him and pretended to tip an invisible hat in his direction. Brett laughed as he passed by, and knew he still had at least one thing to thank Mark for.

SEVENTEEN

A month later, it was Halloween, and for the first time in many years, Chase had no plans on celebrating the holiday at the club or a house party. While Chase loved making and dressing up in costumes, Brett loathed the idea, but always did his best to help Chase design a great one. Last year, Chase won third place in the club's annual contest—beat by an incredible first place winner. A man came in dressed as a banquet table with a full course meal. He had a vase of flowers on his head, with a chinstrap to hold it in place, and around his waist, he wore a fourteen-inch wide table in a complete circle. On the table, were plates, silverware, and goblets all hot glued to the tabletop, along with breadbaskets and a silver fruit bowl? Chase could not stop laughing and pointing at it. Third place won him fifty dollars, which he thought was the best thing he had ever won. It was a great evening, and he and Brett danced until three in the morning.

This year Paul and Jeremy decided to go out just to see the costumes, so Chase sat home with a bowl of candy waiting on the kids in the neighborhood to ring their doorbell and yell 'trick or treat.' He turned on the porch light so parents could see he was home, but no one came. He thought it odd so he opened the main door leaving just the storm door. The dogs stood in the window and barked as the children went up and down the street, picking up candy from all the homes on the street, but not one came to his house.

During the two years Chase had lived there, he had never been home on Halloween. Brett never mentioned the neighbors staying away, so he felt great disappointment that the neighboring adults would not allow him a chance to give their kids handfuls of candy. By nine, he turned the light off and shut the door. He checked on Brett, made notes on his charts, and returned to the den to watch television, and being eating the candy.

Before long, he drifted off to sleep and though sad from the disheartening evening, his mind presented him with a memorable dream of a concert trip he and Brett made to Atlanta. Brett surprised him with the tickets a full month before the trip. Chase was so excited he began marking off the days on their wall calendar in the kitchen. They left after work on Friday afternoon, drove down the mountains on US 25 through the edge of Greenville, and onto I-85 to Atlanta. Brett made reservations at a hotel on the gay side of town so they checked in and hit the streets for dinner.

Chase loved walking along the streets and going in and out of the gay friendly shops. They chose an Italian restaurant with the tables outside on the sidewalk so Chase could see everyone walking by, and they in turn could see him. He loved watching men, and enjoyed flirting, but just when he thought Brett might feel a little left out, he would lean into Brett and give him a squeeze. However, as they ate a grilled chicken and pasta meal, and drank a very nice

225

bottle of wine, from time to time they boldly kissed as if they were back on the gay safe streets of Key West.

After a long bar nap, they hit the shower and took turns washing the other, creating lots of lather on their erections. They carefully dressed and returned to the streets, stopping at one gay bar for a beer, then moved on to another, and finally stood in line to enter the largest gay bar in Atlanta. Inside they found over two thousand people dancing and swaying to the music, and immediately ran into a bar friend from Asheville. It's small world, thought Chase as he grabbed Brett's hand and dragged him to the dance floor.

They danced for about thirty minutes, drank a beer, and danced some more. At midnight, they moved upstairs and enjoyed a drag show with a group of performers who wore amazing costumes, while the host told numerous dirty but funny jokes. Chase loved it, and Brett loved watching Chase enjoy anything. Brett always felt he had never found anyone to love Brett—as much as he loved them. He loved Chase more than anyone on the face of the earth, and cherished every moment with him. All he had to do was wink at Chase, and immediately Chase would smile back at him.

They slept most of the next day, but did find time to go shopping for clothes in several gay friendly shops. Chase bought a new shirt, while Brett bought some funny gay birthday cards. They ate dinner early, changed clothes, and drove to the auditorium for the show. After passing through the ticket gates, Chase realized almost everyone attending the concert was gay. He loved it, and most folks enjoyed smiling back at him.

Rupaul, America's most popular drag queen, hit the stage with song after song. She was gorgeous in numerous fantastic costumes, and together Brett and Chase sang along with every song. Chase often stood up in the chair so he could see, yelling, and singing. Brett held onto the glossy full color program portraying Rupaul's story and rise to fame. She was so good she did various magazine ads for top cosmetic companies.

Afterwards, Chase and Brett stood in a long line so Rupaul could sign their program. When Chase reached the table, he just had the best time flirting and laughing with Rupaul who thought he was so cute. She was also very smart and noted Brett quietly standing behind Chase

"Who is this?" asked Rupaul as she reached out to shake Brett's hand.

"This is my boyfriend," replied Chase glowing with excitement.

"I guessed that, but does he have a name you can recall?" she asked teasing Chase.

"Oh, my gosh! Uh, yea, this is Brett!" Chase's face immediately turned red.

Everyone around the table started laughing. Rupaul held on to Brett's hand as she talked to him. "My goodness you are a good-looking man, and so tall, dark, handsome, and I love those blue eyes. Oh my goodness, am I drooling on you?"

The crowd broke out laughing again. Brett blushed.

"Well, honey, I had better get back to work, but it was so nice meeting Chase and Brett. By the way, Brett, if you need a little help screwing that cute little wild pony of yours, just give me a call. I can jump out of these clothes in two minutes flat!"

The boys and those in line all laughed and drove to the big club to spend the rest of the evening dancing. From time to time, some one would come up and say hi to Brett and Chase as if they had known them a long time. They soon realized Rupaul fans had heard the conversation at the autograph table, making the boys minor celebrities for a night.

Later that night, after taking a shower to scrub off the smoke smell, they began making love. It did not happen too often, but Chase felt like being a bottom. They made out for quite a while, achieving excellent erections. Brett was just about to mount Chase, when suddenly he stopped, and rolled off the bed.

"Where are you going? I'm all hot and ready here!" complained Chase.

Brett returned to the bed with the cell phone to his ear. "I've got to make a call."

Chase grunted, "But we're in the middle of hot sex. Who in the hell are you calling at this hour?"

"Rupaul!" he replied. "She said if I needed any help with you, I was to give her a call. From the look of your big ass, I think I am going to need a lot of help!"

Brett laughed and turned to set his cell phone down and returned to the bed. When he turned back around Chase hit him in the face with a big pillow. "You're funny!" he declared. "Now come on partner, saddle up!"

Chase woke up after midnight scattering the dogs from his lap. In the floor, he found a pile of torn bits of paper. He grinned as he had fallen asleep while still holding a Tootsie-Roll Pop. When he fell asleep, his arm hung over the chair rail with the candy sucker still in his hand. The dogs had apparently licked it until it was gone, then pulled the white paper stick out of his hand, and chewed it into a pile. The dogs both sat on the couch trying to look as innocent as possible. Chase laughed, went over, and started tickling and playing with the dogs. He gave each one many kisses, and then went down the hall to prepare for bed.

Brett's room was dark. He flipped on the bright light and began leaving a trail of shoes and clothes as he made his way to the bathroom. After brushing his teeth, he came to Brett's side, checked the monitors, and wrote down his notes on the chart. Yawning, he made it to the light switch, flipped it off, back peddled a few steps, and fell into his own bed.

As he pulled the covers over his nude body, he absentmindedly said something he had said every night since moving in with Brett before the plane

crash. He said, "Night, Brett. I love you. Don't let the bed bugs bite." He laid his head down, and fell asleep almost instantly.

Brett's brain responded to the sudden bright light, but Chase missed the twitch in Brett's face. When Brett heard Chase's voice say his name, his brain recognized the sound. He moved his feet, his hands, as well as his arm, but the lights were already out, and Chase fast asleep.

Brett struggled for several minutes, desperately trying to open his eyes. He pulled his arm up to his stomach, which he had done several times, but this time, he wished to touch his face and pry his eyelids open. More than once, he tried to pull his arm higher, but his brain could not send the right signals to the muscles Chase worked so hard to keep limber and loose.

Exhausted from his effort, Brett drifted into a deep sleep while his arm slowly slid back to his side.

His senior year, Brett fell in love with a good-looking guy by the name of Alan. Alan was sophomore, but only eighteen months younger, and did not know Brett liked guys, as Brett did everything he could to keep it from everyone. He hoped he would soon grow out of his desires, but he never felt right trying to date, because he feared kissing the girl at the end of the night. He also knew he would never be able to have sex with a girl, as nothing about girls made his dick hard. It just refused to do so. He found a Playboy magazine in a trash can at school, and tried to masturbate while studying the pictures, but it didn't work for him.

Running out of excuses, Brett worked several part-time jobs. His favorite was lifeguarding at the local Y.M.C.A. In this job, he taught swimming to children, teenagers, and seniors. He taught a sixty-eight year old woman how to dive off the diving board. In just six weeks of two nights a week, she completed a single flip. Together, they had their picture taken for the newspaper.

Brett's dream quickly zoomed forward to the Friday night Alan walked into the pool area to swim. Friday nights were dead in the pool with just a couple of swimmers all night. Brett walked along the side of the pool in the tiled gutter, kicking and splashing water. Sensing a change in the room, he looked up, and his eyes went to this high school boy all of five feet six inches tall, with a naturally dark tan and super bright white teeth.

Brett picked up his pace as he walked towards the gate, and asked him if he had swum in the pool before. Alan replied he had, but it had been a while. Brett gave him a quick spin on the safety rules, took his ticket, and stepped aside to allow Alan to enter the pool area alone. He walked down to the deep end with Brett watching Alan's cute butt the entire way. Brett stopped about half way when he realized Alan was walking directly to the diving board. Alan climbed the three steps to the one meter board, stretched his arms a little, looked left and right of the board to be sure no one was in his way, took a breath, walked three steps, and sprung off the board into a dive.

Brett's eyes followed his movement while trying not to stare. Alan's feet left the board as he threw his arms and head forward, and spun into a stunning perfectly executed one and half dive. His slender, beautiful body entered the water with barely a hint of a splash. Brett watched the boy descend to the bottom of the pool, reverse his motion, and push off to swim to the surface.

When his head broke through the water, he saw Brett looking at him with a grin on his face. "Way to go. That was the best first dive of the day. Hi, I'm Brett."

Alan smiled, took three quick strokes, pulled his body out of the water, and stood in the drain gutter dripping. He stuck out his hand, "I'm Alan. It's nice to meet you."

Brett accepted his hand in his, and held it there for a moment as their eyes met. "What else can you do?"

"Pardon?" replied Alan with a puzzled look on his face.

"Dive—what else can you do on the board?" Brett felt his face flush just a little.

Alan laughed, "Oh, I can do a few more things. Will you spot me?"

"It's my job. I am the lifeguard, just don't kill yourself because I hate to get wet," replied Brett sarcastically.

"A lifeguard that doesn't want to get wet?" asked Alan.

"Yeah, it could mess up my hair," replied Brett as he felt Alan's eyes leave his face and wander up to Brett's head. There was not a hair on his head longer than a quarter of an inch in length. He kept it short because he went in and out of the water many times a day teaching.

"Yeah, right," laughed Alan as he turned and walked back to the diving board.

Brett turned back to the shallow in, and saw the last swimmer exit the pool, leaving Alan and Brett alone. He watched him dive again as he sprung the board spinning rapidly into a two and half dive.

"Oh my," exclaimed Brett as Alan surfaced. "That was awesome!"

"I think I'll try the high dive," stated Alan matter-of-factly.

The three-meter board was about twelve feet above the pool. Mostly people climbed the ladder and jumped off the board. At least once or twice a week, Brett would do a beautiful swan dive off the board. Alan climbed the ladder, and checked once again to be sure the area was clear.

"We're by ourselves," stated Brett.

"Right," replied Alan as he prepared to dive. He walked back, took a deep breath, began his steps, and executed a beautiful one and half dive. He came to the surface to see Brett's mouth wide open as he swam up to the edge of the pool beneath him.

"Excellent," said Brett. "How old are you and where did you learn to dive like that?"

"I'm sixteen. How old are you?"

Brett replied, "I am seventeen for now, but in a few months I'll be eighteen."

"Happy early birthday," said Alan with a grin.

"So where did you learn to dive?"

Alan grinned slyly, "My father was diver on his university's team. My whole family can dive."

"Oh, that's pretty neat. You dive very well."

Alan turned and began walking back to the high dive platform for a second dive. Brett turned and walked to the pool entrance and closed the gate, indicating the pool had just closed. He took his whistle off his neck, pulled off his tee shirt, and dove off the gutter into the pool. He took several strokes underwater, surfacing just at the safety rope separating the shallow end from the deep.

Alan waited on top of the diving board for Brett to shake the water from his eyes. Brett gave him a 'thumbs up' sign. Alan took a breath, made three steps, and completed a perfect two and half dive. Brett smiled as he watched Alan's beautiful muscled body descend through the water to the deep end.

Alan reached the bottom, but turned his body towards Brett as he pushed off and swam to him. Brett remained with his legs slightly apart, in awe of this amazing sixteen-year old. To his surprise, Alan swam right between his legs, surfacing right behind him.

"That was another good one. Can you do any other dives?" asked Brett jokingly.

"Yeah, some back flips, jack-knife, and a gainer. How about you?" asked Alan as he squirted some water through his clasped hands at Brett's chest?

"I can do a few dives, but I cannot flip very well. I think I grew too tall too fast."

"You are tall. I wish I was," stated Alan, as he squirted Brett again.

Brett responded with an expert swipe at the surface water with his hand sending a small spray of water right into the side of Alan's face. Alan splashed him back. Moments later, they were splashing each other repeatedly. Alan dropped beneath the water, and tried to flip Brett over. Brett put all his weight on his foot and Alan could not move it. Brett reached down into the water, and pulled Alan up and out of the water by his waist tossing him slightly.

Alan came up grinning, and they began wrestling in the water. They played for a while, and then swam and explored the deep end. Brett noticed Alan had a habit like a baseball player of scratching or adjust his balls every few minutes. Over the course of the next hour, they talked, swam, and became friends. They stayed a long time in the hot showers, soaping their bodies up with lather, then rinsing, and starting again. Their fingers looked wrinkled and

230

waterlogged by the time they turned off the water. From this chance meeting, they became instant friends.

They met between classes, did homework together after school, and every night Alan would visit Brett while he worked at the pool. One Friday night, Brett asked Alan if he wanted to come home after work and meet his mom. Alan did and ended up spending the night. After reaching a height of six foot three, Brett had outgrown his childhood bunk beds, so his parents had bought him a double bed. To their chagrin, he was soon too tall for that as well, but he made it work by sleeping diagonally.

The boys stripped down to their underwear, and climbed into the bed side by side. They talked for nearly an hour before settling down to sleep. In the night, their bodies touched. As the next few weeks went by, they took turns sleeping over at each other's house. They often tickled the other in bed, and slept easily in each other's arms. Nothing between them happened rapidly, but steadily they trusted the other, and felt a special love.

At first, Brett thought Alan felt the same as he did about boys, but Alan talked about girls, and soon had a girlfriend at school that had very strict parents and could not yet date. This made Alan horny. One night Brett awoke feeling the bed slightly moving and instantly, he realized Alan was masturbating with his back to Brett to hide his erection.

Brett slid over with his body tightly against Alan. He slowly slid his arm around Alan's side resting his hand on Alan's chest where he gently moved his fingers back and forth. Alan pushed back against him and continued pumping himself. Brett moved his lips to Alan's back where he kissed him numerous times before moving up to Alan's beautiful, slender neck. Alan pushed his neck towards Brett while moaning with delight at the soft kisses. Alan pumped faster until at last he exploded inside his underwear. Brett loaned him a clean pair, and watched as Alan cleaned himself up, switched briefs, and climbed back in the bed. This time he cuddled Brett in his arms, and they went back to sleep. Several nights later they had began making love. For the next year, they became inseparable friends, but no one knew they had sex almost every night.

The following fall Brett had to say goodbye to his best friend, and head off to college. He did not return home for eight weeks. He and Alan sat alone in Brett's car late one night after the football game at his old high school. Alan told him he had sex with his girlfriend. He told Brett more details than Brett wanted to hear, but Brett pretended to be interested. Nothing was ever said between them about the sex they had shared as boys in high school, but Brett knew it was over. He cried all the way back to his college dorm the next day. The boy of his dreams had left him for a girl. He felt devastated. He never saw Alan again.

As the memory ended, Brett's right hand finger began twitching. He felt the out of control muscle, a cramp, and he felt some pain. He strained to wake himself up, but could not. Defiantly, he fought to control his finger until at last it stopped.

Brett's brain clicked forward to a time not long ago. Off in the distance, he could see Chase's face. He was walking towards him, smiling all the way. Brett waved and Chase waved back. Chase mouthed the words "I love you" and Brett winked, and did the same in return. He reached out his hands to hug Chase as he approached, but just ten feet from him, he suddenly disappeared. Brett's hands slid back to his side.

Hours later, Brett saw Chase again. He was carrying something blue and baggy. It was a carry-on bag. Chase was waving at Brett to hurry up and follow him. Brett put away his laptop, zipped up his bag, and began rolling his cart behind him as he began walking quickly after Chase.

Chase reached the plane and started up the steps. Brett called out his name. Just as Chase turned to see him, Brett snapped a picture. Chase laughed and urged him to come on with a hand wave. Brett put away his camera and boarded the plane.

He saw Chase talking to the people ahead of their seats. He put his bag away in the overhead bin, and sat down in the seat beside Chase. He reached over and patted his lover's knee to reassure him he was there, and everything would be okay.

As usual, Chase checked out every guy walking down the aisle to his seats. Brett elbowed him playfully in the ribs. Chase kissed the tips of his fingers and touched Brett's face.

Chase asked, "How long before we get to Atlanta?"

"Forty-five minutes. It will pass fast," added Brett hoping to calm Chase down.

It failed to work. "Did I tell you I love to fly, but hate getting in the plane?" asked Chase.

Brett gave him a dumb look, "You realize what you just said did not make any sense. How can you fly if you don't get in the plane?"

"In my dreams, I can fly just fine, and I never crash," stated Chase seriously.

"Perhaps, but if you're not in the plane, you're going to get covered with bird shit!"

Chase and Brett laughed as the flight attendant began explaining the emergency procedures. They half-listened as they continued teasing the other.

Suddenly, the dream moved along rapidly as if stuck in fast-forward mode like a video recorder. He saw the plane quickly move away from the ramp and onto the runaway. The lights inside the plane changed, then a bell sounded,

and the plane began accelerating. They lifted off, the tape going faster, he saw a flash, an explosion. and they began to descend.

Brett suddenly tried to scream, but his mouth would not open, and his tongue would not move. He desperately tried again. He had to warn Chase to watch out. He screamed again, but this time a mere grunt came out of his throat. He flexed his toes and tried again. Another grunt sound came out.

Chase moved in the bed beside him, but never really awoke. The ears on the dogs stood up as they turned towards Brett's hospital bed.

In the nightmare, Brett caught a glimpse of the plane coming apart and pieces of the fuselage flying over his head. He tried once more to scream. Another guttural sound came from deep within him.

The dogs barked at him. Feeling groggy, Chase opened an eye. They barked again. Chase turned to look at the dogs in the soft glow of the monitors. He got out of the bed, and left the room, heading down the hall, thinking Bill and Larry were trying to get in the house. He heard nothing, but checked the locks and walked to the kitchen. He pulled on the back door, but it remained bolted as well.

He returned to Brett's room and flipped on the bathroom light, checked the monitors, and sighed slightly as he saw Brett's heartbeat continuing to blip on the screen. He walked to the bathroom and relieved his bladder, gave the dogs a quick rub, and fell back asleep with no idea what had stirred the dogs.

EIGHTEEN

Four weeks passed quickly, with Chase working harder and longer as the holiday season approached. He had worked the last fourteen days straight, offering to do anyone's shift, so he could be off the entire Thanksgiving weekend. The nurses had been wonderful while covering for Chase and watching after Brett, but none of the medical team really wanted to work during the holidays. Chase did not know whom else to call, so he arranged with his boss the long schedule, so he could be home for the turkey day weekend, and give his nursing staff a well-deserved break.

Jeremy and Paul invited him over for dinner for Tuesday by arranging for a friend of theirs to sit with Brett for a few hours. They were worried about Chase. He had lost his tan, and dark circles surrounded his eyes. Jeremy often teased him about a single strand of gray hair coming out of his scalp right in the part line. Chase pulled it out at first, but now he did not have the energy or the desire to even care.

They were proud of the hard work Chase did, and how much he had matured by taking responsibility for Brett's health care. Chase often reminded them, Brett would have done the same for him.

Jeremy and Paul gave Chase a long hug along with kisses to his cheeks. They knew Chase missed all the affection Brett had given him. He never realized how important affection was, and how the loss of it brings a person emotionally down. Paul feared Chase might suffer from mental depression, but emotionally, the job helped him as he gave each customer a big smile, and spoke to all his friends as they passed by his kiosk.

Jeremy and Paul were leaving in the morning for Jeremy's home in Lincoln, New Hampshire. They had an early flight, and already Chase knew he was going to miss them. They promised to call every day, and Chase did his best to wish them well.

When Paul brought the plates of lasagna to the table, along with Jeremy's tossed salad and French bread, Chase quit talking and devoured the food. His normal diet consisted of fast food at work, and frozen food at home. A home-cooked meal was a rarity for Chase, and he savored every delicious morsel. Paul made up some dinner plates Chase could freeze and heat up during the holidays, and Jeremy gave him the rest of the French bread, a huge bag of salad, and made him promise to eat well during the Thanksgiving weekend.

Chase sat in their living room, sipped a wine cooler, and just talked for a while about nothing. Jeremy started telling Paul a story about how he met Chase in the hospital, and when he and Paul looked over at Chase, they found him sound asleep with the wine cooler between his legs so he would not spill it. He looked so peaceful and yet exhausted.

Paul agreed to follow in their car, so Jeremy helped Chase to his car and drove him home. Jeremy fed the dogs, put away the food while Paul

234

checked on Brett, and thanked their friend for staying with him so Chase could be away for a while.

They gave Chase yet another big hug, and promised to come see him on the way home from the airport. He begged them to call him after they arrived safe in New Hampshire. They helped him to bed, turned out the light, locked the door and left. Chase never heard the door close, as he was already deep asleep.

The fourteen straight days of work wore his body down. He did it with little complaint, but his back and legs hurt from all the standing during his shifts in the mall. It had been a long time since he had eaten a big meal, and much like an old bear, he just had to hibernate afterwards.

Chase woke up the following day about two in the afternoon. He looked at the clock through dreary eyes, and at first thought he had awoke during the middle of the night, but forcing his eyes to remain open, he saw sunlight leaking in through the center of the curtain. He stretched in bed, and immediately felt his sore back. He threw back the covers scattering the dogs. They quickly scampered to him, so he spent a few minutes rubbing their ears, scratching their backs, and tickling their ribs.

He groaned as he rolled out of bed, and walked slowly over to Brett's bed. He checked the monitoring equipment, made notes on the chart, changed the IV bag and food bag, and followed up by changing the urine bag. With his chores complete, he walked to the shower and turned on the water letting it warm up while he took a long overdue pee.

Afterwards, he got in the shower and adjusted the water as hot as he could stand it. He washed his hair and his body with one of his favorite body shampoos with a strawberry scent. He decided to shave as well. When the water ran cold, he cursed loudly, quickly turned the shower off, and began drying.

He brushed his hair, put on deodorant, scrubbed his teeth, and finally, he gargled for about a full minute, as his mouth felt like he had been sucking on one of the dog's paws all night. He dressed, made his way to the street for yesterday's mail, and then fixed himself some of the lasagna and bread in the microwave, and sat down to eat after filling the dog's bowls with their high performance, low fat puppy cereal. He grinned as he picked up a morsel that had fallen on the floor, and recalled the time Brett dared him to eat some of the dog's food. They both laughed long and hard as Chase popped it in his mouth, chewed it up, and grabbed another one.

Brett told him a story about his grandmother who had come to visit for the weekend. She had gotten hungry in the night, and took the foil off the top of a can of food in the refrigerator, heated it up in a pan, and ate it. It was canned dog food. Her only complaint was that it was a little salty for her palate. They both laughed at the retelling of the story.

235

At first, Chase thought he would clean house, but still feeling weary, he went back to Brett's room, and began doing his therapy work. He lovingly worked all of Brett's arm and leg muscles one at a time while talking to him. He told him Jeremy and Paul had flown up to New Hampshire. He told him about his job, and when he got tired of talking, he turned on the television and watched a few reruns before heading to his bed for a nap.

He woke up after dark and checked on Brett. He rubbed Brett's feet, tried tickling his toes, but he did not respond. He spoke aloud and asked Brett to move something, but he found no response. It had been several weeks since he had seen Brett move, and though he tried not to worry about it—he did.

The doctor told him there would be 'dry' periods of no movement, but when he began moving again, he should hope for a little more movement than before the 'dry' period, and if so, it would be a good sign of recovery.

Chase did not tell anyone that three weeks had already passed since the last time Brett moved, fearing they might think it was time to give up. He fixed himself some salad in a big bowl, some French bread, a big glass of iced tea on a tray, and watched some television in the living room. He ate everything on his plate, and made a mental note to thank his friends for the wonderful food.

He took the dogs on a walk around the block before dark, and picked up today's mail and newspaper. While Brett read the paper every day before the plane crash, Chase rarely read it. He shut the front door and locked it, a new habit he had picked up since the last time the uncles had tried to get in.

He went through the mail quickly by tossing the junk mail in the trashcan, keeping only a few bills. He saved all the bills and took them to his attorney Michael Evans about twice a month. He had tried figuring out the medical bills, but had long given up. The huge bills scared him, and he had no clue how they would pay them. However, Michael had a sharp eye for overcharged or unnecessary items wandering onto a client's bill, and he knew in the end the airlines were going to pay for all their medical bills—he would see to that. He just kept telling Chase not to worry about the bills, as he would make the airline pay for everything.

Brett had returned to the hospital twice for x-rays, brain scans, and other tests. His reports were always good and each time they found more brain activity. They pricked his fingers and feet with a needle in hopes of him flinching or coming awake, but so far, nothing worked.

Chase once closed an encyclopedia book really fast and loud near Brett's ear, but that did not work either. Jeremy laughed at him, but in the end, Brett remained in the coma.

Chase watched the news for a while on the television in Brett's room, and once bored, he found a DVD movie, and put it on so he could watch and Brett could listen. "Still asleep" is often what Chase said when folks asked about him, so he used the phrase often around Brett. He hated the word coma.

The movie he chose was one of Brett's favorites, and he proudly told friends he had watched it over seventy-five times. The movie, "Torch Song

Trilogy" starred Harvey Fierstein and Matthew Broderick. Brett absolutely adored the movie, but Chase had never heard of it until Brett made him sit down and watch it. Now he was a fan, too.

The movie is in three parts. Chase laughed aloud at the funny scenes and Brett told him to count how many bunny rabbit doodads he could spot in the lead character's apartment. Quickly, he spoke aloud, the napkin holder, the teakettle, the pot pads, the saltshakers, his slippers, and the silhouettes on the wall before the story moved on. Brett could always find the bunnies faster than he could. He knew later on in the story, the father of his newly adopted gay son, would make an urgent appearance at his school while still wearing extra large, blue bunny slippers. It always made him laugh aloud.

When part two started, Chase made a dash for the bathroom to pee, and returned without missing any of the dialogs. Arnold, the lead character, now had a new boyfriend, and boy was he cute, thought Chase.

He walked over to Brett, checked the monitoring system, and began stroking his hair. He wondered if Brett's pupils were right beneath his eyelids or rolled up in his head. He had seen the doctor from time to time flash a pen light into his eyes by holding the lids open, but he had never been close enough to see what the doctor saw.

His curiosity got the best of him, so he gently pushed up an eyelid. He nearly jumped when the eyeball moved a little, and he could now see about half of his beautiful blue eyes. The rest of the eye was indeed up somewhere in his brain. He held it open for a moment, but detected no movement and closed it.

Without thinking and more out of habit than desire, he leaned over and softly kissed Brett's eyelid. Then he patted his shoulder, and decided to give Brett a massage. He took a different approach than the muscle therapy he did every day to Brett. He began rubbing very gently the sides of his head, especially his temples and around his ears. In the past, Brett did the same to help Chase with stress, so he thought Brett might like it.

He then spent some time rubbing the muscles of his neck after climbing up on the bed and straddling Brett. He knew if anyone came in, they would think he had gone crazy, but with Jeremy, Paul, and the nurse gone for the holidays, he had Brett to himself. Besides, Chase really did not care what anyone thought.

Soon he pulled the sheet down to his waist. He reached over to the nearby table, and squirted a big glob of body lotion in his left hand. He put his hands together, and rubbed the palms vigorously against each other warming up the lotion. Softly, he allowed his two hands to smooth the warm lotion all over Brett's chest and tummy. He then went to work by starting at the top rubbing his shoulders and below his neck. He rubbed his mid chest, and down to his belly. It felt good to touch Brett again like this. It was also very sensual, so he stopped and adjusted his crotch as he had begun to harden.

237

Carefully, he moved down to Brett's knees, and sat down gently on his legs. He pulled the sheet down as far as he could. He looked at Brett's soft skin between his belly button and his penis. He used to love to give Brett butterfly kisses all around this tender part of Brett's body. He leaned over, and began kissing him with numerous tiny kisses.

He sat back up and looked at Brett's pitiful crotch. The drain tube was still stuck in Brett's penis, and held there with some tape. His genitals looked squashed, and Chase thought most uncomfortable.

He reached back for more body lotion, warmed it up, and began applying the lotion all along Brett's waist and down his thighs. He spread his legs a little bit so he could run his warm palms down the inside of Brett's thighs. He moved the tube out of his way, warmed more lotion, and tenderly applied it to Brett's balls. Satisfied they looked healthier, he began rubbing a little lotion around the edge of the base of his penis.

Although he had not seen movement from Brett in quite a while, Brett had indeed moved, but usually as a result of Chase turning on the light, heading to the shower, or flashing pictures on the television while undressing, and not looking at Brett. The one area of his body he had not noticed was slight erections to Brett's penis.

The touch of Chase's soft warm skin, stirred something deep inside of Brett. His penis began to grow. It would have to grow a lot to achieve an erection, for it mostly was less than inch or two in length, and completely soft. Chase did not notice right away, and nearly jumped out of his skin when he did.

He continued to rub Brett's genitals and penis with the lotion. Minutes later, Brett achieved certified Vienna sausage length, a bit longer and a bit fatter, but looking much better to Chase.

Chase could not stop himself, as he saw no harm in what he was doing. He told himself if it were he lying in the bed, he would want Brett to do it to him. He continued massaging the boy he loved. Nearly eight minutes later, the erection grew to three and half inches.

"Wahoo!" shouted Chase as the dogs barked in response.

With their favorite DVD still playing, Chase dimmed the lights, and slowly played with Brett's penis to maintain his erection. He was still sitting on his legs looking towards Brett's face, and failed to see Brett's toes push down, and then abruptly up.

"Oh, shit!" exclaimed Chase as the tube suddenly popped out of the end of Brett's penis, and urine began draining back on to the bed. Reluctantly, Chase quit playing and worked until he got the tube back in, and re-taped it into position. He went to the bathroom, got a hot washcloth, and cleaned up the spilled urine.

"That's enough sex for you tonight young man," stated Chase aloud, while wagging his finger playfully at Brett. "If you play with it too much you're liable to go blind," he added mockingly, as his mother had done when she caught him as an early teenager. He covered Brett's body back up with the sheet,

238

picked up the clipboard, and began writing down the numbers. To his surprise, Brett heartbeat was up twenty-eight beats over his normal resting state. The blood pressure machine finished a cycle, and it was up as well. Chase looked at Brett's heart beat on the monitor and smiled, "You liked that, didn't you—you old scoundrel. All right, time to rest. I am pooped, and tomorrow we are celebrating Thanksgiving. We're having warmed up lasagna, and it is yummy!"

He put his face down on Brett's heart so he could hear it, and then leaned up and planted kisses to his face. He gave the dogs a pat, stripped down, and fell into the bed, while turning off the movie and television with the remote control. He felt a little better, somewhat rested, and easily fell fast asleep.

Brett's brain sensed the turning on of the light, and it puzzled him why it was sometimes bright and sometimes dark, but he had no clue as to why. However, this time he heard the sound of something familiar, and his brain went into overdrive trying to decipher the sounds he heard.

A moment later, his left eye became warm, and then the light became even brighter, but soon returned to a medium brightness. Something touched his eyelid. It felt good to him, not harsh, but his brain failed to recognize the contact.

The flesh over his chest began to warm and nerve endings awoke, and started broadcasting numerous signals to his brain. He heard the sounds again. His skin felt warm and cozy, and he liked the feeling.

Suddenly, his brain reacted to the touch of his genitals. Years of flinching when kids threatened to smack him in the balls sent up an alarm to his brain, but processing the appropriate response took too long. He abandoned the thought of fear as the sensation pleased him.

He could not recall feeling so warm down there. He heard the sound of the movie on the television. As the minutes went by, he heard the lead character's voice. It was a distinct rough, course, scratchy kind of voice, but he liked the sound of it—especially when he sang. Who was it? He wondered.

A new signal rushed through his body to his brain. He felt really hot. His blood was pulsing in the veins in his penis. It felt good. Something made him feel very excited. He did not want this feeling to stop. He moved his toes down, and he knew he had. He moved them up again as a sudden hot feeling seared through his abdomen.

Then all of sudden, he became cold again. His flesh felt a chill, then a slight warmness. He felt something touch his face. It felt good. The lights went out, he heard a voice, but it was not the gravelly voice—a softer sweeter one. He knew that voice, but he could not place it. His brow wrinkled hoping the answer would soon come to his brain. He wanted to know the voice, and he wanted the person to touch him again.

His brain crunched all the new data quickly, but it left him spent, and he drifted off into a deep sleep to rest.

Chase woke up mid-morning, feeling thankful for a long night of sleep. He played with the dogs, stretched, and felt his erection. He turned on the television and found the station airing the Macy's Christmas Parade. Last year he and Brett spent Thanksgiving in New York so they could see the parade live. Chase liked the giant cartoon character balloons, but his favorite part of the weekend was seeing the Broadway shows. He felt overwhelmed and under talented as he watched one amazing performance after another. Actors could sing, dance, and bring you to tears with their talents. Chase had always wanted to be an actor, but he had trouble memorizing his lines in some of the small plays in high school, and was afraid he would make a mess of things if he tried out for movie parts.

He settled into the pillow watching the parade and playing with his erection, but soon closed his eyes once more picturing Brett standing before him doing a slow strip as he sometimes did before coming to bed. It always made Chase laugh. He wished he could reach into the dream, hold him, and feel his arms around him again. His recollections produced the desired result, so he leaped out of the bed and walked to the bathroom to clean the mess from his chest, and take a shower.

When he flipped on the light, Brett stirred. His brain could see the light through his eyelids once again. He moved a few fingers on both hands. Seconds later, his eyelids suddenly rolled back for the first time since the day they left on their vacation. He saw the ceiling and stared intently until his eyes finally focused. He then allowed his eyes to follow the ceiling to the light under the ceiling fan. He was afraid to blink his eyes, fearing they will not open again, but finally he had to. He focused on the television on the wall, and it looked familiar to him.

His eyes wandered to his right, and he saw a dresser, mirror, and an empty bed. It took him almost a minute to notice the dogs sleeping on the end of the bed. He heard a noise back to his left. Slowly, almost like a robotic camera, he rolled his eyes around the room to the door of the bathroom. The light was on in there as well. He heard singing and wondered if he was in heaven.

Chase lathered up with the shower soap, and for no reason at all, he started singing a song from the musical Lion King. He always thought he sounded better in the shower, but Brett used to tell him when he sang in the shower, the toilet flushed all by itself. Chase would always throw soap at him for the comment. Brett would then elaborate on the same joke by saying the toilet down the hall also flushed, and so did the neighbor's throne across the street.

He once told Chase that someone was at the door for him. Chase was shampooing and singing, and yelled back who. Brett had said it was the 'bad

singing cops' and they were here to arrest him. Chase would laugh and try to hit Brett with either scoops of water or globs of soap lather.

Brett knew the voice, but his brain did not put a name with the sound. He tried to speak, but his tongue felt like dried silicon. He moved his tongue a little left and right, but no words would come. Desperately, he grunted.

The dogs' ears popped up like an automatic car antenna. They stood still, trying to figure out where the sounds came from. Brett grunted again. They quickly turned their heads towards him and barked. He grunted once more, and they barked again.

"What are you barking at?" asked Chase loudly from the shower. Brett stared in his direction and grunted. The dogs barked. "It's just the television. I bet you see Snoopy and want him to play with you. Well, hang on. I'll be out in a minute," yelled Chase.

Chase finished his shower, dried off, and stepped out. He quickly went through his rapid routine: deodorant on first, as he had forgotten it on several occasions, and felt embarrassed for the rest of the day. He added a bit of air gel, followed by sixty seconds of hair drying. He gargled as Brett always said he went to sleep like an angel, but woke up with the throat of a dragon. Finally, he used his face and eye creams to protect his facial skin from UV rays and the forming of wrinkles. Brett taught him how to avoid the tiny crinkles around the eyes, and he always put the cream in the right places just as Brett had showed him. He then stepped back looking left and right in the mirror.

"Boy, I cannot wait till tomorrow…" he said aloud to no one. It was an old joke Brett pulled on him when they first started dating. "Because I get better looking everyday!" He laughed and cut off the light.

Exhausted from his efforts, Brett closed his eyes and drifted off to sleep.

Chase dressed, picked up the medical clipboard, and walked around to the side of Brett's bed. He wrote down the numbers on the monitor, checked the IV drip and food tube, wrote down the current level, and did the same for urine bag. He set the clipboard down on the bed, bumping Brett accidentally with his arm. He squatted down and turned off the tiny valve, then unhooked the bag, walked to the toilet and dumped the urine in and flushed.

Brett woke again after hearing a new swooshing sound.

Chase returned, reinstalled the bag, and opened the valve. He almost flinched as a squirt of urine descended in the empty bag about the same time he let go of the valve. He made a smirk, and shook his head slightly as if laughing

at himself. He stood up, wrote down the emptying of the bag on the chart, and placed the clipboard on the table by Brett's bed.

He started to feel for Brett's pulse, but instead laid his head down right on top of Brett's heart so he could listen to it. He looked at the second hand on the wall clock and counted the beats. Satisfied, he started to stand up, but decided not to. It felt good to hear his heart. It comforted him. Brett had told him little puppies always sleep touching their mother's side or belly so they can hear her heartbeat and then felt safe. One of their dogs came from the pound, and feared becoming alone again, so he always slept touching Brett's leg when he slept. Chase also slept touching Brett without even knowing he was doing so. He kissed Brett's chest tenderly. Chase felt safe, but very lonely.

He usually read something to Brett everyday, but he was a slow reader, and soon bored of it. Today, he started talking aloud to Brett, feeling he could reminisce about something they had done together.

As he began to talk with his ear still listening to Brett's heart, Brett's nostrils flinched. His nostrils inhaled the aroma of the fresh shampoo in Chase's hair, and the strawberry scent of his body soap. Seconds later, he picked up a faint smell of his deodorant. His brains began sorting out the sound of the voice, along with the fragrances, and his heartbeat picked up a little. He moved a finger beneath the sheet, but Chase did not see it as he continued talking.

After several minutes of talking, Chase decided he ought to check on the tape holding the tube in Brett's penis after playing with it the night before. He slid his hand under the sheet, lifted it up, and partially put his head under so he could see. It looked okay, but he reached down and felt his penis anyway.

Brett felt the warm hand and abruptly awoke. He forced himself to grunt for attention.

Chase was just about to let go of Brett's penis when he not only heard the sudden grunt, but also with his ear still on his abdomen, he heard the sound come from deep inside of Brett. He jerked his head out from the sheet, and quickly turned to Brett's face.

The room was silent. After a long twenty seconds, he saw the muscles in Brett's neck move, and a louder grunt came from his throat. The dogs barked. Chase put his hands to his face in disbelief and gasped.

Another long period of silence occurred. Slowly, he reached out to touch Brett's neck muscles so he could feel the grunt. He moved his hand over the sheet, and just as he touched Brett's soft flesh, Brett's eyes suddenly popped open like the doll of a ventriloquist coming alive.

Chase jerked his hand back, and covered his face like a child watching a horror movie. A strong flash of energy ran up and through his body as if struck by lightning. He peeked between his fingers and noticed the bright blue pupils of

242

the man he loved so dearly. He sucked in as much oxygen as he could, but still no words would come.

Brett turned his eyes towards Chase. Chase's eyes went wide. His heart began racing. He could feel Brett's eyes focusing on him like an auto focus lens on a camera.

A full minute passed before Chase could speak. "Brett? Brett? Can you hear me?"

Brett's ears heard the words and passed the information on to the brain. The brain tried various channels to decipher the sounds. Soon he recognized the world 'Brett.'

Chase slowly moved closer to the bed, and placed his hand in Brett's palm. "It's Chase. I'm Chase." He said it a bit louder.

Brett grunted again. The dogs barked. Brett's eyes moved towards the dogs. The bark was another familiar sound, but the brain failed to give him the right information.

"You've been asleep for a long time, but now you have come back to me," began Chase, as the tears began sliding down his face. "I love you. I love you. I love you," he finished as he leaned over and kissed Brett's face numerous times.

Brett heard the words and they, too, were familiar. His brain sent back a warm feeling that made him smile. He grunted in return. Chase smiled as the tears kept flowing.

Chase pulled away from the embrace, hit the raise button on the bed, and brought the bed up into a sitting position. Brett could now see the entire room. Rapidly, his brain worked to store what he saw, while matching it with the pictures in his memory. His eyes raced and stopped at each object before him. He saw a picture of he and Chase on the dresser, and stared at it a long time.

Chase ran to the bathroom and grabbed the mirror. He held it up in front of Brett's face and pointed to Brett. "You are Brett," he said as if talking to a foreigner. "Brett, you are Brett."

Amazingly, Brett tried to say the word 'Brett,' but his tongue was heavy. Chase was undaunted. "I'm Chase. Me Chase—you Brett," sounding much like an old cowboy and Indian movie. Each time Brett tried to emulate the sound he made a tiny bit of progress.

After a while, Chase wondered if he was pushing him too hard too fast, and told him, he had better rest for a while. As he started to pull away from the bed, Brett raised his left arm and his hand closed around Chase's wrist. Brett grunted.

Chase smiled in jubilation, realizing Brett wanted him to continue. For the next hour, he kept repeating various words, over and over. Little by little, Brett's tongue began to move. Chase took his fingertips and massaged Brett's

lips, making them move when he tried to talk. Brett began to move his lips on his own.

Desperate for words, Chase began looking around the room and pointing at objects and repeating the name of the object over and over. "Television. Television. Chair. Chair. Picture, dogs, bed, light, fan, hair..." When he ran out of objects, he started over again.

An hour later, Chase was exhausted, and so was Brett. Brett closed his eyes, so Chase slipped away to the kitchen. He quickly fed the dogs, ran for the newspaper, made himself a big bowl of cereal, and came back to the bed. He put the newspaper on Brett's bed, and took a bite of cereal. Brett opened his eyes. Chase took another bite, and then began reading the paper slowly to Brett.

Brett's brain recorded each word, and rapidly matched it to the vocabulary stored deep in his brain. Chase crunched another bite of cereal. Brett grunted. Chase stopped reading, and looked at Brett's eyes, trying to decipher what he was trying to say. He took a piece of his cereal, and held it up for Brett to see. Brett grunted.

Chase smiled and moved the morsel close to Brett's nose. His brain recorded the smell. He grunted again.

Chase said aloud, "Open your mouth." Chase opened his mouth wide to show Brett what he meant. "Open your mouth."

Brett struggled for twenty seconds until his lips parted slightly.

"There you go—you're doing it!" beamed Chase. "Open a little more."

Brett did.

Chase put his finger in Brett's mouth and rubbed his tongue. "Do you feel that?"

Brett's eyes brightened. "Do you feel it?" asked Chase again as he rubbed his teeth, the inside of his cheeks, and back to his tongue. Brett grunted.

"That's my boy. That's great!" exclaimed Chase. He wondered if he should feed the small piece of cereal to Brett, but decided to take the chance. He showed Brett the food and dropped it to the back of his mouth. Brett let it sit there a second or two before finally swallowing. "Down the hatch, big boy!" Chase shouted.

Chase leaned over and kissed Brett's lips in jubilation. Brett could feel the soft lips touching his. Chase kissed him once, twice, three times, until he finally felt Brett's lips kiss back. ""Yahoo!" he shouted.

He thought for a second, set the cereal bowl down on the table, and leaned over to Brett. Brett's eyes watched every move he made. He decided to boldly take another chance. He began kissing Brett until he once again felt Brett respond, and then he stuck in his tongue through his teeth and into Brett's mouth.

At first, Brett's tongue did not move, but gently he swirled it around Brett's tongue. Suddenly, Brett's tongue moved to try to touch Chase back. Chase wanted to shout, but did not want to stop. Soon he had the tip of Brett's tongue playing with his.

244

Chase decided to show Brett what the words sound like on his tongue. He laid his tongue down on top of Brett's and tried to say, "Brett." Brett felt the vibrations in his tongue. His brain was now in overdrive. He soon matched the new sound and sensation with words in history. He moved his tongue and attempted to say 'Brett'. He did it three more times until finally Brett repeated the word with a sluggish tongue.

"Hey, hey! That's right. You can do it," exclaimed Chase. "Brett."

Brett immediately said, "Brett."

Chase nearly jumped off the bed he was so excited. The long lonely holiday weekend turned into an all day and night marathon educating and training Brett. Chase picked up everything in the room and said the word to Brett, coaxing him to repeat the word back to him. Sometimes he could and sometimes a word was too hard, but he was not discouraged.

Every hour or so Brett would sleep and Chase would rest. The next time Brett woke up, Chase was watching the rest of "Torch Song Trilogy" from the night before. Chase thought Brett was still asleep when Brett suddenly said the lead character's name sluggishly, "Ar-null."

Chase looked over at him and laughed, "That's right, Arnold. You can do it!"

Brett said the word again, "Ar-null."

Chase came over to him. "Arnold," he said correctly. "Arnold, not Ar-null. You sound like Arnold Schwarzenegger!"

Brett face displayed a puzzled look before he tried to speak, "Ar-nold Swa..., Swa..., Swa..."

Chase laughed, "We'll save that word for later. I have a hard time saying Schwarzenegger, too!"

Chase scanned the room for more words until his eyes fell on the bookshelf. He selected one of Brett's favorite authors, Clive Cussler. He came back to the bed and kissed Brett. Brett's lips puckered a little more each time. He began to read chapter one in his normal deliberate but slow style, which was now perfect for Brett's recovery.

Not long after he finished page one, Brett moved his left hand upward and touched Chase's hair and his face. Chase wanted to shout, but did not want to scare or stop him. He kept reading as the once still fingers now caressed him. Slowly tears slid out of Chase's eyes, tears of joy, and triumph. The tears made it tough for him to read. He had not given up on the man he loved dearly when others might have. He always felt in their relationship Brett was the dominating partner, the one who made the big decisions, the smart one who could balance a checkbook and figure out the real cost of a loan.

However, Brett never acted as if he was the smart one. In fact, he went to great lengths to help Chase learn to make good decisions. While shopping, Chase's eyes would spot something much like a child might and want it

instantly. Brett would smile and enjoy the moment and say, "That's really cool, but why don't we shop around a bit, and see what else you might like."

Usually after shopping for just a few minutes Chase had long forgotten about the object he previously picked, because he already latched on to another. However, near the end of the shopping trip if Chase did bring it up, they would go back to the object, and Brett would simply ask why he wanted it.

This practice helped Chase decide what he needed from what he wanted. Sometimes, Brett would say, "Let's walk and talk." The short phrase told Chase they should move on without offending him or embarrassing him in front of others.

He looked over to Brett's face as he finished another page and smiled at him. He saw the corners of Brett's mouth tighten, trying to smile. Chase winked at him, and Brett instantly winked back. He laid the book down, moved closer, and winked again. Brett responded in turn. Chase kissed him and then winked again. From then on, if Brett wished for a kiss, he only had to wink. His reward came lovingly quick. Chase never felt such intense joy.

NINETEEN

All day during Thanksgiving and late into the nights, they watched movies and practiced speaking. Chase also let him sip some water through a straw. The first time or two, the water leaked out around the edges of his lips. Chase showed him how until he got it, and was rewarded with a kiss. Brett wanted more water and more kisses.

He fed him a little bit of chicken soup, but was afraid to give him too much food until the doctor could see if his intestines were functioning. The urine bag filled up more often as he loved sipping the straw.

Chase read to him often, stopping to pronounce the words slowly, and letting Brett try each one. Brett spoke with a sluggish thick tongue, but hour-by-hour, he was improving. During the excitement of Brett waking, Chase had forgotten about therapy on Thanksgiving, but by Friday, he was massaging Brett's legs when he saw the toes move.

"Do that again," he commanded. "You heard me, move your toes."

Nothing happen. Chase took off his sock, swung his leg up to Brett's chest, and wiggled his toes. "These are toes. Move your toes." He turned to watch as Brett began moving the toes first on one foot and then the other. "Yahoo!" he gleamed as he rewarded Brett with another kiss.

He went back to work moving his joints and coaching him until Brett could bend his knee on his own. Once he learned an action, Chase repeated it, and if necessary, he repeated it again. He felt like he was teaching a baby to walk. He would push one leg to the edge of the bed, and Brett would pull it back to the center. Chase would smile.

He worked on his arms, bending and moving the wrists, elbows, and shoulders. "Touch my face," he would say, and then reach over and touch Brett's face with his finger. Brett would struggle, but with prompting, and a little help supporting his arm, he managed to touch Chase's face. Sometimes while massaging his biceps, Brett would reach up without command, and feel Chase's face, much like a blind person might do to get the feel of a stranger's face.

Friday night, they found only football games on television, so Chase chose another DVD and put it in the player. It was one of their favorite gay stories. About midway through, one lover gave the other a beautiful, sexy massage. Chase recalled how he had done the same to Brett the night before he opened his eyes.

With the movie still playing, he made a show of stripping out of his clothes so Brett could watch him. Slowly, he pulled back the sheet over Brett's nude body. Chase climbed on the bed straddling Brett, leaned down, and kissed him with several butterfly kisses to his forehead, his eyes, his cheeks and over to his ears. He lightly bumped his nose to Brett's nose, and then kissed it. Brett winked at him, so Chase smiled and planted a kiss on Brett's lips. He kissed him

several times, then slid his tongue in, and felt Brett's tongue desperately trying to move as freely as his own. Chase's erection was immediate.

He broke the embrace, squirted some of the body lotion in his hands, and began warming it by rubbing his palms. When his soft hands touched Brett's chest, Brett rewarded Chase with his best smile so far. Chase massaged his chest deep and long, moving and squeezing every inch of his flesh. Brett's hands moved to Chase's bare legs and felt the soft skin. Chase put his hand over Brett's and helped him move and feel his thighs. Soon Brett could move his fingers on his own.

They took turns rubbing each other as Brett attempted to mirror Chase's hands. Brett's hands began exploring a bit farther until the back of his hand rubbed Chase's erection. His fingers felt the sack beneath the penis. His fingers soon surrounded the bag, and he began to squeeze.

Chase's eyes lit up, "Uh, hang on dude, not so hard." He put his fingers in between Brett's, playfully squeezing his balls. When Chase led his hand to his penis, he delighted in the return of the feel of Brett's hand on it. He helped Brett close his hand, pump a little, and when he glanced up and saw the pulse on the heart monitor pick up a few beats, he grinned with great delight.

Chase slid back a little and began playing with Brett genitals as Brett continued playing with Chase. They continued their lovemaking for nearly an hour until Chase lay down beside Brett with his legs intertwined with Brett's, his arm over Brett's chest, and his lips to his neck. Somehow, he managed to cover them up with the sheet, and they slept together for first time since the night before the plane crash. It was the first night in a long, long time neither one dreamed.

Saturday morning, Chase dressed and with a list in hand, he prepared to leave for the grocery store. He kissed Brett goodbye, and promised to be back shortly. He cut off the light and started to leave when Brett began saying Chase's name over and over.

Chase came back over to him and smiled, "I just have to go to the store. I'll be right back." He gave Brett a big kiss.

Brett suddenly said clearly, "No!"

Chase laughed, "Yes!"

"No."

Chase laughed again, "Okay, here's the deal. If you let me go to the store, I promise we will have a big massage party, and maybe sex when I get back."

Chase realized he had said the new words too fast, as Brett's face drew blank as his brain worked on deciphering the sentence. Chase patiently waited, and then his heart broke.

Small tears began weeping out of Brett's eyes, and slowly sliding down his cheeks to the pillow. Chase quickly bent over, kissed the tears, and kissed Brett.

248

"It's okay, honey. I am coming back. I promise. I will be back." He turned on the television and raced through the channels until he found a movie, kissed Brett again, and hurried from the room. He could take a lot from strangers calling him faggot and other dirty names, but he could not take Brett crying.

Chase selected a grocery cart and began running through the aisles. He bought several pieces of fresh fruit and cereal. Then he picked a package of frozen waffles, and when he selected a bottle of waffle syrup, he suddenly had an idea. He turned around, and before him were rows of baby food. He tried to remember which vegetables Brett liked, but his memory failed him. Brett had been gone too long so he picked out bottles of baby food with flavors he liked. He also selected baby bottles of banana pudding. He got two bottles, and suddenly decided he, too, missed enjoying banana pudding. He loaded ten bottles into his grocery cart.

Brett used to make banana pudding from scratch, and Chase's part of the job was slowly stirring the pudding as it cooked. Too slow, and it will burn, warned Brett. When Brett was not looking, Chase would lift the spatula, get a finger full of the pudding, and stuff it in his mouth. Somehow, Brett always knew, because he would say, "Why don't you leave some for the bowl?" They both would laugh. A minute later, Chase would do it again.

Chase rounded the corner and ran into two of his bar friends. They gave fake hugs, followed by fake kisses, and they asked how he was doing. He said fine quickly, while hoping he could move on with his shopping. One of them looked into his cart and said loudly, "Did you have a baby?"

Chase did not skip a beat. He saw his chance to move on, "Yep, I quit being gay, found me a babe, and knocked her up. This is for our kid, and I have got to go!"

The two queens stood in the aisle with their mouths open as Chase pushed the cart around the corner and out of their sight. He bought vanilla wafers, cookies, dog food, and a bag of rawhide chewies, paper towels, and toilet tissue. He grabbed the milk and bread on the last aisle and sailed to the front counter doing the turns on two wheels. He used his debit card to pay and rushed out of the store.

Once home, he quickly set the groceries on the counter and ran down the hall to Brett's room. The dogs came running to the end of the bed to greet him. He quickly patted their heads and looked over to Brett. "Hey good looking, what you got cooking?" he asked with a big grin.

Slowly Brett turned his head towards the voice he recognized, and stared at Chase a second. He opened mouth and said 'Chase'.

"Yes, my name is Chase! Way to go, dude, you did it. Say it again," urged Chase as he looked at the monitoring equipment. "You can do it."

Brett's chest sighed heavily. Chase could almost see his brain working in overdrive behind his eyes, but then suddenly, he eyes held a gaze at Chase and winked. "Chase," he said again.

"Wahoo!" exclaimed Chase as he planted a kiss on Brett's lips, followed by another, and yet another.

Brett reached up, put one hand on Chase's back, and pulled him towards him. The heart monitor hit triple digits, as he slipped his tongue in to Brett's mouth.

They ate a meal of carrots and broccoli baby food. Well, Brett did. Chase made a sandwich for himself. Cautiously, Chase opened the jar of banana pudding and tasted it. It was not as good as Brett's homemade pudding, but it would do. He spoon-fed Brett a scoop from the jar and Brett smiled as he swallowed. Chase broke a vanilla wafer into a tiny piece, dipped it into the jar, and fed it to Brett. He smiled again.

They watched one of their favorite movies on the television. It was one of the best Saturday nights ever, thought Chase. It was, in fact, the best Thanksgiving weekend in Chase's life.

After the movie, Chase began Brett's therapy by moving his joints as he had always done. He was working on Brett's left leg when Brett suddenly started mimicking Chase by moving his other leg with it. Chase grinned and began working on his feet. When he finished with his arms, he gave Brett a kiss. Brett winked at him, so he smiled, and kissed him again. He felt Brett trying to stick his tongue into Chase's mouth. He opened his teeth and began sucking on Brett's tongue pulling, it farther into his mouth.

Chase soon stripped, climbed on the bed, and warmed up some body lotion. In an hour, Chase fell down beside Brett exhausted but happy. He looked at Brett's chest and found it covered with the sperm he had just ejaculated. He smiled, grabbed the tissue box off the table, and cleaned Brett up. He pulled the covers over them. He slipped an arm under Brett's neck, then hit the down button on the bed, turned off the overhead light and the television, cuddled in close and gave Brett one last goodnight kiss. They were both were asleep before the light bulb cooled.

Chase looked at the clock on the wall. It was nearly 5:30 P.M. and Jeremy and Paul's plane should have already landed. He knew they would come by to see him on their way home from the airport. He spent the entire day telling Brett all about Jeremy and Paul. He described each friend in detail and by afternoon, Brett could pronounce 'Paul' but got out a funky sounding 'Jeremy'. Chase thought it sounded more like 'gerbil,' but he encouraged Brett to keep practicing.

He gave Brett a sponge bath, carefully dried him, and even put deodorant under each arm. He brushed Brett's hair, straightened his eyebrows, and used a clean wet washcloth to clean his teeth. At the last minute, he grabbed

a bottle of Brett's favorite cologne from the dresser and put a little on each cheek. Brett looked dashing, thought Chase. He gave Brett a little kiss just as the dogs started barking. He saw the headlights through the windows as he walked down the hall. He met them at the door.

"Hey, buddy. How was your weekend? I hope you rested some," began Jeremy as he grabbed Chase and swung him around in a bear hug, and then kissed him on the cheek.

"Hey, save some of that sweet sugar for me," teased Paul as he, too, gave Chase a hug and kiss.

"How was your flight?" asked Chase. "No problems with the plane?"

"No, the flight was great, but the movie was boring," replied Jeremy.

"Yes, it was, but Jeremy's mom is a fantastic cook and his family accepted me very well. I think his sister's little girl is in love with me," laughed Paul.

"I can see why," replied Jeremy.

"How is Brett?" asked Paul. "Shall I give you a break and do his evening therapy?" Paul began taking off his coat expecting Chase to say yes.

"Well, maybe. I think something is wrong with him," stated Chase quietly.

Jeremy looked alarm, "What is it?"

Chase did not have to answer as Jeremy and Paul quickly began making their way to Brett's room. Jeremy looked at the monitoring equipment and all seemed normal. Paul picked up the medical report clipboard and scanned back through the numbers.

"All seems normal with his charts except for a few times when his heart count and blood pressure went up a little. What's wrong, Chase?"

"It nothing big, but if you look carefully at the bottom of his eyelids, between the lashes, you can just barely see his pupils. Is that normal?" asked Chase.

With Jeremy on one side of the bed, and Paul on the other, Chase moved to the foot of the bed. He hit the button to slowly raise the head of the bed bringing Brett's upper torso to almost a sitting position. When he stopped, and in unison, Jeremy and Paul quietly moved their faces and eyes closer to Brett's face to see if they could see his pupils at the base of his lashes.

"I don't see anything," stated Jeremy.

"Me neither," replied Paul.

"Oh, really, I could have sworn I saw them." Wickedly, Chase grinned, "How about now?" He snapped his fingers, and Brett suddenly popped open his eyes.

Jeremy and Paul both leaped backwards with Jeremy falling on to Chase's bed scattering the dogs. Paul fell into the vertical blinds sending them clinking in all directions against the glass.

Chase busted out laughing and Brett, to all their amazement, did one of his long grunt laughs.

"He is awake!" exclaimed Jeremy as he stood back up.

"When did it happen?" asked Paul as he got to his feet.

"Thanksgiving morning, the best day of the year!" laughed Chase. "Gentlemen, if you please. Brett, this guy on my left is Jeremy, and the other crazy one is Paul."

Slowly, Brett raised both his arms and held out his hands. Timidly, they took his hands in theirs, and looked at Chase's beaming face. "Not bad for an amateur therapist, wouldn't you say?"

"I say you did great. Brett you look wonderful," said Jeremy. "I am so pleased to meet you... finally."

"Me, too," said Paul, "and you smell good, too."

"I cleaned him up a bit, and put on some of his cologne. I fed him some, too."

"Not solids?" asked Jeremy. "His body system may not be ready for that."

"No, I fed him baby food," replied Chase.

Brett struggled, "It...was...good."

"Oh my—he knows words?" asked Paul.

"Yes. We had to start from scratch like learning to speak all over again, but after a while his brain recognizes the words faster and faster."

"It'll be the same when he starts learning to walk," added Paul. "From the way he picked up his arms, I believe our muscle therapy must have worked. You have done very well, my friend, very well indeed." Paul leaned over and gave Chase a hug.

"Watch his eyes," encouraged Chase as he moved to Brett's side, changing places with Paul. "Brett, do you want a kiss?"

After just a half second pause, Brett winked at him. Chase gave him a kiss.

"This is so fantastic! We have to get him to the hospital tomorrow for new neurological tests," urged Jeremy.

Paul added, "We'll also need some more equipment here so we can get him out of bed and start moving him around so he can regain his ability to balance and walk."

Together the friends sat on the bed talking about Brett's recovery and their remarkable holiday weekend.

Brett was very nervous as the medical technicians moved him from his bed to the gurney, but Chase stayed with him reassuring him this trip would be important to his recovery. Chase rode in the ambulance and held his hand the entire way in spite of the dirty look he received from the assistant driver.

Jeremy met them at the hospital, and Brett felt pleased to see another friendly face. Brett had them stop for a minute when they set him down on the

252

sidewalk. He looked up at the sky, saw the birds flying overhead, felt the brisk cool air of late November, and allowed the smells he had forgotten to enter his nostrils and match up with information stored somewhere deep in his brain.

He looked left and right as they pushed him down the hall before transferring him to a regular hospital bed. As they turned the corner, Chase spotted their attorney Michael Evans. Chase smiled, "Boy, I am glad to see you."

"Why?" asked Michael?

"I've already signed my name six times and we have just arrived. How do we get these bills paid for all these tests today?"

Michael patted his shoulder, "All taken of. I just finished visiting with your favorite hospital administrator, Betty Anders. I signed all her forms for you, and I have notified the insurance carrier for the airline. They are thrilled Brett is awake and moving, and most happy to continue paying his bills. They are happy because they hope the bills will soon no longer be necessary. May I speak to Brett?"

"Thank you very much," began Chase as he gave Michael a hug, "and yes, you may. Let me introduce you as he may not remember you at first." They walked over to Brett's bed as he waited outside in the hall for a CAT scan. Brett smiled sweetly when he focused on Chase's face.

"Brett, this is Michael Evans, our attorney. He is solely responsible for getting the money out of the airlines to allow us to take care of you at home. Michael, this is Brett," stated Chase very politely.

"I am so pleased to meet you...again," began Michael as he stuck out his hand. Tears swelled in his eyes as he watched Brett grimace until he lifted his arm up and shook Michael's hand.

"I...am...pleased, too," Brett said shortly and then smiled as he let go and relaxed.

"Your recovery is remarkable. You have a wonderful, determined partner here." Michael put his arm over Chase's shoulder. "He has worked so hard to keep you alive—defending you at all costs."

Michael had spoken a little fast for Brett, but he understood the gist of what he said, "I...love...Chase." Between each word was a slight pause, but Chase knew he was getting better. He had been in the coma for six months and awake only five days.

"I know, and he loves you so much as well. If there is anything I can do please call me. I am so happy you are back," he said slower. "We missed you."

"Thank you," replied Brett slowly. "Please come see me at home." He paused and Michael thought he was done. Brett sighed and added, "How is Betty?"

"You remember Betty?" Michael felt astonished.

"Yes, I do. She always flirts with me," he smiled as he finished the sentence.

"Who is Betty?" asked Chase out of curiosity.

"Betty is my paralegal. She has been with me over thirty-five years and literally runs my office. You've met her, but she is a sucker for a good-looking man, and always had great fun carrying on with Brett. She has been out on grandmother maternity leave, but she'll return soon." He turned back to Brett, "I will tell her you said hello. She, too, is thrilled you are doing well."

"Tell her I will see her soon," he said.

"I will." Michael had to step aside as nurse came up to push Brett's bed into the CAT scan room. "I will see you again soon."

Brett reached out and shook his hand again. Chase quickly leaned down and gave him a kiss. Together, he and Michael watched as she rolled Brett through the doorway. Michael's eyes filled with tears and Chase sensed it. He gave Michael a big hug.

"He looks good, doesn't he?" asked Chase.

"He is a living miracle," replied Michael a bit lost for words.

"Yes, he is, but you were our miracle. You saved him from going to that nursing home and …" he could not say the words. They were too painful. "You kept him alive, and you found the funds for us to live on while we waited for his return."

"He's going to need many experts to teach him how to walk, and I will make sure the best are available for you. Just call me when you need me. I will be there."

Michael and Chase embraced again. Chase smiled as he watched Michael walk down the hall. The experience made him feel all the months of lonely hard work had been worth it.

Brett went from one lab to another for most of the day. He rested in a temporary room while Chase and Jeremy met with his doctor, Steve Albertson.

"Well, fellows, Brett Allen is in great shape. His brain activity is normal, and his wounds have healed up. His muscle tone is amazing."

"It should be. I did his physical therapy four times a day," said Chase.

"Son, from what I have seen so far, you should consider physical therapy a career," replied the doctor with admiration. "His lungs and blood work are good, and his body functions are good. I find his ability to speak words and even short sentences a modern miracle. I took the food tube out. That should make him more comfortable." He paused while looking at his notes, "Okay, here is the plan for getting Brett back to normal.

"Continue his physical therapy four times a day, but we need to get him out of the bed and on his feet. I am scheduling a team of physical therapists, including your friend Paul, to come see him every day." He handed Chase a piece of paper.

"This is a list of the medical equipment you are going to need. The lift will help get him out of bed, the rails to help him walk, and the hoist to start the process. I hope that in due time, he will be able to do this alone, but Chase, I doubt you can handle getting him out of bed on your own. If you dropped him, he could break a bone, and that would be a big set back."

He smiled, "I know you are strong enough to lift him, but at the moment he is like a giant bag of Jell-O, and not strong enough to help you. I am also scheduling a speech therapist to work every day with him.

"He'll also have a memory specialist visit him a few times a week. In addition, we have to start him on solid food to see if his digestive system can handle it. He has been living off liquid food for a long time."

Chase interrupted him, "He likes banana pudding and wafers."

"You fed him solid food?"

"Well, sort of. I bought jars of baby food so he could eat some vegetables and jars of banana pudding. I broke the wafers into small bits, dipped them into the pudding, and he ate it. He also said it was good."

The doctor smiled, "How long ago did you start this?"

"I think it was Friday, so four days so far."

"You fed him every day?"

"He eats everything I can give him, but I feed him just a little every few hours. I have to buy more baby food today."

"Well, has he experienced a bowel movement yet?"

"Uh, no, I clean him every day but no shit yet," replied Chase as he searched for the right word.

The doctor laughed, "Well, when he does you will know it. He will be like a baby, and we'll have to change his diapers often to avoid rashes and such." He wrote down Depends on the list. "Depends are adult diapers. Let's continue the baby food for a few more days and wait for his bowel movements. If the bowels movements occur, then you can feed him soup and crackers, slowly working up to solid food.

"If he isn't..." the doctor searched for the word, gave up, and continued, "shitting, then we could have a problem, and we'll need to get him back over here. I want you to write down everything you feed him including date and time. We must measure the food that goes in closely, and hoping it equals what he craps out, or he could have an intestinal block.

"Do you have stethoscope?" asked the doctor.

"Yes, I do."

"Listen to his intestines. Jeremy can show you what to listen for. Do you have any questions?"

"Do you think he will walk again, and be able to speak normally?" asked Chase.

The doctor closed the file, took off his glasses, put his hands together, leaned on the desk, and smiled, "From what I have seen thus far, Brett Allen is in great hands, and I would be willing to bet he will make a remarkable recovery. Let me warn you, though, you will have setbacks: broken bones, cramps, frustrations, and more. But yes, I think he will make it." He stuck out his hand.

Chase and Jeremy stood and shook his hand, "Thank you doctor. Thank you for everything."

The hospital gave Jeremy the rest of the day off to help Chase set up at home for the next phase of Brett's recovery. It had been a long day at the hospital with numerous neurological and physical exams. All the results were good, and the entire hospital talked about Brett's amazing recovery during their meals and breaks.

Administrator Betty Anders made a point to speak to Chase before they left. She looked much different than Chase remembered. He no longer felt any anger towards her. The last time they met, he managed to vent all his animosity towards her. Today he just smiled.

"I have talked with my staff and everyone is thrilled with Brett's recovery," she said.

"Yes, it has been a long journey, but we are making it work," replied Chase.

"From what I heard, Brett owes his recovery to you. You have no medical training, and no physical therapy degrees. How did you do it?" she asked.

Chase thought for a second, "I had friends show me a few things. What I did not know, I made up. I think when you love someone enough, you find the how and the way, and you do not give up. I knew Brett would be back—even when many others thought he would die."

"I agree, you did very well," she replied as she shook his hand. "Let me know what I can do to help. Anything, just call me," she added.

"Thank you. I appreciate it."

Chase turned to watch the drivers load Brett back into the ambulance.

Jeremy came up and gave him a hug. "I will follow in my car. Are you okay?"

"It has been an exhausting day, but the medical results are so good, I will have to get my second wind for round two, huh?"

"Yes, you will, but you can do it. I know you can."

Chase sat on Brett's bed and fed him a meal of baby food and his favorite desert, banana pudding. Jeremy sat in Brett's office making one call after another ordering the new equipment they would need. When he had finished, he called Michael's office to warn him new bills would soon be in the mail to his office. Michael assured him he could handle the bills.

256

THE WILL

"How's he doing?" asked Jeremy as he walked over to his bedside.

"Great, he ate two jars," grinned Chase.

"Better him than me. I don't think I would like baby food," stated Jeremy as he set down on the other side of the bed.

"Oh, it's not too bad, except for the broccoli. It taste nasty, but Brett eats it."

"You tasted this stuff?" asked Jeremy, as he smelled an empty jar.

"It seemed like the fair thing to do. How could I expect him to eat something I wouldn't?" laughed Chase.

Chase put another wafer of banana pudding on Brett's tongue. He chewed it and swallowed. "It is good," he said. They all laughed.

"There is something we need to talk about," stated Jeremy in a serious tone.

"What?"

"When Brett shits, you are going to be in for a shock!" exclaimed Jeremy.

"You mean like baby shit?"

"No, I mean like adult shit. When we potty in the toilet water, the water keeps the smell contained somewhat, but when an adult shits in the bed, holy cow, it stinks!"

Chase gulped, "So how do I handle it?"

Jeremy explained he would help layer several towels beneath Brett's butt. They rolled Brett to one side, placed the clean diaper down, and rolled him back, pulled the other side flap free, and pinned it into position with the Velcro tabs. "Of course, if he has had a bowel movement, we will roll him, remove the bad one, and sticking it into a sealed bag as soon as possible, and wipe his butt with a warm washcloth, and then rub a bit of lotion to be sure he does not get a rash."

"I guess I can do it," replied Chase somberly.

"You may have to do it four to six times a day. If you don't, he could get sick, and the smell would be much worst. You'll get used to it, and I will help you when I can."

"Okay, thanks, and thanks for helping me today."

"The truck will arrive in the morning. We need to make more room in here. How would you feel about moving your bed into the guest room?"

"If that is what we need to do, let's do it. Do not worry about me. Our goal is getting this big lug up and on his feet." He leaned over a kissed Brett.

Together, they moved out the dresser, the bed, and a bookshelf. When bedtime came, Jeremy said goodbye, and Chase played with the dogs for a while, before returning to Brett. He stripped off his clothes, climbed on to

257

Brett's bed, and began their routine of massage and sex. He slept in the bed with Brett, but rose early in the morning to get ready for the delivery folks.

The men added new features to the bed with an overhead apparatus, which gave it the look of a trapeze set up at a circus. They set up a mat area to put Brett on for more intense physical therapy. They also created a handrail area, so Brett could use the rails to hold to so he could learn to walk again.

Chase was surprised when they rolled in a wheelchair. He knew if he could ever get Brett in a wheelchair, they could get out of the house more. He hoped that day would be soon.

By noon, the physical therapist team arrived. The two men helped Chase put a Depends diaper on Brett after removing the catheter from his penis, and then put on a pair of long john-like pajamas modified with snaps down the entire length of his torso on both sides. They removed the IV tube, capped off the port, and put his hands into gloves like the workout gloves a boxer might use when punching a bag.

To his surprise, the men easily lifted Brett off the bed and onto the mat. Gently, they began working his joints and muscles like Chase had been doing for months. Gradually, they increased to moving his legs on one side and then the other to simulate walking. They especially worked on his hips and shoulders. They sat him up and showed him which muscles to use to hold his body up. They were ready to catch him, as he would fall in various directions. Chase thought Brett looked like a rag doll, but before the workout was over, Brett could use his arms to hold his body still for longer than minute.

A speech therapist came in next. The woman looked like Doctor Ruth on television. She was feisty, energetic, and never accepted the words no or cannot. She gave Brett word exercises to do. She stuck her finger in his mouth and had him move his tongue against her finger. Chase learned a lot and was grateful for her enthusiasm.

By late afternoon, Chase climbed into Brett's bed and together they took a long overdue nap.

TWENTY

Late into the night, Brett dreamed of his first birthday after Chase moved into his life and heart. He had great fun when Chase's birthday came, but on the morning of Brett's birthday, he felt a little worried at what Chase might attempt to do.

Chase offered no hint of remembering his birthday, but he did make Brett run late to work with a last minute hump before showering. He had to skip breakfast, and eat a cold Pop-Tart at work, and even though he walked a little funny all day, his soreness reminded him of the joy he felt with Chase deep inside of him.

For his birthday, an old friend took him out for lunch at Dale's, one of his favorite restaurants. He spent most of the meal bragging on how much he loved Chase, and his friend was smart enough to let him brag. After all, it was his birthday.

By mid afternoon, his secretary called all the staff down to the break room, where she served up the official singing of Happy Birthday, and served brownies and ice cream, one of Brett's favorites.

He arrived home, checked the mail, and made his way back to his room. Chase was asleep in their bed. He leaned over and kissed him.

"Oh, hi, how was your day?" asked Chase with a yawn.

"It was all right. Nothing special, I cannot wait for the weekend," replied Brett.

"Come here," beckoned Chase as Brett leaned down for another kiss.

Chase put his arms around Brett's neck, pulled him on top of him, and kissed him long and deep, while noting the brownie taste. "Happy Birthday big boy," teased Chase. He reached down and squeezed Brett's penis.

"Thank you," replied Brett between more kisses.

"You're welcome. I thought we would have a nice, quiet little dinner at home to celebrate your birthday. What time is it?" asked Chase as he rolled Brett over, and pretended to bite his penis through his clothes.

"Almost 6:30," he replied.

"Whoops! I need to shower. I have not had a shower all day. It was a boring day off." He got up and started pulling off his clothes heading to the bathroom. He turned the shower on. He called back, "The pizza is due here at 6:30."

The doorbell rang. "I think the pizza man is here," said Brett.

"I'm already naked will you pay him for me? There is some money on the dresser. Love you," added Chase yelling through the door. He watched through the crack in the door, while looking at the mirror behind the bed. He saw Brett get up, grab the twenty-dollar bill on the dresser, and head for the

door. Chase then turned off the faked shower, and stepped out of the bathroom fully dressed and looking good.

Brett meandered down the hall, flipped on the den light, flipped on the living room light, and finally reached the door, and turned on the porch light. Normally he looked through the peephole to see who was there, but since Chase ordered the pizza, he knew the driver would be the cute blond boy who always delivered their pizza. Chase always asked for him when ordering.

Chase grabbed the camera he had left in the laundry room, tiptoed down the hall, and waited.

Brett yawned and opened the door.

"SURPRISE! HAPPY BIRTHDAY!" yelled a large group of about thirty-five people. They all started giving Brett hugs as they filed in the door. Chase snapped pictures.

Brett was so astonished he could hardly talk. One by one, they hugged him and brought in food, gifts, and alcohol. He began to laugh as he winked, and smiled at Chase. Brett soon realized everyone who knew he was gay was in his house, including people from work, friends from the health spa, the Big Brother group, the hiking club, the computer club, and a long list of friends from the gay nightclub. There were also members from the Gay Support Group Brett helped sponsor. There was even a reporter from the local paper, and near the end of the line was the cute pizza boy.

Chase led Brett into the living room and out to the deck where the gay friends quickly set up a buffet with all the food they brought in. Brett scanned the food and smiled. Before him was every single dish he loved, and magically cooked with love by friends. This meal would be much better than any restaurant in town, he thought.

They sang Happy Birthday, and Chase kissed him. Everyone clapped until Larry said, "Okay, break it up you two. You are making us horny. Now take this plate, start filling it, and digging in. We have a lot of hungry people ready to dive in, too!"

They ate and danced the night away, and it was late by the time the last of the guests bid goodnight. Their friends always showed they cared in so many little ways. As they closed the door and returned to the kitchen to clean up, they discovered there was nothing for them to do. Their friends had washed, dried, and put away every plate, dish, fork, knife, and spoon. The tables were clean, and even the trash taken to the street for pickup. The place was spotless. They sighed with relief and joy.

Brett wrestled the dogs who enjoyed all the attention they, too, received on Brett's birthday. Chase went to their room feigning exhaustion. Brett turned out the kitchen lights and walked down the hall.

He turned to enter his room, and found at least twenty candles lit and glowing all around their bed. In the center of the bed was a nude Chase, lying most seductively with one arm up and behind his head, his stomach pulled in a

bit to show off his abs, and a bundle of flowers covering his crotch. He had placed a flower bud in his left ear and winked at Brett.

"Guess what I am going to give you for your birthday?" asked Chase.

"I am not sure, but I think I am going to be walking funny again tomorrow!" shot back Brett.

"Yep, you're right! Come here, birthday boy," beckoned Chase eagerly.

The dogs scattered as the boys rolled over while kissing, groping, tickling each other, and scattering the flowers. Soon they settled down, and experienced a long time of foreplay, followed by wonderful sex.

After several months of hard work, the men removed the hospital bed and monitoring equipment, the oxygen tank, the refrigerator, and the shelves of supplies. The railing for his exercises and the mat remained. Brett experienced numerous days of success at walking while holding the railing tightly. His physical therapists continued to work on making him stronger. Already they could see the return of his stomach and shoulder muscles.

At first, Chase threw up after changing Brett's adult diaper, cleaning, and wiping his butt, but as the days and nights went by, he did it with ease. Sometimes, it challenged his patience, as he would have just completed the process only to discover Brett's bowels abruptly let loose again. With no sign of intestinal blockage, his doctor increased Brett's fiber in his diet, and he became more regular.

The next hurdle involved teaching his bladder how to hold his urine again. Chase invented his own training techniques to solve this problem. He sat Brett up on the edge of the bed, inserted his penis in an empty plastic milk jug, and told him to pee. Nothing happened.

"Concentrate," he told Brett. "Think!"

"Think about what?" asked Brett with a grin.

"About peeing, you fool. Tell your bladder to let it rip!"

Brett closed his eyes and thought about his bladder, but not a single drop flowed out. Chase did not understand why his new method failed, but he moved on to phase two of his plan.

"Okay, I'm going to push on your bladder," stated Chase not quite sure where the bladder was inside Brett's body. He pushed on his stomach, his lower intestines, and then tried pushing on his kidneys, but not a drop fell into the gallon jug.

"Nothing," stated Brett.

"Hmm..." replied Chase and then smiling, "I'll be right back. Do not move," he ordered.

261

Chase flew down the hall scattering the dogs, opened the refrigerator, took out a big orange, grabbed a bowl, and a sharp knife. He returned to the room.

"Are you going to cut me if I don't pee?" asked Brett a bit worried at the sight of the knife.

"That's an idea," teased Chase, "but I want you to watch me carefully."

He set the bowl on the edge of the bed, held the orange up, and slowly cut it, allowing some of the juice to run into the bowl. He waited a full minute, but not a drop fell from Brett's penis.

He cut the orange into halves, and began squeezing them, making the juice run down into the bowl. Both boys were surprised when Brett's bladder dropped one big plunk into the bottom of the jug. They grinned.

Chase continued squeezing the oranges until there was nothing left to make a single drop. Brett dropped another drop into the jug.

"Well, that's a start...two whole drops. Let me wash my hands, and I'll be right back."

Chase stepped into the bathroom and turned on the water to wash his hands.

Suddenly, Brett shouted, "Look!"

Chase grabbed the hand towel, but left the water running and rushed over to Brett, "What?"

Brett pointed to the jug and smiled. His bladder was filling the jug. "Yes, we did it!" exclaimed an excited Chase. "I've just invented bladder control water therapy!"

They both laughed as Chase removed the jug, cleaned Brett up a bit, and pulled up his Depends. For the next hour, he gave Brett glass after glass of juice and water. Once satisfied Brett's bladder had to be full, he sat him down on the edge of the bed, pulled his shorts down, and just as he reached to insert his penis in the milk jug, a sudden stream of urine shot Chase in the face.

"Crap!" yelled Chase.

"No, pee!" laughed Brett.

Chase quickly inserted the penis in the jug and ran to the bathroom for a washcloth to clean himself up. He returned with instructions, "Okay, here's the plan. I want you to pee a little and then stop. Then we pee again and hold it. This will teach your bladder valve what we want it to do. Okay pee," commanded.

Nothing came out.

"Pee, Brett! Force it out!"

Nothing came. Frustrated, Chase ran to the sink and turned on the water. Nothing came.

"Dang it!" he said. "It seems your bladder went back to sleep."

Chase suddenly felt his yelling was not helping things. He looked up at Brett and asked, "Have you decided to get into water sports? You enjoy peeing on your lover?" he teased. "You drowned me a minute ago, what happened?"

Brett giggled as he looked on Chase's face and his valve let go. They both laughed as if they had just struck an oil geyser. "Go, Brett. Okay. Stop."

It took a long second but Brett stopped the stream. "Go again, and stop!" ordered Chase.

Brett managed to start and stop again. Repeatedly, they practiced as the days went by until Brett's diapers were usually just spotted with a drop or two, but no longer saturated. When Chase told Jeremy and Paul about his new therapy, they all laughed heartily. Brett made them laugh again when he explained how he played firefighter and hosed down Chase. Brett felt as happy as little child who had just learned to pee in a toilet. He had made it past potty pee training.

Every day Chase began taking Brett for a ride in the car. Soon he was able to get out of the car and into his wheelchair. Chase would push him all over the park, telling him the stories of Brett's childhood, as Jan taught him. Chase dreaded the day Brett might ask about his mom. He knew he had to tell the truth, but all the same, the thought of delivering the awful news sometimes kept him awake at night.

One day as they rested in the shade of an old oak tree, while their dogs ran spirited through the grass fields, Brett suddenly asked. "Where is my mom?"

Chase did not immediately answer as he usually did, but hung his head low.

Brett turned from watching the squirrels leap from limb to limb, looked at Chase, and knew instantly something was wrong. He rolled his wheelchair closer to Chase, reached out, and took his hand in his. Softly, he said, "Tell me about her. What happened?"

With his eyes moist, Chase raised his head and smiled just slightly. "Jan became a friend after I visited you one time in the hospital. She said she could tell I loved you with all my heart, and she admired such a love. I begged her to tell me stories of how you grew up, stories like the one I told you yesterday."

"I remember. That was the one where I carried the flag in and somehow got the pole down through my britches leg and everyone laughed."

Chase smiled again, "Yes, that's right. I loved hearing those stories, and I am sorry I never asked you about your childhood before the plane crash. I want to know all about you so if you remember something – tell me."

"I will, now tell me what happen to my mother," replied Brett.

"Your mother had surgery for gall bladder removal and recovered nicely. I went to see her almost every day in the hospital, and invited her to our home to see you. She came every day, each time telling you and me the stories so you could remember. We believed you could hear us even though you could not wake up."

263

"I'm not sure I heard, but I had many dreams of my childhood, some my mother would know, and many she would not."

Chase continued, "Well, your dad became suspicious of her visits, as he had forbidden her to visit you because I was here. He and your uncles considered me a faggot, the scum of the earth.

"The uncles attacked me several times. The first time was on the day I was leaving the hospital. Jeremy was pushing me in a wheelchair to his car. Bill and Larry jumped us and beat both of us up. Another time they tried to run me over with their car. They came to our house and threatened to kill me."

"Why didn't the cops stop them?"

"Well, I am sure there are some good cops, but mostly, the cops that arrived did not like gays either. Your father tried to evict me from the house. The travel copies of the Livings Wills burned in the plane crash. I had to find the originals. Jeremy and I searched all over the house and could not find them. One day, we found them on the back..."

Brett interrupted him, "Of the calendar, right?"

"Yes, and boy I was thrilled to find those priceless pages."

"Why? What was so important about the Living Wills?" asked Brett.

"Well, for one, the hospital would not let me take charge of your treatment and recovery. Your dad took over. Eventually, he made a deal with the airline's insurance company. They planned to move you from the hospital to a nursing home, remove your food source, and let you die.

"After we found the Wills, attorney Michael Anderson stepped in, we went to court, and we won. He told the court your Will stated I would get the house and everything you owned. He told the judge as your attorney, he knew the Living Wills put me in charge of your life while you were recovering. He hired me to work for you so I could live here, as your dad wanted me evicted. We won.

"I immediately moved you home. Michael got money from the airlines, and we went to work on your physical therapy even while you slept. Jeremy and Paul helped immensely, and we will forever be in their debt for their service." Chase stopped.

"So what happened to my mom?"

Chase looked earnestly into Brett's eyes. "One day your dad followed her to our home, but she had told him she was going to the grocery store. When she returned home, they had a huge fight, and he hit her. She fought back grabbing a knife from the wood block on the counter."

Brett could see the kitchen in his mother's home in his mind. He recalled washing dishes and putting the dried knives back into the block.

"Your father came at her. He grabbed her, and somehow ended up stabbing her with the knife and she died. I am so sorry. She was such a wonderful lady."

Brett sat there motionless for a long period. A slow tear dripped down his cheek. "Yes, she was. She did not deserve the abuse of my father. I saw him

264

hit her on several occasions. When I grew older, I stopped him one time. I told him if he ever touched her again, I would kill him. I wish I had."

"I guess we had better go," began Chase as he stood up, leaned over, and hugged Brett. "She loved you with all her heart."

Brett smiled and hugged him back. "Will you take me to the cemetery? I need to say goodbye."

"Of course," replied Chase. "Come on boys, let's go!" he called to the dogs.

They drove immediately to the cemetery. Chase unloaded Brett, and helped him into the wheelchair. He rolled the windows down in the car and told the dogs to stay. He pushed Brett across the grass with some difficulty, but reached her plot. The grass had grown over the plot. Brett read the stone with only her name, and the dates of her birth and death. He reached out and touched the stone.

He sat silently for a few minutes before speaking. "I will miss you, Momma. I will miss you a lot. I will forever carry your love in my heart. I am so glad you are in heaven, safe from my father. He can never hurt you again. One day, Chase and I will get to see you. We are going to have a grand time when we do. Thank you. Thank you for loving me. Thank you for loving Chase. I love you. I love you. I love you," he finished with tears running rapidly down his face.

Chase reached over and placed his hand on Brett's shoulders as he sat there sobbing. Tears flowed from Chase's eyes, too. He would miss her as well, and he would forever cherish the stories she told him.

A few weeks later, Chase put Brett in the car, and they drove to the mall. With great delight, they shopped as they used to do. Chase picked up various clothes and pretended to model for Brett. Brett gave him a thumb up or thumbs down, and off they went to the next display. When they reached an Abercrombie clothing store, Chase leaned against a large wall photo of four almost naked male models showing off the store's clothes. He pretended he was in the photo, and pulled up his shirt showing his abs. Brett laughed heartily.

A group of high school teens came in the store and saw him. One of them quickly said, "Damn, look at the freaking faggot!" He pointed to Chase.

Another said, "There's a homo on every corner now. They should all be shipped to an island somewhere far away from here."

Chase dropped his smile, and walked over to Brett trying to ignore them.

The group of boys walked over. One of them said, "Get the fuck out of here, faggot!"

Chase's lost his temper, "I have every right to be here. You get lost!"

Another boy stepped in front of Brett, "Is this your 'boyfriend'?"

Chase did not reply.

The boy continued, "I never understood how you faggots have sex any how, but doing it with a cripple must really be sick!"

Chase swung his fist so hard and fast no one had a chance to stop him. He hit the boy who had said the ugly remark between the base of his nose and the top of the corner of his mouth. The boy fell back to the floor, his nose broken, and his face a bloody mess.

The other three boys saw their wounded friend, and then returned their fierce angry gaze to Chase, and charged him. One hit him in the face while another tackled him to the floor. Once they had him down, they started hitting Chase in the face and the ribs. Chase managed to kick one of them in the groin, but the other two continued their fury.

Brett, stuck in the wheelchair, started yelling frantically for help. A store clerk heard him and dialed 911, and then paged the mall security with a code 9.

Realizing the response time for help was too slow; Brett placed his hands on the wheels of his chair and pulled as hard as he could. He lifted his left foot from the metal feet supports and drove the chair into the back of the nearest boy. It knocked him off Chase.

Brett leaned over and grabbed the ear of the other boy, found the earring he wore, and clutched his hand around it as tightly as he could. The boy brought his fist back to hit Chase again just as Brett yanked the earring.

The boy screamed out in pain as the tissue in the lower of his ear came off. He fell to the ground holding his bleeding ear, crying and screaming. Brett looked at the piece of flesh in held in his hand, and then threw it to the boy. "Maybe they can sew it back on, you bastard!"

Two security guards suddenly ran into the foyer of the store where the attacks happen. They found four high school boys on the floor: one holding his bloody nose, another his crotch, another rubbing a bruised sore spot in his back, and the last holding his bleeding ear. They also saw Chase and his bloody face lying on his back almost unconscious. Their eyes then turned to Brett as he continued sitting in the wheel chair.

"What the hell happened here?" demanded one the guards as two police officers joined him answering the 911 call.

Brett turned his face and looked straight at the cop, "My friend and I were shopping. These boys came in and started calling us names."

"What did they call you?"

"They called us faggots," replied Brett proudly. "They wanted to know how homos have sex when one of us is crippled."

The police officers recently attended classes on hate crimes. As part of their training, they had to pretend to be gay men walking down the street holding hands, and experiencing the vulgar slurs yelled in their direction. It was a most enlightening and embarrassing experience that changed the two men forever.

One of the security guards spoke up, "Officer, these four boys have created trouble in the mall before. I have kicked them out several times. I have their names on file if you need them."

"Yes, it would," he replied before turning to his partner, "Get an EMT over here right away."

The manager of the store came up to them, "We can use these to stop the bleeding," he urged. He tossed an ugly orange sweater to the boy with the broken nose, and another one to the boy with the bleeding ear. He then knelt down beside Chase, rolled up a bundle of sweaters, and placed it gently under Chase's neck. He then took a shirt with tiny ducks all over it and began wiping the blood from his face. He ripped off a sleeve and pressed it gently to Chase's split lip.

The officers put on the latex gloves they retrieved from a shirt pocket, and handcuffed the two non-bleeding boys. The emergency team arrived. One began helping Chase. The other put a bandage on the boy with the broken nose. The police immediately cuffed him, too. He then bandaged the boy's ear with gauze and wrapped an ace bandage around his head. Once secured, they cuffed him as well.

He went over to Brett, "Are you all right?"

"Yes, they did not get a chance to hurt me. Chase protected me," he replied as he nodded to Chase as he lay on the floor.

"Chase Fleming?" asked the EMT worker as cleaned up Brett's hand, and wiped his face where a few drops of the boy's blood landed.

"Yes, that's right. Is he going to be okay?" asked Brett, feeling worried and helpless.

"Sure he is," responded the fellow in a calm matter. "I met Chase years ago. Boy, can he dance."

Brett smiled, "Yes, he can and never gets tired."

The man laughed, "That is true. You must be Brett Allen."

"Yes, I am."

"How long have you guys been together?"

Brett opened his mouth to answer, but the information would not spring from his brain. "I do not know. My memory is not so good after the plane crash."

The man patted his arm and smiled, "Well, I think it has been over two years, maybe three because I had a crush on Chase, but I heard he had been snatched away by a handsome devil. I guess that handsome guy was you," he laughed.

Brett smiled, "Thanks."

"Give me a minute to check on Chase, and I will be right back."

He spun around, and stepped on the other side of Chase and asked his partner, "How is he doing?"

267

"He will be all right. He doesn't need stitches, but he is going to be black and blue tomorrow."

"Chase? Chase?" began Chase's old friend. "It's Marvin. Are you okay?"

Chase blinked his eyes twice, stared at an out of focus face for a moment before his vision cleared, "Hey, Marv," he suddenly said, "What are you doing here?"

"Doing my job as usual, but what happened here?"

"These punks attacked us, saying awful stuff. Is Brett okay?"

Brett heard his voice and rolled his chair around so he could see Chase's face. "I'm fine, but you don't look so good," replied Brett trying to smile at his partner.

"I feel like I got run over by a Humvee," stated Chase.

The officer came up, "I need to ask you a few questions."

"The clerk says these boys came up to you and started yelling ugly stuff to you. Is that right?"

Chase nodded, "Yes."

"You hit one of them first?"

"Yes, I did," started Chase proudly. "The four surrounded us. I knew they were going to hurt us. After he said something dirty about having sex with uh, a man in a wheelchair, I popped him in the face. The other three attacked me."

"All three of them attacked you at once?"

"Yes. I managed to kick one of them, but the other two held me down and pounded me in the face and ribs."

"Okay, are you going to be okay?" he asked sympathetically.

"Yes, I have been beaten up several times in my life for being gay. I can take it."

Chase's bravery touched the officer. He smiled and turned to his partner, "Let's get these punks out of here. I think we have a jail cell with some big ugly men in it that will enjoy these little high school bullies."

The four boys' faces turned pale as two by two they led them out of the mall and to their patrol cars. The EMT friend helped Chase to his feet. He was dizzy for a second or two, but managed to walk over to Brett and patted his shoulder.

Chase said, "I think I've had enough shopping for today—how about you?"

"Yeah," replied Brett. "I don't think I can stand any more excitement for today." He turned to the manager, the security guards, and the EMT technicians. "Thank you for helping us. Thank you very much."

They all smiled as they watched a limping Chase slowly push Brett towards the exit.

Jeremy came over after work, took one look at Chase's face, and exclaimed, "What the hell happened to you?"

Brett answered quickly, "I told him if he forced me to pee in that milk jug one more time, I was going to bitch slap him!"

Jeremy looked at Chase as he grinned, and they all busted out laughing.

TWENTY-ONE

Spring arrived with Brett accomplishing improvement in all areas of his therapy programs. No longer did he slur, stutter, or repeat his words, but amazed all with his newly acquired English accent. His doctor told him "Foreign Accent Syndrome" happens very rarely, but there are cases all around the world. Chase went online to search the Internet after getting Brett's speech therapist to write it down for him. British researchers reported the common element in those patients was damage to their brain due to an injury or stroke.

Chase continued reading until satisfied the foreign accent could be temporary or permanent, but in either case, there was no harm to the patient. In fact, most patients lose the new accent after a few years.

Daily, Chase pronounced words Brett could not remember and explained their meaning. He used the Franklin Electronic Dictionary Brett gave him to encourage him to read. Now he was using it to help Brett. He pronounced each word in his Southern voice. Brett responded in a strong English accent as if he was the son of the Queen. However, as time went by, Brett learned individual words in Chase's accent.

From time to time, Brett would say complete sentences trying to use the new words he learned, but the sentence would often become a hodgepodge of an English accent sprinkled with the sound of Chase's Southern redneck country voice. Chase used a tape recorder and played back the sound of Brett's voice. They both got a laugh at the mixed up sentence. Nevertheless, Brett learned, and gradually the accent began falling away.

The rental company's team packed up the last of the physical therapy equipment. Chase announced their bedroom needed a makeover. Chase and Brett spent several days painting the walls and putting down new carpet. Three days later, they moved their bed and furniture back into their bedroom. Exhausted from the effort, they both decided to test the bed by falling on it, cuddling close, calling the dogs for a doggy nap, and quickly drifting off to sleep. The dogs slept on each side of the boys' intertwined bare legs. The ceiling fan turned slowly overhead. They were all asleep minutes later.

The past month had flown by as they made weekly trips to the hospital therapy unit. A few weeks ago, Brett managed to walk without holding on to the railing. It had taken many months to get to this victory, but the long hard days of work made the accomplishment so much sweeter. The staff surprised the boys with flutes of hospital approved non-alcoholic champagne.

Brett practiced one lap on the rails, then stepped around the rails, and began walking freely towards Chase's waiting arms. Patients, nurses, and even some doctors stood in the wings to watch this miraculous event. As it turned out, coming alive from his long coma was the easy part. Learning to be a human again, and a grown adult was much harder, he thought.

He had learned to speak, walk, potty when needed, and pee in the toilet instead of his pants. He did wear a thin panty liner in his underwear briefs for a rare loose single drop of urine. This usually occurred after a hard sneeze or a big laugh. The doctor thought it might eventually go away, but he could need the extra protection for the rest of his life.

His primary doctor gave him a complete physical the other day including chest x-rays and a CAT scan. He pronounced Brett extremely well fit, and encouraging him to keep walking and exercising all he could. Chase winked at him while the doctor continued reading his reports because the boys spent their mornings 'exercising' in their bed. The doctor failed to notice how strong his anus was, or healthy his prostrate appeared. He did not know Brett could once again produce strong erections and loads of sperm. Brett was healthy physically, mentally, and sexually—a miracle indeed for a person surviving a plane crash.

Later that night, Brett dreamed of a special evening Chase planned to celebrate their six-month anniversary. Chase could cook hamburgers or hot dogs on the grill, and Brett taught him how to make breakfast, but for this special day, he wanted to make fried chicken, mashed potatoes, and green beans. He also bought a can of frozen croissants to bake in the oven. He started cooking about three o'clock while Brett was still at the work. Nervously, the dogs lay on the far side of the kitchen to watch the spectacle.

Chase put the green beans in a pot, added some vegetable seasoning, and brought the pan to a boil before covering the pot with a lid, and reducing the flame to simmer. So far, he was off to a good start.

He lifted the big frying pan from the overhead rack, set it on the stove, and turned on the gas burner. He poured three cups of cooking oil into the pan and began letting it heat up. He got a big plastic bowl from a cabinet below the counter, poured about four cups of flour in the bowl, and set it aside.

He looked at his notes his mother had written for him, and retrieved an egg and milk from the refrigerator. Using the flair of a fancy television chef, he tried to crack the egg on the side of the bowl. However, the first time he tapped it too lightly and nothing happen. The second time he hit it too hard and the yolk went all over the countertop and the wall. He sighed, said a favorite curse word, cleaned up the mess, and retrieved a second egg. The pan continued heating the oil.

This time he tapped it to form a crack, then split the shell with his fingers, and dumped the egg into the bowl. He took a fork and beat the egg, added some milk, salt, pepper, and smiled at his accomplishment.

He opened the package of huge chicken breasts. He planned to tell Brett they were called 'Dolly Parton Chicken Breasts' because they were big like hers. He pulled the skin off the chicken, dipped the first breast into the milk

271

and egg mixture, and then dropped it into the flour. He rolled it over until the breast was well covered.

This preparation had taken longer than he thought. Meanwhile, the oil in the pan became very hot. With sticky flour on his fingers, he lifted the breast and dropped it into the frying pan. Luckily, he drew his hand back quickly as the oil exploded into millions of tiny bursting bubbles, shooting out of the pan, onto the counter and all the way up the microwave above the stove.

He ran to the sink and rinsed his hands, grabbed a wet rag, and turned down the gas. He wiped off the microwave then moved to the edge of the stove, saturating the rag with the oil and flour. The tip of the rag came too close to the flame and it caught fire. Chase did not realize it for a second as he continued wiping rapidly. Quickly, he let go of the rag, while smoke bellowed from the burning oil. He snatched the rag, threw it in the sink, and turned on the water. The smoke set the smoke detector off with a loud piercing pulsating sound. The dogs scattered to the living room, but cautiously put just their nose and eyes around the corner to watch the growing disaster.

The screaming smoke alarm drove Chase crazy. He got the stool out and climbed up with a knife to pop the cover to stop the alarm. He pulled too hard and the cover sprang off and landed in the hot pan of frying chicken. Chase dropped his head, feeling totally defeated.

He opened a window to let the smoke out, turned off the heat to the pan, opened the deck door, and angrily threw the pan into the back yard. He opened the refrigerator, took out a beer, and sat down. Slowly, he drank the entire bottle, gathered his strength, and went to work cleaning up the mess. An hour later, he turned off the heat to the green beans. He stepped back and surveyed the kitchen. Satisfied everything was clean, he set the table, added two candles, changed clothes, and drove to the nearest Kentucky Fried Chicken store and bought four big chicken breasts and biscuits. He then stopped at a deli and picked up a bowl of red-skinned potato salad. He stopped at the grocery store and bought an apple pie from the bakery, and a pint of vanilla ice cream.

Later, he welcomed Brett home for work at the door with a deep wet kiss. He took his briefcase from his hand, and sat him down to the table with the candles now lit and the lights low. Chase brought the platters and bowls of food to the table. Brett tasted the chicken and loved it. The potatoes and green beans were good, too. They both ate two biscuits each with butter and honey.

Chase presented him with dessert, and Brett wisely made numerous comments on how wonderful and impressed he was with Chase's efforts as a chef.

Between bites, Brett said, "That was the best fried chicken dinner I have ever had. In addition, the pie was fantastic. You did a great job."

"Oh, it was nothing," replied Chase modestly while blinking his eyelashes.

"Can I ask you a question?" asked Brett.

Chase became nervous, "Sure."

Brett's eyes had adjusted to the candlelight and he pointed up to the smoke detector frame. "What happened to the smoke detector?"

Chase sighed, "It began beeping loudly, and I could not get it to stop."

"Did you tap the red button on the bottom of it so it could reset itself?" Chase had not thought of that. "Uh, no."

Brett got up from the table, "Where is it? I will put it back up for you."

Chase blushed as he began laughing. "It is in the backyard."

"The backyard? What is it doing in the backyard?"

Chase laughed again, "Cooling off."

Brett went out the deck door and glanced across the yard until he spotted their frying pan in the backyard. He went down the steps and walked over to the pan. It was getting dark so he brought it back to the deck so he could see it. Stuck to the inside of the pan was a single piece of chicken, with a melted white plastic smoke detector over it. He showed it to Chase. Chase could not stop laughing.

"I take it this was your first attempt at cooking dinner tonight. I assume we just ate the second attempt."

"Yep," replied Chase, while trying to stop laughing.

Brett laughed as well. He walked to the garage, lifted the lid of the trashcan to throw the pan in. Inside he spotted a crinkled Kentucky Fried Chicken box, the takeout bowl from the deli, and the aluminum pie plate from the bakery. He grinned as he tossed the burnt pan into the trash and closed the lid.

When he returned to kitchen, Chase handed him a cold beer, but said nothing.

Brett took the beer, swallowed a swig, looked Chase straight in the eye, and asked, "Well, what are you cooking tomorrow night?"

It took about three seconds until they both busted out laughing with Brett adding, "I am going to call our insurance carrier and make sure the kitchen is well covered by our policy!"

Late into the night, Chase and Brett slept soundly in their usual spooning position. The dogs slept on the far corners of the bed as if protecting them. Neither Brett nor the dogs noticed, but Chase's breathing became labored. His brow filled with sweat drops. His brain rewound to the morning of their last plane trip. Oddly, he felt like an angel as he could see down from the sky everything he and Brett did to get ready for the trip.

He saw himself load the car and watched as they drove to the airport. In his dream, he saw them sit down in the waiting area near the gate, but when they stood to board the plane—he tried to call to them to stop and not board the plane. Although he called out several times, he saw Brett climb the steps just behind him, and buckled themselves in their seats.

While still dreaming, Chase opened his mouth and took several quick gulps of air. He rolled out of Brett's arms to the other side of the bed. His entire face displayed tiny drops of sweat. However, Brett remained soundly asleep.

The plane began to shake. He imagined seeing the plane from the outside looking down. He saw the engine burst into flames.

Frantically, the pilots struggled to try to keep the wounded plane in the air. He shook with fear when the engine exploded sending the propeller spinning freely into the side of the plane.

From his view above the plane, the rotating blade cut easily through the fuselage like the giant meat-cutting machine at the deli. The plane rapidly began descending to the ground. He glanced to his left and he could see the golf course ahead. He knew the plane would soon crash and explode.

Chase began rocking back and forth in agony as he saw the blade continue on a direct path to Brett's head. He gasped as he saw the plane skid across the ground. He saw a huge broken limb decapitate the pilots. He saw the limb hit the flight attendant in the back of the head, exploding it like a dropped watermelon. Blood sloshed about splattering the walls, the floors, and as the plane flipped over, the red mixture splattered to the ceiling.

Chase started saying 'no, no, no' repeatedly, each time louder than the previous. His head rocked back and forth, as he tried to shake the images from inside his head. He clinched his fists and slammed them into the bed covers. The dogs scattered, frightened at Chase's wild behavior.

"Chase? Chase? Wake up!" yelled Brett as he grabbed Chase's hands.

Chase's eyes suddenly popped open. Even in the darkness of the night, he could see Brett, and gasped as if he saw a ghost before him.

"Chase, it's me, Brett. You are okay. It was just a bad dream. Wake up!" he said again.

Chase fell limp and still. His eyes slowly scanned the room. The plane crash scene had vanished. He saw Brett's face and it looked beautiful. His hair had grown over the scars in his scalp. Brett smiled at him.

"What were you dreaming about?" asked Brett as he went to the bathroom, and wet a washcloth. Gently, he wiped away the sweat drops from Chase's face. "Are you okay?"

"Yes, I'm okay. Wow, that was one hell of a nightmare," said Chase in a whisper.

"Do you want to talk about it?" asked Brett. He lay down beside Chase, put his arms around him, and pulled him close. He planted a few tender kisses to Chase's neck. Chase thought for a second before replying, "No, just a bad dream." He decided recalling the plane crash might not be good for Brett. So far, Brett's memory had blocked the crash completely from his memory. Chase wished the same would happen for him.

He turned slightly until he could see Brett's eyes. Feeling reassured, he wrapped Brett's arms around him just a little tighter.

274

"Do you think you can go back to sleep? It is just three in the morning."

"I don't want to close my eyes," stated Chase, still frightened from the dream.

"Well, just relax in my arms, and I'll protect you."

Chase sighed. For all these months it had been him taking care of Brett twenty-four hours a day, and now in the quiet of the night, Brett returned to taking care of him. It was a meaningful moment for Chase. All the strain of fighting Brett's family, the hospital, and the battles with the police officers, the court system, and learning how to take care of Brett, suddenly fell away from him. He sighed again knowing together they had fallen into a great cavern of tragedy, beginning with the plane crash, fighting to keep Brett alive in the hospital, and surviving the beatings from the uncles. Then the arguing with the hospital administrator, and hiding on the floor while the two uncles beat the door with a baseball bat meant for him. Then there were the moments of triumph as their attorney presented his case to the judge, winning the case, receiving money from the airlines, and finally the first moments of Brett moving fingers, toes, and finally his arm.

He cried many times at Brett's bedside. He had cleaned his butt, brushed his hair, and massaged every inch of Brett's body with the tenderness only someone completely in love could produce. However, not once during the days of the coma had Brett been able to give back to Chase. Only in the recent months of his recovery, did the pendulum of caring and sharing begin to swing from Chase to the middle again, and tonight, Chase felt Brett move it slightly to his advantage.

The euphoric feeling of being in the safety of his lover's arms brought tears to his eyes. Silently, the tears of pure joy drifted down his cheeks. Brett felt a tear on his arm, pulled Chase in closer to him, and kissed the hair on the back of Chase's head. Chase smiled, sniffled twice, and timidly closed his eyes. The dream was gone. He was safe. He was warm. He felt the sensation of Brett's skin next to his. He felt Brett's heartbeat through his back. He marveled at how quickly their hearts and lungs fell into similar patterns. He felt lucky. He felt comforted, but above all, he felt loved.

He let out a soft sigh. He knew Brett would be okay, and now he knew he would be okay, too. Chase soon fell asleep, still surrounded in Brett's arms.

The next few months flew by rapidly. Brett could now safely walk alone. He left the wheelchair, the crutches, and the cane behind. Thankfully, he and Chase returned the final medical equipment to the rental company. He was learning to drive again in empty parking lots, but that would take a little more time as he had trouble lifting his right foot to switch from the gas to the brake and back again.

Daily they walked the mall determined to improve their time with each opportunity. The first time had taken almost an hour, but now they were down to just fifteen minutes. They lifted weights together and swam almost every day at the YMCA pool where Brett used to work.

Brett gradually returned to typing on the computer, clicking the mouse, and practiced writing his name on a pad. His voice produced not a single trace of the English accent created by the brain damage. Chase marveled at the change, but Brett failed to note the difference so Chase started recording his voice again. Every few weeks, he would playback a previous tape to Brett. This always started a playful argument with Brett denying the voice on the tape was his. The doctor explained the loss of the Foreign Accent Syndrome might indeed indicate Brett's brain had fully recovered.

Two or three times a week, Jeremy and Paul joined them for dinner at home or in town. Brett and Chase looked forward to these encounters immensely. Brett always insisted on paying for the meals as a small gesture of his appreciation for their help towards him and Chase during his recovery.

Though thankful, this did not sit well with Jeremy. Each time, Jeremy would tell the server to bring him the check, and each time Brett outsmarted him by silently slipping his credit card to the waiter long before time for the check. Jeremy sighed at the defeat, and they all would laugh.

At home, the couples played board games, charades, and cards, all designed to speed up Brett's mental recovery. While there were things in his past he failed to remember, he easily remembered everything since waking up. He took great care to memorize every person's name he met—especially the staff at the hospital. When he saw them next, he quickly called them by name.

On a recent night, they sat at the table at Texas Roadhouse after finishing a huge meal. They had spent the evening laughing and telling stories on one other, poking fun, and enjoying each other's company. At an appropriate lull in the banter, Brett suddenly said he had something in his jacket for Chase.

"I bought this card and gift a month before the plane crash, and it has taken me a long time to remember why I bought it and what I bought. The moment I opened the card and the box, I knew what I had been up to.

"A few months ago while I was still in the coma, the anniversary date came and went for our third year together. He can never remember what day we actually met each other, but I can, because I wrote it on my calendar, and each January I transfer the date to all new calendars. We're now in our third year—a year we may never forget, but my love and respect for him has grown immensely through this ordeal.

"Therefore," he handed the card and box to Chase, "this is just a token of how much I love you. Happy Anniversary." Brett leaned in and gave him a hug.

Chase did not let on that he already knew about the card and box after he found it looking for the Living Will in the sweaters in the closet. "Oh my!" he exclaimed as he read the card and then passed it to Jeremy and Paul. He then

opened the box and his face lit up as he held up the bracelet. "Help me put it on."

Brett fastened the double claw clasp and they hugged once more. Chase smiled at him, "I love you, but I don't have anything for you."

Brett grinned mischievously and whispered, "Oh yes you do. You can give it to me later tonight—again." They all laughed.

As they left the restaurant in the rain, Brett slipped on the wet pavement and fell hard on to his back to the ground. Chase, Paul, and Jeremy rushed to his side.

Chase exclaimed, "Oh my gosh! Are you all right?"

"Don't try to move yet," urged Jeremy. "Let's check for broken bones."

"I'll check the legs," stated Paul. He began carefully feeling every bone in his feet and legs.

Jeremy felt the back of Brett's head while Chase checked his arms and his ribs.

For about thirty seconds Brett did not speak to anyone. His face displayed a stunned look, but he soon recovered from having the breath knocked out of him. He looked at his three friends and their worried faces. Each one continued checking his body, searching for any sign of damage.

Other customers stopped to watch, assuming a car must have hit him. A security guard began running in their direction. Brett turned his head to the right and saw a car approaching.

Suddenly, he spoke loudly, "If you guys are through feeling me up, and received enough sexual jollies for the evening, I would like to get up and get out of the way of that car," he said with mock sincerity while pointing at the car.

They all stopped instantly. They looked at each other and jerked back their hands realizing the crowd was watching them and probably perceived the situation incorrectly. They all blushed. Brett laughed.

"Get me up, you fools!" he exclaimed.

They quickly lifted him up. He took a few steps, and shook off the fall like a dog shaking off bathwater.

"Are you okay?" asked Chase.

"I'm fine. I really am. Stop worrying. You're going to turn your face into a prune with all those worry lines on your face."

The customers clapped. Brett quickly turned in their direction, gave them a smile, and pretended to tip an invisible hat.

"Are you sure?" asked Chase again.

Brett stepped ahead of the three friends as they walked towards the car, and suddenly leaped into the hair, clicking his heels together out to the side, and then landing safely on his feet like a gymnast in the Olympics and said with a huge smile, "Tah-dah!"

They all laughed and clapped as well.

"Let's go get dessert," Brett suggested. "I feel like a "banana-slip"."

Chase laughed, "You mean, banana split, don't you?"

"No, I mean, "banana-slip as I must have stepped off the curb and 'slipped on a banana'. Don't you get it? 'Banana-slip'!"

They pushed the chuckling Brett into the car and headed for a Basket-Robbins ice cream shop. The dessert topped a great evening of food, fun, and the realization Brett could take care of himself. It was a lot to celebrate and they enjoyed the event immensely.

Chase and Brett drove most of the morning to get to Raleigh, North Carolina. They had not been this far away from home in almost a year. Chase drove most of the way but in a long stretch between major cities on the Interstate, they swapped places, giving Brett a chance to practice his driving.

Brett seemed relaxed and confident. Chase fretted and nervously bit his fingernails. After changing places again, Brett took over the job of navigation, and reminded Chase which exit to take, which street to turn on to, until finally they parked in the visitor parking lot of the North Carolina State Prison. They looked through the windshield at the ominous wall of fences with razor wire in swirls at the top. They saw the guardhouses and the thirty-foot tall cement walls. It was bleak looking place and Chase did not want to go in, but knew he must. His memories of all the prison movies he had seen in his entire life replayed in his head. Weaker men were often beaten and raped in prisons. He also knew many homosexuals died inside these walls. The thought of confinement in this prison created a complete failure in his twenty-four hour deodorant.

"Are you sure you are up to this?" asked Chase almost hoping Brett would say no and they could leave.

Brett smiled and patted his knee, "I'm sure. I need to get this behind me. I need closure, and you're lucky because I also need you with me."

Chase rolled his eyes, "If I was any luckier, I would trip, and break my leg, or both my legs."

Brett laughed, "Come on and do not wink at any of the prisoners. They might assume you want them to jump your bones!"

"Don't worry. I don't plan to even look at anything but the back of your head."

"Not my cute butt?" asked Brett with a sly grin as he climbed out of the car.

"Well, I might be tempted to do that, but nothing else."

"Come on, champ. Let's get this over with."

The guard at the visitor desk checked their driver's licenses, filled out a form, and had them sign it.

"What is this form for?" asked Chase as he began signing it.

"This is a waiver in case there is a prison riot and you get killed. This prevents you from suing us," replied the man with a deadpan face.

278

Chase gulped, "How would I sue you if I am already dead?"

"I don't know," replied the guard, "but there's always a first time." This time he grinned a little.

He took the forms and created temporary badges. He put the name badge in a plastic insert and clipped it to their shirts. He guided them to a table and told them to empty their pockets.

"Okay, step through the metal detector. After that Bill will take you to the visitor room."

Brett went through first and received a green light. Chase went through and immediately set off a beep.

Bill gave him a hard look. "Are you hiding any metal objects?"

"No sir," replied Chase apprehensively.

Bill gave him a stare as if examining him with x-ray vision. Suddenly, he stopped and pointed to Chase's ear. "Your earring probably set it off."

Chase blushed, "Oh, I'm sorry. I forgot about it." He quickly removed the back catch and handed it to Bill. He walked through the metal machine and this time received a green light. Chase sighed heavily.

"Okay, fellows, put your feet on the painted feet on the floor, put your arms out to the side as far as you can reach, and hold still," commanded Bill.

Bill walked to the rear of Brett and began searching his body beginning at his feet and working his way up his legs, his butt, his crotch, his chest, and then his arms. He then stepped behind Chase and began the same procedure. His fingers tickled Chase, but he did not dare laugh.

"Okay, boys, you're clean. Follow me."

Bill led them down a hallway and into a room marked 'visitors'. He led them up to a booth with two stools. On the other side of the counter was a thick glass. A weird-looking phone was on the wall on each side of the glass. Behind the glass on the other side were an aisle, and then a wall of prison bars.

Brett and Chase waited quietly. Off in the distance they heard a man cursing loudly. Suddenly, they heard an electric motor open a door section in the wall of steel bars. A deputy led a prisoner to their area. He told the prisoner to sit down. He gave the boys a hard look through the glass. The deputy picked up the phone and handed it to Henry. He then stepped about three giant steps to the rear to give them just a little privacy, but he kept his eyes on Henry the entire time.

Brett and Chase studied the face of Henry Allen. He did not look at all like they remembered. His hair had turned completely gray, and his face withdrawn and full of new wrinkles. His eyes were red and puffy. Apprehensively, Brett slowly picked up his phone.

Henry spoke first, "Hi, son. How are you doing?"

Brett did not smile but replied, "I'm fine now. It took a lot of work, but I can walk and drive a car. The doctors say I have recovered completely. About the only thing I cannot remember is the accident itself."

"That's probably a good thing. You must have worked hard because the last time I saw you, your head was swollen, and your face pale. I thought you were going to die."

"I was not the one who worked hard," Brett replied as he nodded his head towards Chase. "Chase is the one who cared enough to work twenty-four hours a day, seven days a week for months. He fed me, did my physical therapy, and cleaned up after me."

Henry gave Chase a hard look through the glass, but slowly turned his gaze back to his son. He did not reply.

"Thanks to my attorney, I was allowed to read the transcript of your trial. You murdered my mom. Jan was a good woman. She loved me very much, and only wanted the best for me. Her visits helped me even while still in the coma. She told stories of my childhood to Chase. When I awoke, he told the same stories to me, helping to restore my memory.

"I know I could ask why you did not want her to help me, or why you hated us so, but I will never understand why you killed her. What did she ever do to hurt you?"

He continued without waiting for a reply. "She fed you, cleaned up after you, gave you a great place to live, and you ended her life violently in return."

Brett paused so Henry spoke up, "It was an accident. I did not mean to kill her."

"You hit her with your fist. That was no accident. How could you pick on that sweet lady?"

Henry dropped his head, "It just happened, and I am sorry. I did not mean to kill her." No other words would come to Henry's lips.

Brett gave him a hard stare before speaking. "Chase and I love each other. We respect and help each other, and we never hit each other. He demonstrated his love for me repeatedly through my entire recovery. He dragged me from the plane and covered my body when the plane exploded. He fought for me in the hospital when you wanted to send me to a nursing home to die. He fought you in court and won. He cleaned up my wounds and my shit. He kept me alive until I could awaken once again. He is the main reason I can now talk, walk, and enjoy life once again. He never asked for anything in return.

"But you and your brothers, on the other hand, did all you could to not only stop him, but beat him, threaten to kill him, and locked him out of our house. If it wasn't for Chase, I would not be alive today."

"That's not true. I only wanted the best for you. You should not have been with that faggot!"

"Father, that faggot is the man I love most in the world. That makes me a faggot, too. I do not care what you think. Chase and I are going to have a great

280

life together. One day when the law allows, we are going to get married, we'll have kids, and you'll never see them. You'll also never see me again. I hope while you are alive you feel the agony of what you have done to my mother and to me. In addition, I hope when you die, you burn in hell forever. You and I are done."

Brett set the phone down on the counter, stared into his father's eyes for a few seconds, and then reached over and held Chase's hand. Slowly they stood up to leave. Suddenly, he stopped and turned back to his father and slowly picked up the phone.

"Tell me one last thing. Just how much was the insurance company going to pay you if I had died in that nursing home you planned to send me to?"

Henry's face fell pale. "I don't remember," he replied.

"Yeah, right," replied Brett sarcastically, "just like I don't remember you being my father."

Brett sat the phone down, took Chase's hand once more, and began walking away. Henry watched him walk for the last time. Brett knew he was watching him so he reached back and gently squeezed Chase's butt. Chase was surprised at Brett's boldness inside the prison and turned his head quickly to Brett.

Brett had anticipated Chase's reaction so he quickly and defiantly kissed him on the lips, "Let's go home. I am pooped! And for the record, I love you." Chase blushed and giggled.

They pushed out the door, retrieved their possessions from the guards, and returned to their car. Chase drove as they made their way through the city and back to the Interstate to head home. He had been driving about an hour saying little to nothing. Brett seemed to be exhausted from the meeting with his father. He leaned his head against the side door window and closed his eyes.

"Brett? Are you still awake?" asked Chase hesitantly.

"Yep, just resting my eyes," he replied without moving.

"That was a good speech you gave your dad, but I have just one question."

Brett opened his eyes briefly, glanced over at Chase, and smiled. For as long as he had known Chase, he would always say, "I have a question," when he wanted to learn or know something. "What do you want to know?"

Chase switched to the slower lane after passing a car, "Well, you said we were going to have kids?"

Brett grinned, "That's right. We are going to get married, and we are going to have kids."

"Wow, that's exciting. Do you think I can take care of a kid?" asked Chase.

"Of course you can. You took care of me, didn't you?"

Chase smiled, "Yes, I guess I did."

"Same thing," replied Brett, "only smaller."

Chase paused, obviously thinking hard, "That means I am going to be a daddy!"

Brett laughed, "No, it doesn't."

Chase frowned, "It doesn't?"

"No, I'm going to be a daddy. You're going to be the mommy!" He laughed heartily as he opened his eyes and winked at Chase.

"Why am I the mommy?" asked Chase, half knowing he was not going to like the answer.

"Because only a mommy could cook fried chickens like you do!"

Chase laughed so hard he caused the car to swerve. The stress of the day instantly left their bodies and minds. It had been a necessary journey, but a trip they would never have to make again.

TWENTY-TW0

It had been a year since the plane crash, and two months since Brett returned to work. Chase continued working in the mall and humbly won another award for his sales. Brett could not have been prouder. Chase's reward was a long evening of hot sex.

To celebrate the year and Brett's recovery, they planned a remarkable dinner at Apollo's, his favorite Italian restaurant. Chase designed special invitations using a gay rainbow color scheme. Jeremy and Paul offered to pick them up, so they arrived at the restaurant at precisely eight o'clock. Paulino ushered them to the banquet room in the back of his restaurant. They stepped into the room as Paulino began flipping on the light switches.

"I hope you like the setup," he said.

Brett scanned the room. He had arranged the tables in a big circle so everyone could see everyone, as the guests would sit only on the outside of the table. He had covered each table with a white tablecloth along with dinner settings with his best china. In the middle were the beautiful flower wreaths Brett ordered from Julie, his florist. Chase often received flowers Brett picked at her shop just outside his office.

"This looks beautiful, Paulino. Thank you very much for your assistance," said Brett as he shook the big hands of the short stocky Italian. "I know it will be a great evening. And remember, no one is allowed to pay, no matter how hard they try."

"Yes, sir, we will do our best for you tonight."

Chase laughed, "I doubt he will be able to keep the check away from Jeremy."

"There is no bill for tonight. Mister Brett gave me his credit card several days ago. It is all paid for, including the wine and champagne."

"Very good, thank you," replied Brett.

Chase began putting out the name cards according to the chart he and Brett agreed on. Jeremy and Paul walked over to a wall filled with pictures of Brett and Chase throughout their relationship, and even a few pictures made during his recovery. They smiled at the picture of Brett taking his first steps on the handrails. Memories of the journey filled their hearts as they saw the picture Jeremy had taken of Chase asleep with his head leaning against Brett's chest in the hospital bed. They laughed at the picture of Chase at his birthday party. Brett had attempted to feed Chase a big piece of cake. The icing went all over Chase's face. They found themselves covered in chocolate after a celebratory kiss. They smiled at the pictures of their dogs asleep on Brett's hospital bed, as well as a cherished picture of Jan reading to her son.

Chase had just finished placing the last card when the first guests arrived. He quickly joined Brett at the door to welcome them.

"Michael, thank you for coming," began Brett as he shook his attorney's hand.

"The pleasure is mine, and thank you for inviting me. This is my wife Marie," he added.

Brett shook her hand and smiled, "You have a very smart and wonderful husband."

She smiled back and winked at Brett, "Yes, I know. Thank you for inviting us."

Chase came up to Michael just as he turned from Brett. Michael stuck out his hand to shake it. "You can forget handshakes for me. I'm into hugs," said Chase boldly as he bear hugged Michael.

Michael laughed as he hugged Chase tightly. "See I told you, Marie. This is a great kid."

They all laughed and of course, Chase gave Marie a hug as well, and then showed them to their table. Brett turned around to meet the next guests. He smiled at several ladies approaching together. The first was Mary his intensive care nurse, followed by Mildred, Chase's day nurse, and Jennifer his night nurse. Behind them, he found Sally, Jan's gall bladder nurse along with Mabel, their favorite cook in the hospital cafeteria. Jeremy and Paul showed the group the pictures on the wall and led them to their tables.

The next group consisted of Brett's doctors, his physical therapists, and a cute male x-ray technician he met on many a trip for more scans. Along with this group, they met Brett's surgeon, his wife, and his gay son.

Judge Mildred Clemmons arrived next. Chase had stopped by her chambers unannounced one day, but through her secretary, she agreed to see him for a few minutes. As promised Chase gave her a report on Brett's recovery, and a handed her a picture of Brett. He sincerely thanked her for helping him keep Brett alive.

She looked across the room at the handsome Brett and smiled.

Chase smiled as he saw her step into the banquet room. He quickly grabbed Brett, and together they walked over to her. Chase gave her a hug, "Judge Clemmons, this is my partner, Brett Allen—the boy you saved."

Brett took her hand and shook it warmly. "Thank you so much for saving me, and for helping Chase in such a critical time. He has told me the story about our hearing in your court repeatedly. Thank you for coming."

She smiled, "Chase did not tell me how tall and handsome you are." She winked at Chase, "I can see why you fought for this good looking man."

They all laughed as Chase escorted her to her chair at the table. Brett turned around and met a group of friends from his office including his wonderful mom-like secretary Janie. Chase returned to greet his friends from both work and other stores in the mall. Chase had many friends and rarely could Brett remember them all, so Chase took over, and introduced each one to Brett.

The final group was their close gay friends. Jeremy and Paul led this group to the table while Brett slipped away to give Paulino the okay to start. The

banquet service team soon brought in platters of salad while others began pouring wine. Chase and Brett's careful mix of the guests allowed everyone to meet someone new. The noise of their conversations assured them of success.

The wait staff returned with plates of lasagna, chicken Francesca, and chicken Parmesan, and to keep Chase happy, there were platters of hot Italian subs and Paulino's triple cheese and meat-lover's pizza.

After dinner, Paulino began serving the champagne. Brett gave Chase a reassuring wink as Chase slowly stood, used his spoon to tap his water glass, and waited while the conversations quieted down so he could speak.

"Uh, I'm Chase..." he began, but Jeremy interrupted him.

"We all know that. Everyone in the whole town knows you," teased Jeremy wisely, as the laughter helped Chase relax.

Chase blushed and shot back, "And 'that', my friends, is Jeremy Booker—my ex-best friend." The group laughed again. Chase paused and then continued, "I want to personally thank everyone for coming tonight. To my right is my partner Brett. Not too long ago Brett and I survived the plane crash. In a surprising way, that was the easy part. The hard part came every day as we began to heal. I was lucky and healed quickly while Brett, on the other hand, sure took his time about it!"

The group laughed and this time Brett's face turned a little pink. Chase continued, "Everyone in this room played a special part in our recoveries. From doctors and nurses, to lawyers and judges, to therapist and special friends, each of you helped move us on to the next stage. Sometimes people say I worked hard for so many days massaging Brett's muscles or cleaning up his poop!" The audience laughed again. "But I can honestly tell you, I was the lucky one. Brett has described to me what being in a coma felt like. He had dreams, he saw lights, he heard sounds, and most importantly, he felt even the slightest touch to his skin. He felt like someone might feel buried under an avalanche of snow and could not get out. He wanted to yell, he wanted to move his hands and wave, and say help me, but in the end, his first gesture was so small, so tiny, but so important. It was the drop of a single tear as it left his eye and slid down his tender face. I knew that was more than muscle twitch of his toes or fingers.

"I was able to go work, watch television, talk with my friends, chat with my attorney, and go for a walk. I was lucky while Brett remained trapped inside his body. He felt helpless for many days and many nights.

"He recalls hearing me talk to him. He recalls his mother's stories as she held his hand and sat by his bed. He noted the change in the ceiling light as I turned it on removing the darkness temporarily.

"I cannot describe to you the joy I felt when Brett first opened his eyes, his first attempts trying to speak words, his first time out of the bed, and his first steps. From the moment I fell in love with him, he has told me he loved me at least a dozen times a day. I am ashamed I did not say it as often before the crash.

285

During the many months of his coma, I began telling him how much I loved him, and I longed for him to awake, and tell me he loved me, too.

"After many heart wrenching months, he awoke like Lazarus, and once again said those precious words—I love you. How wonderful that moment was! How euphoric and exciting it felt! I thought my heart was going to leap right out of my chest!

"So tonight, I want to personally thank each and every one of you for the part you played. I know some played big parts like Michael our attorney, or our medical friends at the hospital, or Judge Clemmons, or our special friends Jeremy and Paul who were both nurse and therapist for us. Some of you were simply friends to us, but you probably did not know what an important role you had as well. Many times, I became depressed, but our friends would always perk me back up and inspire me to keep going.

"From the bottom of my heart, I thank all of you!" exclaimed Chase. "Please raise your glasses as I want to say a toast." They all raised their champagne glasses, "Your inspiration, knowledge, and friendship saved our lives. Thank you for all you have done." He took a sip of the champagne, as did the rest of the group.

Brett slowly stood, gave Chase a big hug, planted a kiss on his forehead, and then turned to the room to speak. He said nothing at first, but allowed his eyes to move from one guest to the next, smiling silently at each person—one at a time. "When I was in my coma, I could not speak, but yet benefited from the friendship from most of you. I want you to know, inside my cocoon, I wished I could see you as I do now, and smile back at you. I owe every one of you my life in some form or another.

"Chase has told me the roles many of you played. Jeremy became a new friend I had not yet met. He helped sneak Chase in to see me in the hospital. He and his partner Paul helped take care of me when I came home. They taught Chase how to take care of me, and thankfully, miraculously, Chase did not kill me!

"Hey...." began Chase with a grin before Brett continued.

"The reason I say that is not long ago, Chase decided to surprise me by cooking dinner. Those of you that really know him will understand how scary that was. He attempted to fry some chicken, but the oil was too hot and splattered everywhere. The cleaning rag caught on fire and smoked the kitchen. The smoke alarm went off giving him a huge headache. He solved the problem by attempting to remove the battery but knocked the lid of the smoke detector into the hot frying pan." The group laughed.

"However, by the time I arrived, I found a table set for two with candles, and a beautiful platter of fried chicken, green beans, and red skinned potato salad. It was a wonderful meal. Imagine my surprise when later when I took out the trash and found an empty box of Kentucky Fried chicken and a plastic bowl from the deli. When I asked him what happened, he told me the story. He then showed me the frying pan still lying in the backyard. In the pan

286

was the smoldering lid to smoke detector. We had a good laugh about it, and to this day, it is one of our favorite stories to recall.

"Chase learned how to read the vital sign monitors, how to administer my IV bottles and feeding tube, how to do my physical therapy, and he did these chores over and over again, twenty-four hours a day. He was also inventive with his treatments. I have a confession to make to our medical friends. If Chase were a licensed nurse or therapist, there would be grounds for lawsuit because he went way beyond the normal realms of therapy. He used sex to motivate me!"

The group chuckled, "Yes, if I moved a toe, I got a kiss. If I moved an arm, I got another kiss, and if I spoke three words in a row, I got a blowjob!" The group howled with laughter, and Chase's face turned a bright shade of red.

"So you see, it is because of Chase's 'special' talents, I improved so quickly!" They all laughed again.

Brett let the giggles die away before continuing, "Seriously, I owe all of you so much, and if there is ever anything we can do for you, we will. Nevertheless, to Chase, I owe my life. When others wanted to let me die, he refused to allow it to happen." Brett reached into his coat pocket and produced a folded paper. He unfolded it so they could see what it was. "This paper is the tool Chase used to save me. I urge you all to get one. Michael can help you with it. It is a Living Will.

"Unfortunately, the extra copy was lost in the plane crash. Jeremy, Paul, and Chase searched repeatedly all over the house until they found the original one, which became a turning point in my recovery. Please, please get a Living Will done, and encourage your friends to do the same.

"I have been thinking for some time for a possible way to reward Chase for his efforts on my behalf. This has been a tough one for me, perhaps tougher than my first steps on my own. I mean, how do you thank someone for saving your life, and working as hard as he did?

"He was amazing, tenacious, funny, and charming every step of the way. He made me laugh when I did not feel like laughing, and he made me want to try harder so I could kiss him back, hug him, love him, and finally walk over to him and tell him how much I loved him.

"To thank him, I have decided to devote the rest of my life to him and to us. To accomplish this, and with Judge Clemmons help, I have decided to marry Chase!"

The group cheered. Chase remained almost speechless. "How can we marry? It's still illegal for gays to marry, isn't it?"

"Chase brings up a good point. It is illegal for us to marry, so we don't have a marriage license, but in front of our faithful friends, we'll be married by our word, our pledge, and our love. Is that okay with you?"

The group cheered again. Brett took Chase's hand and led him back a few steps from the table. Paulino entered the room with a large bouquet of

flowers. He gave them to Chase. His staff quickly went around the room pinning corsages on the women and boutonnières on the men. Paulino brought numerous wreaths on stands placing them behind and beside Brett and Chase. Judge Clemmons stood and walked to Chase and Brett and shook their hands and then stood between them.

Brett spoke up, "With Chase's blessings, I have asked Jeremy and Paul to be our best men, one for each of us." He then turned to Chase, "Unless of course you would rather have a bridesmaid?"

Chase took a playful swing at Brett's shoulder while the crowd laughed.

Judge Clemmons spoke up, "It is a shame it is illegal for them to marry as this would have been my most spectacular wedding ever. However, there is no doubt these two guys absolutely love and cherish each other. So unofficially, I am going to marry them.

"Brett, do you promise to love, honor, and cherish Chase to death do you part?"

"I do," responded Brett gladly.

"Chase, do you promise to love, honor, and cherish Brett to death do you part?"

"I do," he said quickly.

"Then by the fellowship of this group, the loyalty of your friends, your devotion to each other, and your love, I pronounce you husband and..." she stumbled a little, "I pronounce you husband and husband!"

The crowd cheered. Paulino and his staff stepped into the room and cheered. They raised their glasses and saluted them. Brett leaned over and kissed Chase on the mouth. The group cheered again. Brett retrieved two gold rings from his pocket and placed one on Chase's finger. Chase took the other and placed it on Brett's finger. They kissed again. The crowded cheered.

Paulino pushed a cart in the room with a big cake with two grooms on the top. "Dessert is served!" he said with great flair. They cut the cake and passed out plates. The champagne flowed freely as they all celebrated the recovery and the wedding.

After the conclusion of the party, Jeremy and Paul took them home. As they pulled up to their house, Chase spoke up, "Guys, could you do Brett and me a favor?"

"Sure," replied Jeremy. "Anything."

Brett cleared his throat, "Chase and I want to take a vacation, and we're leaving tomorrow. Would you mind feeding the dogs for us?"

"Of course, we will," said Paul. "Where are you flying to?"

Chase and Brett looked at each other smiled.

Brett spoke up first, "We are not flying this time."

"We're taking a cruise," added Chase with a grin.

"Yep, no more flying for us for a while!" exclaimed Brett.

Jeremy thought for a second before replying, "Uh, have you guys seen the movie Titanic?"

Brett and Chase pelted him with playful punches. "Don't jinx us!" said Chase.

"If you don't mind, could you come in the house for a second, we have something to show you?" asked Brett.

They all got out of the car and went in the house. As they stepped inside, Chase flipped on the lights. "Brett and I have been redecorating." He showed them Brett's office wall. It was covered in numerous new copies of their Living Wills. He flipped the calendar around and there was two more attached there. They both opened their wallets and produced small laminated versions of each other's Living Will. Then Chase reached beneath his chin and produced a small penlight brass barrel, held by a chain around his neck. He twisted it open and shook out a miniature version of their Wills.

"Oh my!" laughed Jeremy. "You guys have it covered this time."

"You guys are so funny," added Paul.

"Okay, group hug," encouraged Brett.

The four made a circle and putting their arms around each other's backs. "Brett and I thank you and love you," said Chase.

"We are proud you are our friends—our best friends," added Brett.

"And you guys are ours," replied Jeremy.

"Have a great vacation," said Paul, "and please don't crash in to anything. Not a car, a boat, a jet ski, a sail boat, or even crash into a waiter!" He paused for second before adding, "Unless he is really cute!"

They all laughed as the dogs barked and ran in circles around them. It was the beginning of a new adventure and they were ready for it.

TJ Johnson
December 2008

Acknowledgements

I keep a journal as I write new stories, but when I looked back on the journal of *The Will*, I find myself shocked the rough draft was finished in May 2, 2002. By the time the final edition hits the press, many years will have passed. Years ago I felt the pain of becoming an outsider while the person I loved most was dying. Deep inside, I always knew I would write this fictional story to express with my characters what I felt in my heart.

Author TJ Johnson

TJ spent most of his early years hating to read, and thinking even less of his senior English class. Fortunately, a special teacher insisted he write a fictional short story, a two-page tale about something he found interesting. Instantly, TJ became hooked on the fun of writing fiction. Thankfully, he now reads constantly, going from one book to the next, with several in queue waiting their turn. His favorite part of writing is the crafting of a rough draft. A period in the process when the words fly from the storage center deep in his brain like a movie stuck on fast-forward. The agonizing part begins with the painstaking restructuring, as TJ edits one sentence at a time until he is either happy, or exhausted into believing he is happy with his conclusion.

His new release is **The Raceboys** about a national champion forced to come out as a gay driver. Also available is **The Will** and **Stranded**.

Coming Soon: TJ is currently polishing "**A Writer's Fantasy**" about his favorite college sport basketball, as well as his favorite player. In the story, he plays himself as he writes about the fictional Taylor University's historic basketball program, and the circumstances that led up to meeting their star player. The story tells how they fell in love, and TJ begins writing a book called "A Backstage Pass to Taylor University's Basketball Championship." It is meant to a be a funny, improbable, love story, but as TJ states in the beginning, "It's MY fantasy, and I'll write it anyway I please," which means in the story TJ is thinner, has more hair, and far better looking!

Currently TJ is editing **The Blackfeet Boys** set in the northwest in a time when two young warriors must abandon their home with the most feared and blood thirsty tribe in North America, and search for a safe and isolated world together. Followed by **Gay Grifters**: Chris Connors learns his new friends not only steal your wallet and gold, but also your heart and soul! With little honor among thieves, these young gay men take pleasure in robbing their tricks, while aiming for bigger scores. Will the biggest thief in America give up a life of crime for a lifetime of love? Only the tale will tell.

Fans of the War Series (**The War Apart - Part 1**, **The War Ahead - Part 2**) will be pleased to know that the research is finished, and the writing has begun on **The War Beyond - Part 3**.

Future works include several new stories: Followed by: **Forever Alone...Again** a funny sentimental tale about a man's countless attempts to find real love, only to watch his new perfect relationship self-destruct before he can move their love from third base to a home.

Tom Flack

Requests for additional information and Inquiries can be obtain from Hard Title Publishing, at Info@ItsFiction.com

WWW.ItsFiction.Com

Tom Flack

Requests for additional information and Inquiries can be obtain from Hard Title Publishing, at Info@ItsFiction.com

WWW.ItsFiction.Com

292

Contact TJ Johnson at:

Info@ItsFiction.com

1. I try to answer all my email myself; however please read "Bio & Info" before writing as your question – saving time for all! Many readers ask the same questions repeatedly.

2. Please do not add my email address to any group for jokes, thoughts, prayers, or riddles, etc. I always delete these without reading.

3. I do not open any emails with attachments as these may contain viruses or other nonsense!

4. Please do NOT write suggesting plot lines as I delete these quickly, too. I like to write my own stories. If your plot is good, write it yourself! Do not send your manuscript to me – I am a writer, not a publisher, and I do not have the time.

5. All characters and names are part of my imagination and indicate no one particular. If I like a person's name, I may use the first or the last name but never both at the same time. It is true some of the events in my books are historical in nature but many are not. Choosing which to believe is your job, but this is why fiction is fun.

6. If you do not receive a reply, perhaps "Bio & Info" contain the answer already, or your email address is not functioning correctly.

7. If you have read all the above, I cannot wait to hear from you!